DEATH, DISCOVERY & CARNE ASADA

DEATH,
DISCOVERY &
CARNE ASADA

THOMAS CURRAN

Published 2020
Printed in the United States of America
ISBN: 978-1-7346748-0-4
E-ISBN: 978-1-7346748-1-1
Library of Congress Control Number: 2020903754

Cover and interior design by Stewart A. Williams / stewartwilliamsdesign.com
Author photo by Karen Musselman

For information, address:
Thomas Curran
www.thomascurran.com
thomas@thomascurran.com

Dedicated to my son, Holden
his mother, Leslie
my mother, Margie
my father, Tom
and my dog, Wink,
who walked the first 1,396 miles of my journey by my side.

On May 15, 2019, after a grueling 29.5-mile day in extremely high heat, Wink and I set up camp at the edge of Lake Eufala just outside Checotah, Oklahoma. That was the last day Wink walked with me.

Wink: *"The rest is all you, man. I gotta go home; it's too damn hot!"*
Me: "I'll see you at the ocean, buddy."

I finished the remaining 2,000 miles without my co-pilot, and I missed him dearly.

This is for you, Wink.

CONTENTS

Prologue xiii

POST-WALK
Confession 1

PRE-WALK
OCTOBER
Thomas 8
Jesse 10
Annie 13
My Motley Crew 17
The Nose Picking Incident 21

NOVEMBER
Buckethead 27

DECEMBER - FEBRUARY
Aftermath 35
Annie/Kennedy 41
Becoming A Hunter 45

THE WALK
FEBRUARY
First Steps 53
First Blood 56
Google Made Me Do It 67
The Art Of Walking 72
La Casa De Morgan 80
Whiteville 84
Sprinkles 89
Joshua 95
Jenny 104
Tyler, A Bridge, And A Yellow Bear 111
Somewhere Over The Rainbow 128
Momima 131

MARCH

    The Thieving Mud Hole.. 158

    Peggy Sue.. 166

    Lung Saw 175

APRIL

    Natchez Fright Night 188

    4,000 Aprons & A Place To Bury Toenails 193

    Forever Together In A River 202

MAY

    Toad Suck & A Masshole 214

    Hunting A (New) Killer 223

    The Alibi 228

    Tornadoes 101 249

JUNE

    The Texas Panhandle 258

    Road Trip 264

JULY

    Knock, Knock! 270

    Sleeping Burritos & Tiger Town 274

AUGUST

    The Prineville Coffee Murder 232

    A Teepee, Leigh? Really? 285

    Erika...289

    Welcome To California 298

    Lost In Dehydration..304

    My Old Law School Buddy 310

    Rita The Shrink...321

    Getting Moore 332

    A Killer's Killer 343

    Hello, Again, Annie 349

SEPTEMBER

    If I Never Touch The Water... 364

The Big Thank You Page 370

About The Author.. 373

PROLOGUE

Johnny: "So, tell me, what happened to the dick?"

Me: "Huh?"

Johnny: "Did they ever find the dick?"

Me: "Nope. Or the rest of the body. Just a frozen, floating head and balls."

Johnny: "Damn."

Me: "Yeah. Poor kid."

Johnny: "So, if I can find info on this crazy bitch, what do you plan to do with it?"

Me: "I'm gonna hunt her down."

Johnny: "Hunt her down? So, now you're Dog, the Bounty Hunter? What are you gonna do when you find her? Call the cops?"

Me: "Probably not."

Johnny: "You're all of 160 pounds dripping wet. What are you thinkin', man?"

Me: "You don't want to know what's in my head right now."

Johnny: "Can you hear yourself? This chick overpowered a pretty good-sized guy, killed him and hacked his body up into pieces, and you're gonna go find her? Dude, she put his fucking head and junk in a bucket of sauce and stuck it in your freezer. She's fucking crazy!"

Me: "Yeah, I don't know, I kinda admire her artful approach to murder. Maybe I'm just losing my mind."

Johnny: "You think?"

Me: "Are you gonna help me or not, Johnny?"

Johnny: "My life is so damn boring, why not? But with one condition. You don't approach anybody before I pick them apart. Let me know who you're headed to meet and let me find out if they're crazy, normal, an ex-convict, ex-military, married to the mob, Dahmer's brother, linked to any crazy shit or whatever."

Me: "Deal. How's life?"

Johnny: "It's fuckin' boring."

POST-WALK

SEPTEMBER

CONFESSION

COSTA MESA, CA

33° 37' 47.4" N

117° 55' 13.7" W

MILES WALKED: 3,235

I didn't plan on killing people when I walked across America.

TO-DO WHEN I WALK ACROSS AMERICA:

1. Master the art of cold-soaked top ramen.
2. Learn to dig a cathole and perfect my aim.
3. Wrestle a bear.
4. World's largest ball of twine.
5. ...
6. ...

Murder was not on the list.

Yes, I killed people.

A lot of people.

When you kill people, any number of people, when does it become "a lot" of people? Is three a lot? Eight? A baker's dozen?

And what is the definition of serial killer? Mass murderer? Spree killer?

se·ri·al kill·er *noun* a person who commits a series of murders, often with no apparent motive and typically following a characteristic, predictable behavior pattern.

mass mur·der·er *noun* The FBI defines mass murder as murdering four or more people during a single event with no "cooling-off period" between the murders.

spree kill·er *noun* The U.S. Bureau of Justice Statistics defines a spree killing as killings at two or more locations with almost no "cooling-off period" between murders.

cool·ing off pe·ri·od *noun* The period of time within which a killer blends back into his/her seemingly normal life.

Definitions often confuse me on this matter because all murderers are killers, but not all killers are murderers. To murder requires malice aforethought and some killers do meet that criteria, but not all of them. However, the names and definitions above, which come directly from the Department of Justice, use the words murderer and killer interchangeably.

So, what am I?

I confess to many killings; however, they were not in series and I had motive, albeit *most* of the time it was self-defense or in defense of another, and my behavior was far from predictable. Therefore, I am not a serial killer.

I am also not a mass murderer. I did not kill a mass of people during a single event and I certainly cooled down quite a bit between those that I did kill.

I for sure killed more than two people in different places but over long periods of time and with lots of cooling-off time in between. So, no, I am not a spree killer.

Some of my killings were in self-defense and, therefore, perfectly justifiable. I can rest my head and sleep soundly without a bit of guilt over them. However, reflecting back, I did put myself in every one of those situations knowing that they could end up with someone dying. Had I not, no deaths would have occurred.

Some people died by my hand in order to protect others. I would inject myself into some stranger's bad predicament out of the kindness of my mushy, warm heart and, had I not, an innocent life may have been lost. I say justifiable.

And some of the dead people in my path were just assholes who needed to die. Completely unjustifiable and certainly not ok in the eyes of the law.

I am a killer, or murderer, or both, of many people over a long period of time, for many different reasons and with lots of cooling-off time between deaths.

Therefore, I will identify as an unidentifiable killer.

I'm going to tell you a story, a (somewhat) true story about two killers and a hunting adventure like no other. A story that should never, ever, encourage you to walk across America. However, if my story does, for some sick reason, inspire you to lace up some sneakers and attempt to do what only a dozen or so people accomplish each year, I'll throw in some pointers to help you out.

I am a murderer, but I am also a giver.

PRE-WALK

OCTOBER

THOMAS

'm not a hiker, camper, walker, cyclist, bodybuilder, work out person, yoga enthusiast, Pilates guru, circuit training asshole, or any of those types of people. I shower twice a day, I'm a bit obsessed with clean fingernails, I fear and loathe body odor, and I don't piss or shit in front of anybody. I like my bathroom door closed when nature calls; that is not a group activity. I don't make my bed every day, and I don't freak out if there are a few unwashed dishes in the sink; however, my living area is clean, and I like my stuff where I like my stuff. I've lived in the same house for thirteen years and could have bought it by now with all the rent I've paid. I'm friendly, likable, and pretty good looking for a fifty-year-old man. And I'm modest.

I'm not Mr. Outdoorsy. Well, I wasn't before my journey. I was Mr. Indoorsy. I was a chef, through and through. Two culinary schools in two countries, years of getting my ass handed to me by far superior culinary geniuses, two failed marriages, and far too many defunct relationships got me to where I was when my life was flipped upside-down by a woman I'd never slept with.

I'd spent my entire adult life in kitchens, most without a window to see the shining sun. I'd lived thousands of days entering the kitchen before sunrise and exiting long after the streetlights came on. I was a chef and restaurant owner and that's the life you sign up for. I was fifty years old and all I knew how to do was cook, drink, and break up with girls. That was my legacy. Well, that's not all true. I raised a great kid who made it through college in four years, and, even though I screwed that marriage up, I maintained an excellent friendship with his mom and her new husband. Unfortunately, for my son's lower back and his bank account, he's pursuing a career similar to mine. Chip off the ole' block?

I used to love being a chef. I mean, I still love what I accomplished in my career, and the social benefits were pretty damn excellent, but the pay absolutely sucked. You don't become a chef to get rich; you do it for the love of cooking and free drinks. Normal people benefits? No way. No medical insurance, vacation, or paid sick days. Forget family holidays cuz those are out. You kiss those bennies goodbye when you put on the coat (unless you work at some boring as fuck corporate restaurant). I loved hot kitchens, neck-deep in the weeds, ticket rails twenty deep, long hours, late nights, free drinks, and lots and lots of women who thought it was cool to date a chef, most of whom would quickly realize that we have no money or much time for them.

Being a chef defined me. It's all I knew; it was the only career I ever wanted, and I was good at it. After the discovery in the freezer, there was no more room in that world for me, so I walked across America. I didn't know I'd have to kill people to do it.

JESSE

Jesse was a line cook in my restaurant. He was a real piece of shit but also a badass cook and monster prep guy and he had a damn good work ethic. His ridiculous and not very well executed *I'm a chef* tattoos attempted to tell a story that he wanted everyone to believe - "I'm tough. I'm hardened. I've done my time on the line. Respect to Chef, Goddammit!" That was Jesse's fantasy story. Jesse's reality was that he was barely out of his culinary school diapers and Jesse was not Chef. That was me. I was Chef. Check your bad boy at the door, get in here and cook and shut your damn mouth, Jesse, you're not impressing anybody. Fucking rookie

Jesse was maybe, barely, twenty-six years old. Jesse could cook, no doubt, but his mouth, temper, and ego were a bad mix. Toss in some booze and weed (and who knows what else) and you get Jesse on the Rocks. Tons of salt. He was one of those kids who went to cooking school, got the obligatory chef tattoos within a week of Basics 101, stopped shaving to look cool (till his tough as nails Austrian baking instructor kicked him out of class for looking like an asshole), cherished his knife roll and warned everyone not to touch it.

Jesse grew up one of nine boys. Nine. Let me list the ways that Jesse was screwed from the moment his mom plopped down on their filthy lime green linoleum kitchen floor and blessed him into the world. He was the youngest, so you know he fought for every pancake he ever ate, and I'll bet the Log Cabin bottle was bone dry by the time it got around to him. I watched him eat sometimes and I can guarantee my presumptuous fake maple syrup musings are spot on. If you tried to sneak a fry off his plate, I bet he'd break your arm. His two oldest brothers were in prison when he was born, and he didn't get to know them till he was in 1st grade. Both were serving time for being dumbasses together and thinking that robbing the liquor store where they also happened to stock up on booze and smokes every day was a good idea. Welfare? Yes. Dad? No. Anybody around to help him with homework or, hell, for that matter, just get him to school every day? No way.

Jesse was born into, grew up, and still lived in the same three-bedroom double-wide trailer in a long-ago forgotten part of the city. I'm not even sure you could call it a double-wide because that would imply that there were two smaller vessels purposely joined together to make for a more enjoyable trailer park living environment and done so by a company that performed that kind of work professionally. No, this was a bit more, shall we say, homemade than that. Someone, presumably Jesse's long-lost dad or some other random sperm donor, had sandwiched together two not so similar in size or color trailers, hoisted them up somewhat evenly and adjacent to one another and connected them with glue or tape or screws or magic. There was a fantastic amount of coppery blood-red rust dripping around the jagged edges at the seam that almost certainly caused spasms and lockjaw amongst the too poor or lazy to vaccinate teenage tyrants in the park. There were so many scraggly, prickly weeds of all colors, makes, and models growing up, around and through the dozens of joint connections that you couldn't really tell how the two shelters were held together. Several large, multi-colored yet faded and lifeless tarps were haphazardly taped together and randomly laid out over the top of the connection to help avoid water from leaking inside. The tarps were held down by old, bald tires and a massive, rusted anvil. How that anvil was possibly hoisted up to the trailer roof and by whom was unknown. And how it hadn't fallen through the shabby roof after all these years is a miracle in physics. Inside, a giant, somewhat square hole that was not part of the original trailer plans created a walking space between the two living vessels. Whoever cut the holes in the two trailers was either drunk, high, or a pre-school drop-out. The hole on the left trailer was a pretty decent square about six feet wide. It appeared that the cutter then drank a case of beer and went to work on trailer two. This hole was a sloppy square with rounded corners, and it was a foot wider at the top than at the bottom. It was also much larger than the more skillfully crafted opening on trailer number one, all of which created a walkway between the trailers that looked to be out of a torture chamber. I imagined several scrapes and cuts were had in that shabby little hallway. Within this home lived nine children, a woman and, at some point, maybe the man or men that Jesse didn't like to talk about.

Outside this palatial estate and, once upon a time long, long ago, someone attempted to pretty up the place by lining up now dead and rotted out potted plants along the base of the trailers. This was clearly a failed attempt at hiding wheels that would never, ever roll again, and to provide a safe place for dogs, cats, and other assorted farm animals to shelter within. Several rusted BBQs, broken down lawn chairs, an old mustard yellow refrigerator, and the obligatory automobile carcass finished off the exterior landscape design.

Although four of Jesse's siblings were well into adulthood when he was born, not one could afford their own place, and they still lived with Momma. Are you gettin' the gist? Jesse had a rough go as a kid. I have no clue how he paid for culinary school, and I didn't care to know. I got his whole life story over a beer his first night on the job, and I kinda felt for the kid. He hadn't chosen to grow up like that, and I can't imagine that he'd had many opportunities for a normal childhood. I liked Jesse because he persevered through his early years and found something that he loved doing, and he did it well. If only I could get him to grow the hell up and keep his mouth shut, I'd be in pretty good shape.

ANNIE

When badass Annie appeared out of nowhere at our back door one day, she eyeballed my whole crew, settled her gaze on Jesse, and, after a brief stare down and under her breath, said, "Asshole."

And that's when it all started. Annie was thirty-eight years old and she'd been working in kitchens for well over a hundred years. She was hardened. She was tough. She had done her time and she eyed Jesse with a scary blend of curiosity and contempt. I could see the cogs in her brain turning the moment she showed up on our back loading dock. We were all outside smoking cigarettes (a killer habit I ditched when I started my walk) when Annie, decked out in clean baggies, well-worn but spotless clogs and a chef coat fresh out of the dry cleaner's plastic, walked up and said, "Hey Chef." Her knife roll was a well-worn, soft creased leather job, and it looked like she got it for her first birthday. That roll had seen some good line time. I wondered if this was interview cleanliness or if she genuinely respected her position enough to show up that way every day. I would learn quickly; it was the latter.

Annie didn't have an appointment, or an interview lined up, and I wasn't hiring. But, from moment one, she exuded confidence and reliability and showed respect.

Annie: "Are you Chef?"

There were four of us back there, and I guess she picked me out because I was the elder in the group, and I didn't look intimidated. The other guys, yeah, all guys, eyed her with worry.

Me: "Yeah, this is my place."

Annie: "I'm a hell of a cook. You're Chef. I'm good, I'm clean, and I'll have your back. Got my own setup, I keep my mouth shut and I show up to work."

Well, that's more than most of my guys could say. She said all this right in front of my crew without a worry in the world. She couldn't care less about what they thought of her. She was there to work.

Annie: "When can I start?"

Me: "Right now."

That was it. Annie didn't need to say anything else. Anybody with that kind of confidence got a shot on my line whether I needed them or not.

Back in the kitchen, my guys were pissed. They always bitched about how overworked they were, and here was someone with no agenda ready to help and, all of a sudden, they didn't want another set of hands on the line. But, fuck them, she was there, I was intrigued, and it was my place so they could piss off.

Annie wasn't beautiful, but she was cute in a tough girl kinda way. A little bit of makeup, hair in a ponytail and super clean, short fingernails. I have a thing about dirty nails - NOT IN MY KITCHEN (or my bed). She was tall. Taller than all of us. And not big tall, more like model body type tall. Maybe six one. Her coat covered only some of the art on her arms. Unlike Jesse's strategically placed, flash tattoos of knives and shit, Annie's were different. Her approach to body art was all about her history of being a line cook. Jesse's tats said what he was going to do in his career when he grew up. Annie's were a memoir. She tattooed her scars. She didn't try to heal them with vitamin E oil or whatever people use. She fucking tattooed them. "Here they are. Here's how they got here." It sounds contrived and proud, but that wasn't it. They were simple line tats that, from more than a few feet away, looked like tiny scratches. And there wasn't a ton of them - maybe half dozen or so in all. There was another, more substantial work of art on her shoulder, the bottom of her neck, and chest, but I had no clue what it was. It appeared to be the same piece stretching great distances, but I wasn't positive. It was colorful, and what I could see was very well done. Every time she would catch me looking at it, she would move her body or tighten up her jacket to try to conceal it. Ten years ago, I would have asked to see it, but now that will end you up in court. So, I let it go. I'd learn later what that tattoo was and how relevant it was to this story.

The guys warmed up to Annie after a few days. She wasn't lying about what she could and would do. She worked her ass off. She could follow a recipe, and she looked for stuff before asking where it was. She didn't talk much, and she kept her station clean - so clean - like she wasn't even there. I don't typically subscribe points to people's behavior or work ethics, but she earned at least nine points for cleanliness (she sometimes got that coveted tenth point when she cleaned up after me) and a few more for not showing up with the typical attitude that most punk line cooks have.

About a week into Annie's time with us, I saw her laughing at her phone when she was outside on a break. I'm not one to ever ask personal stuff, so I didn't. Can you tell that I'm a little fearful of employees suing me for bullshit stuff? Anyway, I was back there, and she was laughing pretty hard.

Annie: "Oh, hey Chef. Sorry for being so loud."

Me: "No worries. Happy is good."

Annie: "My wife sent me a video of a cat with its head stuck in a Kleenex box, and it's fuckin' hilarious."

Me: "Yeah, I've seen that. That's a good one."

So, Annie is a lesbian. Or bi-sexual. Or whatever. No label needed. And I don't give a crap, but it's good to know for no other reason than curiosity. I wasn't attracted to her like that, but, as an owner, you never get to ask about people's lives outside of work unless they bring it up first. Thank you, California, for creating this environment. Here's my obligatory justification for Annie's sexuality not being a big deal - my sister plays for both teams, my Grandma was a lesbian, I lean left and have many gay friends. Hell, my fiancé broke up with me to be with a woman and she's happier than ever and I'm happy for her. So, there, can I be done with that now?

But Annie having a wife is a critical fact in this story and guess who it has to deal with? Jesse. Oh, Jesse, why did you let it get so messy?

Let me explain kitchen life to those that haven't experienced it. I know everyone has seen reality restaurant TV shows, and you may have read Bourdain's Kitchen Confidential. If you have read it, you can probably skip this part but read it anyway because I took the time to write it. If you haven't, then definitely keep reading. Small restaurant kitchens haven't evolved that much ethically, morally, or legally in the past eight thousand years. Big corporate restaurants are well protected with mandatory behavioral classes, Human Resources and counseling, zero-tolerance policies, thick, colorful employee handbooks, security cameras, narcs, snitches, drug test kits, safe places, eye cleansing stations, all legal paperwork hanging where consumers can see them, spic and span hood filters, gender-neutral bathrooms well equipped with diaper changing stations and non-slip floor mats in the kitchens. Yippee for them. But, I can tell you that small restaurants are run by mom and pop who are broke, bust ass for fifteen hours a day and don't always put the amount of time and money that they probably should into prevention of horrible things like harassment, injury, high employee turnover and bullshit lawsuits from former line cooks that claim they lost their big toe after accidentally kicking the leg of a prep table. Yes, that happened in real life. That piece of crap was wearing kitchen shoes, so kicking a table, no matter how hard, would NEVER hurt your toe so much that, two days later, you'd have to have it amputated. Maybe he should have taken better care of his diabetes and pampered those blisters he always got on his heels and toes from wearing the wrong shoes on his two-mile journey to and from work. Nineteen thousand dollars later, Hector took a hike. Anyway, it's all those little chores and tasks that owners put on the back burner because they can always get to them tomorrow, right?

Wait, where was I going with all this?

MY MOTLEY CREW

So wanna-be badass Jesse and full-on badass Annie started getting along alright. It took a few weeks, though. The other guys in the kitchen took to her much faster. I had a small crew and, until Annie, it was made up of all guys. That was not by design at all, so back off with your social justice accusations of sex discrimination. When I opened up, I placed an ad, and, for some reason, the only girls that showed up to apply were for the front of the house. So, I hired a bunch of guys and, except for Hector (the toe guy), the rest have been with me since day one. The downside to this unintentionally lopsided gender make up in my kitchen is that they had a lot of bad habits I had to break when Annie showed up.

Funny, when you're not so worried about someone being offended, you don't notice the comments or jokes as much. The guys that worked for me weren't bright by any stretch of the imagination, but you don't have to be brilliant to work on a line, wash dishes or bus tables. You do have to be fast, clean, pleasant in front of guests, and punctual.

Hipolito, who we affectionately nicknamed Polo, had almost all of those qualities except the whole "pleasant around guests" thing. Perhaps because his name's origin meant 'destroyed by horses', his unpleasantries were baked in at birth. He had an invisible leash around his neck that I verbally yanked if he got anywhere near the door to the dining room. Polo was one hell of a dishwasher and prep cook, though. I never had greasy pans or dirty spoons to deal with when Polo was in dish pit. He was also a super nice guy with a huge heart. I didn't know him that well because he was a bit shy, but he never argued with anybody and was always willing to cover a shift, drive someone home or loan someone a few bucks even though he was flat broke. I liked Polo, and I liked him around my kitchen.

Jose was another line cook. He had a loud mouth, huge smile, and he worked two full-time jobs to pay for his four kids. Jose talked so much shit about his other boss that it made me wonder what he said over there about me. Honestly, he talked more shit than anyone in my kitchen, but it was always in a joking way. He didn't have an enemy in the world, and he was a well-oiled food-prep machine. No knife roll for this guy. He had one big ten-inch blade that he hid in a different place every night, and the man knew how to use it. This guy could small dice an onion faster than any machine in my kitchen. No overpriced Robot Coupe for me-- I had Jose. As I said, everyone loved him; he liked Annie and Annie liked him.

Billy was my all-around back-up guy-- part-time dishwasher/prep cook/busboy/parking lot sweeper/bathroom cleaner/occasional ass kisser. There isn't much to say about Billy. He was a wallflower. Sometimes I forgot he was even there. He knew his job, came in and got it done. I had to send him home a few times for showing up looking like he just rolled in after an all-night bender but, other than that, he was alright. I don't even think that Annie knew his name for the first few weeks. Billy was a big, big guy. He was a good six six and took up lots of real estate when he moved around my tiny kitchen. He had bushy dirty blonde hair that was usually unkempt but in a surfer boy kinda way, so it worked. He was also very modernly Christian. He wore WWJD bracelets and talked a lot about his ultra-modern church but, when he was in the dish pit, he always listened to pretty hardcore rap, not of the Christian persuasion, with his headphones on and was not shy about singing along. WWJD? -- definitely not sing those songs. Billy was an odd guy but incredibly kind and caring.

Besides me, that was pretty much my kitchen crew. I had another ten servers and bartenders and a few more busboys, but those positions are transient. I had one bartender that'd been with me since the beginning but, as soon as a hot new restaurant opens, those positions jump ship for more tips.

Although she didn't care much for Jesse's attitude, Annie did appreciate being his line mate because Jesse was fast and never fucked up orders. But he was also a messy line cook, and that bothered her. She was regularly cleaning up behind him and, at the end of the night, had to go out back, take the cig out of his mouth and drag him back in the kitchen to help break it down. But, when the ticket rail was full, and they were weeded, she didn't want anybody else next to her. Line mate comfort and trust is a good thing. Yeah, Jesse was a hell of a worker and a generally good guy.

But he was also a dumbass who had nine brothers with zero respect for any woman other than their momma. The stuff that came out of Jesse's mouth about women was unbelievable. In an effort to not offend my readers, I will limit myself to only three examples of his favorite "Jesse-isms," which is probably three too many. If Jesse ate or smelled something he didn't like, it was "like some nasty bitch." If someone screwed up a ticket, it was "just like a damned chick would do." If a line mate or customer complained, "Quit bein' a little bitch girl." These were his three favorite sayings, and he used them even when they made absolutely no sense at all.

OK, I realize you're probably wondering why I kept this kid around, let alone hiring him in the first place. And, all I can say is, I know. I'm part of the problem. I get it. I traded morality for hard work and put my business in legal jeopardy at the same time. Do you have any idea how hard it is to find someone to show up every day and work hard at the rates small restaurants can afford to pay line cooks? It's fucking hard. So, yeah, I made a morally lousy choice to keep him around, but I kinda liked my restaurant to be open, and nobody else was banging down my door to earn fourteen dollars per hour and sweat the whole time. Until you've been there, don't judge. An old wolf hunts with the teeth he's got.

Jesse and Annie had become like brother and sister. They bickered a lot but genuinely liked each other. Not the kind of like that would bring them together outside the workplace, and they certainly didn't go bar hopping. They joked, laughed, yelled with and at each other but always closed up the night as friends.

Long after the fact that Annie was married to a woman was known to all, Jesse changed his tune. He started to flirt. It was so sudden that I thought maybe something had happened outside of work between the two of them. Jesse began making teenage boy type compliments and going out of his way to help her. He would take a minute to leave a prep list for her or offer to place the produce order. This was not like Jesse. He didn't usually think about other people's feelings, and, all of a sudden, he seemed smitten.

I watched this closely yet from afar. As long as I didn't see anything that would be considered harassment, I let it go. But then Jesse crossed the line. One day he put his arm around Annie's waist and kinda pulled her in close like a friendly hug but maybe just a little bit too friendly. She didn't seem to care, but I did. No touching in my restaurant. Period. I pulled Jesse aside later that night and warned him to keep his paws off and to stop flirting. That was the first time I ever had to have words with him, and he was not happy about it. He got very defensive and claimed it was all just friendly stuff, but I didn't care.

Later that week, I walked into a fecal blizzard.

THE NOSE PICKING INCIDENT

'm not sure what set it off but, when I arrived, Annie had vengeance in her eyes. I asked Polo where Jesse was, and he started laughing and stole a look at Jose. Jose nodded his head towards the walk-in refrigerator and joined Polo in whatever hilarity he was enjoying.

Annie was on the line with a bowl of fresh ground pork and another bowl of hog intestine. She was tense, her face hot with rage, and she was standing tall and stoic, staring and seething at the wall. She had a knife in her hand, and her bony knuckles were stark white. She needed to lighten that grip and step away from the sausage stuffer. I asked her out back for a smoke, hoping to get an idea of what was going on, but she was tight-lipped. She was not a kiss and tell type girl. Whatever happened between them was between them. I told her to take a break and cool down.

I found Jesse standing in the walk-in, literally cooling down, with a bloody towel up to his nose. Like Annie, Jesse wasn't giving up the ghost, so I had no idea what had happened. I just assumed Annie went Ali on Jesse's nose; I know I had wanted to a few times in the past. Maybe I had a little more patience than Annie. I put the kitchen on a thirty-minute break, asked them to all get over what happened and come back ready to work. I cranked, stuffed, and twisted the sausages myself. When Jesse came back, besides the big bandage on his nose, he seemed to be perfectly normal and OK. Back to work, no bullshit.

That was the quietest shift ever. I was the only one who spoke, and I kept it all business. Order, fire, pick-up. That was it. There was no room in the air for pleasantries, compliments, or jokes about bitchy diners.

Jesse and Annie both left in separate directions the second the kitchen was broken down. Polo, Billy, and Jose were cracking their shift beers, so I figured I'd join them and see if they'd spill the beans. Billy said that Jesse showed up to work with a hickey on his neck, and Annie made a joke about it. That sent Jesse into asshole ego mode, and he started laying on the flirty touchy bullshit pretty thick. He was saying things to Annie like, "Don't get jealous, baby" and "Maybe it's time you had some of my goodness between those long-ass legs, baby" and "How about I go over to your place after work and show you and your girl what you've been missin'."

Annie was in the middle of grinding up the pork when, according to Polo, after Jesse's comments, she picked up his precious knife roll and threw it in the deep fryer. Then she grabbed her blade, pushed him up against the wall, and took a little nip off the tip of his nose. Jesse was screaming and bleeding into his apron while hearing Polo, Jose, and Billy cracking up as his precious knife roll melted in the hot oil.

The next day was almost like nothing had happened. Jesse was quieter than usual, and a much smaller band-aid had replaced the massive bandage from the night before. He and Annie even joked a bit, but there was definitely some tension from the elephant in the room. I watched, curiously and cautiously, to make sure there wasn't going to be a repeat performance by either of them, and there wasn't. After a few days, I had pretty much forgotten about the whole incident, and it seemed like the crew had, too.

I met with Annie and Jesse separately after the incident. I told them that I knew what had happened, and, to cover my ass, I wrote them both up - Jesse for harassment and Annie for picking his nose with his own knife. First and final write-ups for both. If Annie complained about harassment or if I witnessed it, Jesse was out. If Annie took to violence again, she was out. Annie was confident that it was just a moment, and she had spent enough time in enough kitchens to know that some guys just think it's OK to pull crap like that. Jesse apologized to Annie, and they even laughed a bit about his melted knife roll and how I had made Polo clean the fryer.

By now, you get the deal in my kitchen - it's pretty loose. I find no need to crack the whip when the food is coming out right, it's coming out fast, and we're on wait most nights. Jesse and Annie seemed to work their situation out on their own, and I didn't hear a peep out of Jesse that would even come close to harassment. So, why rock the boat? Well, because I should have, for one. But, despite the intense nature of the line when you're in the weeds, we all laughed it out over beer and a smoke at the end of every night. Weeks went on like that, and it was nice to be back to normal. We were a tight crew.

We were.

NOVEMBER 2

BUCKETHEAD

COSTA MESA, CA

33° 36' 26.7" N

117° 55' 46.6" W

MILES WALKED: 0

Until Jesse made his final move on Annie. Polo and Jose had been warning him for a few weeks, since the nose picking incident, to back off his comments and advances on Annie. Jesse, as brilliant as he was, decided enough time had passed. He just wouldn't succumb to the fact that he couldn't convince Annie that HE could get her to play on the hetero team. Honest to God and I swear on all that's holy that, since the nose picking incident, I didn't know about or witness any issues between Jesse and Annie until after Jose found Jesse's head and balls frozen solid in a twenty-two quart container filled with our secret recipe carne asada marinade in the walk-in freezer. Coincidentally, the discovery was made on the same day that Annie pulled her first, and last, no show.

Finding Jesse's head and junk took a while. Something didn't seem quite right that morning. I walked into a not so clean kitchen, which was pretty unusual when Annie closed up shop the night before. The floor looked like it had been cleaned, then something spilled on it, and it was hastily cleaned again. One of the pot scrub sinks was full of dark, murky

27

water, but I assumed it was one of the hood vents soaking overnight to de-grease. And there was a funk in the air. Sometimes that happens in a restaurant, so it doesn't cause too much concern. You go looking for the piece of shrimp that fell under a table and avoided the broom and get it out to the dumpster. Problem solved. But this didn't seem like that. Anyway, I didn't mind. Jesse would be in soon, and he'd figure it out. But he didn't show up. I was in my dinky office doing payroll or some crap and lost track of time when Polo poked his head in.

Polo: "Hey, Chef, where's Jesse? And what's that smell?"

Me: "Huh? He's not here?"

A glance at the wall clock confirmed that the whining little maggot was late for the very first time. Must have been a big night out. Jesse never showed up late and never called out sick. So, I called his phone. Nothin'. I called his roommate (one of our servers). Nothin'--hadn't seen him since yesterday at work and assumed he went out, got drunk, and met a girl with lousy decision-making capabilities or a very low bar for a one-night stand.

Me: "Grab a prep shirt from the locker. It's you and me till Annie shows up. Let's get prepped and then clean up whatever that is soaking in dish pit."

Polo: "Yes, Chef."

I love that answer.

We were an hour into prep and pretty much ready to go. Annie, despite her questionable cleaning job, at least got Jesse to help prep us up for that day. Polo emerged from the dish pit, looking confused.

Polo: "Nothing in the water, boss."

Me: "Goddammit. What did they do in here last night? The place looks like crap, smells like ass, and they left a sink full of dirty dishwater?"

But then Annie no showed. That's when I knew something was way off. Wait, did those two fuckers go off and hook up? I'll be damned! I'm not one to condone people cheating, but I'd be lying if I said a small smirk didn't cross my face. Did Jesse actually convince Annie to switch teams, if only for a night? Whatever was going on, they were both on my shit list. I started to panic a bit and called Jose in for lunch service. Luckily it was his day off at his other job, and he grudgingly agreed to come in. I also called Billy in to lend a hand.

Lunch was a little slow, and I didn't care. I called Jesse and Annie every ten minutes with no luck. I was a bit worried, but more pissed off because I was going to have to pay Jose, Polo, and Billy overtime to help me get through dinner if neither of them showed up.

Between lunch and dinner, I called my buddy, who's a cop a few towns over, and asked him if I should be worried enough to file a report. He told me not to call one in but that he'd call his friend who was a cop in my town and ask him to stop by today. Officer Adam pulled in around four thirty, and we sat at the bar. I told him the whole story about the incident a few weeks earlier and how things were back to normal. Then I filled him in on Jesse and Annie's disappearing act. Adam started to tell me that these things happen all the time; maybe they were secret lovers. "HOLY SHIT!" Jose's voice boomed through the kitchen and into the bar, and he came barreling through the door to the dining room, followed closely by Polo.

Me: "What the hell, Jose?"

Jose: "Chef, dude, what the fuck is in there? The marinade! The goddamned marinade! I opened the frozen tub of carne asada marinade, and there's a dude in there staring at me, and he looks just like Jesse!"

What the hell was Jose talking about? The cop looked at me as he pulled back his face in a confused look. Like me, he clearly didn't understand what Jose's out of breath ranting could mean. There was a dude in the marinade staring at him who looked like Jesse? I shook my head, clearly annoyed, and invited the cop in to see what Jose was yapping about.

Sure as shit, Jesse was in the frozen marinade, and he was staring straight up at me. Well, at least his head was. The tub was a frozen solid block of orange juice, lemon juice, lime juice, garlic cloves, low sodium soy sauce, chipotle in adobo sauce, chili powder, cumin seed, paprika, oregano, black pepper, canola oil, and Jesse's head. It had floated to the top of the liquid and froze, eyes wide open without any distinct look on his face. I was perplexed at how someone could die so horribly yet have such a serene, peaceful appearance after their head had been removed. It would be a few hours before we learned that his balls were also a part of the new recipe.

This would explain the mediocre floor cleaning job and murky water. Polo was in the bathroom puking for ten minutes. It turns out he had his bare hands and arms down in that water, and this fact was not settling well with him.

Me: "So, do you want me to thaw this out or…?" I asked the cop.

Officer Adam: "No, leave it there and get your team out of the kitchen but don't let them leave. You won't need a sign to tell diners that you're closed tonight. They'll figure it out."

And figure it out they did. No less than a dozen squad cars with flashing red and blues, news vans with their phallic satellite poles (I do love how those things pop up out of the tops of those vans), about a hundred people crowded around the sidewalk and a cadaver sniffing dog was apparently enough to warn off would-be diners.

Guess what boards up an eatery faster than the health department publicizing the discovery of a cockroach infestation? That's right, a severed head and a pair of nuts in your marinade. Besides the obvious hurdles like a murder investigation, police tape, reporters, and the well-marinated body parts, the main reason this type of problem shuts down a restaurant is that everyone will forever wonder where the rest of the fucking body is. The news played out the murder particulars, so everyone knew what had been found in the marinade and what had not. So, people will want to know about the rest of the parts, especially the dick. Forget the torso, feet, hands, arms, and legs – where's the dick? See the problem? Let's just pretend that I did happen to re-open, and someone actually came back to "help support us," how could they take one bite of our Monday night meatloaf special without pause? Without wondering just a little bit?

The comical irony that our menu's focus was hand-cranked sausages was not lost on me.

Closed. Permanently. Wouldn't be surprised if they just leveled that building. No restaurant would ever gamble on that site. Sorry asshole property owner guy, but my insurance didn't cover this one, so I gotta file the ole BK and be on my way. Good luck on that corner, you slime ball.

BONUS!

If you've made it this far, still have an appetite, and want to make some delicious carne asada, here's a recipe for you - minus the body parts.

Just mix all these ingredients together, toss in a big Ziplock with some skirt steak and refrigerate for at least four hours (overnight is even better). Fire up a BBQ, get it as hot as you can, remove meat from marinade and grill over the flame for about eight minutes per side. Slice thin against the grain and serve on warm corn tortillas with your taco toppings of choice.

- 1 ½ cups Orange juice, fresh squeezed
- 1 cup Lemon juice, fresh squeezed
- 1 cup Lime juice, fresh squeezed
- 6 Garlic cloves, crushed up and minced
- 1 cup Soy sauce, low sodium
- 1 Tbsp Chipotle in Adobo Sauce, smashed
- 5 tsp Chili powder
- 5 tsp Cumin seeds, toasted and ground fine
- 5 tsp Paprika
- 5 tsp Mexican Oregano, dried
- 5 tsp Black pepper, fresh ground
- ¾ cup Canola oil

DECEMBER - FEBRUARY

AFTERMATH

Annie was in the wind. It had been a few weeks since I shuttered the windows at the restaurant, and the nightly news had carried the unsolved story for about a week. After the hunt for Annie failed to produce any leads whatsoever, The Buckethead Killer story was lost in the shuffle of all the other chaos that was Southern California news. Occasionally there'd be a *Breaking News, This Just In* update about the case teased all day, but they were always random comments about sightings of Annie or interviews with her friends, and, get this, her estranged husband. Yeah, you read that right. Annie was not married to a woman. Some random LA guy called up with all the evidence to support his marriage to Annie. Apparently, they met and married within a month and, just as quickly, she was gone. He hadn't appeared to be horribly broken up over his loss, rather, he seemed more relieved that his body was still supported by a healthy set of nuts.

Three weeks after the discovery in the freezer, the cops got another bombshell call that sent the case further into a tailspin. The anonymous female caller suggested that the girl plastered all over the news wasn't named Annie and that they could probably find her on Instagram under the name CarbonEdgeKenn. Ha. That made me laugh because her blades were fucking sharp. Sorry, Jesse.

Because the cops and news outlets were focused on finding a gruesome lesbian killer named Annie who chopped off some poor kid's head and balls, it took investigators three weeks and two jaw dropping calls to figure out that 1.) Annie was not a lesbian, 2.) she was not married to a woman, and that 3.) Annie Fox wasn't her name. Her real name was Kennedy Rose Quinn.

Who the hell was this girl that I hired? She had all the legal crap in her wallet that showed her name as Annie Fox. No middle name. She had a California driver's license, social security card, and I even saw her damn Costco card with the same info one day when we went shopping together. She even had *Annie* engraved on her blades. Of course I had given all that info to the cops including her bank account that I direct deposited her paychecks into (which was drained to zero the day after the murder) and her mailing address from her I9 form (which turned out to be the address of a long-ago boarded up halfway house a few miles away).

Luckily for me, I had saved up a little bit of cash, but I was utterly lost without my restaurant. I had spent over a year planning it, building it, perfecting the recipes, and, over the past four years, had built up a pretty damned respectable eating and drinking establishment less than a mile from my house. I had every chef's dream ripped away from me with one swift slash of a blade. OK, that's a bit overdramatic. I'm sure it took far more than one slash to do the work she did on Jesse.

The rest of Jesse's body was never found, which was difficult for the cops to understand because Annie, errrrr, Kennedy didn't have a car and there was no trail of blood out of the kitchen. They even went so far as to test all of our house-made sausages for traces of human flesh. Nope. None. We pride ourselves on using only the finest, all-natural pork and seasonings and firmly believe that there is no room for additives or fillers in our fine charcuterie.

For days my entire staff was called upon time and time again to meet with investigators to talk about Kennedy. The news didn't know what to do. They had made so many splash screens and clever nicknames for the elusive lesbian killer known as Annie and, all of a sudden, she wasn't a lesbian, and her name wasn't Annie. Annie is such a catchy little name that's so easy to make into clever nicknames. What the hell do you do with Kennedy and murder that some won't find offensive because of the assassination of JFK? You can't make clever names using Killer and Kennedy; it just doesn't fly with the public. And the juicy tidbit of Annie being a lesbian was now gone, too. So sorry news teams, but you're gonna have to put in some overtime if you want this story to sound sexy now. I hated the media during all this crap. They made snarky comments and dropped innuendos about my restaurant and missing body parts and homemade sausages and, of course, painted the picture of an owner who ran a circus in his kitchen. And, of course, the story of the nose-picking incident surfaced, so I must have known that Kennedy was violent, and I should have been more proactive. Yadda yadda yadda. Back off asshole anchor news dude, you have no idea who I am or how I ran my kitchen.

OK, maybe I should have seen this coming, but I didn't, or perhaps I thought they would fight a little, but I certainly never anticipated this. I guess, in hindsight, asshole anchor dude was a little bit right.

I filed for bankruptcy two months later. I had no choice. I had a personal guarantee on the building lease, and it was my only way out of not paying the jackass owner nearly ninety grand in penalties for breach of contract. He had no chance of finding a new tenant, so I was on the hook for three more years. I didn't care. I carried about fifty thousand in credit card debt, so I got rid of that as well. I owned my car and rented my little beach house and had no ambition to buy a place, so what the hell did I care about bankruptcy on my record?

Life was grim. I didn't go out in public because I was known to most in my town, and I couldn't even get a beer without strangers staring at me or familiar people coming up to offer an unwanted, uninvited hug. These feigned moments of communal grieving would inevitably open the door to long conversations about the murder, and I was over it. I heard so many rumors that I didn't even try to dispel them any longer. Everyone could piss off for all I cared. I was the guy that busted his ass and bankroll to create a place where everyone had fun and felt welcomed and where my employees were treated well. In the blink of an eye, I became the guy that had a head and balls floating in his marinade and a dead employee on his conscience. I had to get out. I had to get away from this circus and figure out what the hell I was going to do with the next fifty years of my life. Yes, I wanted to live another fifty years, but I knew I wasn't up for even one more day of this life.

By the time the news had pretty much tired itself with the Kennedy/Annie story, I had become a hermit. I was running out of money, I hadn't spoken with my friends or family in nearly a month, and I was holed up inside my shack of a house for days on end. I stopped shaving and cutting my hair. I looked like a hundred miles of really hard road. I'd sneak down to the beach when nobody was there to enjoy the sun and waves and, when necessary, I'd cover myself up as much as possible and attempt an incognito trip to the grocery store for cheap wine and whatever frozen entrees were on sale. I was sinking quickly to a bottom that scared me to death. Just a few months earlier, I was eating great food, drinking good wine, and hanging out in my bar with friends. Now I was an unemployable fifty-year-old chef who knew no other trade and had no desire to learn one.

The bottom of a bottle can't possibly drown sorrows that have already learned to swim. I needed to escape.

I came across a book by a guy named Tyler Coulson while killing an afternoon at the library; it told the story of a man who walked across America with his dog Mabel. Tyler wasn't a philanthropic journeyman, and he wasn't out to prove anything to anybody. It wasn't an athletic endeavor, and, for the most part, besides Mabel, he did it alone. He spoke of the endless highways and millions of minutes he spent in his head, trying to discover what kind of man he was. He walked with his dog, talked with his dog, and he listened to his dog. He learned how to care for another living being and how to let another living being take care of him. He braved the elements, intense loneliness, wild animals, and gut-wrenching gas station food. And then he wrote a beautiful book that was deep and intense and so far from a mundane, boring memoir that it was hard to believe that it was non-fiction. His words riveted me. I wanted to be him or be like him. I wanted to be that brave, and, for the first time in my life, I wanted to be that alone.

The day I finished his book, I decided I was going to go for a walk. A long, long walk. And I was going to get a dog, so I'd have someone to talk with. I knew from reading his book that if I didn't have a damn good reason why I was going to walk, I would never make it. So, I thought long and hard about why I wanted to do this. Escape wasn't enough. That reason would wear out quickly, and I'd end up quitting. I thought about a lot of things I had royally jacked up in my life, things I had always told myself were not my fault but knew they were. And there were some unpleasantries that happened to me as a kid that I had packed up years ago but had never thrown out. It was time to dig out that box and examine its contents.

But all of this noise that I attached to my "why" could be done anywhere and certainly in less time than it would take to walk this old, overworked body across America. There had to be a reason I wanted to do this particular walk. What was pulling on me to do this? What was nagging me to get away from my hometown and wander, somewhat aimlessly, down a bunch of highways and county roads?

And then I knew why. I needed to find that bitch Annie. Kennedy. Whatever the hell her name was. I'm gonna call her Annie because it was Annie, not Kennedy, who cut that kid's head off and ruined my life. Well, and his, too, so I guess I was going to do it for both of us. I knew I'd be able to cover a lot more ground more quickly in a car chasing her down, but that wouldn't allow me the time I needed to sort out all of my other dominoes, get them all lined up straight and pretty and stack them nicely back in their little wooden box. I still needed to do that on this journey and driving around aimlessly would take away from that. Besides, I needed to sell my car so that I wouldn't run out of money and gas was too damned expensive.

WALKER TIP
TO DOG OR NOT TO DOG?

Walking with a dog has its ups and downs. Wink provided companionship and protection. He was warm in the tent on cold nights, he reminded me that I was loved, and he gave me purpose on days when I struggled. We talked a ton and, yes, dogs will talk back. I have zero regrets about getting a dog for my journey.

The downsides to walking with a dog are many and should be considered before you make that decision. Food and extra water are very heavy. For as much water as you carry for yourself, you have to bring the same for a dog. Depending on size, you will be buying dog food in seven to ten-pound size bags which can get expensive. Buying a forty-pound bag is far cheaper but pushing that much extra weight is tough. You also better make sure your dog is healthy and can handle twenty miles per day regardless of the weather or have a small enough dog and big enough cart to put it in. I would recommend getting pet insurance for about forty dollars per month. I had to use it twice and it saved me a ton of money.

A dog will slow you down and set the pace so be prepared for that. Oh, and forget about eating in restaurants or cafes, a dog immediately converts you into an outside diner. It wouldn't hurt to make sure your dog obeys all normal commands like heel, come and sit. No point bringing an untrained dog that's gonna be difficult to handle. It's hard enough getting strangers to help you on the side of the road and if you have an aggressive dog, forget it.

To sum it up, I quote Section 13, Part C (6)(C) from Tyler Coulson's
How To Walk Across America and Not Be An Asshole

The Walker with a dog must repeat this mantra: "I know and accept that, by bringing my dog on a walk across America, I am agreeing to let the dog set the pace."

ANNIE/KENNEDY

I hadn't watched the news in weeks. I had already tuned out before the discovery and identification of hetero Kennedy. By then, I had lost everything and didn't care what the cops were up to, what they knew about her, what her friends were saying about her or what leads they had fruitlessly followed up.

But now I was obsessed with gathering as much info as I could on her. So, I dug in deep. I was Dick Fucking Tracy. I should have bought a yellow trench coat and fedora. I researched every article, every interview, every news clip, and started my own little investigation. Stones left unturned - zero. The number of people I cared about pissing off by digging into this girl's life - zero.

I called my old buddy Johnny, a former private investigator who lived in Idaho, and asked him to help me out. He didn't do that kind of work anymore, but he had heard bits and pieces about the strange murder investigation out in Southern California. He had no idea that I was the poor sap who had lost his entire well-being and life savings after her brutal attack.

He agreed to do some work for free because he thought the whole case was quite funny with the chopped off balls angle and because one night, back in high school when we were young punks, I introduced him to the woman he ended up marrying so I guess he felt like he owed me something. Hell, I just took him to a party and said hi to my friend Shannon, they hooked up a few nights later, and that had lasted over thirty years.

Johnny called me about a week after our initial conversation and not only dumped all kinds of useful info in my lap, he also dropped a bombshell. The cops had screwed up. Her name was not Kennedy Rose Quinn; it was Kennedy Quinn Rose.

Me: "What the hell are you telling me, Johnny? Quinn is her middle name, not her last?"

Johnny: "That's what I'm telling you, man. The cops fucked the names up. Quinn isn't a ubiquitous name for any girl, so they just assumed, I guess, that it was her last name. I don't know what to tell you."

Me: "Who gives their daughter the middle name of Quinn?"

Johnny: "Don't be so old, dude. It's an up and coming name for girls these days, but it certainly wasn't forty-four years ago. If you're gonna be out there chasing her and the cops figure out her real name, they're gonna get there before you. If you show up after them, you could be in real danger."

Me: "Fuck them. I'm gonna let 'em hit a dead end with the wrong names and, eventually, they'll cold case it."

Johnny had all kinds of info on the movement of Kennedy Quinn Rose, but Annie was a ghost with zero paper trail. She was also older than I thought. She was forty-four, not thirty-eight. She was tall, which I already knew, and had no living siblings. She was born in Whiteville, North Carolina, a small up and coming town about two hours north of Charleston digging its way out of disastrous flood and economic hardship in the south. Her family was scattered from multiple divorces and was difficult, but not impossible, to pin down. Her mother, Peggy Sue, was living in a small town called Monroe, GA, and worked as a bartender in an Irish pub at the ripe young age of sixty-two, which means she was only eighteen when she popped out a murderer. She was a washed-out hippy with wrinkled tattoos and deep lines in her face from years of smoking Lucky non-filters and shooting Jack behind the bar. Annie's sixty-seven-year-old father, Lester, lived in an even smaller town called Rockmart, Georgia. I don't know why he landed so far away, but Rockmart was a good five hundred miles west of the Whiteville trailer park he used to call home. Maybe he just needed some distance. He had owned an auto parts salvage yard just off the main highway that was now boarded up but still full of rusted out tractors, cars, refrigerators, and whatnot. Annie had random, distant cousins from coast to coast along the south in both Carolinas, Mississippi, Arkansas, Texas, Arizona, and California. Only a few of them had crawled out of the blue-collar life and made something a little more for themselves. He gave me all their names, occupations, and last known addresses.

Johnny then gave me a timeline of Annie's whereabouts for the past four decades. Her parents split up when Annie was five. Annie and her mom moved around a bit in the Carolinas and eventually settled down in Monroe, GA, when Annie was in seventh grade. Annie was a high school dropout and had worked as a line cook in the same Irish pub her mom still tended bar in. She meandered west and worked in various kitchens but never held a position that would require her to practice any management skills or allow her a fancy title. She was a wallflower to most former employers. She was a hard worker, punctual, dependable, and likable. The only consistent storyline besides her stellar work ethics that followed her from town to town was that she slept around with a lot of her co-workers, and then she would disappear. She got into a few scraps with other female employees, and they were always over her promiscuity. The common theme was that she didn't seem to care if someone was hurt by her screwing around so long as her needs were met.

Kennedy Quinn Rose dropped off the radar in Albuquerque. Her name never surfaced again. And neither did the name Annie Fox. She was a nobody until she showed up at my restaurant. She had made it across the US via the southern states as Kennedy until she appeared on my doorstep in her crisp white coat, well-worn clogs, and badass line skills as Annie.

I struggled with hating her for ruining my life. I didn't know why she had done what she did to Jesse, and I wasn't sure if I'd ever find out.

I may never have found her. Jesse was a lot to take and, not that anybody deserves what she gave to him, I can only imagine what pissed her off so badly that she took his body apart. And, why the hell did she leave him the way she did? It was pure hatred. But why would she do that to me? I had always treated her well and even bumped her pay a bit after only a few weeks. She had to have known that by leaving Jesse's body parts in the freezer would shut me down. She had to have known that I would lose everything. She knew my restaurant was my life, my wife, and my lover, and that no doubt it defined me as a man.

I was becoming a prey driven hound. I needed to find that bitch, not for justice, but for answers.

BECOMING A HUNTER

For my walk (and mostly just on paper), I planned for pain, loneliness, crap weather, wild animals, crazy people, flat tires, boil in a bag food, sore muscles, defecating in the woods, caring for a dog and everything else on my long list. I bought the right gear, clothes, first-aid kit, double-wide baby jogger, cook system, shoes, flashlights, and all kinds of other stuff I figured I'd need. I read at least a dozen books by people who had walked across America. I planned my route to the day, created a fancy spreadsheet and became a Google Maps pro. On paper, I was ready to go. I would later learn that my body and my mind were not as well prepared, and they certainly were not in lockstep with my heart, which ached to go.

I have to spend a minute on my ridiculously cool cart I affectionately named Alexa. No, it's not a shopping cart I lifted from the local market; it's a double-wide baby stroller/jogger made by Thule. I named her Alexa because, at my house, I have one of those completely unnecessary gadgets that does shit for you when you ask it to. You don't even have to ask nicely; you just have to say her name. You all know them as the Amazon Alexa. I love that thing. But I had to leave it at home, of course, so my cart became Alexa. Alexa is top of the line, and, had I not found one used, I wouldn't have had it. They're about $1,000 new, and I didn't have that kind of money. Luckily, those are the kinds of things that people buy and never use and end up selling for cheap on Craigslist. I was the benefactor of one of those consumers.

I modified the hell out of it. I cut out the baby seats and removed any piece of aluminum and metal that wasn't vital to the stability of the cart.

I installed drum brakes on the rear wheels which were already attached to a badass suspension system, purchased a backup wheel/tire assembly for quick flat changes, installed a four-panel solar set up on the top, added a few lights, a nifty cell phone holder, an aftermarket rain protector, attached my safety gear in a way that was easy to access and even installed a Camelbak water system so it'd be easy to hydrate without reaching for a bottle. Alexa was beautiful and, considering all the add on goodies, was still pretty lightweight. After she was completely loaded with all my gear and water/food, she weighed a little over 125 pounds. Alexa was solid. I knew she'd get me across the country. If you're one of those people that is offended because I attached a gender to Alexa, feel free to dispose of this trashy novel now and slam me on social media. I don't care.

I couldn't wait to meet the countless strangers on the road. I knew in my gut that, for the most part, Americans were good people. Hell, I was a decent looking guy, easy to talk to, outgoing, had a sweet looking dog, my cart was pretty much brand new and super shiny, and the gear on it confused those that would normally think I was homeless. I also knew I'd meet some real pricks and would have to accept being judged by them, stared at by them, and harassed by them, but I never thought I'd have to kill some of them.

I quit smoking, although I did start using a stupid little vape pen to get my Nic-fix when I needed it. I started eating better and walked about seventy-five miles per week completely geared up so I'd build the muscles I'd need to succeed. I got a dog specifically for the walk. I wasn't planning on bringing a dog, but I was talked into it by family and friends who felt I needed companionship and protection. I named him Wink because he winked at me when I asked him at the shelter if he wanted to go home with me. That was easy. I had no intention of falling in love with him; I didn't even like dogs, but I loved Wink. He was my new best friend, my co-pilot, my protector and my motivator. He would not let me be lazy on the road. He would out walk me every day and be waiting by the tent or motel room door every morning ready to leave.

WALKER TIP

GUNS AND WEAPONRY

If you want to carry a gun, carry a damn gun. BUT you better be a gun person and know how to use that thing because, when you would need it on a walk, you won't have time to hesitate or consider if you really want to shoot someone. And it better be well concealed yet easily accessible, and that can be a tricky combo to accomplish on a baby stroller. Easily accessible on a cart means exposed to the weather, so you better KNOW that your wet gun isn't going to fail you. And, lastly, every ounce counts, so don't go all Dirty Harry and try to pack around a .44. You don't need to blow someone's head off but get something powerful enough to stop a human and large animal. Oh, and you might wanna check the laws about bringing that thing across state lines - pretty sure you can't do that.

Whether you carry a gun or not, definitely have weaponry available for protection and have them readily available. Bear spray, pepper spray, knives and a stun-gun were my weapons of choice and I did have situations where they could have come in handy had things escalated. Bear spray will stop pretty much any predator from a good, safe distance. It's not cheap but it's worth having should you meet up with a bad guy. Or a bear.

The most common question asked before and during my walk was, "Do you have a gun?" The answer to that was, "Maybe." What's the point of telling everyone you have a weapon that is illegal in a lot of states and certainly not legal to carry over state lines? But I didn't have a gun. I had everything possible to protect myself up to having a gun. I'm not a gun person, and I don't think I'd use one, and it would probably be used against me. So, no, no gun.

I should have brought a gun.

When I said I had everything else, I did. I had multiple knives and a stun gun strategically placed on my cart. I had bear spray, which is designed to stop a grizzly at full speed so you can imagine the damage it would do to a tweaker who wanted to steal my stuff. I had a walking stick that I only carried for protection. I had an air horn and even a cute little "pull this pin" alarm thing that would burst your eardrums if you held it too close to your head. But, most importantly, I had Wink, common sense, the gift of gab and could talk my way out of most bad situations.

But I should have brought a gun.

Since Annie started life near the east coast, that's where I was gonna start hunting. Hunt and, of course, sort through all my demons and see which ones I still enjoyed having around. But, for now, I'll focus on those miles that pertained to the hunting of a murderer and how the road made me a killer.

I planned my start for early February. I learned, from reading all those damn books, that you have to start walking from the east coast no later than the first week of March if you want to avoid snow in the Rockies and Sierras soon after late summer. Since I was a good twenty years older than most of the authors I read, I planned my start for the first week of February to give my older body a little extra bonus time. I knew I'd need more days off, and I'd walk a slower pace than those whose advice I was using to plan this thing.

THE WALK

FEBRUARY

THE HUNT BEGINS

HOLDEN BEACH, NORTH CAROLINA
TO
AIKEN, SOUTH CAROLINA

FIRST STEPS

HOLDEN BEACH, NC

33° 54' 50.8392" N

78° 16' 1.632" W

MILES WALKED: 0

After selling all my worldly possessions, packing up my gear, crating my dog, and flying to Charleston, I took a week to hang out with my son who lived there. I knew this walk could kill me, and I knew I needed some time with him before I took those first steps. We were close. We were more like friends than we were like father/son. I started getting antsy after a few days, so I asked him to take me up to North Carolina to a small beach town that bore his name and was just a few days walk from Whiteville, the small town in North Carolina where Annie was born. I would start hunting there.

The weather on the morning I started walking couldn't have been more perfect. The sun was out, it was a bit chilly, which is good for walking, and the water in the Atlantic Ocean was reasonably warm for early February. I knew this because I took off my shoes and socks and went out there and stood, near knee-deep, and watched the sunrise. It was the first time I had seen the sunrise over the Atlantic, and it was magnificent. I thought it would look just like a sun setting over the Pacific Ocean, but it was remarkably different. The sky in the east, coming out of the night, was ash grey with long streaks of a hundred hues of orange emanating from a fiery ball that was still invisible behind the water. It seemed to take forever before I saw the tip of the massive orb peek over the horizon. Dozens of seagulls stopped flying and landed nearby on the sand that still shimmered from the last wave of water that had washed over it. I looked down to see bubbles coming up through the sand and, at my feet, was a small yet perfectly designed shell about the size of a quarter. I picked it up and put it in my pocket. I would later wear it around my neck to remind me that it was going to have a new home on the west coast when I got there.

I stood, Wink at my side, seagulls all around, and every living animal with a breath within my line of sight was motionless. I had never seen this sunrise before. I knew Wink had never seen it either. I had this odd wonder about the fish in the sea, and the absurd thought that, maybe, they, too, stopped swimming every morning to witness this beautiful spectacle. Slowly the sun made its acquaintance with me, and we shared a stare that lasted several minutes. We both knew it was our first and final moment together. The birds flew away to continue whatever they were doing a few minutes earlier, Wink had lost his gaze on the horizon and started digging in the sand, and I knew it was time to turn around and get on the road. I pulled out a little wide-mouth bottle I had brought, dropped another small shell and some sand inside, and scooped up some water. I sealed it up tight and walked back to the road.

Wink: *"Are you ready?"*

Me: "Yeah, I think. Let's do it."

After drying my feet and spending several minutes making sure that every grain of sand was out from between my toes and from under my feet, I put on my socks and shoes, and my son and I started walking west. I was only five feet in when it finally hit me that I had over three thousand miles to go until I got home and that it was going to take me at least eight months to get there. Maybe more, depending on how the hunt went.

My son walked a few miles with me, then we stopped, hugged,

dropped a few tears, and said goodbye. My son didn't know I was going hunting. He thought I was having a midlife crisis, and I probably was. That was the hardest moment of my life. I had said goodbye to him a hundred times as he grew up, became a man, and went off to college, but this time was the most difficult because I had a pretty strong feeling that it would be the last time I ever saw him. Your odds of dying increased astronomically when you walked thousands of miles with several hundred tons of steel flying by within inches of your body. Doing the walk while hunting a cold-blooded killer pretty much sealed the death deal.

Wink: *"Are you done sniffling? You'll see him again. Come on, let's go. We're not even close."*

FIRST BLOOD

MILES WALKED: 14

Twenty-four hours. I became a killer within twenty-four hours of starting my walk. It was one of those self-defense killings, though. I hadn't gone crazy that quickly. Day two would turn out to be a pivotal moment, and it pissed me off because it delayed me a few weeks.

I had stayed at a small motel in a near coastal town called Shallotte, about fourteen miles from the ocean where I had started hunting the day before. I got up early so I could get Wink through his morning bio process (and me through mine, which takes a cup of coffee) and out on the road right at sunrise. My destination, which would take me about three days, was an old church near Whiteville that I found on Google Maps about fifty-three miles away on the edge of Hwy 130. I planned to sleep behind as many churches as possible between here and there. To do so, I planned my days to arrive somewhat near dusk and slip behind any church that offered some cover so I could enter unnoticed to set up camp. This is called stealth camping. I not only hate it, but I also suck at it. More on my stealth camping struggles later.

WALKER TIP

AIR HORNS MIGHT SAVE YOUR LIFE.

The biggest issue I faced, and I know from multiple conversations was true for every other walker I've met, was stray dogs or unleashed guard dogs. Although a problem everywhere, it was abundant in the south. EVERY single day I walked during my first four months I had dogs chase me and nip at my ankles. It was hard enough controlling Wink and my cart while playing dodge-car all day, then throw in a raging pit bull trained to protect a piece of property, and my days could have turned to shit really quick.

Not all dogs are pets in the south; some are unleashed and there to protect and they will chase you and they will die by a truck doing it if they have to. I saw more dead dogs on the sides of the highway in the south than most other animals. However, dogs HATE air horns. Buy a two pack at Wal-Mart and have that thing strapped to your handlebars or in a pocket in your hi-viz vest. Whenever you can, grab it and fire it off quickly. I used mine every day. I bought new air horns almost every other week. The second a stray or unleashed dog gets too close, just point and shoot.

I also fired mine off a few times before bed when I was camping in areas known to have bears and mountain lions. I don't know if it kept them away, but I never encountered either while sleeping so maybe it worked?

The route I should have taken was southwest on Hwy 17 a few miles to northwest Hwy 130. But I was leaving from this motel that was a few miles out and up in that wedge, so I looked for a shortcut on an angle and found one rather quickly. With the help of Google Maps, I found a rural road that headed northwest at an angle that would shed off about four miles. Perfect! I wasn't in this to chalk up as many miles as possible. This was not a competition for me. I was a walker and a hunter, and efficiency, safety, and speed were everything. It was a Sunday morning, and the beautiful weather I'd had the day before was gone. I had grey skies, low clouds, and persistent drizzle that, within an hour, had turned to rain.

On this rural road were homes and trailers about every hundred yards or so set back about fifty feet from the blacktop. Sunday morning is a lonely time when you're walking down a rural road in the south. Everyone is either at church or in their homes, getting ready for church. I didn't see a soul for the first mile. I would learn to love walking on Sundays. There were very few cars on the roads and, despite the daily dose of stray, unleashed property guard dogs, the roads were mine.

After a few miles, the road started to get a little questionable. The asphalt was breaking up in places, the rain flooded the holes, and I had to weave Alexa through the maze of mini lakes of unknown depths. The road eventually got so pockmarked that I couldn't avoid one hole without hitting another. Several times I would power over one of the mini lakes, and nearly half of my rear tire would sink into water and gravel mud. OK, so now I knew they were pretty deep, and I definitely didn't want me or Wink stepping into one. I became far more cautious with my steering. This went on for a few hundred yards and got progressively worse. It got to the point that the entire road was just one big muddy lake a few inches deep, and my feet were soaked. Surprisingly, Wink didn't seem to give two shits about the rain, mud, or holes. He'd shake the water off his pelt and keep on walking, but I was already trying to figure out how to clean him up before I allowed him in the tent with me that night. No way that mudball mutt was sleeping next to me.

We approached a bend where the road started to curve so much to the left around a grove of trees that I couldn't see much further ahead. According to Google, it would continue to curve for about a mile to the northwest, where it would connect to Hwy130. I stopped and wondered if this was a good idea. The road was no more than a vast, curving lake with little islands of dirt and mud and occasional asphalt chunks poking through the surface. I was debating whether I should turn around and take the known, safe route, but I was already several miles in, and I wasn't giving up that easily. It was during my contemplation when two men simultaneously exited the two homes on either side of me and walked to the road. I was getting ready to ask them if the road was safe to walk when one of them stepped directly in front of Alexa and put his muddy boot on her wheel. Wink and I both immediately sensed danger. This was not a friendly meeting by those good-natured people in middle America I had read about.

We'll call the boot guy Mr. Boot and the other guy Mr. Quiet because he didn't say a word. He was a big man, though. Much bigger than Mr. Boot, but Mr. Boot was the big kid on the block. I was standing behind Alexa, hands-on handlebars, and said, "Hey guys."

Mr. Boot: "Where you think you're goin'?"

His accent was astonishingly thick with equal parts dumb and twang. I had been in the Carolinas for over a week and had yet to encounter the odd sound coming out of his mouth. Fearing banjos, I replied in my most friendly voice avoiding any words over two syllables.

Me: "Up this road to Hwy 130."

Before I continue this story, let me tell you a few more things about myself. I am not a fighter. I have been in two fights my entire life. The first was in third grade when a kid named Mark Cartwright became mad at me while we were playing soccer. Mark was a nerdy red-headed kid, and I actually liked him but, because of his fiery mop and Coke bottle glasses, he had decided that third grade was the year that he was going to prove to the school that he was not a geek. Before computers, it was not cool to be a geek. He got into a lot of fights, and I kinda felt sorry for him. Anyway, he got mad at me and punched me in the forehead. Yep, in the forehead. And that doesn't hurt much. But I couldn't hit him back for a few reasons – first is that we had been friends and I still liked him despite his new third grade attitude and, second, because he wore these ridiculously large, thick glasses and I just couldn't. So, I let him punch me about five times in the forehead, and the whole thing fizzled out at that point.

The second fight in my life was a dumb bar brawl when I was twenty-two, and, during that fight, I hit another human being for the first and last time in my fifty years of life. Experienced fighter, I am not. I am also not a big guy. I stand five feet ten inches according to my driver's license, but I'm a hair shy of that. I weigh-in, after eating a few cheeseburgers, just south of 160 pounds. I'm not intimidating by any stretch of the imagination. I'm also not a manly man, and some would say I'm a bit effeminate. Several strangers I've met in the past have told me they thought I was gay. Maybe it's because I've never really cared about being macho, I dress rather nicely when I need to, and perhaps I have feminine gestures or whatever. I couldn't care less, to be honest. I'm very comfortable in my shoes, and I'm very heterosexual but, if you want to think I'm gay, that's cool, too. My point is that these two rednecks were not intimidated by me at all. They'd just as soon shoot my dog, kick my ass, get out of the rain and eat their Cap'n Crunch.

Mr. Boot: "No, you ain't."

Me: "I'm sorry. Why? Is this not a road?"

Mr. Boot: "Oh yeah, it's a road, but you ain't goin' down there."

Me: "Is this a public road?"

Mr. Boot: "Boy, you see that No Trespassing sign over there?"

Mr. Boot was pointing a very greasy finger with filthy fingernails at a tree on his fence line. Indeed, there was a No Trespassing sign there.

Me: "I'm not gonna cut through your property. I'll stay on the road."

Mr. Boot: "You ain't from around here, are you?"

Clearly not, dumbass. Have you ever seen me on this hick road before?

Me: "No, I'm not. I'm just a guy walking across America with his dog to take a break in life."

Mr. Boot: "Well, if you ain't from around here, you should assume that when you see a No Trespassing sign on someone's property that it means the road, too."

Wink: "*This guy is an idiot. Keep your mouth shut and let's just turn and leave.*"

I had no reply. I couldn't attach any logic to what was coming out of his mouth, which, by the way, was missing more teeth than it still harbored. Those that were still magically attached to his jaw were lookin' pretty bad. If I were one of his remaining teeth, I would have begged to be yanked.

Me: "So, you're saying I should turn around and head back the way I came and not walk down a public road that I should be able to walk down?"

Mr. Boot: "Don't you get smart with me, boy."

I'm not sure why he kept calling me boy. I was clearly older than both he and Mr. Quiet, who, by the way, had not moved a muscle since he took his firm stance to my right and had crossed his arms across his barrel chest and beer belly. Did I mention that Mr. Quiet was wearing nothing but a pair of yellowing thermal underwear with the leggings tucked into work boots and a cowboy hat? Mr. Boot had at least dressed up in jeans and a t-shirt before he came out to harass me.

Me: "Sorry, guys. I'm good. No harm intended. We'll spin around and head back."

Wink: *"Finally."*

Mr. Boot: "Good call."

And that was that. The rednecks stood there in the rain and watched me leave until I was a good ¼ mile away. On my way back down that road, at least one resident from nearly every house was standing out on their porch, watching me pass. I approached a few guys leaning against a beaten-down old mailbox and asked if the road was public.

Mailbox guy: "Yeah, it's public."

Me: "Then why did those two guys tell me I couldn't walk down it?"

Mailbox guy: "Cuz, you cain't."

I think these guys ditched class with Mr. Boot and Mr. Quiet.

Me: "OK, well, thanks, I guess."

About another ½ mile into my backtracking and near a long bend in the road that turned into a small bridge that crossed a quick moving creek, I heard a truck pull up behind me. I moved the cart to my left and kept walking, but the truck didn't pass. It was several feet back, matching my speed. I could hear it creep along, and Wink was going berserk. He was pulling on the leash to turn around and bark, and it was all I could do to hold him back and keep walking like I didn't have a care in the world. One step off the bridge, the truck came around and swerved to a stop in front of me. Mr. Boot was staring me down, and every few seconds stole a glance at Wink. I had a firm grip on Wink's collar, and I was ready to release him if necessary.

Wink is an excellent protection dog. He looks super sweet and gentle, and he generally is. But, if he senses danger or feels like he needs to protect me, he turns into a formidable attack dog. He weighs sixty pounds, and he's all muscle. He's predominantly beagle and German Shepherd but, born a wandering street dog in Mexico, I was told he probably has at least ten breeds in him, and a lot of it is a mix of pit bull even though he looks nothing like that. Before leaving on this journey, I had some professional training with him. Nothing too serious, but just enough to be able to control and release his guard dog desires as necessary. When Wink was leashed to my hip, he was alert and aware and would bow his chest and growl and bark when danger was near, but he would not lunge. One release of the carabiner when he was tense, and he'd be on top of someone in a split. In the situation I found myself in, the release of the clip was imminent.

Wink was sensing danger and was ready to go. If I released his leash, he would attack. Mr. Boot and I stared at each other for what seemed to be several minutes but was probably only forty-five seconds. He got out of his truck and had a stick in his hand that was the size of a small baseball bat. So, this was it, huh? Day two of my journey, my hunt, and I was going to get my skull bashed in by some dumbass redneck who was pissed off because I was walking on his street. My first thought was, "Thanks a whole hell of a lot, Google. You know everything about everything in the world. Why didn't you know that this asshole lived down here and didn't want me walking down his street?"

Mr. Boot: "Where you goin', boy?"

Really? This again?

Me: "Fuck, really? I'm just heading back to Hwy 17, so I can continue my walk that way."

Mr. Boot: "No, you ain't. Not today."

Me: "And why is that?"

I was starting to get pissed. My initial fear was quickly turning to anger. It may have seemed that I was just out on a Sunday stroll but, Goddammit, I had a killer to hunt down, and this jackass was taking up valuable time.

Mr. Boot: "Cuz, you may have seen sumpin?"

I think he meant something, but I heard sumpin.

Me: "Listen, I didn't see shit, and I'm going to walk down this goddamned road back to the highway, and you don't need to worry about me anymore. I'm just a dumb motherfucker who decided to walk across the country. I don't know who you think I am or why I would care what's down your dumb hillbilly road, but I don't. OK? So, get back in your truck and leave me the fuck alone!"

I was one hundred percent certain that he did not expect this hostility from me. This rage was coming from a place I hadn't visited before, and I kinda liked it. This guy could take me down without a second thought, but, all of a sudden, I felt pretty badass.

Mr. Boot: "What did you say to me, boy?"

Me: "Quit calling me boy, you dumb fucking redneck!"

Whoa. Who is the person that took over my body just now? Whoever it is, he's gonna get my ass killed.

Wink: *"Please tell me you didn't just say that."*

By that time, I had my stun gun in my hand but concealed where he couldn't see it. My hunting knife was in its sheath but strapped just under my handlebar within easy reach, also not visible to him. In his mind, I was defenseless with only a dog who was ready to rip his throat out. He looked at Wink and saw my thumb on the clasp of his leash and knew it would only take a split second for me to release him. Wink was on my left and slightly in front of me near the rear wheel of Alexa. Mr. Boot was in front and somewhat to the right. My advantage, however, was that he probably thought Wink was my only weapon, so he kept himself positioned with Alexa between them. He looked at me and back at Wink, and I knew he was contemplating a move.

Wink: *"Release me. I got this. Just pull the clip and let me go."*

Keeping an eye on Wink, he charged quickly. His stick was cocked behind his head and came around to my right. Instead of unleashing Wink, which is what he thought I would do, I ducked quickly under the handlebars just as his weapon connected with my left temple and down I went. Wink's leash was only 4' long and just short of allowing him to get to Mr. Boot as hard as he tried. I was seeing some flash of light from the blow but could still hear Wink barking clearly, so I knew I wasn't going to pass out. I looked up to see him looming over me and watched him raise the stick again, and that's when I zapped that ass crack right in his upper thigh next to his balls. Mr. Boot dropped hard to my right, his eyes wide open either out of pain, shock, or surprise. I zapped him again in the belly, and he started to flop around on the ground like a fish out of water.

I was still seeing stars and didn't have the senses about me to get to my feet, but I knew I had bought myself a little bit of time. I was afraid if I zapped him again, he'd have a heart attack and die, and I didn't want that to happen. I just wanted to get the hell out of there, but I still couldn't stand. I looked around for help, but there was nobody in sight. Not one car drove past us on that lonely, wet Sunday morning. We were both on the ground, racing each other to recovery. First one up wins. I saw Mr. Boot get to his knees, very slowly. He was coming around, but I was starting too as well.

I grabbed onto Alexa and pulled myself up to one knee. On my right, he was on one foot and getting ready to stand completely. The stick was between his legs but easily within his reach. I pulled my hunting knife from its sheath and held it close. As he reached down for the stick, I zapped him again, but this time my aim landed right in his crotch. I was off balance and fell onto my back, looking up at Mr. Boot, scrambling to gain footing. I wrestled to get up but saw him stumble and fall towards me. There was no way on God's redneck earth I was letting this guy land on top of me. I'd be trapped, and I'd be dead. I raised my knife just as he started to stumble, and it found a home right under his rib cage. I barely had to push as the force of his falling weight did all the work. The blade was buried to the hilt, and down on top of me, the hillbilly fell.

I felt his hot blood pool over my chest, and my hand was warm and wet. I was still holding the handle, but the entire eight-inch blade was fully embedded somewhere in his gut. He was heavy, his body was going into spasm, and it was hard to get him off of me in my condition. I looked over at Wink, who was completely wrapped up in his leash and nearly immobile because of it. He wasn't barking at all now. He was calm, looking at me with his big, sad puppy dog eyes like he knew something horrible had just happened. He was trying to tell me he loved me, he understood and that everything would be OK. It was on the side of that rain-soaked road where, with a dying man collapsed on top of me, I fell in love with Wink. We would be together forever, and we would hunt.

Mr. Boot didn't die like they do in the movies. Blood didn't spurt out of his mouth, and it seemed to take forever. I just laid there with him on top of me. We looked at each other a few times, and we both knew that he was going to die under those grey clouds that were soaking our bones. I knew he was in pain, and his eyes told me that he had regret. He almost looked like he wanted to apologize. I hated him, but he was a human being, and he was suffering. His breath was heavy and hot and smelled of stale cigarettes, coffee, and halitosis. I winked at him and yanked that knife up as high as my strength would allow hoping to hit his heart and put him out of his misery. He gasped in pain and then died a few seconds later, staring at me with a tear slowly creeping out of his eye. I rolled him off of me, pulled my knife out of his chest, and watched the blood pool beneath him. I stood over him for a few minutes. I wasn't wondering what I should do or whom I should call, and I didn't even consider running. I stood there, holding a huge, bloody knife in one hand and my stun gun in the other, and I watched him be dead.

I felt like fucking Superman.

I should have felt horrible for taking another person's last breath, but I didn't. I mean, I didn't like what had just happened, but it made me feel invincible. Powerful. Like no man I had ever felt like before. I looked at Wink, and he looked at me and said, *"Hey. Are you OK?"*

Me: ""Yeah, you?"

Wink: *"I'm good. We're gonna be OK."*

GOOGLE MADE ME DO IT

Not surprisingly, I had no cell service at that little spot on the road, but I wasn't too far from the motel where I'd stayed the night before. I planned to call the police, tell them what happened, take a nap or, better yet, crash one more night in the motel and start walking again tomorrow. I put my knife in the sheath, pocketed the stun gun, washed some of the blood off of me the best I could in the creek and pushed Alexa forward. I didn't make it far. Within a few minutes, three more trucks came barreling around the bend from where Mr. Boot was lying dead. Oh, shit, here comes the posse. I grabbed my phone and begged it to have service, and it had enough to dial 9-1-1. I quickly screamed into the phone that there had been a stabbing, that the situation was about to escalate rapidly and that they better get some cops out there pronto.

And that they did. The trucks were already stopped, and I was flanked by redneck neighbors of Mr. Boot. The highway was about ¼ mile away, and, thankfully, there was a sheriff nearby. He arrived, gun drawn, within seconds of something even more terrible happening. Here's what the cop saw: one blood-soaked guy standing by a baby stroller with solar panels, a dog chained to his hip, and four other guys all holding knives except one who had both a tire iron and a shotgun, surrounding the bloody guy with the stroller. The cop was probably wondering how bloody stroller guy was still standing. With his gun drawn, the cop yelled for the rednecks (he didn't address them like that) to drop their weapons. I had already put mine away, and my hands were way up in the air.

Weapons down, the cop ordered us all on the ground on our bellies. He must have known by then that the blood wasn't mine because I was moving pretty well. He radioed for back up and, within minutes, his buddies were everywhere. A few ambulances showed up shortly after the other cops, and, by then, they had learned the whereabouts of Mr. Boot, who, by the way, was named Donny Jonathon Gainer. Not knowing what the hell was going on, all of us were searched, cuffed and put in separate cars. The only thing I was worried about was Wink and Alexa. We sat there for quite a while, and I watched them put Wink in the county's animal services van. Alexa sat, all alone, on the road as they surrounded the scene with crime tape. I assumed she was now evidence, and they'd rip her apart and box her up.

Knowing that he had a real name should have created some emotional connection between me, my hands, and the death of a real human being. I tried to feel sad about Donny and what I had to do to him, but I didn't. He was a tough-guy bully about as smart as a potato who went looking for a fight, and he got one. No guilty conscience here. If not from me, it would have happened someday. Fucker had it coming. It turns out that Donny had a long history with the cops and had spent several nights in the can recovering from too much booze and too many bar fights. It was not surprising to the local PD that Donny violently met his maker, but I think they were a little surprised that it was a skinny city boy from California pushing a baby stroller who introduced them.

I was stuck in town until further notice and spent two full days being interviewed by countless cops. The media was everywhere, but I wasn't talking to them. The last thing I wanted was my face in the news, but that was inevitable. If Annie learned I was near her birth town and had just gutted some guy, it could spook her into hiding. This little incident didn't help matters with the cops back home, either. Now, suddenly, I was the link between two dead people, both of whom died in bloody, horrific fashion. My alibi for Jesse's death was airtight; they knew there was no way I killed him. Annie had disappeared but, now, there may have been some suspicion that I could have been an accomplice. I spent a lot of time on the phone with cops back home, and I could hear the apprehension in their tone. Dig all you want coppers, there's no connection, and Mr. Boot was a fluke encounter.

During my first interrogation, it was clear the detectives on the case were perplexed by my presence in their town. Their questions defined their confusion: what I was doing, why had I chosen to pass through Shallotte, did I have any history here or with Donny, why did I choose his road to walk down, why didn't I take the highways that day to begin with, etc. Here's a tidbit of our interview that never seemed to stop spinning in the same circle.

Cop: "Why were you on that road?"

Me: "I was walking."

Cop: "But why that road?"

Me: "Google told me to go that way."

Cop: "Google told you to go down that road?"

Me: "Actually, yes, it literally told me to go down that road. Have you ever used Google maps? I use it every day, with the sound on, and on this particular day, it told me to go down that road."

Cop: "I don't think you're being honest with me, son. How could your phone tell you to go down a road?"

Is it possible that this cop also ditched class with Donny?

Me: "You're kidding, right?"

Cop: "Don't get smart with me, son."

Me: "OK, but why do you keep calling me your son?"

Cop: "Why were you in front of Mr. Gainer's home?"

Me: "I was walking."

Cop: "Where were you walking?"

Me: "Down the road that Google recommended."

Cop: "I meant, where were you walking to?"

Me: "California."

Cop: "California. You and your dog are walking across the damn country to California, and Google told you that Mr. Gainer's road was the fastest way there?"

Me: "No, that's not how this works, and Google doesn't care about the dog."

Cop: "Do I look like an idiot to you?"

Me: "I don't believe that idiots have a specific look. That's more of an IQ, inside the head kinda thing."

Cop: "You better be very careful, son."

Me: "OK."

Cop: "Now, why did you go down that road instead of just taking the two highways to get there?"

Me: "Because Google told me to."

Cop: "Why didn't Google tell you to take the highways?"

Me: "Because Google's job is to show me the shortest, quickest route, not the longer, out of the way route."

Cop: "Do you always listen to Google when it tells you to do something?"

Me: "Why are we talking about Google? Google had nothing to do with this."

Cop: "I want you to explain to me in a way that I can understand what the hell you were doing this morning on that road that caused all of this to happen."

Me: "I was walking. On a public road. Is that a crime here?"

This conversation actually happened, and it went on like that for hours.

When I retrieved Alexa from the stroller pound, she was a mess. They'd taken her apart and searched through all my gear which sparked a whole new wave of interesting small-town cop questions. Why do you only have three pairs of underwear if you're going all the way across the country? Why doesn't your baby stroller have seats in it? If you're walking west, do the solar panels work when the sun is mostly behind you? Does your dog ever wear those booties? Why do you have a hunting knife?

Are you going hunting? (Yes) Why do you have bear spray? We don't have bears around here. (Do you think I'm just walking in circles around your shitty little bear-less town or, perhaps, is there a chance that somewhere across this vast nation I might run into a bear? Or a tweaker? Or a Donny?)

It just seemed too coincidental to them that a guy would spontaneously decide to fly to the east coast with his dog and walk across the country a few months after he had lost everything, was in the middle of a gruesome murder investigation back home, and had just gutted a guy with a hunting knife. They were desperately trying to connect the murder back in California with Donny falling on my knife in North Carolina. They knew Donny was a piece of crap, but I guess the thought of some damn liberal beach boy from Californ-I-A strolling through their red as hell rural neighborhoods and ending up wrist-deep in the gut of their local bad-boy just couldn't possibly add up.

"I lost everything, and sometimes you just have to wander." I said this to multiple investigators during my Shallotte vacation. It was always met with suspicious stares, but I didn't care. I didn't need them to understand why I was walking. I just needed them to let me hunt.

THE ART OF WALKING

'm no pro, but there is an art to surviving a walk across America. I didn't know jack when I started, and all my preparation was purchasing gear and taking notes on paper. Although I walked quite a bit before I left to build up the right muscles, I've spent my entire life on my feet and figured my body had been toughened through years of standing, stooping, carrying fifty-pound boxes of meat and chasing girls. How wrong I was. I should have trained a hell of a lot more and learned some minimal yoga at best. Waking up on the floor of a tent or a different bed every day after walking a few dozen miles then eating a power bar, squatting against a tree to take a crap, striking camp, making cowboy coffee and then doing it all over again takes a toll on your body. Not to mention your mind. Most, but not all, trans-con walkers are considerably younger than me, and I should have just planned a little better for aches, pains, and stretching.

Once you start walking, most aches go away pretty quickly. The pains of the journey either work themselves out or get worse and become chronic battles you deal with daily if you don't let them heal. For example, my feet were usually swollen by the end of the day, and it felt incredible when I took my shoes off, but the next morning, it was almost as painful to lace them back up. However, within a half-mile, they felt great, and I wouldn't feel the pain until I'd take my shoes off later that day. My lower back, however, hurt all the time. It was an age thing. To help, I popped ibuprofen like a fiend and rubbed CBD cream all over my aches. That's good stuff.

WALKER TIP

LUKO TAPE

One of the most useful, cheap things you can carry with you. Forget blister pads, blister kits, and band-aids. Luko tape is like an awesome combination of tightly woven cloth like they use for band-aids but with adhesive as strong as duct tape. The minute you feel a hot spot on your feet, you gotta stop, peel off your shoes and socks and put a few layers of luko tape over it. Luko tape will stay put for days if you want it to. It won't go anywhere, and it's comfy and flexible. And it is dirt cheap – far cheaper than any blister specific aids. I also use it to wrap my handlebar grips, and I've used it to patch some holes in my tents and Alexa's rain cover. The stuff is magic.

I was never fearful of walking so close to death. If I were to die, it would, more than likely, come from some jackass in a car barreling towards me who wasn't paying attention. Maybe they're playing Words with Friends or Candy Crush on their phone, doing their make-up, eating a Sausage Egg McMuffin or perhaps they had too many martinis at lunch. Most people think you walk with traffic, but that will get you killed on day one. You always walk on the left side of the road against traffic. You do not break this rule ninety-nine percent of the time. The only time you would ever cross the road and walk with traffic is if you have no shoulder at all, and there is a sidewalk on the other side. Period. A shoulder on the other side is not a sidewalk. I would push my cart and dog through foot long wet grass, mud, and piles of roadkill on the left before I'd cross over and walk on a clean shoulder on the right. You have to be able to see what could hit you and react because those assholes I described above will not. If you plan on surviving a three-thousand-mile walk on highways, you have to know your options and how to react to cars and drivers. I learned the art of "reading the gap" within my first few miles. Nobody can teach this, and it doesn't take lessons to perfect it. It's trusting your gut, and you better be sober and well-rested to do it right. Here's what I mean: every car coming towards you has a driver behind the wheel, making decisions when they see you. As a walker, if you're paying attention and want to survive, you keep your eye trained to the middle of the space between the car's front passenger tire and the white line you are following. That's the gap. You can see it as soon as you can see the car. Most of the time, the gap widens a little or a lot. This means the driver sees you and is giving you more space. As I made my way across the US, I tried to wave to every single car that widened the gap. People like recognition for their good deeds. Sometimes the gap narrows, and you immediately adjust left off the shoulder, into the mud or grass or down an embankment, whatever is necessary depending on how narrow that gap gets. Drivers tend to let the car drift to where their eyes go. They're looking at something odd coming at them and, without knowing it, allow the car to drift to the right. It's unintentional, but it's dangerous for you. This is why so many officers are killed on the side of the road while writing speeding tickets. And sometimes people are just being assholes and like to scare you. Luckily, on most highways, state departments of transportation build into the roads that strip of indentations along the shoulder to alert drivers when they start drifting to the right. Despite how annoying those divots are for a walker, they probably saved my life countless times. So, when the gap narrows, you adjust left. The worst scenario is when the gap doesn't change at all. You have no idea if the driver sees you or not. If they don't, that means they're preoccupied because, unless they're driving blind, they cannot possibly miss a person wearing a yellow reflective vest leashed to a sixty-pound dog while pushing a double-wide baby stroller with a flashing bike light directed at them. And, if they are preoccupied, anything could happen at the last minute. They could see you just as they're getting to you and react by swerving, which could be right into you or away from you, which could cause a horrible accident. Or, if the gap doesn't change, it could be that they do see you but feel there's already room for both, so they stay their course. Which is fine if you know that's the deal, but you don't. When the gap doesn't change, you adjust left every time. You make these decisions thousands of times every day.

WALKER TIP

HOLY SHIT, THAT WAS CLOSE!

Get a rear-view bike mirror attached to the right side of your cart's handle-bars. I learned on my first day that the cars coming towards you are not the only vehicular dangers. If you are on a two-lane road, the vehicles coming from your rear will want to pass each other, which means the passer will come flying from behind in your lane that you might be walking in if you don't have a shoulder. Being able to see that car coming at your rear right is critical if you are not on a shoulder well to the left. Even if you only have one wheel in the lane and someone coming from behind is passing another car, you become roadkill, vultures will eat you, flies will lay their eggs in you, and you will become a maggot pond. So, get a mirror and don't become a maggot pond.

After only a few miles on the road, I was a master gap reader. There could be a line of ten cars coming at me, and I knew, within a few seconds, which one could be a problem, and I'd adjust. You would think that having a giant eighteen-wheeler barreling down on you would be the worst, but I would take a highway full of truckers over cars all day, every day. Truck drivers are the best road companion to a walker. They're trained to move left if they see anything or anybody on the shoulder. They do it for their safety, not the walker's, because suicide by truck is a thing, and they have no interest in being the bumper that some down and out, suicidal person sees just before they meet their maker. Although truckers, ninety-nine percent of the time, move to their left, I always moved to mine as well to let them know we had mutual respect and I wasn't thinking of jumping in front of their rig. And I always waved thanks. The only time a trucker doesn't move left is if they simply cannot because there's no room or if they're a wide load because it's too dangerous for them to make that move. Wide-load trucks got the whole road from me. If I saw that coming, I moved as far left as I could, stopped walking and put my hands up so they could see that I had stopped, and I was giving them the space they needed. Mutual respect. It made me feel like I was part of a team.

Although it's legal to walk on most highways in the US, they're not designed for walkers and drivers just aren't expecting us out there. We're in their territory and you need to understand that to survive. On roads where I didn't have a lot of options to my left, I would talk to the drivers coming at me. Out loud, I would say, "Show me you know me. Show me you know me." I just tossed that out in the universe, hoping they would hear it and give me some indication of what their plan was. I think it worked. I should trademark that.

Every walker is different, and we all have our own set of rules and boundaries. Here are just a few of mine that I adopted rather quickly.

- No headphones or earbuds. I had a Bluetooth speaker for music, but it was never so loud that I couldn't hear what was going on around me.
- I set a timer for two hours, and I stopped on that timer so Wink could drink water and have a little snack. If it was hot out, we stopped more frequently.
- No trespassing. To understand the importance of this rule, re-read my story about Mr. Boot. I would have rather not slept than go onto someone's property without permission.
  - I saw a sign in Arkansas that said: "If you trespass on this property, be dressed to meet Jesus!" That would not be a wise place to stealth camp.
  - I did break this rule when I would stealth camp behind churches. I generally felt safe that Pastor Bill was not going to approach me with a shotgun.
  - I also did not have to stealth behind churches all the time because, if the pastor was there, I'd just asked permission, and they always said yes.
- No alcohol while walking. Period. As much as a cold beer at lunch sounds great, I don't trust my judgment after that. I would wait till

the end of the day and, oh, it tastes so good after twenty miles.

- No walking in *severe* weather. No matter where I wanted to end up that day, thunder equals lightning and, in a lot of the south during the season I was there, equals the potential for tornadoes. I would blow my money on a motel or hunker down behind a building till that crap passed.
- No walking on the right side of the road. We've already discussed this. I didn't want to die.
- No political or religious conversations with strangers or house hosts. I'm a moderate lefty from California who doesn't believe in God walking through the very red Bible Belt. I presumed that I was a political and religious minority down there.

Those are just a few boundaries I had for myself that helped guide my decision making every day. My first few months out were riddled with horrible storms, and I made a few bad decisions that ended up putting me in pretty bad situations, which is when I adopted my weather rules.

In the beginning, walking twenty miles was daunting. I just didn't have it in me. If I knew I had to walk twenty to find a good place to sleep, I was bummed. But, after a few weeks, twenty miles was standard. If I dipped too far below that, I felt like I didn't accomplish much. And then there were days where I'd hit the thirty to forty-mile mark and those days were mistakes. At my age with my body, twenty miles was a good number for me. It didn't kill me, and I was always OK to move forward the next day pretty much pain-free. It also worked well for Wink. He could go further, but longer mile days ended up hurting him, too. So, we found our groove at twenty.

Mentally, I had no idea how to prepare for this journey. I'm a very sociable person, and I don't like to be alone. There's a big difference between being alone and being lonely. Alone on the road can be amazing. I started with music playing all the time but, rather quickly into the walk, I learned to love, and need, the silence of the road. It was more comfortable and allowed me to work on the stuff that was mushed up inside my head. Walking for eight to ten hours in silence is the best therapy I'd ever had. I got through some pretty heavy shit my very first month and felt like I was genuinely accomplishing the goal of digging into it. Loneliness, on the other hand, was a bitch. I'm a person that likes to share and, although I love Wink and I talked to him all the time, it wasn't the same. I missed human companionship a lot. I missed being touched, and I missed sex and kissing. I missed sitting over good wine and having a meaningful conversation. Although I met hundreds of strangers, those moments mostly only cured being alone. I struggled to find a replacement for loneliness.

I think it's hard for most people to understand the enormity of walking across the country. I don't fault them for it, it's hard to fathom doing it and, like most humans do every day, it's just walking, right? People would ask, "Hey, what day will you be in Atlanta? I'm looking at flights, and I'll meet you there." Huh? I'm six hundred miles away, and you want to know what day I'm going to be there? I could, at best, give a week that I might be there. But unless you're out on the road, you can't fully understand the day to day work it takes just to get through those twenty-four hours, let alone thirty-two hundred miles for eight months. It's a tough job.

Unless you are super-wealthy, have lots of financial support, or a Rolodex of potential host families, you camp quite a bit. Ninety percent of those camp nights are stealth, which means you are sneaking into a place that you are not supposed to be and, in the near dark, pitching your tent. You can't watch shows on your phone unless you can completely cover it up because the glow of the screen will illuminate your tent, and that kind of defeats the definition of stealth. It's not too hard to spot a glowing orb sitting in a grove of trees fifty feet off a highway. So stealth camping is also very lonely because you typically get set up in the early evening, and you end up with a lot of time to kill. Then you set your alarm for about an hour before sunrise to strike camp and get the hell out. You can make your coffee and take a crap after you're safely away from where you are not supposed to be. I didn't have a lot of money and knew very few people on my route that hosted me, but, for the most part, I lived in a tent, and I got really good at finding hidden gems of land that allowed restful, safe sleep. However, as I stated earlier, I hated stealth camping, and I did suck at it. It took me a few months to get comfortable with it, but I still wasn't good at it. I sucked at finding just the right place. I let my fear of getting caught make me too cautious, and it took me a long time to trust that Wink would hear danger before I would.

Finding food to eat was easy. Finding good food to eat was not. Finding good food to eat with a dog attached to your hip upped the ante. Fresh fruit? That required an act of congress. Some days all I wanted was to sit in a booth and be served a hot meal but, with a pup, that didn't happen often. I ate on the tops of garbage cans, leaning against a building or, very uncomfortably, sitting on the front wheel of Alexa when I was too lazy to pull out my folding chair. Anytime I saw a closed business with a bench or chair in front of it, I would stop for a rest. You take these things for granted when you're in a normal environment, but finding a comfy place to sit, hopefully out of the sun, when you're walking down a highway all day is tough. Most days, you will never find a comfy seat unless you set your course to find one. Happening upon one was rare. Try living on gas station food propped up against a building for a few weeks. Go ahead, do it. Not only will you train your gut to be rock solid in any situation, but you'll also collect some spare change and a few dollar bills every now and again from people who think you're destitute.

LA CASA DE MORGAN

ASH, NC

33° 59' 41.5" N

78° 35' 28.0" W

MILES WALKED: 24

After five days of redundant interrogations, interviews, and binge-watch-ing The Office reruns, I was released from my Shallotte motel prison. It felt like I had been locked up and, after walking out of my room with Alexa reassembled and organized, I felt like a new man. I headed towards Whiteville, via the highways this time, to restart my hunt for Annie. I knew she hadn't lived in Whiteville since she was a little girl, but it seemed like the right place to start looking for cousins, family friends, buckets of heads, or whatever could lead me to my next destination. I had a contact for a place to stay in a town called Ash not far from Whiteville but, based on my plans, wasn't sure I wanted to be tied to a home where I would be expected to eat and socialize with people. I was more eager to get on with hunting.

The road can be a real a bitch. We fell in love, but it took a while. Ten miles into my day, she coiled up, struck fiercely and latched her gnarly fangs around my ankle. The joint in my heel popped, and a pain shot through my leg and torso that can best be described like this: take a six-foot-long metal BBQ skewer and get it nice and red hot over an open flame. Then shove it up through your foot, into your calf, and all the way through your gut and brain and out the top of your skull. But before the pain even considers subsiding, slam a twenty-pound sledgehammer into your Achilles. Yeah, that about sums up how awesome that felt. Down on the highway I fell with all of my strength and sanity drifting away. With pain so fierce I was brought to tears, that bitch of a road dropped me flat on my ass on the side of a lonely highway and begged me to surrender. I dried my eyes, swallowed the pain, locked my stare upon her unforgiving face and said, "No way. We were meant to be together."

And just like that, after idling in Shallotte for nearly a week, I was down again. Would my walk never actually happen? I was only twenty-four miles into my journey and was going to be delayed again. I made the call to the family that had offered to host me for a night. Richard and Lisa Morgan lived on a large piece of land in Ash with their daughter Jessie. They had hosted another trans-continental walker I had met when planning my journey, and she hooked me up with them. Richard drove out and met me on the side of the road, loaded us up, and took us to their home. I was an emotional wreck. I was sure my journey was over and that I would never find Annie. I wasn't very social my first night there and slept hard and long after drinking a few beers on the porch with Richard. The next day I was far more friendly.

The following morning, Lisa was calling everywhere, trying to find a foot doctor that could see me on such short notice and on a Friday. Guess where she found someone? Back in Shallotte. Just my luck. But, hey, I just had to drive there and meet Dr. Kibler who was willing to see me at 4 p.m. on a Friday. Long story short, Dr. Kibler was a marathoner and, when Lisa had told him that I was walking across America and had an injured foot, he was excited to have me come in. Doc took x-rays and showed me my problem, which wasn't an injury after all but, instead, a heel spur that was rubbing against my Achilles. He also said it shouldn't have hurt as badly as I described earlier, which means that maybe he was calling me a wimp - totally legit judgment. I can be a baby when I'm sick or injured. He gave me the green light to continue walking but told me to rest for a week, get some different shoes, and I should be good to go.

That's when I learned the true definition of road angel. The Morgan family didn't bat a lash. They offered their house for as long as it took to heal. They even knew about my run-in with Mr. Boot and Mr. Quiet, how it unfolded, and, just when I thought they'd kick me to the curb, they grabbed me another beer and cheered on my heroics. I ended up staying with the Morgans for four nights. I had five days of cold Bud Light, good food, a lot of tears from sharing tough life stories while sitting in rocking chairs on the patio, and some fun times on their quad.

During those four days, I spent a lot of time in the kitchen with Jessie. We made French rolled omelets and lemon cream Napoleons. They took me to their local oyster and beer joint where our fingers got messy and our bellies got full. The Morgans became a second family to me and, had

WALKER TIP
TENTS

Don't rush out and buy a bright orange or red tent. Search around till you find one that blends in with nature. For normal camping situations, it's good to be seen and easily found, but the point of stealth camping is to be stealthy.

If you think bigger and roomier is better, you're wrong. If you're solo, get a one-person tent. If you have a pup, maybe a two person if your pup is big. I had the MSR Hubba Hubba NX2 and loved it. It was a dark maroon color with a grey fly. It was the best one I could find that didn't double as a locator beacon. It blended well; Wink and I fit perfectly inside, and it was lightweight and easy to set up and strike. The only time it failed me was when I screwed up my placement under a roof line and you will read about that a little later. Yes, my mental breakdown fiasco behind the church in Mississippi really happened exactly as I described.

I not met them through a chance meeting with a friend, I don't think my journey would have made it past that spot on the road where my ankle took me down.

The Morgans were the first family to save my butt. They wouldn't be the last.

WHITEVILLE

34° 20' 21.9" N

78° 42' 15.4" W

MILES WALKED: 53

t was a Tuesday morning when I said goodbye to Richard, Lisa and Jessie and rolled Alexa down the driveway away from the safety and comfort of Casa de Morgan. The long road, my girlfriend once again, succumbed to my presence. Over time we would learn to compromise, wield to each other's passions and respect our mutual destiny. She cradled me when I was lonely and fed me endless miles of adventure when my life had left me empty. She relieved me of the burden that was awaiting me back home and, upon her, I accepted the most fundamental job known to man – survival.

Wink: *"I think we should have stayed. I kinda liked it there."*

Me: "Me, too, buddy. We'll see them again. Sooner than later."

I was headed to Whiteville to see the birthplace of a murderer and, despite not having walked for several days and still in a bit of pain, I needed to cover the twenty-three miles in two days. Thursday was a perfect day to roll into town and restart my hunt because I was planning on stealth camping behind a church, and there's not much that goes on behind them during off-God hours. I knew that, if needed, I could even crash back there for a few days if necessary. My walk was brisk despite the light rain that never let up. This area had suffered through a severe hurricane about three months earlier, and the ground all around me was still horribly saturated. Finding a place to stealth camp is hard enough. Then you factor in swampy conditions, and it takes away a lot of options. I was seriously hoping that this church was going to work out. To my delight, it was exactly where I was expecting it to be, and it was all boarded up - closed for business. The brush around the building was overgrown, and the rear of the place provided multiple options for setting up camp. Hell, it was so perfect, I could probably even watch some Netflix in my tent without getting caught. There wasn't another building for about half a mile, and that was a volunteer firehouse, so there wasn't going to be anybody there.

I didn't even wait until dark to set up. I looked all around for paraphernalia like freshly emptied beer cans, hypodermic needles, fast food bags, other camping gear, etc. If I saw that stuff, there could be some issues with teenagers or tweakers using that area to get high or drunk or homeless people using it to camp. Thankfully there was nothing significant. I was so far from town, and the back of this church would be a nuisance for any of the above-mentioned groups of people to get to. I was safe. With my camp all set up, I unfolded my chair and sat down on a landing under the rear door awning safely out of the rain. I also got Wink set up for dinner and put him on a long lead so he could roam around and do dog things. For the first time since I started my walk, I was alone, in a safe place, and I could think.

I had no idea what my actual plan was to find Annie. I'm not an investigator, and I have no investigating skills. I'm not even that good on a computer, so it was gonna take some time learning how to stalk someone online and gain knowledge of their life, family, and friends.

Luckily for me, Johnny, my buddy in Idaho, was game for helping me out. He was excited about doing this, so I used him a lot. My first order of business was to figure out what my cover story was. There was no way in hell I could successfully walk up to a stranger's door and start asking questions about a family member and expect to leave without a few new holes in my back. No, I needed a story and one that would work no matter where I went. I had no idea how close her family was, if they talked to each other, if they would call and warn others about me and my inquiries or if they were just as dangerous as she was. I also had to remember to call her Kennedy when I was talking to them. Any slip up on the name, or if my story didn't seem plausible, then red flags would start flying.

I decided to go with the old "I'm an old friend from high school, having a mild midlife crisis and decided to walk across America and seek out my old buddies for nostalgic purposes. I want to reconnect with the place where I grew up and the friends I had back then." Unfortunately, for this to fly, I had to find the name of a real person that Annie went to high school with, and it would be even better if they were friends or acquaintances and even super better if they didn't live anywhere near the south. Monroe, GA, where Annie attended middle school and then dropped out of high school as a junior, was nearly 350 miles away. At my pace, that was three weeks of walking. I had time and a few cousins to follow up on between here and there. I called Johnny.

Me: "Hey, buddy. I need to be Annie's old high school friend."

Johnny: "Need more than that, man."

Me: "My cover is old friend, midlife crisis, walking across America and reconnecting with my past blah blah blah. I need a real person she may have known in high school."

Johnny: "Got it. Give me a few days?"

Me: "Yep."

The sun was down by the end of my call and the walk that day, despite only being about fifteen miles, kinda kicked my ass. Wink and I climbed into the tent, got comfy, and we watched the original Dirty Harry on my iPad. Damn, I love Clint Eastwood. I set my alarm for 5:38 a.m., precisely one hour before sunrise the next day. I wanted to be prepared to vacate the church before the sun came up if it was necessary.

Wink: "*So, this is the way it's gonna be from now on? We walk a ridiculous number of miles then hide in a tent behind a building and then do that over and over till we get home? That's your plan?"*

Me: "I wouldn't call it a plan, really, more of a mission."

Wink: *"I'm not so great with maps and distance. About how many days will this take?"*

Me: "I really don't know. Maybe two hundred days?"

Wink: *"When you met me at the shelter, did it ever cross your mind that maybe I didn't really want to do that?"*

Me: "Honestly, Wink, no, I didn't. I figured every dog loves an adventure."

Wink: *"That's very presumptuous of you. We'll see how this goes for a few days and I'll let you know if I decide a different sort of life is right for me."*

Me: "That's fair. Can we sleep now?"

We slept like two rocks.

The next morning, I decided to wander into town and do some minor investigating. I wasn't going to ask any specific questions of anybody. I just wanted to see where Annie lived until she was seven and get a feel for her life as a small child. Johnny had already given me the address where they lived back then, and, according to Google Maps, it was a trailer park. Shocking. Thankfully, this particular trailer park was not like most I had walked by on my way to Whiteville. Most of those were broken up places down dirt roads where it would be impossible to wander around without drawing suspicion. I had no desire to run into Mr. Boot's intellectual equal in one of those places. The park she lived in as a child was pretty run down and shabby, but it was right on the road that led into town, so walking by very slowly didn't raise any eyebrows. I had hidden Alexa in a grove of thick trees and bushes behind the church, and I walked with Wink, like any other person in that town. The park was big, and I had no clue which unit she had lived in because I had no plan or desire to meander into the neighborhood of mobile homes. I was sure there wouldn't be anybody there to talk to about her. I just needed to see what her pre-murderer life was like so I could feel her.

In my mind, I attempted to date the trailer park backward thirty-seven years and feel what it felt like the year Annie's family moved away. Have you ever looked at an older person's face and mentally scraped away years of aging to find the younger version under the folds and wrinkles? That's what I was doing. What was this place like back then?

SPRINKLES

stopped at a small counter-style café down the road a bit and asked my server about the town's history. According to her name tag, she was called Sprinkles, and she unloaded some pretty amazing and fucked up details about the little town of Whiteville way back when.

Sprinkles: "Please tell me you ain't thinkin' of movin' your sweet little butt here."

Me: "Would that be bad?"

Sprinkles: "Only for you, sugar."

Me: "Why is that, Sprinkles?" Was she flirting with me?

Sprinkles: "This town used to be wonderful. Used to drip fun like honey. Small-town boys chasin' small-town girls. We had a few bars and even a roller-skatin' rink, although it was pretty small. But then with the internet, the kids started learnin' that there was much more life outside of Whiteville. All the younger folks who grew up here and who should have stuck around to keep the town alive moved away for better candy. They left behind nothin' but the old people who don't make babies no more and the town started to go sour. Then the floods came and pretty much wiped out the entire downtown area. Whiteville just kinda died after that. This went on for a few decades until our property values dropped so low that, all of a sudden, some young families tired of city life decided to buy farms and properties for dirt cheap. With that came more families, and some new businesses started to pop up again, like this café which had been closed down for years."

Me: "Well, that doesn't sound so bad to me, Sprinkles."

Sprinkles: "For you, it would be bad, cuz you ain't southern. You're a city boy, you ain't got no ring on your finger, and you're kinda cute. You're a danger. Even the new, younger families don't want a city boy around town makin' their money, and the boys around here don't want you gettin' their women. No, you should enjoy your vacation here but keep it a vacation. I personally don't care cuz I sling coffee, ain't got no money to be afraid of losin' and, as I said, you're kinda cute but it ain't up to me sweetie."

I liked Sprinkles. I liked how she couldn't complete a sentence without including sugary sweet additives. She took her name a little too seriously.

Me: "I'm not movin' here. Tell the boys to calm down. I was thinking about investing in some property down the road that I heard might be up for sale. Do you know the trailer park just south of here about a quarter-mile?"

Sprinkles: "Today is your lucky day city boy. I've lived in that trailer park my whole life. What do you mean it's for sale?"

Me: "It was a rumor, so I thought I'd look at it. Probably nothin'."

Sprinkles: "Well, if it is for sale, I hope a cute boy like you gets it but doesn't mess it all up. I know it ain't much to look at, but it's got history, and we like our history 'round here."

Me: "Don't you worry, pretty girl. If I buy it, you are safe. It would just be a land investment. Tell me about the park you grew up in."

Sprinkles: "Well. I don't think that much about it. I just always known it as home. There's a small creek that runs back behind it that used to flood every year. My pop would threaten to move out every time the water came up and flooded around our trailer. We would all just laugh at him because he grew up right here in town, and he was one of the first people to live there with my momma. He wasn't goin' nowhere; he just liked to sound tough. They were so in love, my parents. They couldn't wait to have a bunch of kids runnin' around and playin in the creek. Me and my li'l sister were born a year apart, and we were the first kids in the park. When I was about three years old, a couple moved in a few trailers down. The lady had a baby inside her, and a little boy clingin' to her leg. He was maybe two years old then. I was so excited to have new kids to play with, but it took a while before Christopher, that was the boy's name, took to likin' being with a couple of older girls. Then Kennedy was born, and we couldn't wait to play with her. By the time she could walk, we had her down at the creek chasin' turtles and makin' mud pies."

Me: "Seems like a nice place to grow up. And here you are, still in town after all these years. You must be fond of this place."

Sprinkles: "I never really thought of leavin'. Where would I go? I always wanted to chuck it all and move to Hollywood and become a big star. I guess that's every little girl's fantasy. Hell, a big city like that would chew a girl like me up. I'm better off here."

Me: "Well, it sounds like you had a good childhood friend. You said her name was Kennedy?"

Sprinkles: "Yeah, her name was Kennedy. And she was a good friend, till she moved away. More kids came and went through the years, but you always remember your first real friend when you're a little kid."

Me: "Where did she go?"

I lost Sprinkles for a few moments. Her bubbly spirit had been replaced with a sullen sorrow that washed over her face.

Sprinkles: "Kennedy was a sweet little girl and my best friend. Christopher, on the other hand, was not so sweet. He made me think of sour apple suck-em sticks, which I did not like cuz they was sour. That boy did not like his sister comin' into his world and takin' up his momma's attention. Sometimes, when we was playin' in the creek, he would be mean to the turtles and frogs we would catch. He'd turn those turtles upside down and make them lay there in the sun. We'd have to chase him off to turn them right side up in the water. Kennedy became Momma's girl, and Christopher became Daddy's boy. And that wasn't so good because their momma and daddy did fight a lot. We could hear them screamin' at each other almost every night about food, laundry, money, and sex. He was a mean man to her, and we'd often hear the momma cry on the steps of their trailer."

Me: "Sounds like Christopher needed an ass whoopin'."

Sprinkles: "I remember one day down by that creek my sister and I heard some screamin'. We went down there to find that boy sittin' on top of his sister with a big snake in his hands. She was pinned down under his legs, and he had that snake by the head, and it was hissin and flingin' its tongue out and whippin' its body around his arm, and he was holdin' the head of that snake right in front of that poor girl's eyes. He was yellin' that he was gonna let that snake eat her eyeballs right out of her head, and she would never see her momma again. I ran up and tackled him into the creek and punched him in the face, and he started cryin' like a baby. Kennedy was already runnin' home callin' for her momma. That night we heard those screams and yellin' like no other night. And we heard some hittin', too. You know that sound of fist on flesh and bone and the screech that comes after and the slammin' of the front door. I heard that little boy yell after his daddy, "Papa, where you goin'? Don't leave me here. I wanna go with you!" Then came the sounds of his car revvin' up and dirt flyin behind his wheels, and then he was gone. The night fell silent all except for that boy sittin' on those steps cryin' for his daddy, who never came home. A month or so later, that boy was gone, too. We all figured his daddy had come for him in the middle of the night, but not long after, they found that boy in pieces out in the woods all eaten up by animals. The police said it was not an animal that took that boy apart."

Sprinkles was gone. Her mind was somewhere dark. She held the coffee urn in her hand through that whole, horrible story, and she never looked at me. Her gaze was fixed on the windows, looking out on the highway. She snapped back after a minute with a tear in her eye. I doubt she had thought of that story in years, and it clearly upset her.

Me: "Are you still friends with Kennedy?"

Sprinkles: "Never again were we friends. Her momma kept her inside and didn't let her down by that creek and didn't let her play with us kids.

A few years later, Kennedy musta been 'bout seven years old or so, they up and blew away like the wind. Never seen her again."

Me: "I don't know what to say. That is one hell of a story and a lot more than I was expecting. I'm sorry that happened to you, Sprinkles."

Sprinkles: "Don't you mind pretty boy. Stories like that make up small towns like this. You look achin' to go, so you get on your way, I got your coffee. And, if you do buy that park, maybe you come look this old lady up?"

Me: "Are you hittin' on me, Sprinkles?"

Sprinkles: "Take your pooch and get on outta here."

I had forgotten Wink was at my feet. It was as if he had been listening to Sprinkles and was as stunned as I was. Sprinkles shot me a mischievous grin and a wink and moved into the dining room.

Holy crap. That's all I could think after I left Sprinkles with her memories. Something terrible went on inside that trailer where Kennedy was born. Something far more sinister than her brother holding a snake to her eyes. What had that boy done to her that nobody ever saw or, if they had, had decided to ignore? Sprinkles was a bubbly, sweet-tooth lady with a mile-wide smile and some sexy, flirty eyes, but telling me about that day down by the creek changed that woman's whole world if only for that moment. I had a feeling she knew more about that trailer and that boy and his daddy, but I didn't need her to go there. I would piece it together on the road.

What was I chasing? Who was I hunting? Was Annie a confused, mentally unstable woman who was never able to get over something horrific in her childhood and, thus, turned to violence against men who wronged her? Or was she a killer who used her past as an excuse for her violence? How could a five-year-old girl kill and dismember an older, bigger boy? Was she abused by the boy? By the father? Mother?

As Wink and I walked back to my temporary church shelter, he chimed in.

Wink: *"That was too easy."*

Me: "What do you mean?"

Wink: *"Just seems odd that the first person you meet in town just happened to be friends with the girl we're hunting."*

Me: "Yeah, I guess. But it's a pretty small town. People like Sprinkles don't move to towns like this, they're born and raised here. Not too far of a stretch that a single, fifty-year-old woman living in the small-town trailer park she grew up in would be working at the local diner."

Wink: *"If you say so. Next time we hit a spot like that, you mind getting me some bacon? The smell was killin' me."*

Me: "Sorry, buddy. For sure."

I didn't know how to feel. I was completely conflicted. Was I now hunting her for revenge, justice, or just to give her a hug and let her cry it out? I needed a breather. I needed the road. I'd only been walking for two real walk days, not counting my Shallotte vacation, but the road had already grown on me. There was nothing left for me to see or hear about here in Whiteville. The next day I would walk and gather my thoughts.

Back behind the church, I fed Wink, and we walked around a bit so he could run and get some exercise. He'd been tied to me on a 4' lead all day, and he needed to break free for a bit. I didn't sleep well that night. We got straight into the tent at dark, and I didn't even think of watching a program. My mind was racing with feelings of sadness, anger, and a desperate need to find Annie.

JOSHUA

awoke the next morning after a few snooze hits on my alarm. I cleared my eyes, checked email, and, after sifting through all the crap, found one from Johnny from the night before. The next lead he offered was a 40-year-old first cousin to Annie on her mom's side. Her married name was Jennifer Lincoln, but her friends called her Jenny. She was the outcast in the family because she fell in love with a boy her senior year of high school whose skin was a little too dark for the family to accept. She was born and raised in a small town called Turbeville, SC, but moved a few miles east to Lake City immediately after graduation to escape both her racist parents and life in a dry town. She chose Lake City because it was a little more accepting of mixed-race couples, and she was in love with her man. She married Joey when she was 19, and they were still madly in love. Jenny hadn't spoken to her family in nearly twenty years, despite them still living only twenty miles away in the next town where she grew up.

Back in Idaho, Johnny was keeping a spreadsheet updated with names, addresses, careers, criminal records, marriages, kids, arrests, and anything else he could come up with on as many people associated with Annie over the years. A quick call to him and I learned that Jenny was not only the odd man out in the family because of her marriage but also one of the few cousins who became something more prominent than the rest of the family tree. Touché! Jenny had started working as a receptionist at a reasonably large insurance company in Lake City when she was 20. Her employers quickly realized that she was an ambitious, brave young woman who was going to either push hard to move up in the company or move on to bigger and better things. Her boss mentored her, softened her hard edges developed as a child living with abusive parents, and promoted her to the accounting department. Bored to tears but still young and immature, Jenny wised up and started befriending the sales team and knew right away that she was a born salesperson. She admired the insurance sales team for their cute clothes, fancy cars, and the smooth, polished way they spoke. She would hide out in the bathroom and practice talking to herself in the mirror so she could work on her smile and broaden her vocabulary. Within a year, just shy of turning twenty-four, she was one of them. By the time Jenny was thirty-five, she had opened an insurance franchise of one of those big, nationwide companies. Her face was now plastered on highway billboards pitching auto, home, and life insurance. Joey was no slouch, either. He trained to be a corrections officer at Turbeville Correctional Institution when he was just twenty-three years old. He was a go-getter, a man who wanted to right the wrong and change the world. By the time Jenny had her own insurance business, Joey was a senior corrections officer and well respected by other officers and most inmates. In Lake City, Jenny and Joey were upper-class material. They owned a charming home, had three children in private school, and were well known in the community as a kind, honest, hard-working couple who had beat the odds despite their struggles as a mixed-race couple in the south.

I had no idea how to approach these people. Why couldn't they be simpler and more approachable like Sprinkles? I decided to call Johnny to get my cover story in line.

Me: "Hey, man. I gotta approach Jenny and Joey in a few days, and, based on your intel, she's a bright woman, and he works in a prison surrounded by habitual liars, so they're gonna sift through bullshit pretty quickly. What did you come up with?"

Johnny: "Well, lucky for you, Annie and Jenny didn't grow up together or in the same town, so it should be a bit easier. Do you wanna be dead or alive?"

Me: "Huh?"

Johnny: "If you want to take on the identity of one of her classmates from her school days without raising too many suspicions, you have two options, and one of them is dead."

Me: "That's just great. A dead guy. OK, tell me both."

Johnny: "Joshua Owen was an acquaintance of Annie's in middle and high school. They weren't besties but, in small-town America, everyone knows everyone. He was a shy kid and joined the Army right out of high school. He came back from his duties overseas, became a recluse up in Vermont, went off the grid, suffered some PTSD, and died a few years later while camping in a thunderstorm. A damn branch broke from a tree in strong winds and crushed him while he was sleeping in his tent."

Me: "Widowmaker death, huh? You'd think someone like him would know not to set up camp under an aging tree. Damn shame. Who's next?"

Johnny: "Shane Gutierrez was a kid that got a lot of crap for having a Norwegian mother and Mexican father even though he took after his mom and was pasty white. Kids can be real assholes at that age. He and Annie were friends but, when she dropped out of high school, that friend-ship naturally faded. Shane went off to college in Colorado and now lives in Durango selling weed at several dispensaries he owns out there. He's pretty well known in that community but, from what I can tell, estranged from anything in the south since his folks left Georgia after he graduated high school. They're now down in Boca Raton with no relationships left in Monroe that I can find."

Me: "Are you sure Shane does not look Hispanic?"

Johnny: "Oh yeah. But he was heavy as a kid, and, from what I can find online, he still carries some extra pounds. You, my friend, do not. My advice? Go for Joshua. He has zero ties to Monroe, parents are also dead, and there are no siblings. He does have cousins spattered about, but his last ten years alive were either overseas or in a cabin in the woods. He died more than a decade ago, and the story was barely brought up in any media that I can find. Just some poor vet found dead in the woods."

Me: "Deal. Joshua, it is. Send me everything you have on him. This has to be as airtight as possible, and I hope to God none of her family kept up on his life or heard about his death."

Johnny: "Give me a few hours, and I'll email you everything on him. I do know that he hated to be called Josh, so do not slip up on that one."

OK, so I became Joshua Owen. Ex-military, private and quiet, left Monroe at eighteen to join the Army, came home, and went to hide out in the Green Mountain state. I waited for the info from Johnny. Lake City was about eighty miles from my current home behind the church in Whiteville, so I had a good four days to walk and tighten up my story. I was eager to leave but spent the next few hours striking camp, eating some breakfast (boil in a bag breakfast skillet), feeding Wink and doing that morning stuff. I smelled horrible. I hadn't showered since I left the Morgans, so I did some cowboy bathing back behind the church. I found a garden hose and filled up one of my water bottles, stripped down and, using baby wipes, cleaned my necessary parts and attempted to wash the road off my body and out of my hair. It was a decent attempt at cleanliness, and I didn't smell homeless, so, I guess, mission accomplished.

I got on the road around 10 a.m. and headed up Hwy 130 for a bit then took rural roads that would, in a few days, get me to Hwy 378 west to Lake City. My first few days were pretty uneventful on the road. It was frigid, and we had off and on rain. Being off the highway was good and bad. The highway provided better shoulders and more options for food and water, but the side roads offered far better scenery and much less traffic. I played dodge-car on and off the grassy, muddy shoulder when cars didn't widen the gap, which slowed us down a bit. Wink didn't seem to care, but he was muddy, and he needed a real bath as much as I did. We camped behind a few more remote churches with no problems and even found one that had a completely covered area in the back that was well hidden from the road. Unfortunately, we had to get out of that gem of a spot the following day so that churchgoers wouldn't freak out at early Sunday service.

On our third night, we found a secluded spot in a vast, triangle-shaped median that separated two highways and a road. There was some construction going on, so traffic on one side was not going to be an issue. There weren't many houses or buildings around so wandering into the middle of the median went unnoticed. Wink and I set up camp before sundown, wrestled around a bit, went for a nature break walk, and crashed early. Around 3 a.m., Wink abruptly stood up and started barking furiously. A few seconds later, multiple flashlight beams were on the tent, and I could hear feet slowly approaching. I could hear voices, but the words were hard to make out over the sound of crunching leaves and branches. I couldn't contain Wink's barking, and he was clawing the tent and pushing his body into the zipper flap in an attempt to get out. The footsteps stopped, and one of my visitors called out to us.

Visitor: "Control your damn dog."

Me: "I've got him on a leash. He's just barking. Who are you? What do you want?"

Visitor: "Come out of the tent but hold on to your dog. We don't want any problems."

Wink: *"You want me to handle this?"*

Me: "No, be cool. You'll know if I need you."

I pulled on my sandals, put on my hat, held Wink firmly in one hand by the collar as I attached his leash, and unzipped the flap door. It was difficult to contain him and ease my tired, sore body out the door, but I eventually got there. Finally, on my feet, I looked out but was blinded by several beams of light.

WALKER TIP

I know its extra space and weight but bring camp sandals. You will, every day and night, need to climb out of your tent to go pee, get food, take a walk or confront strangers shining flashlights on you in the middle of the night. There's nothing worse than having to squeeze your resting feet into shoes just to take a leak. If you take my advice and bring camp sandals, they should not be flip flops with the thing that goes between your toes. You're probably going to wear socks to bed on cold nights and, well, you know what I mean. Get sandals that you just slide your foot into.

Me: "You mind not flashing those in my eyes?"

Visitor: "What the hell are you doing out here?" Beams still shining at my face, Wink was firm on his lead and growling but also blinded by a flashlight.

Me: "Getting some sleep. I'm walking across America. I found this spot, assumed it was public land, and pitched my tent. I'll leave before sunrise. I mean no harm to you; I'm just a guy taking a break in life to walk around a bit."

They lowered their beams and, after my eyes adjusted to the now slightly illuminated darkness, I could see four guys wearing the same hi-visibility vests that I wore walking the sides of the highway.

Me: "Thank God. I thought I was about to deal with some tweakers or teenagers looking for a place to party."

Visitor: "Dude, seriously, you're walking across America, and you just decided to camp here tonight?"

Wink: *"That's what I said."*

Me: "Seemed like a good place."

Visitor: "All good, man. We really don't care, but we gotta dig a ditch through this median out to that construction zone, so, unfortunately, you gotta pack up and move on."

Me: "Fair enough, guys. Sorry to startle you."

Visitor: "As I said, all is good. We probably startled you and your dog more."

Wink: *"Hey, I was not startled."*

By then, Wink had figured out that these guys weren't a threat, but he was still on high alert. I clipped his lead to Alexa and, as quickly as possible, broke down my gear and got it packed up. My bio clock was all fucked up by then and, even without coffee, nature was calling. I asked the guys if I could use their porta-potty and spent a few moments alone in there. Ahhhh.

It was about 4 a.m. when we started walking, and we were well onto Hwy 378 at that time. Lake City was still about twenty-two miles away, but I decided to cover in one day. I needed a shower, a real bed, and a hot meal. I was also low on supplies and needed a decent breakfast buffet at which to stock up on essentials. The highway was barren so early in the morning except for the truckers who also enjoyed the lonely, dark roads and we were able to cover some serious miles quite quickly. I had all of my lights flashing to give the truckers plenty of warning, and we walked without any near-death, late-night experiences.

We rolled into Lake City around 2 p.m. The last few miles were brutal, and Wink and I were both slow by then. I hadn't fully recovered from my injury week of not walking, and what would have been a six-hour walking day for someone in better shape took us ten, and my body was seriously revolting against me. I found a decent motel that allowed dogs, got into my room, and quickly dragged Wink into the shower with me. Wink hates baths and, weighing in at sixty pounds of muscle, he's not easy to coax into one. I lathered him up and let him out to shake off the water. I cranked up the hot water and let it burn my skin and smooth my muscles. While waiting for a pizza to be delivered that I had ordered before the shower, I tended to a few hot spots on my feet to prevent blisters from forming and shaved my face nice and clean. I needed to be as presentable as possible when I approached Jenny the next day.

With a full belly, clean body, and soft bed, sleep came early and deep.

WALKER TIP

STEALTH IS ONLY FOR CAMPING AND "NATURE" BREAKS

When you walk, wear a hi-visibility vest. Period. I know they look ridiculous, but, hopefully, your goal is to survive, and you need to use all the tools at your disposal to make sure drivers see you. And you need to buy the right kind, or it will suck when you wear it. Make sure your vest is made of breathable mesh, and it's a bonus if it has pockets where you can store stuff like your phone when it's raining, snacks that are easy to reach, and protective devices like an air horn and mace. More on those two things later.

It's also advisable to put strips of reflective tape on your cart but not too much. You'll want to cover up that tape when you're stealth camping so don't go overboard.

I vaguely remembered one dream when I woke up the next morning, well after sunrise, and it had something to do with a goldfish eating my nose off my face. No clue. I left Wink in the room and ventured down to the "free continental breakfast" bar. I made two Belgian waffles, a plate of sausage and bacon. Extra bacon for Wink. I took my food back to the room, devoured it quickly, and returned to the breakfast bar with a jacket that had many pockets. The place was a veritable mini-mart and, when not being watched, I stuffed them with fruit, pre-packaged Danishes, hot cocoa mix, single-serving peanut butter and jelly, nondairy creamer packets, oatmeal, napkins, and plastic utensils. Boom! I was loaded up. Never again would I pay for those items and I made a note to myself to read the breakfast bar reviews when booking future motel rooms.

I decided that the only approach to Jenny was direct and to the point. Wink would be a benefit in this endeavor because he was so damn cute, and girls just loved him. I made sure he looked clean and smelled nice and, of course, did the same for myself. I even took the time to iron my one clean pair of walking pants (I only have two), and I hung my shirt in the shower to get rid of road wrinkles. I cleaned and clipped my fingernails and even trimmed my eyebrows for maximum viewing pleasure. It was a Tuesday morning when we strolled into Jenny's insurance offices.

Me: "Hey, Wink, listen to me. I need you to be cool and cute, ok? Stay by my side, don't pull on the leash, and flash your cute puppy dog eyes as much as possible."

Wink: *"Great, now your exploiting me. Would you like me to sit on my butt and crash cymbals together like a wind-up monkey?"*

Me: "Can you do that?"

JENNY

LAKE CITY, SC

33° 52' 14.8" N

79° 45' 08.2" W

MILES WALKED: 117

Receptionist: "May I help you?"

Me: "Good morning. I'm hoping to meet with Jennifer Lincoln. Is she available? I don't have an appointment, and she doesn't know me, but I'm an old family friend. My name is Joshua Owen, and I just need a few minutes of her time."

She called Jenny's office, announced who I was, and nodded her head a few times while listening to the reply that I could not hear.

Receptionist: "Mrs. Lincoln is finishing up some work, but she'll be out in a few minutes. Would you care for some coffee?"

Me: Oh, hell yeah. "Yes, please, black would be fine. Thank you."

A few minutes later, a very tall, beautiful woman who was well put together introduced herself as Jenny Lincoln. I recognized her instantly from the billboards I'd seen the past few days. We shook hands, she patted Wink on the head, took us into her office, and closed the door.

Jenny: "Well, well. Joshua Owen. Is it Joshua now? I do recall, very clearly, that Kennedy used to tell me about a cute boy from school named

Josh Owen way back when and here you are, all grown up, sitting in my office. Where have you been all these years, and what brings you to me in little ole Lake City?"

Shit. She either honestly did not know that Joshua was dead, or she was one cool poker player. This could have headed south really quick.

Me: "Yeah, I hated Josh as a kid, but everyone insisted on calling me that. So, Kennedy used to talk about me? I thought she barely considered us friends. I always had a thing for tall girls, and she was a tall girl. I see it runs in the family. Kinda puts a smile on my face that she told you about me. I was a pretty shy kid. Kind of a loner, actually."

Jenny: "Kennedy always preferred the quiet, non-aggressive boys, so maybe that's why you stood out. So, what can I do for you?"

Me: "I left rather abruptly after graduation and joined the Army. I couldn't wait to get out of Monroe. But, after being overseas for several years and then settling down in Vermont, I realized that I had left without really saying goodbye to my friends. I decided last year that I was going to walk across the country, re-discover myself and, if possible, track some of them down and say hello. I don't know, maybe I'm having a midlife crisis, but something just compelled me to come back to the south and, maybe, see how it would feel to visit. Kennedy was high on my list, and maybe that's just because I had a crush on her but also because she was always kind to me when others weren't. I have no idea where she is, but I did know that she had cousins around these parts, so I figured I'd start there. Gotta love the internet. So, here I am, in Lake City talking to you."

Jenny: "You walked here? From where?"

Me: "North Carolina. The Atlantic Ocean. Took me a few days." Small laugh.

Jenny: "Well, I guess I can't turn you away after that journey. I'm not sure I'll be too much help, though. After high school, I pretty much disengaged from my immediate family and, with that, comes distance with relatives as well. It's fine, though, because most of my family are people I don't want to be around anyway. They hate the fact that I have a black husband and that I've littered the world with my mixed-race babies. Screw them. Ignorance is pretty rampant in my family, and I prefer not to be around it."

Me: "Well, it appears you've done well for yourself. And good for you for not caving. Your husband must appreciate your loyalty."

Jenny: "He's a hell of a man and a great father."

Me: "Did you know Kennedy very well as a kid?"

Jenny: "We were as close as we could be as distant cousins. She's a bit older, but I always liked older kids, and we got along well during the holidays, and the few times we'd visit each other."

Me: "She was a special friend to me, but I always felt there was a little bit of mystery about her. There was a side I never quite knew. Maybe that intrigued me a bit."

Jenny: "Well, she grew up with tragedy in a broken home. That's gotta be tough."

Me: "I didn't know about any tragedies. She didn't open up like that with me."

Jenny: "I was far too young and have no memories of when her brother died and her parents split up. I imagine that could break most kids but, according to family talk, Kennedy seemed happier and more carefree after all of that. What did you think of her as a teenager?"

Me: "I guess she seemed generally happy. But she could turn quickly. I remember a few times she'd be friends with someone one day and done with them the next. It never seemed to bother her though."

Jenny: "I didn't know her like her friends did. I'm family so I knew the occasional Kennedy at familial gatherings. I saw her much more when she and her mom moved to Monroe, but then it tapered off as she became a teenager. You know how that goes; I would see her a few times every year, and we'd sneak cigarettes and sweet wine outside and talk about boys. That's when I learned about you. You came up several times for a few years. I think Kennedy had a crush on you, too. Missed opportunity there, my friend. You could have had your tall girl."

Me: "Damn my shyness. She was just so pretty, and all the boys liked her. She was probably fully grown by ninth grade, which meant she was the tallest kid in school, I'd say. Every boy wanted to be with Kennedy. It was like they could be with the model girl in school or something. I never had the nerve to say anything to her other than what friends say to each other normally. I guess looking back now, my crush was probably pretty strong."

Jenny: "Well, here's what I can tell you about Kennedy outside of school. Kennedy wasn't super smart, but she wasn't dumb, either. Call it average for book smarts. But she was tough as nails. I'm not sure exactly what life was like inside that trailer when she was a little girl, but I can say that she moved to Monroe with a super soft, friendly smile but a toughened, calloused heart. You didn't know that about her unless you tried to get close but, by then, it would have been too late. She didn't let people get close, especially boys. She got around with the boys alright, which confused a lot of hopeful, horny naïve young men. Yeah, boys could get inside her body, but they never got inside her heart.

"Kennedy loved her mother about as much as she hated her father. I tried to pry for information, of course, but she would shut me down with a glare that almost scared me a few times. I know she didn't mean to make me feel afraid, and I don't know if it was fear or hatred in those eyes of hers, but it was clear she was not going to share anything about her father with me. And the same went for her brother, Christopher, when his name would come up, which it rarely did. I never knew that boy. I think he died right around the time I was born, but you know how families talk, especially after a tragedy. If you believed what you heard, you'd think that little boy was evil as sin. Personally, I choose not to have an opinion. As I said, my family are not people that I attempt to relate to, and their beliefs are so incredibly twisted and ignorant that I don't ever try to understand them. That boy could have been Christopher Robin, and they'd still turn him into something evil after all the rumors that flew around about him."

Me: "That's pretty harsh. Did your family not like them?"

Jenny: "Who knows. My family is filled with judgment and igno-rance. If something is worth getting all worked up over, my family will jump right on it."

Me: "What about her parents? Did you know them well?"

Jenny: "Not Lester, her dad. Barely remember him but all I ever heard was bad stuff about his temper. I do know Peggy Sue, her mother, very well. She is a lovely, caring woman who would stop at nothing to protect her little girl. Kennedy loved her mother but, as she got a little older, she realized it was overbearing, and Kennedy started to distance herself a bit so she could feel a little more free from her grasp."

Me: "I didn't know much about her home life. I knew her little broth-er died when she was young and that her parents were divorced, but that's about all she shared with anybody."

Jenny: "As I said, nobody was allowed too close. I've never been clear on the rest of this story, but something happened when she was in high school, and Kennedy suddenly dropped out. I figured she was just bored or being dumb, but, of course, rumors had to fly around the family. She picked up some work at the bar her mother worked at in Monroe, and, within a few years, she was gone. The cops came to me way back then, asking around for her, but I honestly had no idea where she had gone. I was still in high school and chasing boys and ditching classes. My time with Kennedy was less and less by then. Apparently, some local boy had gone missing, Kennedy was a friend, and they thought I might be able to help locate her."

Me: "Do you know who that boy was? I wonder if I knew him?"

Jenny: "He was a bit older if I recall, but you'd have to dig around to get his name. I don't remember if I ever even knew it. I'm not sure if he ever turned up."

Me: "So, the odds of me finding Kennedy around here sound pretty slim."

Jenny: "To say the least. Last I heard she was in Los Angeles but that was a year ago at least. You could go to Monroe and see her mom. I bet she still tends bar at that same Irish pub. It's the only one in town so it shouldn't be too hard to find. And Peggy Sue is easy to spot. Picture an older version of Kennedy but a lot more wrinkled, messy, and tattooed. She might talk to you. She's a nice lady. Would you like me to call her for you?"

I knew she was going to call her the minute I walked out the door.

Me: "That would be great, thank you. I would hate to blindside her as I did you."

Jenny: "It was a pleasure meeting you, Joshua. Good luck on your journey."

Me: "It's gonna take me about three weeks or so to walk there so, if you do talk to her, tell her I'll see her when I see her."

Jenny: "You are one crazy boy. Happy trails."

And, just like that, I learned a few fascinating tidbits about Annie. She had a crush on me, which felt cool even though it wasn't me she had a crush on. I lived vicariously through Joshua for a few minutes and let her crush happen. She also did an excellent job of hiding or trying to forget her childhood, and anybody attempting to get in suddenly found themselves very much out. She was promiscuous as a teenager, which I knew she carried into her adult life, and she was into boys, not girls. Just more confirmation of that lie she told. She was close to her mom and hated her dad. I think Mom and Dad might shed some good, if not very different, ideas on where Annie could be. I just had to figure out how to handle them.

I wasn't even a block away from Jenny's office when I got Johnny on the phone.

Me: "Dude. Search for a missing young man in Monroe, GA, a few years after Annie dropped out of high school and right around the time she up and left town."

Johnny: "What's up?"

Me: "Don't know. Might be nothing but I just sat with her cousin Jenny, and she told me that, a few weeks after Annie left Monroe, cops came to see her looking for Annie because she was friends with a guy who was a little bit older and who'd gone missing."

Johnny: "A lot of bodies around this girl. You sure you want to keep this up? Plot's pretty thick, man, and you haven't even met the parents yet. This shit could get dangerous."

Me: "Are you kidding? I'm fucking loving this."

Johnny: "It's your body, man. I'm on it."

TYLER, A BRIDGE, AND A YELLOW BEAR

COLUMBIA, SC

33° 56' 49.8" N

80° 37' 38.5" W

MILES WALKED: 172

was anxious to meet Annie's mother in Monroe, but I had a little over three hundred miles to cover before I would get there. For me, that's about three weeks of walking. At three mph, that's a ton of time to think. Since I have so much time on my hands, let me tell you about Tyler.

I had no idea if Tyler Coulson was a nice man, a good man, an honest man, or if he was a complete asshole. From his books, I took him to be a lot like many dispirited people but, instead of writing a book to bitch about why, he wrote about his attempt to figure it out and move on. He wrote a few books that changed my life so, naturally, he was my hero even if it turned out that he was an asshole.

Tyler was a very successful young lawyer and clearly not thrilled about it. Money can't buy happiness, right? So, he ditched that life and walked across America. He didn't do it for charity or notoriety. He didn't blog or boast on social media. He wasn't walking to change anybody's life. From what I took, he walked to change his life and escape what he had created for himself and did not like. His first book, *By Men or By The*

Earth, is the finest, most raw story I have ever read and, given where I was in my life at the time, it struck a significant chord deep in the cockles of my heart. Although it recounted his journey in great detail, it didn't read like a memoir. I struggled to believe it was non-fiction the first time I read it because the adventure seemed so unreal and not at all plausible. I knew of the countless people that hiked the Pacific Crest Trail, The Appalachian Trail, and the Continental Divide, but the thought of someone walking across our country, coast to coast, saltwater to saltwater, without an actual trail to follow just seemed ludicrous and fictional.

Then I read his second book, *How To Walk Across America and Not Be An Asshole,* and the reality that not only do people, although very few, actually hoof it coast to coast, but that I might be able to do so myself.

WALKER TIP

If you're going to attempt this journey, read both of Tyler's books. If you can only read one, *How to Walk Across America and Not Be An Asshole* is mandatory. My walker tips are fun and real, but this book will tell you how to adequately prepare, both physically and mentally, for this journey. You will not regret buying this book and studying it several times. Just do it.

Remember, I read these books before I found Jesse in my marinade, and, at that time, I put the idea of doing this in the fantastical dreams bucket. Within a few months of reading them, Annie had hacked up a body and turned my world upside down. It wasn't until after I was attempting to lose my sorrows in the bottom of bottles that the idea re-surfaced. And that's when I reread them. But, this time, it was from the "I'm definitely fucking doing this" angle, and the books took on new meaning. Highlighter pens, sticky notes, Amazon shopping lists, wall maps, computer mapping programs, and an REI membership quickly replaced my knives and secret recipe books. But, more importantly, they replaced the bottles. I was hyper-focused on getting ready and hitting the road.

I had tried to message Tyler a few times but was unsuccessful. I learned from those attempts that Tyler, unlike most crossers, kept to himself as he built his new life with his wife in Chicago. It was a while before we actually connected. He was officially off social media, and his website was defunct. That's cool; I'll leave the man alone. He'd done enough for me just writing the books. I referred to him often with my friends and family as I planned my walk. I would often, jokingly, but kinda seriously, steal a line from *Fight Club* as I was figuring out my route or deciding if I really needed bear spray and, in my head, would ask, *"What would Tyler do?"* I guess you could say I idolized him. One day, quite surprisingly, Tyler answered one of my many messages about gear and stuff. His reply was all I needed to hear from him. In just a few simple words, I knew it didn't matter what Tyler would do about anything. Those few words granted me freedom. He simply said, "Hike your own hike, man – Best, GTC."

But what Tyler's books didn't teach me was how to be a hunter. I was going to have to learn that on my own. And they definitely didn't teach me how to be a killer. Oddly, that came naturally.

NOTE TO READERS:
Tyler Coulson is not an asshole. We became friends during my journey and he's a really good guy.

I left Lake City and headed west on Hwy 378 towards Columbia, which would take me about a week, then I'd head south on Hwy 1 to Aiken, where I'd cross the Savannah River into Augusta as I entered Georgia. A few more days on Hwy 78, I'd pass through Athens and drop down into Monroe, home of Peggy Sue Rose. That was my plan, and I executed it flawlessly. But not before I had to kill again. And again.

About thirty miles shy of Columbia on Hwy 378, with rain pelting me endlessly, I decided to stop early in the day. I was tired, the highway absolutely sucked for walking, and I was done playing dodge-car and walking in muddy weeds. I approached a very long bridge that crossed the Wateree River. It was under construction, and workers, in their hi-visibility vests similar to the one I was wearing, were still guiding traffic through a maze of orange cones and porta-potties. Formerly known as Garners Ferry Landing, this looked to be promising for a quiet night of stealth camping. I veered off on a frontage road down a steep, dirty gravel path that was scarred with deep tire tracks obviously caused by the construction trucks from above. The trail, which was difficult to navigate due to recent flooding, led to a choppy, concrete landing under the bridge. On either side of the slabs and muddy tire ruts were thick groves of dense trees. If I could magically erase the bridge, concrete, and years of graffiti, it would have been a beautiful, peaceful patch of riverfront land. However, because there was a bridge, columns, concrete, mud, piles of trash, and evidence that shady shit happened down there at night, it was not peaceful or beautiful, but it would do.

At the water's edge and slightly to the right of the artsy bridge columns were the remnants of what used to be a bustling little ferry business. A rotted out, half sunk wood dock bobbed precariously as it clung to life to the concrete pylons jutting up from the shoreline. Across the river, I could see the opposite side of the defunct ferry crossing, but few remains were still there. Under the bridge on the other side, strategically hiding between two columns, was a small red car idling with its lights on. I could barely make out a driver, and he appeared to be sitting there killing time. It seemed odd, but perhaps there was another person in the car that I couldn't see, maybe resting her head in his lap for a nap. I speculated the worst in people. The road can do that to your mind.

I left the edge of the river so the lovebirds across the water could have their privacy and trekked around to look for the best place to pitch my tent. To the left of the bridge, the concrete gave way to dirt and weeds as it neared the woods. Searching that area, I found a small path into the tree line that came to a tiny but perfectly situated clearing about ten feet into the woods. I tried to determine why this barren patch of land was here, but nothing gave that away. It didn't lead to any power stations or any other clearings; it just appeared to be a spot on the ground where trees decided they didn't want to grow. It was fine by me, I'd take it.

As I set up camp for the night, the sun was a few hours from setting westward, and, in the thick of the woods, it felt later than it was. I could tell from the heavy sound of traffic on the bridge above that commuters were making their way home from work. The sound was loud, and the steel connectors that were sandwiched between the tons of concrete slabs that made up the bridge crashed together as the plates made contact with each other. It was a constant drum of metal on metal bangs as if someone was hammering a steel spike into the ground. I hoped that the frequency would die down considerably later in the evening or sleeping might have proven to be a bit difficult.

Wink: *"This is not a good place to camp. I mean, I'm fine but I'm tough and have sharp teeth. But you...I don't know. This place is pretty sketchy."*

Me: "After what happened back on day two, you don't think I can handle myself?"

Wink: *"I'm just offering up my opinion that I think you chose a shit spot to camp. That's all."*

I left my erect tent and grabbed my little foldable chair, my JetBoil pot and fuel, a few cans of chili, a foil pack of tuna, some crackers and a gallon of water and made my way back under the bridge and onto the concrete slabs where I'd play dinner host to myself. I dumped both cans of chili in the pot, fired up the fuel, and, while it heated, devoured the tuna right from the pack. I didn't realize how hungry I was until I smelled my entrée simmering away next to me. I got comfy, pulled the pot off of the burner, and sat, watching the quiet, serene river run by and listening to the constant banging above me. Life was grand.

Wink: *"Can I have some of that?"*

Me: "No chance I'm giving you chili and sleeping next to you."

Wink: *"But I have to sleep next to you after you eat it?"*

Me: "You can sleep outside the tent if you'd like."

Wink: *"Jerk."*

I walked back to Alexa and fetched a Slim Jim for Wink which he scarfed down in two large bites. Then I fed him his normal food.

Wink: *"Thanks, buddy."*

Me: "Love you, big guy."

It's in those moments, the ones before sundown when you make your way into your tent, and after you've taken care of all the essential business like eating, cleaning up, taking a leak, and performing the best cowboy shower possible, that loneliness sets in. Sometimes there are options: walk into town and see what's going on, write in a journal, watch crap on your iPad or sift through endless dribble on social media. After several days on the road living for a few hours during each of those days in this exact moment, I started to miss my life back home. I missed my restaurant, my bar, and all of the regular customers I had become friends with. I missed game and wine nights. I missed my local spots where I'd meet my friends. I missed girls I could call and, hopefully, hang out with for the night with no guilt afterward. Although the journey, even so young in its beginnings, allowed me to find happiness when I was alone, the road couldn't replace everything from home. Maybe if I were twenty-two and journeying across America before I had settled into mature adult life, the road would have never failed to give what I needed emotionally. But, at fifty, I was pretty set in my ways, and I knew what buttered my bread: human connection.

As I was sitting peacefully, despite the clanging, enjoying the river, a glass bottle came crashing down about five feet away and nearly gave me a heart attack. Startled, I found my chair toppling backward, and I landed with my head on a baseball-sized chunk of old concrete. Immediately, I knew that I was bleeding because my head was sideways, and I could feel warmth trickling down my scalp through my hair towards my left cheek. You know when a kid cracks a pretend egg on your head and then lets his fingers lightly trickle down your hair, hoping you think its gooey egg innards caressing your scalp? It felt just like that. I reached up to find a pretty good gash on the back of my head and cursed the asshole that tossed the bottle out their car window and over the bridge. As I got up and shook off the dizziness, I sensed company. Turning around, I saw what appeared to be a yellow arm, or yellow sleeve, peeking out from behind one of the bridge columns. The person was standing, facing the column, but all I could see was his right arm. It moved slightly, and I now had confirmation that the bottle had not been tossed out of a car. Looking back at the shattered glass on the ground near my chair, I could see that it had come from the direction of the yellow arm, so now I knew who the asshole was.

Wink: "*Whoa!*"

Me: "What the fuck was that?"

Yellow arm: "I've been watching you."

Me: "Why don't you step out and talk to me like a man?"

Wink: "*Let me go! Let me go! I got this.*"

I watched the yellow arm fidget and pull something out from inside his jacket. I couldn't quite make it out, but it wasn't a gun or even a pipe. It was fatter than a pipe, maybe a foot long or so, it was an odd maroon color, and it was kind of shiny. I strained to see what it was with no luck. He was gripping it tightly, and it made me a bit nervous. If I knew what it was, I might be able to prepare a little better for what was coming. He wasn't moving, and he couldn't see me, so I quietly walked over to the edge of the woods where Alexa sat with Wink clipped to her wheel. He had been sleeping before the loud crash and was now taught on his leash, ready to attack. Leaving him there, I unclipped the bear spray and hunting knife. I was now on the other side of the column and could see that his left hand was empty. I shouted again, demanding him to come out, and I could tell he was startled at the change in the direction of my voice. He jumped a bit and darted around the column in an attempt to hide a bit better. Or, maybe from his perspective, he moved to get a better attacking position. I scooted left, as quietly as possible, and our eyes connected. Very still, my visitor stood tall and statuesque, and stared at me with crazy anger in his eyes. You know when you see booking photos, and you can almost tell by the eyes if the person is guilty or crazy? This guy had those eyes. Fuck. I had a crazy bottle-throwing guy with a shiny maroon something or other in his hand locked in a stare down with me. I felt like I was at the OK Corral waiting to count to ten except, in this country-western flick, I had bear spray, and he had…something??

He slowly emerged from behind the column and I took in the full size of his tall, overweight mass. His hair was well-trimmed but slightly unkempt. I put him in his early sixties, but years of working the highways could age a man. Maybe he was in his fifties. However old he was, I was younger by at least a few years, and I was in pretty good shape by this point in my walk. I was undoubtedly quicker than his size would allow him to be. His jeans were dirty, but his camel-colored work boots looked fairly new. I realized that he wasn't wearing a normal yellow jacket, he was wearing a hi-visibility coat. He was a highway worker from the bridge, and he'd been watching me. He was a lot bigger than me, and I was trapped with the woods on my right, lots of concrete above and below, woods way to my left, and a river behind me. My only option was to be the aggressor. I unclipped Wink and held him close as he strained to attack.

Me: "What's your fuckin' deal, man? You get off on cornering other men down by the river, big boy?"

Him: "You're kinda trapped down here, fella. Unless you're a good swimmer."

Me: "Trapped? Not at all. Let me clue you in on a little something. I'm walking across America hunting a killer. I've already dealt with a few bears and a shit ton of assholes like you, so if you think you're scaring me, you might wanna think again. My dog here doesn't seem to like you too much, either, and he's pretty pissed that you woke him from his nap. Do you think I'd be down here if I didn't have the means to drop you on your ass, you dumb son-of-a-bitch?"

Wink: *"A few bears? Really?"*

OK, I lied. You've been following my story from the beginning and know damn well I haven't fought off any bears. But I think I sold the lie pretty well.

Him, fake laughing to show me he wasn't intimidated: "Well, well. You are gonna be a lot more fun than I thought. Today's gonna be a good day. Why don't you do yourself a favor and not do anything stupid little man."

He inched forward slowly. I stood perfectly still, weapons in hand, leash ready for release, waiting for him to make his move. I still didn't know what his intentions were. Did he want to steal my gear? Murder me? Fuck me? I had no idea. None of those were options. I could almost taste Mr. Boot's blood as yellow man continued to move forward. I remembered feeling like Superman when Mr. Boot died on my chest. My courage was swelling, and I almost wanted this fucker to come at me. I let my thumb and forefinger find the safety measure on my bear spray, and, as discreetly as possible, removed it and slid it into my pocket.

Me: "I'm going to give you a decision to make. You may or may not like your options, but they're the only ones you've got. If you take one more step forward, I'm gonna drop your ass. Forever. If you wait longer than a ten count, same result. Or, you can turn your ass around and get the fuck out of here, and we'll call it a day. Everyone wins. Ball's in your court, big guy."

Wink: *"Or, you can just unclip my leash and we can end this really quick."*

Yellow man was rocking from foot to foot as he contemplated the rest of his life. He inched forward but quickly retreated a few inches back. I was sure he'd made the right decision, but then he stood, big and bold, staring. Maybe he was counting to ten in his head. I knew his decision before he did. His eyes and the slight smirk across his face gave him away. I wished we were playing poker instead of this game of bear spray roulette. In an instant, he lunged, and I emptied half of the canister of spray dead on. His body hit an invisible brick wall and dropped, hard, onto the concrete. His head hit the ground, and, for a moment, our bloodied faces almost mirrored each other. His shiny maroon weapon, whatever it was, launched from his hand and rolled several feet away. He was gasping for air and clawing at his eyes and throat as his body twisted, turned, and flipped around in agony. Suddenly, he stopped moving altogether, his hands clenched to his chest as if he were trying to excise a demon from his heart. His eyes, swollen, red, and tearing were locked on the underside of the bridge when he stopped breathing.

Holy crap! I knew the spray would stop him but, kill him? No friggin way. I stood, watching him be lifeless and knew I had to call this one in. I was alone and could easily get out without being noticed, but all of his construction buddies had seen me walk down here with Alexa and, trust me, I'm not too inconspicuous in small towns. I'd be pretty easy to find. I pulled out my water bottle and sat down. Sip. Another sip. I was in no hurry. I had to figure out how to best explain this mess.

9-1-1 operator: "What's your emergency?"

Me: "There's a dead guy under the bridge at Garners Ferry Crossing. I think he had a heart attack."

Wink: *"That guy's dead?"*

9-1-1 operator: "You think he's dead? Did you see him have a heart attack, or did you find him like that?"

Me: "I hit him with bear spray, and then he died. I presume it was his heart. This stuff isn't supposed to kill people. Or bears."

9-1-1: "What side of the river are you on, sir?"

Me: "East side. Under the bridge that's under construction."

9-1-1: "Please remain where you are, stay well away from the body, and, please don't touch it."

Me: "Yes, ma'am."

Wink: *"Dude, that was badass. I mean, sucks for him but he kinda had it comin'."*

Me: "Wink, this is not good. I didn't want to do that."

Wink: *"I know. Just trying to help you feel ok about it. I love you, buddy."*

Me: "I love you, too."

I walked over to the shiny maroon object and laughed. Are you kidding me? A fucking re-usable metal coffee tumbler with a screw-on sippy lid? I know I wasn't supposed to touch anything, so I didn't, but I did kick it with my shoe to see if it was filled with lead or a chain or something that would actually make it a viable weapon but all I got was a dribble of coffee when the opening in the sippy hole gave in to gravity. He liked his coffee with cream. I noticed the logo on the tumbler as it rolled. It was scratched up but easily identified as coming from one of those convenience stores that's open from 7 to 11. Does that place even exist around here? I hadn't seen one yet on my walk. He was planning to attack me with an empty, dirty, metal coffee tumbler. I was completely perplexed. He was either a rookie attacker, incredibly dumb, or this was a completely impulsive decision.

I straightened up my folding chair, finished my cold chili, ate a roll of Ritz crackers, and sat back to await those who were sworn to protect and serve. I was about thirty miles out of Columbia, and I imagined they weren't roaming around on the highway waiting for something like this to happen, so I probably had at least fifteen minutes of peace.

Should I have been feeling bad? That's what I contemplated as I finished dinner and hydrated. I could hear sirens in the distance closing in on me. I got up, folded and stored my chair, and cleaned up my dinner mess. I didn't want them to know that this situation wasn't bothering me in the least bit. By the time the red and blue lights appeared flying across the bridge overhead, I was standing in the exact spot where Ms. 9-1-1 told me not to move from. I'm a rule follower.

Cop: "Sir. Put your hands in the air where I can see them."

Me, hands way up: "Hey, I'm the victim here. Not this dead asshole. This was self-defense."

Cop: "I really don't care, sir. I'm here to secure the scene. You can tell your story to the detectives at the station."

Me: "I don't want to go to the station. I walked a lot of miles today, and some guy decided to mess with me and ended up dying. I'm tired, and that's my story, so I don't want to go to the station."

Wink: *"I don't wanna go, either, if it matters."*

Cop: "Nobody wants to go to the station, but you're going, so get comfy."

Me: "See that glass over there? Take a picture of the angle from where it broke to where all the pieces landed. That's critical to my story."

Cop: "Sir, please, we know what we're doing."

More cops, a fire truck, and two ambulances arrived, followed by a car that was so detective cliché I was sure I was in a movie. Out of cliché car stepped cliché detective. I swear to all that's holy, he was wearing a trench coat and had a small flip pad of paper in his hand. This was getting fun.

Cliché detective: "Good evening, sir. My name is Detective Blah Blah Blah." Sorry, I forgot his name for the life of me. "Can you give me a one-minute synopsis of what happened here tonight?"

Me: "Easy. I was down here sitting in my chair watching the river flow by. A bottle came crashing down beside me. I got up to find that big guy hiding behind that column. He stepped out with that coffee tumbler in his hand, but I didn't know that's what it was. He was gripping it tight and threatening me. He kept saying I was trapped down here, and he was gonna have some fun. Well, before he came from around that column, I grabbed my bear spray and disengaged the safety tab. I warned him that if he came at me, I was gonna drop him. He did, so I did. I sprayed him to stop him, but his heart didn't like that too much, and, well, there you go."

Wink: *"I can vouch for all of that."*

Detective: "Do you sleep down here under the bridge?"

Me: "Excuse me? What the fuck kinda question is that?"

Wink: *"Yes, we were going to, even though I told him it was a bad idea."*

Detective: "Are you homeless?"

Hm. That's the first time I realized that I actually was homeless. But a different kind of homeless that this cop may not understand.

Me: "Is that relevant to what's happened here?'

Detective: "Maybe. Maybe not."

Me: "So you asked me for a sixty-second synopsis because, I guess, any more than that would be a waste of your valuable time, but then you start drilling me, the victim, with offensive, irrelevant questions as if my time is less valuable than yours. Listen, I could have up and left, but I called you, alright? "

Detective: "Hey, why don't you bring it down a few notches. I'm just piecing together what happened, alright? You're saying this was self-defense and that's fine, we'll sort through the details at the station and get to the bottom of it."

Me: "No, I don't want to go to the station. I told that cop over there the same damn thing."

Detective: "Nobody wants to go to the station, but you're going."

Me: "Huh. That's exactly what the other cop had said. Verbatim."

Detective: "Break down your tent and pack up your gear. You are not sleeping here tonight. We'll get it loaded up and take it and your dog to the station. You can retrieve them if or when we finish tonight."

A few hours later, I was sitting, dead tired, in a small room at a cold steel table that had an empty chair on the other side. There was a rickety old camera up in the corner. Picture any interrogation room that you've ever seen on TV, and this is where they filmed that episode.

Detective: "Tell me what you were doing down under that bridge."

Me: "I'm walking across America, and it looked like a good place to pitch my tent for the night. It's public land, I assumed, so I chose to stop there."

Detective: "Why are you walking across America?"

Me: "I don't know the answer to that question yet. But I'm working on it."

Detective: "Why Columbia, SC?"

Me: "Google told me to come this way."

Here we go again.

Detective: "Can you help me understand that a little better?"

Me: "I decided to walk across America. I chose a starting and ending point. Google did the rest."

Detective: "So you just walk for no reason but to walk?"

Thank God we didn't do the Google back and forth thing like before. This guy wasn't as green as the cop back in Shallotte.

Me: "I do. Can we get past the fact that you don't understand my life decisions and discuss the asshole who attacked me so I can get out of here?"

Detective: "I can go all night if you're gonna be an asshole. I'll decide what we talk about. Why are you carrying bear spray in this area? We don't have any bears around here."

Me: "Are you serious? I just said that I'm walking all the way across America. And I prepared for all of America, not just Columbia, South Carolina. No disrespect, but Columbia didn't even enter my preparation equation. Just didn't."

At the silent conclusion of my bitchy little attitude moment, the door opened. A uniformed officer peaked in, looked at the detective, and something unseen or unheard happened between the two and the detective up and left without saying a word. I was pretty sure I could leave without getting into any trouble; I wasn't under arrest, and I was tired, but wasn't sure where Wink and Alexa were being held. I deserved more than a tent, so I pulled out my phone and booked myself a hotel room about a mile away. A nice place, too.

Then the door opened, and I was graced with the presence of Mr. Detective again. You know when you watch a movie where there's someone in an interrogation room, and the detective is vague and sometimes leading with his or her questions and then gets called out for some unknown reason and then reappears with a file folder in his or her hands and changes the direction of the conversation? All of that was happening, with movie-like precision, in my life at that moment. Yeah, Mr. Detective had a file folder in his hands, which he set very precisely in the middle of the table and sat down.

Detective: "How's your walk going? Meet any interesting people along the way?"

Me: "It's OK. I think it's a young man's sport, though. My body hates me. I've met some cool people, but I keep to myself for the most part. I'm out here to re-discover myself, think about some stuff I've been ignoring, and dealing with some personal issues. I really don't feel like getting caught up with other people's crap. Not right now."

Detective: "What state have you enjoyed more, North or South Carolina?"

Me: "I don't know yet. I'll let you know tomorrow."

Detective: "Tell me about Shallotte, NC."

OK, I can play this game of he'll pretend not to know about Mr. Boot, and I'll pussyfoot around precisely what he wants me to bring up. Fuck him. If he wants to treat me like a suspect in a crime, I'll play along.

Me: "I stayed there the first night of my walk. Days Inn, I think. Decent motel. Oh, and my ankle was hurting, so I stopped in and saw a podiatrist."

Detective: "That's it? Nice motel, good doctor?"

This was getting boring; I was tired and starting to get pissed.

Me: "Oh, yeah, and I killed a guy there, too."

Detective: "Yeah, I know. Read all about it."

He tapped the top of the file folder. I knew he knew as soon as he asked about Shallotte and, instead of showing me any respect and just asking, he played asshole cop because he thought he was on to something big. Time to turn the tables.

Detective: "You've walked through two states, and, according to your version of events, have had to kill two separate people to defend yourself. Now, I'm a detective, so I say maybe you attract problem people to you. I'm not saying you killed two good, hard-working, stand-up citizen of the month award winners but, still, two people. Dead."

Me: "Coincidence?"

Detective: "No such thing."

Me: "Maybe Carolinians aren't too keen on people who walk. I'm in the Carolinas, walking, and have been attacked by two people that I've had to kill to protect myself. Is that a Carolina thing, or just a coincidence? It must be a Carolina thing because you don't believe in coincidences. Maybe I did you and your buddies up north a favor by luring out the only two assholes in both states who don't like people who walk and took 'em off your hands for you. How about you start treating me with a little more respect, more like a victim, and less like a suspect. And, while you're at it, talk to your state department of transportation and your city planners and tell them to put in some goddamned sidewalks. Maybe then people will walk around a bit more and you guys won't be so uptight about it."

Detective: "Well, that is one passionate, angry response. Do you always get this angry?"

Me: "Only when people try to kill me. And when I get locked in a small room for hours and treated like crap. That makes me angry, too. And no sidewalks. Huge anger when that happens. I could go on for hours about the lack of sidewalks and beat up roads, but I'll stop now."

Detective: "That door's not locked. Leave whenever you want. We thought you wanted to help."

Asshole. Totally called my bluff and won. Well done.

Me: "Oh, yeah? Where's Alexa?"

Detective: "Who's Alexa?"

Me: "Sorry. Alexa is my cart. Someone put her in a van down by the river, but I haven't seen her since."

I actually did my best to imitate Chris Farley, but he either didn't get it, didn't care, or I sucked at imitating Chris Farley. I thought I nailed it.

Detective: "Alexa is outside the door. We didn't touch anything. You're free to go. Do yourself a favor: next time cops need to talk to you after a tragic event, don't be such a condescending asshole, and maybe you'll get that respect you want."

Good point. I could be a condescending asshole.

Me: "Heard. And I apologize. I'm tired, I walked all day then found myself cornered by some crazy motherfucker who ended up dying right in front of me. It's almost midnight and I just want to sleep then get on with my walk. I meant no disrespect even though I know I was disrespectful."

Detective: "We're good. We know how to find you if we need to."

Me: "Yeah, I'm pretty easy to find. Tough to outrun the law at three mph. Hey, think I could get a ride to the Holiday Inn about a mile from here? It's been a long day, man."

Detective: "No, I feel confident you can walk there. Have a good night."

Me: "Oh, and my ankle is fine in case you were wondering."

Detective: "Good. You'll need it if you ever open another restaurant. Yeah, we know about that, too. That's three dead bodies around you."

Me: "Anything else?"

Detective: "Just one more thing. Do me a favor and waltz on out of town tomorrow. I don't need any more bodies, and you, asshole, seem to attract them."

I totally deserved that. I needed to check my attitude at the door the next time I kill someone and have to talk to the police.

SOMEWHERE OVER THE RAINBOW

LEXINGTON, SC

33° 54' 32.9" N

81° 13' 26.3" W

MILES WALKED: 231

ead bodies suck. Despite feeling like a total badass, getting to Monroe to meet Peggy Sue was a much needed, anxiously awaited vacation that was just three weeks away. If it were Hawaii or Paris or any other exotic or erotic destination and any other time in my life, I'd have been pouring over tour books, but it wasn't that kind of vacation.

I'd end my days in the Carolinas in a town called Aiken, but I had to travel down Hwy 1 to get there. It was mid-day when I passed through a town called Lexington, where I met a friendly family at a Sonic Burger. If you don't know this fast-food burger chain, they've re-created the drive-in with auto stalls and digital menu boards, and your food is brought out on trays that attach to your window just like the old A&W stands I remembered from my childhood. When you're a walker with a cart and a dog, finding a comfy place to sit and eat and be in the shade can be a challenge. Welcome to Sonic Burger. I loved rolling Alexa into those stalls between other cars, pulling out my folding chair and Wink's food, pressing that button, and placing my order. But the best part was when the delivery person strolled out and saw me, no window, sitting there. It was the same every time. They'd pretend like they saw that every day and would say it was no big deal, but their face couldn't hide their confusion.

So, it was at a Sonic Burger, fully sprawled out eating a burger in a stall, where I met the Wall family. They were piled into a big minivan kinda thing having a special family day out for lunch. I rolled up and parked next to them, set up my chair, laid out Wink's food and water bowl, placed my order and glanced over to see four faces suspiciously staring at me. One of the kids in the back, whom I would soon learn to be the daughter named Emily, was in the back seat looking out the window at Wink, and they seemed to connect pretty quickly. The father, Philip, rolled down his window and inquisitively asked what my deal was and if I needed some money for food. I kinda laughed and declined his offer, explaining that I was on an amazing life journey across America and doing just fine. After he got over his initial concern for either his safety or my desperation, we ended up having a pleasant conversation. Emily, and her pre-teen sister Sarah Grace, piled out of the van to meet Wink and check out Alexa and all her cool gadgets as I talked to Philip and his wife, Joli. It turned out that Philip liked craft beers and fancied himself a great cook, and they invited me for dinner and offered their backyard for camping.

Did I mention to you that I did not mention to the Walls that I had killed two guys in the past few weeks?

After walking off the greasy burger a few miles to their home, parking Alexa and putting Wink in their huge backyard to run and play with the kids and their two dogs, Philip and I went to the grocery store to gather the ingredients he would need for a meal similar to a crab boil but with sausage, shrimp, corn and potatoes. We cracked some cold beers, prepped the ingredients together, then simmered everything together outside in a giant turkey fryer that was filled with a broth that smelled a bit spicy and a lot like fresh herbs. I was starving by the time dinner was plated. It was during dinner when it came out that I was a chef and, instantly, they were worried that I was judging their culinary talents. No matter how many times I told them that the meal was amazing, which it was, they assumed I was just being nice. They were so wrong. Philip was an awesome cook and I crushed three plates of grub.

Barely able to move after stuffing my face, I plopped down on the sofa to finish my second beer. Sarah Grace appeared from her upstairs room with a ukulele, sat down on the floor across from me and, with the confidence of a seasoned veteran musician, belted out *Somewhere Over The Rainbow*. Her fingers glided along the fretboard and her soft, young, innocent voice filled the room with grace and love. Her name served her well.

Somewhere over the rainbow. Where exactly was that? Was I headed there? Sara Grace sang so beautifully of bluebirds and lullabies and, with tears threatening to wash down my face, I wondered: if I just wished upon a star, would my troubles melt like lemon drops? Is that all it would take?

There would be no rainbows, no trees of green or red roses, too. The next day I would kill again. But it wouldn't be to save my ass.

MOMIMA

MONETTA, SC

33° 50' 44.5" N

81° 36' 16.8" W

MILES WALKED: 260

left early the next morning with the Wall family standing on the porch, waving me off and cheering me on. There was only one more town separating Aiken and me, and that town was Monetta, which was known for one thing and one thing only, Big Mo. Go ahead, guess what Big Mo was.

I'll give you a second.

Time's up. Big Mo was a drive-in movie theater, and I had been hearing about Big Mo since I left Columbia. It was the only drive-in movie theater for a million or so miles, and it was a big deal. People had told me that the owners were prominent in the community, everyone loved them, and that I should contact them when I got close because they would definitely let me camp at their theater and it would be safe and known. I liked safe and known camping. Big Mo it was then.

About five miles outside of Monetta I sent a message to the Big Mo Facebook page letting them know who I was and that everyone in the last three towns had told me all about their drive-in, what a wonderful family

131

they were and how great they are for the community and blah blah blah. Could I please pitch my tent, I'd be out by sun up, they wouldn't even know I was there, etc.?

I walked and anxiously awaited their reply.

As I started to see signs of a town, I got a message that said, "Sorry. We're not comfortable with that." That was it. I was kinda shocked after I had heard what amazing people they were and how letting someone walking across America stay at their theater would be something they would totally be into. But they weren't.

As I approached Monetta, Big Mo, in all its glory, appeared on my left. I wanted to spit on it. I pondered sneaking in and going stealth (maybe even leave a little something behind in the morning after my coffee) when a super cool old guy in a pickup truck pulled up beside me and rolled down his window.

Truck guy: "What in the world are you up to, dude?"

I instantly loved this guy. He was a total hippie without a care in the world. He was wearing a super bright tie-dye shirt and a green beat up trucker cap. Several skinny braids with colorful beads randomly popped out from the mop of dusty grey and brown hair that flowed from underneath his cap. I guessed him to be about sixty or so, but I felt like I was hangin' out with my old buddies when I was much younger. He was smoking a cigarette and somehow spoke, smiled and puffed all at the same time. He was the coolest person I had met so far on my walk.

Me: "Me and my dog are just walking, man, what are you up to?"

Truck guy: "Drivin' around, enjoying the sunshine, brotha."

Me: "That cigarette all you been smokin'?"

Truck guy: "Right now it's all I'm smokin'. Seriously, what are you doin' out here?"

Me: "We're walking across America, my friend. I'm on my way to Aiken and hope to be there tomorrow or the next day."

Truck guy: "Wow, that's groovy man. Aiken is a really nice place, especially if you're into horses. Lots of horses there. And cute girls, too, cuz of the college but when you meet Sally don't tell her I said that. She'll kick my butt."

Me: "Sally?"

Truck guy: "Oh, yeah, I was gonna tell you, but then something happened, and I forgot."

Me: "We've only been talking for one minute. What happened?"

Truck guy: "Huh?"

Me: "Never mind. Tell me about Sally."

Truck guy: "Oh, she's the prettiest girl in town, man. Seriously. Monetta is known for three things: Big Mo, South Carolina peaches and Sally."

SIDE NOTE:

They call Georgia the Peach State, but South Carolina grows more peaches than Georgia, and South Carolinians will make sure you know that fact. Especially in towns like Monetta, where they grow a lot of peaches.

Me: "Is Sally your girl? Wait, what's your name?"

Truck guy: "I'm just Bill, but townies call me Hoover. Ever since I was a boy in high school, I've had that name. One night all of us were out behind Big Mo smokin' some weed, and we got busted by the Sheriff. When he walked up all sneaky and quiet the bong was well affixed to my lips and I was sucking down a big barrel of smoke, so my friends started callin' me Hoover cuz I guess that's how the Sheriff described me and my sucking on that bong to all those who would listen."

Me: "That's a rad legacy, man. So, Sally, why am I gonna meet her?"

Hoover: "Oh, yeah, right. So, Sally and her husband own the only market and cafe in town unless you count that damn Dollar General store which I refuse to patronize on accounts they hurt Sally's business when they opened up next door."

Me: "I promise I won't go to Dollar General. Sally is married then?"

Hoover: "Oh yeah, she's been married since right outta high school.

He's alright. You know how it is, pretty boy gets the pretty girl."

His eyes were fixed on his windshield, and he disappeared for a moment or two.

Me: "You ok there, Hoover?"

Hoover: "Ha! Shit. I think I fell asleep for a second. Yeah, dude, I'm groovy. When you see Sally, you tell her that Hoover said that thing about the three things that come outta Monetta. She'll get a kick outta that."

Me: "Sounds like maybe you have a crush on Sally?"

Hoover: "Hell yeah, I do, brother. Since I was about three years old, man. Only about fifty kids in this town and families don't move here, so the pickin' is slim. I'm just lucky we were friends and still are. You tell her what I said; she'll like that."

Me: "I will, Hoover. I'll make sure she hears that."

Hoover: "Hey, if I see you around later, I'll bring you some weed, ok?"

Me: "Hell yeah, I'd like that."

Hoover: "OK, dude, I gotta go. Hike in peace, man."

Me: "Be good, Hoover."

That guy's only job, and Monetta should pay him a ton of money to do it, should be sitting at the beginning of that town to greet every damn person that drives, walks, bikes, or crawls in. The Official Greeter of Monetta - Hoover! That guy lifted my spirits so much. And then reality settled back in, and I still didn't have a place to camp. I should have asked Hoover but was too wrapped up in Sally talk.

I walked straight to the City Hall/Police Station/Fire Station/City Park. It was all the same building and space. I parked Alexa and clipped Wink to the wheel, fixed my hair a bit, made sure I didn't look homeless, and stole a quick sniff of my pits. Golden. Deodorant was still working.

Lady behind the glass: "Can I help you, Sir?"

Me: "Hi, how are you? My name is Thomas, and I'm walking across America, and I was kinda wondering if I could camp somewhere in town? I'm super clean and just need to pitch my tent for one night. I'll be gone before sunrise, and I won't leave a mess."

Lady behind the glass: "Well, I don't think it'll be a problem for you just to set up your tent behind the station here but let me call the mayor to make sure."

Me: "Oh, you don't have to disrupt the Mayor for me. I'll figure something else out."

Lady behind the glass: "This is a small town. The Mayor is also our Chief of Police, drives the school bus, and owns a couple of acres of peach trees. It ain't like the big cities. He's just a local and doesn't mind bein' bothered. Besides, he'll wanna know you're here and where to keep an eye out for ya."

Me: "Ok, then. Make that call. Thank you. I'll step outside and wait. My dog is leashed up out there."

I had only waited about five minutes when the lady from behind the glass came outside and gave me the thumbs up to set up camp behind the multi-purpose building. As Wink and I got everything ready, I looked around for cameras and lights. I was curious if I would be watched all night and even more curious if I was going to be sleeping under a flood lamp. Not that the light would bother me much, I'm a pretty heavy sleeper, but those damn things attract all kinds of winged critters that I had no desire to battle with buzzing against my tent all night. Known camping can sometimes be as nerve-wracking as stealth camping. If you're in the middle of a town, even in a place that appears to be safe and known, you run the risk of local teens or creepers finding you pretty quickly. You let your guard down and think you're safe and you're known by local authorities to be there. But, on the flip side, you're pretty exposed to whatever lurks around after small-town chief of police lays down for some zzzzzs.

Wink and I were well fed and set up for bed, but it was barely 5 p.m., and mosquitoes were buzzing around. Despite bathing in bug spray with the highest legal limit of deet available, the damned things still buzz around your head, and it's completely impossible to sit and relax. So, I decided to visit the market and maybe meet Sally. The Monetta Mini Mart, known by its sign as MoMiMa, was a quaint little place on the southern edge of town. I'd pass it again the following morning heading out, but I needed to hit it that night for food and water since most of those places didn't open up as early as I typically started walking. I leashed Wink to an old, rusted but still functioning ice freezer by the door and made my way in. There was a very pretty woman whom I'd guessed to be about fifty behind the counter. She greeted me kindly and, might I add, a little flirtatiously.

Pretty woman: "Well, hello stranger. Hello, pup. What can I do for ya?"

Me: "I'm just passin' through town, need some stuff and to deliver a message. Are you Sally by chance?"

Pretty woman: "Hell, I wish. She's far prettier and has lots more money than this country girl. What's a handsome boy like you lookin' for Sally for?"

Me: "This is a pretty small town, and if what you say is true, that Sally is far prettier than you, then this town breeds a lot of pretty women."

Wink: *"Really? Did you just say that?"*

Yeah, that was corny, but it worked. She was all smiles, and her cheeks blushed bright red. Yeah, I flirted back for sure. I was a lonely guy on a lonely highway, and if a pretty woman wanted to flirt, I was game. I wasn't about to tell her I was living out of a cart camping behind the damn police station. Nothing more guaranteed to kill a moment like that than to admit I was a vagabond.

Pretty woman: "Well, thank you, Mr. Charming. My name is Rosie, like my cheeks right about now. What's your dog's name? Sally is out runnin' some errands with her husband. They should be back later. You can sit in the cafe, and I'll get you something to drink while you wait. If that's your pleasure, of course."

Wink: *"My name is Wink. Nice to meet you."*

Me: "Yes, that would be a pleasure, Rosie. My name is Thomas, and this is Wink. Tell me, is this a dry town, or is there a cold beer in my immediate future?"

Rosie: "Dry my ass. Wouldn't be here if it was. Beer's on me. Sit your butt over there at the counter, and I'll bring it right over."

Me: "Thank you, but no need to treat."

Rosie: "You look like a city boy. Probably bought drinks for girls a thousand times. It's a new millennium, Thomas, and this girl's gonna buy you one. Maybe more."

Me: "Well played. OK, then."

I found a counter seat towards the other end of the cafe bar. Since my run-in with Mr. Boot and Yellow Man, I'd had a tendency, no matter where I was or what I was doing, to place myself where I could see as many people as possible with as few of them at my back. It wasn't a fear thing, though. I had started to feel dangerously invincible. I'd had that feeling before.

When my son was a young boy, maybe seven or so, we were driving on a small island in Newport Beach where his mom lived so I could drop him off. It was her weekend, and I had a date, a first date, with a girl I had met a few weeks earlier. I was pretty excited for the night because I was intensely interested in this girl. She was flirty and beautiful and a little bit crazy, and she made a living as a nude model at the art institute near my work. She would come in often to have lunch, and she'd be with the students who, just minutes before, got to stare at her naked body without judgment or fear of being called a pervert. I was quite envious of those kids and often wondered if I could take just that class. I guess I was the pervert, huh? Anyway, she intrigued me. I've always had a thing for confident, ambitious girls who'd lived a bit on the edge, and Rosie was all that rolled up into one crazy red-headed body.

OK, back to the island story. We were driving and, up ahead on the right where most of the waterfront homes had apartments on the top that you entered from a set of stairs that ran up the side of the house to a front door balcony, I saw smoke pouring from the stairwell. I pulled up to see flames all over the balcony and halfway down the stairs. In hindsight, everything I did after that, I should not have done in front of my young son.

Although heroic, it was dangerous, he could see everything, and it could have gone horribly wrong. I stopped the car and let it run and told my son to stay put. I jumped out and, without even thinking, ran up the stairs hugging the handrail to avoid the flames that were chewing up the wall on my right. At the top, the balcony was engulfed in fire and the front door was entirely ablaze. Across the balcony, crouched down in the only corner not yet consumed by flames, was an old man shielding himself. I ran to his side, lifted him to his feet, and half carried, half dragged him down the stairwell. Within a few seconds of getting to the bottom safely, the fire department showed up, and neighbors were out of their houses watching in fear. Firefighters jumped from their truck, took the old man from me and brought him to the back of an ambulance. They asked if I was ok to which I said I was and, well, that was it. I got in my car to see my son's eyes bulging from his head and a smile so big it almost required plastic surgery to remove it from his face. I had just saved a man's life. I dropped my son off, and, as I drove to meet my date, I couldn't quite comprehend what had just happened.

Despite smelling horrible, I had a good night. I guess there's nothing sexier than a true hero. Or maybe it was my smell. Or my smile. It didn't matter. The date went well. For several weeks following my heroics, I found myself looking for people that needed help. I wanted to save a life or a kitten from a tree or anything that would let me feel that powerful and special again. I guess I kinda felt that way my whole life after I saved him.

About a month after I played Superman in the fire, my son and I were, again, in my car when we witnessed a bunch of teenagers run out of a music store with armloads of CDs. One of them had a pillowcase that was stuffed full. This was not a life-saving event, but I hated paying $10 for a CD, and these punks, thieving hundreds of them, were part of the reason they were so damned expensive. Stores had to account for shrinkage in their prices, right? So, as they ran down the street, we followed them. They were oblivious to our pursuit. I called 9-1-1 and told them about the situation. The operator asked if I could follow them until the cops showed up, and I said, "Hell, yeah!" My son knew we were gonna be having some fun.

We followed them to a parking lot where they jumped in a car and slowly drove off. They didn't haul ass as if to make a quick escape. They meandered their way through a few lights and got on the freeway with us in hot pursuit! I was on the phone with the operator the whole time giving updates on our location and the other car. Within a few miles, I started to get upset. Where the hell were the cops? The operator kept saying they were moments away, but they were nowhere in sight. The car exited onto a frontage road, came to a red light, waited for the green, and then turned left under the freeway where they hit another red light. There we were, stopped directly under the overpass, waiting for the green. The cars exiting the highway on our right passed through our intersection as we waited. Finally, after several long, annoying minutes and me getting angry with the operator telling her that we were going to bail out and head home, our light changed to green, and the thief's car started to go. Suddenly, BAM! A car coming down the offramp on our right ran the red light and t-boned the car we were following. It must have been going full speed because it totaled the car and carried it a few lanes over. I was on the phone screaming, "You better send an ambulance, lady, cuz that car just got nailed!" My son's eyes were about to fall out of his head, and the shocked look on his face was priceless. We stopped and watched as the car door opened, and the teenagers and hundreds of CD cases rolled out of the car. Out of everywhere came the cops. It was like they were waiting in the trees and dropped from the sky. There had to have been a dozen of them. Red and blue lights and sirens filled the air with crazy excitement.

I got out of my car, told my son to stay put, and found the nearest cop to explain everything. He asked me to positively ID the kids, and I said I would but only if they couldn't see my face. One officer sat in the back seat of my car with my son to keep him calm while I sat in the front seat of one of the cruisers. He turned the forward-facing spotlight on as another officer walked the three kids over. They were blinded by the light and couldn't see me behind it in the seat. I did my civic duty and made the identification. The kids were arrested, and we went home.

I'm not saying that this little fiasco came close to the feeling I had when I saved the old guy in the fire, but, once again, I felt heroic. And, once again, my son was beaming, and I could see in his eyes that he thought I was the most awesome dad in the world. Well, I was, but it's cool to see it on your kid's face.

We've told those two stories a hundred times over the years, and they never get old. His recollection and mine are a little different, but it doesn't matter. We will always have those two crazy moments together.

As I sat and waited for pretty, flirty Rosie to return, I scoped out the scene. Small towns always intrigue me. I guess I've lived in big cities for so long that lacking any sort of anonymity is entirely foreign to me. Towns like Monetta, although loosely connected to its neighbors by a highway, contained their people. You were either from Monetta or you weren't, and you never would be, despite years and years of residency. If you were, chances are you were locked in for life.

Rosie: "Alright, sugar, here's that beer. Cracked one myself and hid it behind the saltshakers over there. Don't' tell Sally and definitely don't tell Teddy."

Me: "Teddy? As in bear?"

Rosie: "Sally's husband. Yeah, as in bear, but Teddy Bear he ain't. Maybe one day, long ago, he was cute, cuddly and lovable but not so much these days. But I didn't say that."

Me: "Your hide-a-beer-from-Teddy-and-Sally secret is safe with me. Got any tequila you're hiding from them as well?"

Rosie: "I'll tell you what, travelin' man, let's buy a little bottle with my employee discount, and I'll see to it that it gets hidden real well. You game?"

Wink: *"Think I could get one of those Slim Jims you got up there on the counter?"*

Me: "I'm game. Can I grab a Slim Jim for Wink?"

Rosie: "If you're just passin' through town, you sure you wanna flirt with the worm?"

God, I loved this girl.

Me: "Since I'm just passin' through town, you sure you wanna flirt with me?"

Wink: *"Where do you come up with these lines?"*

Rosie: "Let me get that bottle. And I'll get you that jerky, Wink."

Wink: *"Thanks Rosie. She's cool - I approve."*

So that was how I met Rosie --the flirty, beautiful hometown girl from Monetta. And that was how a flirty hometown girl from Monetta and a bottle of tequila turned me into a killer of a different sort than I had already become. A killer, whose outrage over witnessing another person's pain, put self-preservation as a justifiable and defensible excuse for killing on the back burner and took a life for the benefit of another. Mr. Boot, way back in Shallotte, made me a killer. Yellow Man in Columbia cemented my confidence. Teddy in Monetta made me a murderer.

Rosie: "Alright, pretty boy. The bottle is ready, and so am I. Been a hell of a week around here, and this girl could use a drink. I'm not off yet but screw it; let's do a shot and talk about what happens later."

Me: "Line 'em up."

Rosie poured us shots in red plastic cups typically used for beer pong and tailgate parties. It would turn out to be a very long night filled with booze and blood.

I was sitting on a black plastic milk crate that doubled as smoke-break furniture with my back against the rear of the building. Rosie was in front of me. We had been drinking beer and tequila for a few hours, laughing, telling stories, and, by that time, I had confessed to her that I was crashing in my tent behind the police station. She found that fact to be sexy in a bad boy, vagabond, gypsy kinda way. Rosie was a small-town girl, had only been out of Monetta a handful of times, and those travels hadn't taken her too far from home. She was mesmerized by my crazy, fantastical tales of frozen heads, gutted roadside rednecks, and a deranged, dead yellow man under a bridge. There was no fear in her eyes and, before Sally's arrival, I was pretty sure that I wouldn't be sleeping in my tent that night. Rosie had started the rear-of-the-cafe tequila fest sitting across from me, cross legged on the ground, but had inched her way forward through my stories and was now planted in front of me at my feet, with her hands around my calves staring up into my eyes as I recounted my tales. That's when Sally barreled through the back door of the market with a trail of blood trickling from the corner of her mouth, blew right by, and disappeared into the not gender-neutral bathroom door. I had heard from Hoover and Rosie how beautiful Sally was but, when I saw her face, beauty had been replaced with messy hair, a torn sleeve on her blouse, a swollen lip, and terror. Sally had seen better days, and Rosie was on her feet in a split.

Rosie started pounding on the door to the bathroom and was begging Sally to let her in or tell her she was ok, but all we could hear was sobbing and wailing that sounded like a child who'd lost their first pet. Water was running and splashing behind the door, and then a scream of pain like I'd never heard broke Rosie's pleas. It was a scream of severe emotional pain. I was frozen. This was a highly charged, deeply personal moment, and I was witnessing something horrible that I couldn't understand. I was an outsider with no history with these people. I had only heard the one comment that Rosie had made about Teddy not being so delicate these days, but our conversation had shifted away from them and on to my stories. My knowledge of Sally and Teddy and their relationship was just about zero. All I thought I knew was a small-town boy married a small-town girl and, maybe, small-town boy got a little feisty sometimes.

Rosie: "Oh shit, Thomas, he's finally done it. He hit her, or worse. This is bad. You have to leave. Now. Before he gets here. Leave! You don't want to see him like this."

Me: "Rosie, calm down. What the hell is happening?"

Rosie: "He's all kinds of jealous, Thomas. Always has been. Always warning boys to keep their eyes off her, but she flirts as all girls do, but she's never done nothin'."

Me: "You say he's never hit her before? You just said he's finally done it. What's that mean, Rosie?"

Rosie: "She'd never admit it. She'll disappear for a few days at a time sayin' she's goin' to visit family and can I run the market and I always knew he was hittin' her but, through all these years, I ain't never seen it. She hid it really good. I tried to know for sure so many times, but she would never tell me. I've seen him with that anger in his eyes when he's had a few drinks, and I've seen him go after some boys and whoop their asses, but never have I seen her hurt. Now I know, now I can see it. You gotta go. If he sees you, he's just gonna think you're here for her. He's crazy, Thomas. Go."

Me: "Should I call the police?"

Wink: *"Yes, that would be the right move."*

Rosie: "Oh, hell, no. They love that boy no matter what he does. They'd just blame her for making him do it for some damned reason. No, you go. It's time this gets handled here, between us, no police."

Me: "OK, I'm out. Shit. I can help!"

Wink: *"No, you can't. Let's go. This is none of our business."*

Rosie looked at me with sincere, pleading sympathies and tears flooding her face. She loved Sally, maybe like a sister, and she was going to protect her. Her eyes begged me to leave.

Me: "You have my cell. Please let me know that you're ok. Promise me you'll let me know."

Rosie nodded her head and ran into the cafe. Moments later, she emerged with a key strung up on a large soup ladle and went for the bathroom door. I left her as she wished.

I was only a few blocks from my tent. I grabbed Wink and raced back, where I planned to tie him up and grab my weapons. When I arrived at the police station, I ran into the mayor/sheriff as I rounded the building towards my campsite.

Mayor/sheriff: "You must be the traveler campin' out back?"

Me: "Yes, sir. My name is Thomas, and I greatly appreciate you giving me a safe spot to sleep tonight. I promise to be out early and keep it clean. You won't even know I was here tomorrow."

Wink: *"My name is Wink."*

Mayor/sheriff: "My name is Steve, and we aim to keep people safe here in Monetta, so it's my pleasure."

Wink: *"Hey, Steve? There's a girl behind the market who's not so safe right now."*

Me: "So, do you go by Sheriff Steve or Mayor Steve?"

Steve: "Just Steve. An old small-town guy like me needs no title. Everyone here knows who I am, where I came from, and what I do. We're all just a big happy family. Not a lotta reasons to have the police around here but, then again, we do get people passin' through, so enforcement is sometimes necessary. Tell me, why does someone walk across the country? Since my secretary called and told me what you needed, I've been perplexed. Just didn't know people did things like that."

Me: "I guess sometimes you just have to get lost to get found, you know?"

Steve: "Yeah, I guess that makes sense. But it's my job to keep my town folks safe, so I did some callin' around…"

Here we go again.

Steve: "…and talked to a few friends up in Columbia, so I know what happened up there. And they told me about Shallotte and what happened back at your home. So, let me be clear, Thomas. The only reason I'm letting you camp here is so I know where you are. Keep your enemies closer, you know? Now, I'm not sayin' you're my enemy, and I know what happened in Columbia and Shallotte were self-defense, but I would be lyin' if I didn't say I'm not too thrilled about you bein' here. But, because I've got no reason to assume you're gonna cause problems and because I don't want you campin' out where you shouldn't be, I'm gonna keep you right here where I can keep an eye on ya if I feel I need to. Have I been clear about what I expect of you tonight?"

Me: "Yes, sir. Crystal clear."

Steve: "I don't have the legal right to ask this of you, but I'm going to anyway. Would you be willing to relinquish any weapons you may have in your possession, legal or otherwise, until tomorrow morning when I promise I will return them to you myself?"

Wink: *"Don't do it."*

Me: "Steve, I would normally decline that request because, obviously, I've needed them the past month to save my ass a few times. I'm kinda attached to them if you know what I mean. But, if it will make you feel more comfortable and, since you're doin' me a favor, I will reluctantly oblige. I feel safe here and trust that you'll keep your eyes on me. Come on over, and I'll give you what I got."

Steve and I made our way around back where I removed all of my weapons from Alexa and handed them over. Minus my spent can of bear spray, there were three knives of varying sizes and styles, my taser and a small keychain pepper spray I had picked up on my way out of Columbia. Replacement bear spray was harder to come by in these parts but was high on my list of must-haves in the very near future because that shit works.

Me: "That's it."

Steve: "No guns?"

Me: "No, sir. No guns."

Steve: "You are a brave man takin' on this journey without a gun."

Wink: *"He's got me."*

Me: "Wouldn't know what to do with it. Probably kill myself tryin' to figure it out in the heat of the moment."

Steve: "Smart man. Sleep well. I'll be back first thing. You'll be alright. Everyone in town knows you're here and that I'm watchin' ya."

Me: "I feel safer already. Goodnight, Steve."

With that, he left me alone, defenseless. At least he didn't confiscate Wink. He's my most badass weapon, anyway. I got into my tent and thought about Rosie and Sally. I sat silently, waiting for the sirens to erupt and commotion from down the street, but nothing ever came. About an hour after the sun went down, I thought I heard a scream but chalked it up to fantasy or birds. I had decided to let them handle their domestic dispute the way they saw fit and without my interference.

Wait a damned minute. How the hell could I let those two women, one beaten and bloody, deal with some crazy, wife-beating bastard by themselves? I knew Teddy was a big guy. I had heard all about him from Hoover and Rosie, and those two girls probably weighed about 225 pounds combined. And one of them was already hurt. I wasn't a big guy or a fighter, but I was a pair of unexpected hands and, quite frankly, pretty proud of my most recent victories on the battlefield.

I woke Wink up from his lazy slumber, clicked on his leash, and slithered out of the tent.

Wink: *"Where are we going?"*

Me: "You know where."

Wink: *"Oh, no. Come on. We just barely escaped trouble two days ago. Take a break!"*

Me: "You know they need our help."

Wink: *"Alright, then. Here we go again."*

I did some stretches and walked around a bit to appear like I was taking my dog for a stroll. I purposely walked in the opposite direction of MoMiMa, down a side street, and circled back. I stopped and sat on a park bench by a baseball field and checked my messages on my phone. If anyone was watching, I was just that stranger that everyone supposedly already knew about wandering around town, getting some fresh air. When I got back to the main road, I turned left towards the market. It had been a few hours since I had left Rosie at the bathroom door in tears and had no idea where to find her after hours. I walked past Dollar General, strolled around back and headed in the direction of my tent again. I was behind the market where I saw Sally and Rosie sitting in the same spot I was earlier smoking cigarettes and drinking out of those red cups.

I found a spot to lean in the shadows where I had a pretty good view of them. I pulled a pig ear treat out of my pocket to keep Wink occupied and quiet. As I watched, I learned that Sally and Teddy lived in the house behind the market. It was a charming, well-decorated home with a pristine fenced in yard. This was one of the nicer residences in Monetta; it looked comfortable, inviting, and well-loved.

Nobody lives in your four walls, but you.

I saw Teddy for the first time through the front windows and confirmed that he was a big man. Not big as in fat, big as in tall and well-built. This former athlete had not let his body go to waste. He was also very good looking. I still hadn't seen Sally at her best, like the Sally I had heard about, but I was able to sift through the blood, messed up hair and fat lip to see the beautiful woman people spoke of. Teddy and Sally were kind of an oddity in small-town America. I had been through many towns in just a few weeks and these two just didn't fit the mold. Their bodies and their home were too perfectly coiffed for small-town life. But I shouldn't judge.

Teddy made his way to a sofa with a glass full of brown liquor and turned on the television. He flipped through the channels for what seemed like an eternity, never landing on any of them. He stopped, with the guide still on the screen, and made his way to a side window where he gazed over to the girls behind the market. I saw him smile, or smirk, or maybe it was a look of disdain. His mouth curled up on its ends, but his eyes and body language were not smiling. Back on the sofa, he surfed some more. He finally chose a channel and, if I wasn't mistaken, landed on a kid's cooking competition show. Huh. Interesting choice. But there I was judging again. I needed to stop doing that. As I scolded myself for being a judgmental prick, Teddy stood up and made his way to the window again. This time he was quick and deliberate like he heard something outside. He gazed towards the women, and, just as he took his drink to his lips, the fury surfaced. After one large swallow, he threw the glass across the room, directly through a window on the other side of the house. I heard the window shatter and the glass explode on the driveway. A few dogs barked in the distance. Wink had stopped chewing and grew tense, but I calmed him and turned him away to redirect his focus. I didn't need him adding to the noise and giving us up.

As I watched Teddy storm through the front door towards the market, I repositioned myself closer and behind a large bush next to their house but still hidden in shadows. Wink could sense my anxiety and was tight on the leash. Scratching him under his mouth kept him quiet, but he remained vigilant. I peered around the bush and saw Hoover, about ten feet away from the girls, near the opposite edge of the market. He was speaking to them very quietly when Teddy came roaring around the house and made his appearance.

Teddy: "Oh, Hoover. You are a brave man for comin' here tonight, my friend."

Hoover: "I was just heading to the General when I heard the girls talking out here and thought I'd stop to say hi. I wasn't expecting to see anybody out here at the market this late and, hearing voices back here kinda concerned me. All good, Teddy. All good, man."

Teddy: "You know, Hoover, all these years you've been kissin' my ass, pretending to like me, pretending we're friends from way back. We ain't never been friends, Hoover. You are, were, and always will be that stoner loser kid that wouldn't leave town. I see how you look at my wife. You been lookin' at her like that since we were kids. I let it go all these years cuz, well, look at ya. What's gonna happen? Sally gonna run off with a guy like you when she's got me? Hell, no. I kinda liked it, actually, watching you drool all over yourself when she's around. You're pathetic, Hoover, and no girl, especially my girl, would ever waste her time with you."

Hoover was frozen in stance with a burned-out joint between his fingers. I don't know if he was afraid or had succumbed to the free flow of diarrhea coming from Teddy's mouth, but Hoover looked defeated. As I watched him stand there, legs slightly trembling beneath his weak body, I saw fear wash over his face. The joint slipped from his fingers as Teddy took a step forward and then stopped. Hoover took a half step backwards and found stability against the wall behind him. Teddy walked over to Rosie and lifted her off the milk crate by her blouse as she trembled and cried.

Teddy: "You sit here, consoling my wife, but, Rosie, this is just as much your fault, you bitch. I know you tell her how bad I am, and you like it when she flirts with all the guys in this town because you're lonely and you want her lonely with you. Yeah, she gets power from you and your bullshit words. It's 'bout time I put an end to that. Keep your butt on that crate, Sally. I'll deal with you at home. And, hey, stoner boy, get your skinny ass over here. I don't want you goin' off tryin' to be a superhero, now. Come on, come on over here, and sit down. You get to watch."

No way I was watching this unfold. I slowly made my way, as quietly as possible, across the driveway and into their house to look for a weapon, and in the kitchen were plenty of them. I chose a hefty, eight-inch chef's knife. Oh, it felt good in my hands. If there was a weapon I was good with, it was an eight-inch chef's knife. In the movies, you always see people test the blade to make sure it's sharp by scraping the pad of their thumb across it. Now, maybe if you plan on going all Annie and slicing someone's throat, that's important but, in attack mode, you're probably going for the stab in the gut and even a fairly dull blade will make its way in nice and smooth. I checked for an edge anyway cuz that's what you do, right? It was pretty sharp.

I crept outside and back to my hiding spot behind the bush. I had missed a few minutes of Teddy's somewhat drunken assessment of some fantasy he had cooked up in his head. When I rejoined the argument, Teddy had Rosie up against the wall with her blouse twisted up in his fist. He was yelling about some guys with a boat earlier in the day and something about Sally helping them load beer in the back. Teddy swore she had unbuttoned the top of her blouse a bit and was bending down in front of them or some dumb shit. Teddy was furious and, apparently, had gotten into a fight with her earlier on the drive back to the market when he grabbed her by the hair and had punched her a few times in the face. He was reliving that experience in a proud, arrogant, wife-beating way. His hand had moved up from Rosie's blouse to her neck and chin, and she had tears streaming down her cheeks as he yelled. Bits of spit were flying in her face. Sally was begging him to stop and Hoover was sitting there in absolute fear doing nothing.

Wink: *"He's really hurtin' Rosie. Come on, let me have him!"*

Wink was at the ready, pulling on the leash, waiting for me to release him. He's a smart dog. He knew what was going on. He knew because I knew, and we were a team. I walked out slowly, from behind the bush and onto the sidewalk, just as if I was out taking a stroll. Wink was in attack mode, and my thumb was on the latch of his leash. Teddy turned around and saw some strange guy about ten feet away with a dog. His hand tightened around Rosie's throat. She looked at me, begging me to both leave and help. She feared for Wink and me but knew the outcome of tonight if help didn't arrive.

Teddy: "Who the fuck are you?"

Me: "Just a guy walking his dog. Is there a problem here?"

Wink: *"You know there's a problem here. Let me go, I got this guy."*

Teddy: "I think you might want to just keep on walkin'. Maybe right out of town would be an excellent idea. Nothin' here concerns you, understand me?"

Me: "Looks to me like a few fine folks got mixed up in a good ole fashion wife beatin'. If you ask me, of course."

Wink: *"He didn't ask you, actually."*

I slowly inched forward. I was within six feet of Teddy, which made him turn his head away from Rosie while still holding her neck.

Teddy: "Well, I'm pretty damned sure I didn't ask you. This is private property and a private matter. I suggest you turn around. Now."

Me: "Maybe we can talk this out?"

Distracted and confused, exactly how I wanted him, Teddy became angry and flustered, and, as soon as he turned to yell at Rosie, I released

Wink, who covered six feet in a split second. Wink took Teddy down, who was caught off guard, and I ran over and sucker-punched him in the kidneys, leaving him gasping for air. I quickly leashed Wink and handed him off to Hoover, who took him about ten feet away. Wink was growling furiously, and it was all Hoover could do to hold him back. Teddy was on his knees, trying to get back to his feet when I slid the knife deep into his back and found a lung. I gave it a small twist for good measure. He was down, fighting for air with blood flooding around his knees, and then he was dead.

I stood, hands horrifically bloodied, looking at three lifelong friends frozen in shock. In a fraction of a moment, I took a life and released three people from years of pain and fear.

I was a hero, again.

Sally looked at me with confusion and horror. Hoover was shaking from anxiety and joy. Rosie, with tears streaming down her pretty cheeks, stared into my eyes with adoration. I was, once again, a hero.

Hoover: "I killed him! That's what happened here. Leave. Go back to your tent. You weren't here, man. This has been comin', and it makes sense comin' from me."

Hoover's anxiety had been replaced with a smile from ear to ear as if he'd already convinced himself that he was the brave man who'd saved his childhood fantasy girl from the big bad wolf. He wanted this victory to call his own. He wanted to be the town hero who saved Sally.

Sally: "Who the hell are you? You just killed my husband!"

Me: "I'm just a guy. I'm a nobody."

Sally: "Rosie? Hoover? Do you know this man? Rosie, who is he? What just happened?"

Rosie: "It's all over Sally. Teddy's not gonna hurt you anymore. Or me or Hoover. You're ok. You're gonna be ok."

Sally: "Oh my God. What just happened? I don't know what to do. Rosie, what do I do?"

Rosie: "It's OK, sweetie. I'll explain but right now he needs to leave.

He just saved you, Sally. And me."

Sally: "Thank you. I think. I don't know. Just leave. I'm ok. We're ok. We're gonna be ok, right, Rosie?"

Rosie: "Yeah, baby. We're gonna be ok. Hoover, you sure you did this? This is big! Are you sure? I could have done this. He had my neck. I could have done this."

Hoover: "It makes sense, Rosie, that I did this. Hey, Thomas, you gotta go! Now. We got this."

Wink: *"There is no way we're gettin' away with this."*

Me: "Hey, Rosie, maybe another day, huh?"

Rose: "Yeah, maybe. Thanks for the tequila. Now go on."

I reached down and smeared the handle of the knife and told Hoover to come over and grab it like I had when I stabbed Teddy. I had to get my prints off that knife and his prints on it. I was back in my tent within ten minutes. I laid on my sleeping bag, heart-pounding, just waiting for the sirens, cuffs and a jail cell. It took forever for the action to start. I assumed they sat and hashed out their story for a while before calling 9-1-1; a story that, hopefully, didn't involve a guy with a cart and a dog walking through town. The town came alive for the rest of the night.

A few cop cars and an ambulance wailed down the main road about twenty minutes after I was in my tent. Wink was tense from the sound but had probably already forgotten about the incident behind the market because I gave him just about an entire bag of his favorite treats when we got settled in. I could hear lots of voices and people scurrying down the street to see what was going on. I stayed put. No chance I was going out there only for someone to say they saw me walking around not too long ago. Nope, I promised no trouble, and I had nothing to do with this. Nobody ever approached my tent.

Deep sleep didn't come that night. I dozed off a few times, but the police station was loud and active all night with cars coming and going, and I could hear people crying loudly outside the front doors. As long as I was lying here in my tent, I knew their story was holding up. I had heard all three of their voices approach the police station and go inside hours earlier but didn't hear them again. I wasn't sure if they were locked up or had left while I slept.

As the sun began to rise and shine, Steve was at my tent.

Steve: "Hey, Thomas, come on out. Leave your dog."

I unzipped the floppy tent door and eased my body out. At the tender young age of fifty, this took a few moments longer than it would a more youthful, agile man. My bones creaked and ached as I took those first few steps on the cold, hard earth.

Me: "Mornin', Steve. It got a little chilly out here last night."

Steve: "Yes, it was a cold night. Very cold, indeed. How was it out here? Any disturbances?"

Me: "Apart from some sirens, I slept quite well, thanks."

Steve: "Sirens. Yeah. Had an incident in town last night. Know anything about it?"

Me: "Not a thing, Sheriff. Figured you boys were chasin' teens in fast cars."

Steve: "So, you were here all night? In your tent?"

Me: "Well, aside from a few nature breaks for me and my dog, yeah, buttoned up all night. We're getting used to tent life and lots of downtime."

Steve: "Someone saw you over at MoMiMa yesterday around supper. Were you there?"

Me: "Yes, sir. I had some dinner and a few beers and met Rosie. Nice lady, but you already know that."

Steve: "Did you happen to meet the owners of the place? Sally and Teddy?"

Me: "No, didn't have the pleasure. I went there to deliver a silly message from some guy named Hoover. I ended up staying for dinner."

Steve: "What exactly was that message, Thomas?"

Me: "He told me to tell Sally, if I met her, that there were only three good things that ever came out of Monetta: Big Mo, Peaches and Sally. Something like that, anyway. He told me all about his childhood friendship or crush on her and that she'd get a kick out of that. I didn't meet her, but I passed the message on through Rosie."

Steve: "Yeah, Hoover's been pushin' that line for years. Good guy, Hoover is."

Me: "You should hire him. As a greeter for the town. It made me want to hang out for a while."

Steve: "Well, turns out that he and Teddy had a little scrap last night, and Hoover ended up killin' the guy with his own damn kitchen knife. He says it was self-defense. Says Teddy and Sally got to the market, Sally was beaten up a bit, and Teddy started yellin' at Hoover about always flirtin' with her. From there, the story is a little questionable. Hoover says Teddy came after him with a knife, and, somehow, Hoover got it away from him and dug it deep into his back. It probably took Teddy a while to bleed out. Shit way to go, you ask me."

Me: "Well, this must look pretty suspicious, me bein' in town and all on the night this happened after my past few week's experiences."

Steve: "You were the first person I thought of when I saw the body. Naturally, we're tryin' to figure out if we should be charging Hoover with a crime or if it truly was in self-defense. You see, Hoover is a little guy, as you have seen, and Teddy is a big, big man. Now, I know Teddy had been drinkin' but, it is still hard to imagine Hoover could get that blade away from him."

Me: "Don't know what to say, Steve. The body can do some inexplicably powerful and courageous things sometimes."

Steve: "I guess it can. Hoover's not denying anything, so this is probably a shut case here pretty quickly but, I have to admit, I'm not sure I'm gonna go to my grave thinkin' I know the whole story here."

Me: "How are Sally and Rosie? Did they see it happen?"

Steve: "Oh, yeah, they were right there. Back up Hoover's story one hundred percent. They are better than one would expect, to be honest. I imagine Sally's gonna inherit a lot of money and Teddy wasn't the nicest guy in town. Not sayin' he deserved what he got and all, but I would understand if she wasn't too broken up over it. If you know what I mean."

Me: "I'm just an outsider, Steve, so this is just one asshole's opinion, but some people just need to die."

Wink: *"I agree."*

Steve: "That's one way to look at it. Listen, the sooner you head out of town, the better off we'll be in sortin' all this out. There's nothin' here for me to hold you on and no evidence to show that Hoover's been lyin', but I have my doubts. I know how to find you should I need to."

Me: "No invitation needed to vacate. I'll pack up and get on my way. Hey, is there coffee somewhere in town? I presume the cafe isn't open today?"

Steve: "That's correct. There's some inside. Help yourself."

Me: "Thanks. And thanks for the campsite. Good luck with Hoover."

And, just like that, I was free to go. In reality, I was always free to go. No in-depth questioning, no metal tables in small, bleak interrogation rooms, no cuffs, no cells. Hoover took the shot, and I'll never know why. Perhaps to impress his girl with his bravado and courage. Maybe because he wished it had been him who drove that blade into Teddy's back. Who knows? The human mind and heart are fucked up and mysterious.

Wink: *"Dude, you just got so lucky."*

Me: "I know. We gotta knock this shit off."

Wink: *"We?"*

I got packed up, brushed my teeth, took care of nature duties, and made my way into the station for a second cup of coffee. With nobody manning the front window, I peered through the glass to see if anything interesting was lurking around the corner. I saw Hoover, cuffed to a rather comfy looking chair next to a desk. He was facing my direction, and Steve was on the other side of the desk with his back towards me. Hoover and Steve were both in the same clothes from the night before, and both looked a bit rough around the edges. Hoover caught my eye, and we connected for a very long moment. Without words, we exchanged thanks - his with a slight grin and nod, mine with a nod and salute.

As I walked out of town, I had hoped to catch sight of anybody at the market, especially Rosie, but it was a taped off ghost town. Whatever the cops needed, they had already retrieved. All that was left was a dark interior and ribbons of yellow sealing the place off. No Rosie.

I wasn't far from Aiken but decided not to stop anywhere but at a motel. No bars, no cafes, no stealth camping. Twenty-five miles to Aiken then over the state line into Augusta, Georgia. I had to get the hell out of this state. No more Carolina blood. No more Carolina bodies. No more Carolinas. I would cross into Georgia with two states walked and three dead bodies under my belt. Before Teddy, I was just a killer. After Monetta, I was a murderer walking free.

MARCH

THREE BODIES LATER

AUGUSTA, GEORGIA
TO
FLORENCE, ALABAMA

THE THIEVING MUD HOLE

AUGUSTA, GA

33° 28' 13.9" N

82° 06' 22.1" W

MILES WALKED: 311

needed Georgia to be completely uneventful. Four deaths in as many months was taking its toll on my psyche. As empowered and heroic as I was feeling after Monetta, my soul needed a break from death. Hopefully, my time with Peggy Sue would be loaded with fun facts and history that would lead me to that other murderer in this story.

My father was a big-time golfer. He played several times a week at either his club or that of his brother. He played at Pebble Beach and even did a vacation of golfing around Scotland, and he'd told me many stories of beautiful Augusta, Georgia, where the PGA Masters Tournament is played each year. In my naive mind, I was going to cross the Savannah River, which acts as a state line between South Carolina and Georgia, and roll into a green, grassy, upper-class city where people just golf and do golf like things. Wrong. Perhaps it was the path I walked but, except for a cool coffee shop in the downtown area, Augusta was a shit hole. I will repeat this so as not to offend anybody from Augusta who might read this book - maybe I took the worst route through the worst parts of the city. I did not see the whole city. My goal was Monroe, 180 miles from the state line, and I begged Google Maps to show me the most direct way there. It obliged by giving me a path through Augusta that was not green or golfy in any way.

The entire city of Augusta, as it appeared to me, was poor and under construction. Sidewalks, bike paths, and any other safe way to travel by foot were dug up, and the holes were filled with water from the constant rain that never wanted to stop. Not only did I have to play dodge-car all day to get to the other side of town, but I also had to curb jump my cart about a hundred times. Even Wink, who was usually pretty chill with any surroundings, seemed pissed off. I swear I heard him say, "Ah, crap. Another goddamn hole."

I walked as quickly as possible to get across town. I had booked a hotel room on the other side of Augusta, and I had no desire to sightsee. I wanted to go through and out in one day. Traffic sucked, it was raining, I was constantly banging my cart into things, falling into muddy holes, jumping it up on curbs and trying to keep Wink from eating through his leash and bailing on me completely, which I wouldn't blame him for doing. It got so bad that I decided to call a few of my buddies on a conference call so we could shoot the shit and lift my spirits.

Adam, Brett, and I were having a good laugh on the phone when, suddenly, my whole cart jerked and came to a grinding stop. I looked down to find my entire front wheel missing. Disappeared. The brackets that held the front wheel had fallen to the sidewalk, hit a crease, and stopped me instantly. What the hell?

I grew up in the San Joaquin Valley in California in a city called Stockton. I'd never heard one good thing about Stockton as an adult but, when you're a kid, it's just where you are, right? It's just a neighborhood with a creek and a cul-de-sac where you ride your BMX bike over rickety homemade ramps. Stockton, in the summer, was hot. Real hot. And I used to love taking my paper route money and getting missile pops from the ice cream man. Those things, you had to eat them fast, or you ended up with red, blue, green, and purple juices running all over your hands. I remember one particularly hot day when I raced down the street on my sweet Torker bike to catch up to the taunting music ice cream trucks blared over the tin can loudspeaker mounted on the top. I threw my bike aside, raced to the window, and got my missile pop. As I sat on the grass eating my treat, I noticed that it wasn't melting that much. I licked and sucked my way down the pop, and, when I got near the bottom, it still had some of those freezer burn mini icicles around the base. I was confused, even perplexed by the scientific anomaly occurring in front of me. Why didn't it melt? What the hell was up with my missile pop? I don't know that I had ever been more confused in my life.

Until my wheel went missing. One second I was strolling along with my dog and my buddies on the phone, and the next second, the entire wheel was gone. I looked around to find nothing but the giant sidewalk crevasse I had just cruised over. I tied Wink to the cart and walked around, looking in the gutter and bushes but no wheel. I did find parts of my axle about eight feet back. Two pieces, actually, that used to be one. The axle had broken in half and slowly worked its way out of the wheel as I curb jumped all day. When I lifted the front tire to go over the hole, and since I was on my phone and not paying attention, it had simply fallen off and sunk into the brown abyss.

It made me laugh a little bit. The fact that my entire wheel was submerged in dirty water on a rainy day in a shitty town about five miles away from my motel all added up to a pretty good chuckle.

Me: "Guys, you're not gonna believe this. My front wheel fell off and disappeared into a giant hole of brown water, and my axle broke in half."

I have good friends. Friends who care deeply about me. In that moment, neither of these guys found this to be anything other than fucking hilarious. They already knew I was having a day from hell and, you know how guys are: anything to dig the dagger in a little deeper so long as it doesn't kill, you gotta push on the blade. Yeah, this was good fun for them. Anything that allowed them to say, "Well, you know, you don't have to be walking across the damned country." I still loved those guys, but, right then, in my miserable state of moisture and frustration, they could go to hell. I hung up.

As I was about to remove my raincoat and dig into that thieving mud pit, something told me to stop and take in the moment. Where the hell was I? A few months earlier I was serving beer, sausages and tacos to my friends, and now I was standing in Hell Hole, Georgia on rain and mud-soaked broken-up sidewalks with a dog I barely knew, and I was about to reach down into a wet brown mess to fetch a fucking stroller tire. How did I get there? I barely remembered even walking to the cracked and busted up patch of concrete upon which I found myself contemplating my existence. Life had sure taken a turn since I had last considered my whereabouts.

As I focused on my butchered-up life for that brief space of time, I landed my eyes on a small red shack looking building that was off to the side of the road and down by a fast-moving creek. There was a small parking lot next to the shack, which was filled with cars, and there were a few more waiting for space. On the side of the shack facing out to the creek and about four feet off the ground, a pipe jutted through the wall from the inside and from it poured water at a pretty fast pace. People were lined up with large plastic bottles waiting to fill them with the never-ending rush of water, and the people in the cars who were waiting for a place to park no doubt had empty vessels in their trunks awaiting the same finale. I had never seen this before. I'd never seen a wanna-be barn next to a running creek in the middle of a large city with a never-ending flow of water jetting out of a pipe from its side and a line of people standing in the rain to get some of it. Where was this water coming from? Surely not from that disgusting city creek, which was littered with trash and mountains of evidence of homelessness and drug paraphernalia? If so, why would you want to drink it? Who knew what was in that murkiness? On the opposite side of the creek from the watershed was a swimming pool. At some point in ancient history, it was probably a cool little gathering spot for local kids to pee. It was not a private pool behind someone's home; it was just a big, rectangular mass of green water with a broken diving board at one end. It looked like it had just dropped out of the most frightening chainsaw massacring, hockey mask and knife blade glove wearing, scar-faced, striped sweater, Halloween movie set and landed on this busy street with zero fencing around it. All of the concrete surrounding the pool, the diving board, the ladder coming out of the side, and even the tree branches floating in the murky brown water were completely covered in dark green algae. Nobody had dared to even dip a big toe in that pool for years, but I was ninety-six percent certain that people had been laid to rest in it. I witnessed no floaters, but there were definitely long lost loved ones weighted down at the bottom.

You know the Dr. Seuss book *And To Think That I Saw It On Mulberry Street*? I felt like Marco with my disappearing wheel, that weird water spigot cabin thing, the parade of people and cars waiting patiently in the rain to get their fill and that super creepy pool.

Deal sealed. I double-checked my list of places I'd love to live, and Augusta appeared nowhere on it.

A honking car horn snapped me back to reality.

Wink: *"Good luck, man. I wouldn't put my arm down there."*

Off came the jacket and down into the water my arm went.

Wink: *"Oh, that is so gross."*

With my mind in a funk from the happenings of that day, I contemplated what the hell else could be down that hole. Dog poop. Hypodermic needles. Nessie. Hoffa. Earhart. Cooper. It was deep. Anything was possible. When my elbow reached the water, my fingers found a spoke, and, without much effort, I pulled out my prize, just like a box of Cracker Jacks. None of the other above-mentioned possibilities surfaced with it.

The next five miles of walking, as you can imagine, was an act of deep determination to get to a dry, warm place, hot bath, cold beer, and cozy bed. The art of getting there was me dealing with all the shit I had from the previous several hours getting across town and now had the added fun of pushing Alexa in a constant wheelie position for nearly two hours. I was already used to the judgmental stares from people thinking I was home-less, but now those stares were mixed with smirks and laughter. Assholes. I was doing a noble thing hunting down a murderer, thus providing them a safer living environment. What the hell had they done for society lately?

Dry. Warm. Bath. Beer. Burger. Bed. Goodnight.

Turned out the axle on those strollers was a standard bike part. I wasn't stuck in Augusta. An Uber ride across town to the bike shop and back to buy two new axles (an extra, just in case) took less than an hour the next morning. I even braved leaving Wink in the hotel room so I could move more quickly. I was on the road, well out of Augusta by 11 a.m., and on my way to Monroe. If I hunkered down with no alcohol, ear-ly bedtimes, early to rise, ate well, and stopped losing cart parts, I could be there in five days. Or I could rent a damn car and be there by tonight but, no, I still needed to be tender with my soul searching, and all that self-help crap I'd been ignoring because of all the murder and stuff.

Eighteen miles to Harlem. Nineteen miles to Thomson. Twenty-six miles to Crawford. Twenty miles to Athens. Screeeeeeetch. Guess. Who. Was. There? Right there, waiting for me on the side of the road as I walked into town. Nope, not Annie. Rosie! Great, now she gets to see and smell me after rain walking and camping with a wet dog. Tenting that night was no longer on the docket. Hotel time it was. This boy needed a shower.

Rosie: "Hey, homeless."

Me: "Surprise, surprise. What in the hell are you doin' here, and how did you find me?"

Rosie: "Not too hard to track you down. From Monetta, there aren't many directions you can head, and I knew you were goin' through Au-gusta. I just kept drivin' till I saw your cute butt back there a few miles. Tequila?"

Me: "Oh, yes. But first I need a hotel and a shower."

Rosie: "Already took care of that first part. Let me know if you need help with the second. Meet me there. Four blocks down, turn right. You can't miss it. I'll be out front."

Forget that sentence a few paragraphs ago about hunkering down with no alcohol and all that other crap. My body needed a rest, and Athens was just as good a place as any to get it. Athens, GA. Home of the University of Georgia Bulldogs, REM and the B-52s. Athens became a city in the early 1800s and blah blah blah. Do you really care?

Rolling into a nice hotel with a beautiful girl, wet dog, and an insanely odd-looking stroller garnered lots of good stares. I didn't care. An hour earlier, I thought I'd be stealth camping in the rain in the middle of wherever and there I was, at a fairly swanky hotel, and I had a pretty good idea how that night was gonna go.

Rosie: "Not to be presumptuous, but I looked into dog boarding places if you need a break for the night. Just a thought."

Wink: *"Wait, what?"*

Me: "Hm. I haven't done that before. Do dogs like places like that?"

Wink: *"I'm not sure they do."*

Rosie: "Probably more than walking around town after already putting in twenty miles. They've got a dog playground and a small pool. It's supposed to be a pretty cool place. Your call."

Wink: *"I like playgrounds and swimming."*

Me: "Yeah, let's do that. Maybe they'll bathe him, too."

While I showered, Rosie took Wink a few miles away to the overnight place and checked him in. She was back before I was out. That steaming heat was too damned good to rush. She waited on the bed as I finished up and got dressed. We hadn't been physical before, so barging out of the bathroom fresh from the shower wrapped in a towel was maybe a little too forward.

We ate dinner at a loud but dimly lit wine and small plates bar on a busy downtown corner. I had read about a bar called Sister Louisa's - It's A Glory Hole! that I wanted to check out, and it was only a few blocks away. If you were to gather up a couple dozen religiously satirical artists and writers and pay them to design a bar that would be highly offensive to any catholic in the world, Sister Louisa's would be the result. It was a relatively small place with walls lined floor to ceiling with hundreds of religious pieces of art adorned with words and sayings painted on them that made even a devout non-believer as me cringe. It was incredibly original and clever, and my mother would not approve. But the drinks were strong and straightforward, it wasn't too loud or too crowded, and it gave us time to ease into after-dinner activities.

I'm not one to kiss and tell, but it's safe and respectable to say that Rosie didn't drive back to Monetta that evening. Or the next, although Wink did join us for slumber party night #2. I'm not sure how she paid for that room, but she insisted. And I got a massage. From her. Nice.

Rosie didn't ask much about my walk or why I was doing it. Perhaps she sensed it was something I didn't want to talk much about. Not to say I was secretive, but I was just vague enough that she probably got the hint. We did talk a lot about the days following the MoMiMa murder, though. Hoover was never charged with any crime and, while in custody, got a few discreet pats on the back from some of the other officers and town officials. It seems Teddy hasn't been the town favorite for quite a while and, although nobody wished a painful, horrific death upon another person, things might settle down a bit now that he was gone. Sally seemed to bounce back fairly quickly, as well. It had only been about a week since everything happened, but the market and cafe were open and doing quite well. Nothing like a little blood and guts in the defense of a hometown girl for the local folks to rally around. Rosie said Hoover was the new town hero, or so he felt. Maybe someday I'd revisit Monetta and get a feel for what my actions had accomplished.

Me: "You know I gotta go today. I have to get to Monroe by tomorrow. I'm already a few days late, but with no regrets."

Rosie: "I thought I might be able to talk you into coming back to Monetta, but maybe that'll have to wait."

Me: "It will."

PEGGY SUE

MONROE, GA

33° 47' 37.8" N

83° 42' 47.0" W

MILES WALKED: 470

I was first-date nervous when Wink and I approached the pub where murderer mother Peggy Sue tended bar. Look at me name calling. We found ourselves a few feet from the door after walking from Athens to Monroe, showering in a cheap ass motel, and steadying our nerves. I say "we" like Wink was nervous. He couldn't care less where we were as long as Slim Jims were involved.

I got a few interesting stares as I sauntered up to the bar, saddled a seat and settled Wink with some jerky. I was watching a much older, much more talkative, and far worse wrinkled version of Annie throw back a shot of a smooth, brown liquid followed by a large swallow of beer. Several men at the bar followed suit, and I guessed from the toast, someone close to all had recently died. Bottoms up, stranger.

Peggy Sue: "What'll it be?"

Me: "Whatever you were having."

She eyed me with curiosity but didn't move. Her stare was cold and fierce.

Me: "Whiskey and a beer back, please."

Peggy Sue: "Is your pup gonna be a problem?"

Wink: *"I'll be cool, lady."*

Me: "Is he a problem for you?"

Peggy Sue: "I guess we'll see. I've been waiting for you, *Joshua.*"

The way she said my fake name kinda creeped me out. So, Jenny had called Peggy Sue the minute I left her insurance office back in Lake City.

Me: "And you must be Peggy Sue."

No reply. Peggy Sue, without ever breaking eye contact, pulled a Bud Light from the cooler below her, lined up two shot glasses, poured us each a finger of Jack and slid mine over to me. The whiskey went down hard and hot. I'm not a brown liquor drinker, but I wanted to be on the same drinking page with her, so I suffered through the heat and fought back the urge to cringe a bit. The cold beer helped.

Peggy Sue: "So, *Joshua,* Jenny tells me you're an old schoolmate of Kennedy's who's walking around the world or some dumb shit, and you happened into her office looking for her. That about right?"

She was hard to read. The friendly woman I saw throwing back shots at the other end of the bar was gone. The woman in front of me was all business, and her face didn't convey much trust when meeting strangers asking about her daughter.

Me: "Pretty much sums it up. I met a woman back in Whiteville who remembered your family. I think she lived near you, and she and Kennedy played together as kids. She said she knew of a distant cousin of Kennedy, and that led me to Jenny."

Peggy Sue: "Sprinkles is still slingin' hash in that diner, huh?"

Me: "Ha! Yeah, she is. Feisty woman, too."

Peggy Sue: "Listen, *Joshua.* I don't know you. You say you're an old friend of my daughter and maybe you are. But why in the hell are you walkin' around the world lookin' for her?"

Me: "I guess that is weird, but, first of all, I'm only walking across America, and it's not to find Kennedy. Just happened through Whiteville and thought of her. I'm kinda aimlessly roaming for some self-evaluation time and, when Sprinkles led me to Jenny then Jenny led me to you, I figured I'd route my way here. I always liked your daughter, Ms. Rose, and don't mean to worry you."

Peggy Sue: "I think I remember Kennedy mentioning you back in her school days. Been a long time and, well, I've been in a bar for most of it, so you probably understand if my memory ain't so great. What is it you want with Kennedy anyway?"

Me: "Nothin', really. I think I'm going through a midlife crisis. Kinda hit a wall last year. I used to live on the west coast and decided to chuck it all and just go wander and maybe find myself. Thought I'd pass through my hometown and then I started thinkin' about my friends and, of course, Kennedy was right there at the top of my list. Probably wouldn't surprise you if I admitted to a boyhood crush on your daughter."

Peggy Sue: "You wouldn't be the first."

Me: "I'm just heading westward, back to California, and figured if Kennedy was anywhere on that path, it would be nice to say hello."

Peggy Sue: "Probably not gonna happen. Kennedy is kinda like you, a wanderer. She headed west years ago and, last we spoke, she was out in California, but I haven't heard from her in several months, and she got rid of her phone. I miss that girl. We were close her whole life until about five years ago or so. She started disappearing and reappearing all over the place and kinda dropped out of communication. Last we spoke was around the beginning of the year. She was somewhere near LA workin' at some restaurant. That was the last I heard of her."

Me: "Is her dad still around? Think he might know anything?"

Peggy Sue: "What? Are you kiddin' me? Didn't you hear anything about him from Sprinkles or Jenny? He's probably dead and, if he ain't, he should be. She would never call her daddy. Piece of shit, that man is."

With that, Peggy Sue meandered over to her lonely bottle of whiskey and brought us each another shot. At this pace, tomorrow was gonna be a rough day of walking.

Peggy Sue: "This one's on me for makin' me laugh. Hell, 'Is her daddy still around?'. You crack me up, Joshua. The things that man did to her and my boy back when we was married would turn your gut."

Me: "Sorry. I didn't know that was taboo. I don't remember Kennedy ever mentioning anything bad about her dad. We can drop it. I was just hopin' to say hi to her, no big deal."

Peggy Sue: "You finish your drink up, son, and get on your way. It's gonna start to get busy around here, and I'm not too keen on your dog stickin' around for it."

Me: "Yes, ma'am. And, hey, Peggy Sue? It was nice to meet you. You and Annie look a lot alike."

Peggy Sue: "Annie?"

Shit.

Wink: *"Way to go, Joshua."*

Me: "Kennedy. Sorry. Damn whiskey! Shouldn't have had that second one."

Peggy Sue: "I guess not, *Joshua*."

I went bottoms up and got the hell outta there. No doubt, Peggy Sue knew where her daughter was and that she had gone by Annie. Her look wasn't one of confusion. She had the eyes of a momma bear staring down a hiker who got too close to her cubs. I rushed back to the motel, heart pounding, locked the door, and pushed Alexa up against it. If Peggy Sue wasn't dangerous, I'm sure one of her drinking buddies was. If I was able to sleep, I planned on getting up long before sunrise and hoofin' it out of town pronto. But first, a call to Johnny.

Me: "Sorry it's so late. I kinda fucked up, but maybe it shined a light on something."

Johnny: "Good to hear your voice. I was starting to check the news for stories of a murdered homeless guy and his dog down in the south. What happened?"

Me: "After a few shots, I slipped up and accidentally referred to Kennedy as Annie to her mom. She knew. I tried to backpedal, but she knew.

No way that's a coincidence. Any chance you can look deeper into Peggy Sue? See if there are any communications with Annie or, I don't know, anything? Not sure what to look for, but I know she knows about her daughter and her fake name, and she probably knows more than that. You should have seen her eyes, Johnny. She scared me."

Johnny: "Well, after killing three people, it must have been pretty bad to get a scare out of you. Gimme a few days."

I decided to get a visual on pops. I had to see what that monster looked like. Rockmart was ninety miles away - about three days if I kicked ass. I jumped on Hwy 78 west around 5:30 a.m. and never looked back. By that time in my walk, my tolerance for alcohol was pretty low. I was eating crap food, not enough of it, was generally always in a state of mild dehydration, and anything more than two drinks was enough to give me a pretty good headache in the morning. That morning was no exception.

I knew I had to go straight through the heart of Atlanta, which I was not looking forward to. I could skirt around it, but that would add more miles. One hotel on the western edge of downtown Atlanta and one more day's walk got me to the Silver Comet Trail.

I was on trail about ten miles from Rockmart when I met a really cool couple. They were curious about Alexa and Wink and what I was doing so I lied. I told them I was walking across America for a charity and they thought that was great. I asked if they knew of a place in Rockmart or near there that was safe to camp, and they offered to let me set up near a small lake on their property. In Rockmart. Boom!

We walked and talked a ton, and I had to make up a bunch of crap stories to fit my lie. They told me about Rockmart, how small it was, and how they couldn't wait to sell their farmhouse and move someplace bigger. The Silver Comet Trail runs right through Rockmart and, as we were leaving the trailhead, I saw what appeared to be exactly what Johnny had described as Lester's old salvage yard right there on the road going into town.

Me: "What's that place?"

Carla: "Crazy old man's junkyard is what we call it. A real eyesore for the town. First thing you see when you drive in from the east."

Kenny: "Everyone in town wants to burn that place down and bull-doze it. The old man who owns it, when he's around, sits out there all day yellin' at everyone walkin' by as if we're gonna jump his fence and steal his rust. Yep, there he is right there. Check this out."

Kenny, with a laugh, walked up to the fence and put his fingers through the links like he was planning on scaling it.

Old man: "Hey! Hey! Get outta here! I will shoot your ass if you come over that fence!"

Kenny: "Ah, Lester, ain't nobody ever steal any of your crap. Who'd want any of your rusted-out junk anyway?"

So, that was murderer daddy Lester. That was too easy! I made a point to come back in the morning and get a closer look. We walked off laughing as Lester continued his barking from his all-weather Barcalounger.

Kenny and Carla were super cool and let me forego the tent for a far more comfortable sleeping environment on their sofa. I guess when people think you're doing a good deed, they'll go out of their way to make you comfortable. I felt terrible for lying, but the steak dinner I had that night was out of this world. No doubt, Kenny knew his way around a smoker and grill. Fed, fat and happy with a few glasses of wine in me, I crashed out by 9 p.m. Wink was sharing an insanely large dog bed with their equally insanely large Doberman, who was quite lovable despite my predisposition to animals that could chew my face off. I kept my pepper spray handy just in case he changed his temper.

I woke to the smell of chorizo, eggs, toasty tortillas, and coffee. Just before my eyes opened, I fantasized that I was in a Mexican paradise. Carla had prepared breakfast burritos, and I wolfed one down in about four bites. As I was packing up to leave, she handed me two more wrapped in foil for the road. It was gonna be a good eating day for me.

Lester, in the same clothes from the night before, was still in his recliner. Maybe he slept there? He wasn't moving, and his eyes were closed, so that was a pretty good possibility. Or maybe he was dead.

Lester: "Get the fuck away from my stuff!"

He belted that out as I was walking by and without ever opening his eyes. Yes, they needed to burn that place down. I walked by without turning my head much, past the yard about a hundred feet, turned around, and headed back. Wink was a bit confused as we made the U-turn but fell quickly into step. We stopped at the very beginning of the fence line to watch Lester from afar and hopefully not draw his attention. As I watched him sit, eyes still closed, he suddenly got up, looked directly at me, and walked very quickly towards me with more speed than I thought he was capable of.

Lester: "What do you want? Huh? Two days in a row, you've walked by here lookin' at me. You and that damned cart and dog. What do you want?"

Me: "How much for that old toilet?"

Lester, turning around to look at an old, yellowed porcelain crapper half buried in the dirt, furrowed his brow as his gaze landed back on my face.

Lester: "It's not for sale. Not to you. What do you need a toilet for? People like you just shit where you want. You're the problem these days. Messin' up our cities and our towns. Takin' all our government money cuz you ain't got your own. No. That toilet ain't for you. Like you got any money anyway. Now leave me alone."

Holy crap, Lester was nuts! He was also tall, like his daughter. I hadn't planned on talking to him but, since he was there and being an asshole, which I wasn't in the mood for because I had a delicious breakfast burrito in my belly, two more in my cart, and I was happy. And since I didn't want his grouchy old man attitude to ruin my happiness, I decided to fuck with him a bit.

Me: "You know, you're right. I usually do shit where I want. But I've been thinkin' about putting a toilet in my cart, so I'd have a more comfortable place to handle my business. Someplace that might remind me of home. I miss my home and my mommy. I just thought maybe I could buy that toilet and install it in my cart."

Lester: "You can't just put a toilet in a cart and shit in it. Where do you think it's gonna go? Are you dumb or on drugs or somethin'? Yeah, must be those drugs you bums are always takin'. Fine, I'll sell you the toilet for fifty bucks. I'll even help you install it, you dumbass."

Me: "I'll give you five, and you don't have to help me."

He stared with amusement and dismay. Five dollars would probably buy him his beer for the day.

Lester: "Fine. Five. But I ain't liftin' a finger."

Me: "Glad I caught you on a good day. Folks I was with yesterday said you aren't always around."

Lester: "Oh, they keepin' tabs on me? Waitin' for me to leave so they can steal my stuff?"

Me: "No, I just think they walk by here a lot and notice that maybe you're not always here."

Lester: "Maybe sometimes I go visit my kids."

Me: "That's very nice of you."

I handed him a five dollar bill and walked away.

Lester: "Hey! You forgot your toilet!"

I didn't respond. Just kept walking to the trail. Figured I'd let the old drunk stew on that whole exchange for the rest of his life. If he had any friends, he would have one hell of a story to share.

Me: "Johnny, me again. Anything on Peggy Sue?"

Johnny: "Dude, getting phone records takes time."

Me: "Add a name to your inquiry, would ya? See if you can dig into any communications between Annie and her dad, Lester. Also, research his travels. He's drunk off his ass and said that sometimes he goes to visit his kids. Plural. Not kid, but kids. They only blessed the world with two, and one of them became kibble for forest critters when he was a little boy."

Johnny: "Well, you did say he was drunk. OK, I'll get on it."

That was that. I was near the end of my third state, and I could proudly say that I hadn't killed one person in Georgia. I still had twenty-four miles to the Alabama state line and one decent-sized town so that could change. I thought, maybe, I could set a record by crossing America and, without getting convicted, kill one person in each state. Shit, my mind was messed up. Those aren't even good joking thoughts. I needed to walk, be alone, like really alone, and cover some ground in peace and harmony. This lifestyle was starting to get to me.

Nineteen miles to Cedartown, another seven to the Alabama state line where the Silver Comet became the Chief Ladiga and about another seventeen or so to a campground on the trail that promised to be quiet and peaceful. It was exactly that. I set up camp in super cold temperatures about fifteen feet from a wide, shallow, and fast-paced river. We arrived near sundown, which did not allow for much sightseeing. It was creeping down into the thirties, and all I wanted was some hot cocoa (doable thanks to my JetBoil cooking system) and some delicious dehydrated chicken and dumplings. I ate in the cold of the night just outside my tent, cleaned up, climbed in, fired up Netflix, and crashed in about five minutes. Wink was bundled up like a burrito under his blanket. It was our coldest night yet, and I had three layers covering my entire body, including my wool beanie and face gaiter. The only visible skin came from the slit in the fabrics where my eyes were.

Wink and I slept like two rocks.

I didn't kill anybody in Georgia.

LUNG SAW

loved Alabama. I loved the roads, the scenery, and the people. Hell, I even loved the cops. I thought about buying a billboard in the dead center of that state that just said I LOVE ALABAMA! I almost died there, but I still loved it.

Best of all, I didn't kill anybody. If you're keeping score, that's two states in a row where I didn't kill a single person.

The next several days were long, stunning journeys through what turned out to be the most beautiful state on my walk. I hiked up and over several steep hills and deep down into a gorge to see the Noccalula Falls, and the following day learned a little lesson about how they name their streets in that stretch of the state. Despite its beauty, Alabama had some pretty severe hills that kept coming and coming. Just when I thought I was done with a set, a whole new range appeared. After three or four summits, I finally picked up on the cues that I was about to climb another damned mountain. The roads at the base of every hill or mountain or whatever you want to call them (I don't know the technical difference and have no desire to Google search it right now) are called "Street Name Gap." Gap being the keyword here. Gap in the road name means precisely this: "You are about to climb a big fucking hill right now." There were way too many roads with the word Gap in them. Beautiful, wide, and lacking a lot of traffic, but they said Gap, which meant climb.

Guntersville was a killer resort town. Not killer because I had to kill there but killer because I had a safe, known place to camp next to a big ass lake at a yacht club thanks to a very kind guy named Philip whom I met through my friend Lindsay. After all those Gap hills, I needed a day off. Since Guntersville offered such sweet sleeping arrangements and plenty of places to eat delicious hot food, it worked out to be a perfect place for some R&R. Turns out, I needed that rest because, on my walk out a few days later, the reaper came a knockin'.

Leaving Guntersville required a pretty legit two-mile uphill battle but on a well-paved, wide road with perfect shoulders. I got a late start because I was only planning on going 23 miles to an area that looked to offer lots of accessible stealth camping opportunities. I was well rested, well fed, generally happy, and the weather, when I started out, was pretty nice. All that awesomeness disappeared about five miles into my day. Dark grey, ominous clouds rolled in from the east, and the temperature started to drop. I checked the forecast, and it didn't look promising. A one hundred percent chance of severe thunderstorms did not appeal to me. I didn't like camping in thunderstorms. I didn't mind the rain so much; it was the lightning that kinda freaked me out. I was new to the whole outdoor living lifestyle, and, being that I had no idea exactly how people died from lightning strikes, my brain made up all kinds of juicy "what if" scenarios, and I started to believe them to be true. I found myself Googling, "Will my tent poles attract lightning" and "How many people die each year from lightning strikes." Shit like that. Turned out that most people who die from lightning don't typically get hit by the bolt; rather, it strikes nearby, and the ground electrifies and ZAP, down you go. Camping in a thunderstorm means you're basically sitting on top of water, which, we all know, loves electricity.

So, this damned storm was coming in behind me, and I didn't want to camp in it. I only had one option, and that was to double up my day by walking forty-two miles and blow some cash on a motel in a town named Priceville. The thought of covering that much land sucked almost as much as the thought of soaking in a jacuzzi with an electrified toaster. I went to Wink for advice.

Me: "OK, boy. Thunderstorm camp or forty-two miles?"

Wink: *"Uber."*

Me: "Not an option."

Wink: *"Hitchhike."*

Me: "With a cart and dog? Not gonna happen."

Wink: *"You're the chicken shit. I say camp."*

Me: "Thanks. We walk."

Wink stopped, sat back on his ass and glared up at me.

Wink: *"I'll do it for a Slim Jim."*

Me: "Deal."

NOTE:

Slim Jim did not pay for product placement in this book and did not contribute even one stick of that meaty mess during or after our journey.

So, we walked. I estimated my arrival in Priceville to be near midnight. We were going to go as fast as possible to stay ahead of the storm, so I stopped at a gas station, bought a bunch of Slim Jims for Wink (his treat for dealing with my bad decision making), gulped down a large coffee, stretched for a second and off we went. Since I was feeling pretty good that day, I decided to do some running. If I could get my speed up by one mile per hour and hold that pace for half the distance, we could arrive by 10:00 p.m. Another mistake. That day was filled with bad decision making.

We stayed ahead of the storm for the first thirty miles. Jog three, walk one, repeat. All day. At mile twenty-nine, my body started to revolt. My left hip flexor sucker-punched me with pain that shot down my leg, and then my entire hip froze up. Attempting to walk normally prevented me from pushing off with my left foot in its normal position. So, I limped. And I hurt. From my knee up, my muscles contracted and twitched and screamed at me to stop. I started yelling at my leg, things that might come out of a crazy person's mouth as they stared at a wall talking. "Oh, you think I want to be walking forty-two miles today? Why don't you quit fuckin' whining and get with the program? Why can't you be a team player? You don't hear my right hip flexor bitching and moaning, do you?"

I was losing it. It was nearly sundown when I passed through a highway junction that had a gas station that was quite busy. I knew nobody would randomly help a guy with a dog and a cart get a ride into town, so I pulled out a $20 bill and offered it to no less than four cars for help. I was in so much pain I was actually offering to pay anybody with a truck to put my shit in the back and give us a lift to town. Nobody helped - not even a moment of contemplation. It had started to rain, and I was limping terribly.

Twelve more miles in the rain. I had made a huge mistake. I should have just found a place to pitch my tent before the sun went down, but by then it was pitch black, the highway was soaked, Wink was on high alert, and I was barely able to walk through the pain. I was furious at myself for making that terrible decision. A wise man once wrote, "The problem with walking somewhere is that the only way to get there is to walk." So, we did.

As I crested what I knew to be my final hill before Priceville, I saw the lights of the town in the distance. It was the pot of gold at the end of a dull, grey toned rainbow. It was a good three to four more miles to the motel, but a renewed energy took over my body. The pain was unreal, but my warm, dry room was somewhere down there below the flickering yellow streetlights. I stopped to stretch my leg in hopes of some relief and powered on.

In my heightened state of anxious happiness, I had no idea that death was right behind me.

Wink was already on edge for so many reasons: it was dark, he was tired and sore, and he was always on high alert walking after the sun went

WALKER TIP

SOLAR PANELS AND CHARGING BANKS.

When I started my walk, I had a foldable, lightweight four-panel solar set up on top of my cart. By the end of the first month, It was stuffed inside my cart. I used it one time across the country. I say it's better to be safe than sorry but, solar panels...I don't know. I just didn't need it. I was glad I had it, just in case, but I never found myself so far away from power that my charging bank didn't keep me covered.

My charging bank, on the other hand, I used every single day. I purchased a 30,000 mAh charger on Amazon. It was pricey but worth every penny. If there was a 40,000 mAh charger available when I walked, I would have paid for it. I had a phone, iPad, two flashlights and a Bluetooth speaker which all needed charging. I used Google maps so much that my phone ran down mid-day. I would charge it while I walked. The charge on my pack typically lasted two to three days but anytime I was near an outlet I plugged everything in.

down. That was the protector in him. It was his job, he knew it, and he did it well. He was soaked and muddy and had to stop to shake off the water every so often. He was tired, like me, and probably hurting as well. I wouldn't have been surprised or offended if he'd hated me that night. We had walked forty miles in wet, cold and perilous conditions, and it was completely unfair to him. But he never complained. He powered on. He would walk until he dropped before he would stop and complain.

Walking downhill into town with little light around us, we both sensed the presence of another person nearby. I could hear footsteps, and, as I searched for the mystery person's location, I saw the dark silhouette of our follower about a hundred feet or so behind. We were on the outskirts of town where shabby trailer parks began to appear on both sides of the road; the kind of areas you worry about as a walker after dusk. During the day, they probably seemed rather harmless; at night, they were bogeyman motels. You could hear dogs barking in the distance and see random beat-up cars slowly crossing into muddy driveways. Their headlights illuminated broken down mobile homes in horrible disrepair. The fear of stray guard dogs was my first concern; the guy behind me was my second. I had to give him some benefit of the doubt, though. I was walking in an area where people are probably known to roam. He was far enough back that I allowed my fears to be present and was mindful of my surroundings but didn't dwell too heavily on him. I was still more concerned about dogs in the dark.

Within a quarter mile, my follower had gained some ground. He was close enough now that, when I glanced back to check on him, I could see that he was of slight build, maybe a few inches shorter than I, and his head was covered with a black hoodie. So cliché, right? I guessed him to be about twenty feet behind us. Wink was going crazy and wanted off the leash. He wanted to protect me, or maybe he just wanted to protect the stash of Slim Jims he knew were hiding in Alexa. My hands lowered to my knife and stun gun; I unsnapped the safety. I could hear his footsteps gaining ground. I heard the distinct sound of a lighter and, seconds later, I could smell cigarette smoke. It smelled comforting and familiar. I'm a former smoker, and, like all vets of that nasty habit, you never quite lose that craving, especially in moments like this.

All I wanted was for this guy to make his presence known and offer some reassurance that he's just walking into town like me. Something like, "Hey man, no need to worry. I'm just walking to Carl's Jr". There was a Carl's Jr. coming up on the left and, not only did I hope this was his destination, it made me realize that I was starving. He was close enough now that he was invading that socially acceptable space where strangers either avoid or introduce themselves.

And, suddenly, he was gone. He completely disappeared. I didn't hear him bail out, but I'm sure Wink did. We were next to several rows of closed up storefronts and industrial buildings, and I guess that was his destination. I kinda laughed a bit at how paranoid I was and admitted to

Wink that I was being a real wimp. He agreed, but I think he was just as relieved as I was.

The attack came fast and out of nowhere; Wink didn't even sense it coming. As the blade penetrated my skin and dug deep into my back just below my right shoulder, Wink had sprung into action and was starting to shred the leg of my attacker. I'd never been stabbed, and it fucking hurt. It was odd, though, because it wasn't as debilitating as I thought it would be. I was down on my knees in pretty severe pain, but I wasn't gasping for air or spitting blood out of my mouth. Wink was covered in blood and on top of the attacker whose leg was shredded. Wink's leash, which was still clipped to my belt, pulled on me, which sent sharp pains through my chest. I had to unclip him from my belt and re-attach him to Alexa. I wasn't sure how badly he was mangling that guy, and I didn't care. The attacker was kicking and screaming in pain, but he was no match for Wink, who held him down under threat of ripping his throat out.

I rolled over to my stomach, grabbed my phone, and dialed 9-1-1. The attacker was still on the ground and not going anywhere, anytime soon. He was bleeding, far worse than I, from his shredded legs. Wink was standing over him, almost daring him to move. Wink is a loving dog, and I want to believe that he felt a little sorry for the guy but, hey, you play you pay, right? I watched every drop of rain as they made their way to my face. It was a light drizzle, and it felt good. It was peaceful. I could feel my jacket warm from my blood and wondered if this was where I was going to die. I guess it wouldn't have been so bad; my hero was standing guard, guiding me to the light. The worst part of dying here would be that Wink would know that he didn't save me, and he would carry that guilt for the rest of his dog life. I didn't want that to happen. I cried for him. He came to me and licked my salty tears and laid down next to me but kept a vigilant eye on our attacker. I hugged him and kissed him and thanked him. As my head began to get sleepy and the cold and wet no longer bothered me, I drifted off into darkness.

Flashing lights, piercing sirens, shouts of anger, ferocious barking, and boot steps snapped me out of my slumber. All I could see was red and blue, and someone was above me, flickering a flashlight in and out of my eyes over and over again.

Me: "Where's my dog? Where's Wink?"

Wink: *"I'm right here. I'm OK."*

Flashlight person: "We have your dog. He's OK. He's just a few feet away. Can you tell me what happened? Where do you hurt?"

I tried to sit up but was immediately held down by flashlight person.

Flashlight person: "You need to relax. You've lost a lot of blood, and we're trying to determine where your wound is."

Me: "That asshole next to me stabbed me in the back. Below my right shoulder."

Flashlight person: "My name is David, and I'm a police officer. This is Carmen, and she's a paramedic. She's going to take care of you while I ask you a few questions. Then we'll get you to the hospital and get you patched up. We can finish up there. Who is the man next to you, and what happened?"

Me: "I'm walking across America with my dog. We were walking into town. We're staying at the motel next to Carl's Jr. I can't remember the name. This guy appeared out of nowhere and shoved a knife or something in my back. My dog attacked him and took him down. He saved my life."

David: "Your dog has a lot of blood on him, but we don't think any of it's his. There's another paramedic checking him out. I think he's more concerned about you. He was in major protection mode when we arrived. He was practically laying on top of you. If he'd had his way, he would have taken me down trying to get to you. It must be good to have a companion like that."

His words were calming. He was talking to me like we were out having a beer, but both of them were working on getting my shirt off without moving me too much. Wink was OK, and I was breathing. That's all that mattered.

Me: "What about the attacker? Did you get him? Did he get away from Wink?"

David: "The first ambulance took him. He was in far worse shape than you. Your wagon is on the way."

Me: "He's still breathing, then?"

David: "Barely. Listen, I'm a cop, and she's an EMT. Her job is to save people. My job is to protect them. Your buddy is a local problem child like many we have around here. Meth, weed, alcohol, fights, petty theft, etc. Nothing too bad, but he was headed that direction. I'm surprised he targeted someone with such a big dog. Not smart."

Me: "That's my boy. Hopefully, the kid will walk again. Before I passed out, it wasn't lookin' too good for him. Lots of blood. Wink had his entire thigh in his mouth, and his bite was deep and strong. That had to hurt."

I spent the next few days in the hospital. The knife that ended up in my back was the jagged edge blade from a multi-tool thingamajigger. Not sure what the kid thought he was going to accomplish with that unless he planned to saw me in half. I took a peek at the repair job the doctors did, which was pretty good considering the edge of the wound was pretty roughed up. My attacker had shoved it several inches deep and pulled it down and out, which ripped and tore at my skin and muscle. The stitches were all over the place, and it was going to make for one hell of a walking trophy.

The attacker, whose name was Richard Wheeler, didn't fare so well. The kid bled out before he got to the hospital. Wink had bitten straight through his femoral artery. He didn't have a chance. It was kind of David and Carmen to not tell me about how bad his situation was while I was lying on the ground on the side of the road. I didn't want that kid to die. I hated him for stabbing me with a mini hacksaw, but, whatever. I can't let my mushy heart get in the way of life's little shitty realities.

Of course, while I was lying in the hospital my second day, I had to talk to the cops. This conversation wasn't like the others, though. These guys were cool and understood without a doubt that Richard was the aggressor, and I was the victim.

Me: "Before you even begin, let's get something straight. I have no energy or desire to play any cop interrogation games, so let's not dance around the fact that Mr. Wheeler is the fifth person to die an odd death because of me or near me in the past few months. I know you know this already, so let's just cut to the chase."

David: "Of course we checked you out and, yes, we learned about the murder in California and the mysterious deaths in the Carolinas. Your name did pop up in a separate police report in South Carolina but only as a possible witness."

Me: "OK, just so long as we don't need to rehash all that crap. I wish I could replay a conversation I had with a cop in Shallotte, NC, about murder and Google Maps. I should write a fuckin' book about it."

David: "One time and one time only. Spill it all, and we'll be done."

Me: "I used to be a chef in California. I owned a restaurant, and one of my line cooks chopped up another line cook. The one that got away was never caught. I lost everything. I decided to walk across America to clear my head. A toothless redneck in North Carolina tried to kill me on a rural road because he was afraid I witnessed something. I have no idea what because I killed him before we got to that tidbit of info. A few weeks later, near Columbia, SC, a guy dressed in all yellow cornered me under a bridge and, when he tried to attack me, I nailed him with bear spray, and he fucking died of a heart attack. A week later, in Monetta, South Carolina, I just happened to be in town camping behind the police station, with permission, when a couple of guys got into a fight over a woman, and the one that was the husband ended up with a knife in his back. Kinda like me. I had nothing to do with it, and I didn't witness it, but I was nearby when it happened, and when the shit about the first three dead guys came up, Monetta's finest wanted to question me. Then last night happened and that's it. That's all the dead bodies."

David: "That's quite a few. I've been a cop in this town for fourteen years, and I've only seen about a dozen bodies that weren't caused by nature or autos. Have you maybe considered a different hobby?"

Me: "Walking three thousand miles across a country isn't a hobby; it's a job. Every day you have to problem solve. Where am I gonna sleep? What am I gonna eat? Do I have enough water? This is life in its most primitive form. I've chosen the most basic, fundamental job ever. Survival. Nothing more. My job is to survive, and every day I walk to work."

David: "That's pretty fuckin' heavy. Oh, sorry. We're not supposed to swear on the job."

Me: "A tweaker nearly sawed my lung in half with a pocket multi-tool. Rules can piss off tonight."

David: "You're a weird dude, Thomas. Maybe not in California but in Priceville, Alabama, you're a weird dude."

Me: "Thanks, I'm cool with that."

David: "Alright, here's the deal. As soon as the doctors release you, you're good to go."

And that was that. He didn't ask me one time why Google Maps sent me to Priceville. Thank God. I was exhausted, in severe pain, stayed overnight, and was released the next day. I had to make my way to the pet impound place to get Wink, who smelled like he'd rolled around in salmonella ridden chicken thighs and moose poop and then sunbathed for a few hours.

Wink: *"Get me out of here. Seriously, this place is disgusting."*

Me: "Excuse me, but why the hell does my dog smell like this?"

Pet impound lady: "Because that's what it smells like in here."

Honesty is always good, I guess? I didn't aim for the motel. I went straight to a coin-operated car wash and pretended Wink had four wheels. Yes, I got some strange stares but, hey, in the end, he was Armor All clean and it only cost me $2.00. And, yeah, I know that maybe the car wash soap wasn't ideal for his skin but, if you wash your car, you get it all over your hands, and nothing terrible has ever happened, so one dog car wash wasn't gonna kill him. Wink had a blast as he jumped around and splashed in the puddles so please don't send me any hate mail about animal cruelty. He wasn't complaining.

APRIL

ARE THERE CHAINSAW ZOMBIES OUT HERE?

FLORENCE, ALABAMA
TO
CONWAY, ARKANSAS

NATCHEZ FRIGHT NIGHT

FLORENCE, AL

34° 53' 45.3" N

87° 52' 47.2" W

MILES WALKED: 869

needed a day off to rethink this whole adventure, what I was doing out here, and where the hell I was going next. I had no clue in which direction to walk now that I had met Annie's family, which really got me nowhere and almost got me killed multiple times.

I sat in my room all day working on my iPad, trying to figure out my next move. I had walked about eight hundred miles, and, if I made a straight as an arrow dash home, I only had, wait, let me Google Map it, OK, 2,017 more miles. Damn. That's a long way. Eight hundred miles took me two months. Two thousand more, let's say five more months. That's assuming I don't get stabbed or cornered under a bridge or fall in love a few times. The route from here also put me straight through Albuquerque. Coincidence? Wait, did Annie walk, too? Is that how she got there?

I decided to stay the course. Keep heading west, keep Johnny on the search, and see what happened.

Western Alabama was super cool. I stayed in Florence for a few days with a guy named Kevin. He let me crash at his house and took me downtown for some cocktails and good food and introduced me to a bunch of his friends. He was just an all-around good guy. And he also saved my ass from a significant detour that would have jacked up at least three days of walking.

When I left his place, I was headed kinda northwest towards the Natchez Trace Trail. I was way out on some long, winding country roads when, of course, the one I needed to turn down was blocked off by a giant DETOUR sign and gate. Dammit. I did a quick Google Map check and there was no way around this mess that didn't add a good thirty miles to my walk. I was way out there. The fence had been up for a long time. This was a more, shall I say, permanent closure. Thank you again, Google.

What to do, what to do. I called Kevin.

Me: "Hey, Kev, it's Thomas. I've got a problem and I hope you can help."

Kevin: "What's up? You OK?"

Me: "Yeah, yeah, I'm fine, but I hit a roadblock. I'm at the corner of Dowdy Rd., and Natchez Trace and I'm supposed to turn left except it's closed and looks like it has been for years. Any chance you can dig around and see why it's closed and if it's at least walkable?"

Kevin: "Yeah, for sure. I know a guy who works for the county. I'll call you back."

Minutes later:

Kevin: "Hey, I got some answers."

Me: "That was quick."

Kevin: "That road has been closed for a few years. There's a bridge about two miles down that's kinda broken up from the flooding. I remember that bridge because I've kayaked that river a few times. That thing's a mess, but it's still there. You might be able to cross it."

Me: "How deep and fast is the river right there?"

Kevin: "You don't want to fall in. Let's just say that."

Me: "I'm goin' for it. Thanks. I'll catch you on the other side."

Kevin: "Power on. Don't fall in."

I had to completely disassemble Alexa and toss her and my gear over the fence. This was not easy given the fact that I still had a stitched-up back that was pretty damned painful. Wink and I squeezed through the edge of the gate, and I spent the next half hour putting Alexa back together and reorganizing my shit. Although the road was littered with leaves, rocks, and tree branches from not being used in a few years, it was the most peaceful I had been since leaving the Atlantic. There wasn't a soul in sight, not even the sound of squirrels. It was eerily quiet with just the slightest crackle of leaves from a gentle breeze.

As I approached the broken-down bridge, I had to laugh at what came next. The gigantic tree trunk that spanned across the road and blocked forward momentum was, presumably, laid to rest there to prevent any car from attempting to cross. It was just too perfectly placed. The width of the trunk was about four feet, way too big to get Alexa over. I walked to the edges, but they spanned well into the rocky riverbanks. I looked across the bridge to see the gate closing off the road on the other side. Once again, I disassembled Alexa and heaved her and her belongings over the tree trunk. This time, instead of putting her back together only to do the whole thing over again at the next barrier, I carried everything, piece by piece, over the bridge, and chucked it all over the top. Back and forth, about fifty feet or so, took eight trips. The bridge itself was a mess with deep crevices where you could witness the rage of the water below. Kevin was right; I didn't want to fall in that river.

Wink and I managed to get through a thicket of bushes on the edge of the gate and out to freedom where the yard sale of scattered cart parts and camping gear littered the road. I sat and, once again, made Alexa whole. As I took my first few steps, I heard laughter and loud applause. I looked up to my left to see the balcony of a large home where a half dozen or so people had been watching me. They had a pretty good view of the bridge. I smiled and took a bow. Jerks didn't even offer me a beer.

I made my way to the Natchez Trace Parkway. I include this story because I like to poke fun at myself, and I promised to give funny anecdotes of why I know I suck at camping. The Natchez Trace Parkway is a 440-mile, two-lane road that runs from Nashville, TN to Natchez, MS. It's open to cars but not to commercial vehicles, and the speed limit is maxed at fifty mph. The section I was planning to walk also had no buildings or homes within a quarter mile or so from the road. As far as I could see on either side was lush forests and pastures of flowers. It was remarkably beautiful, quiet, peaceful, and an excellent place to stealth camp.

During my second night camping off the trail, I was just settling into a Netflix binge-watch session when I heard a noise that was so eerily screechy and haunting, I was certain I was going to die. Wink didn't seem bothered by it, but his ears perked up.

Wink: *"We're in the woods. It's just a sound. Relax. You're such a wimp sometimes."*

Then it came again. And again. It was like the sound of a screeching bear but with a bit of a growl to it. It didn't sound close, though, so I wasn't too concerned, but it was creepy, and it was insanely dark outside. Did I mention that there were no lights on the parkway? Pitch black. So, I laid there and listened. And I kept hearing it for about thirty minutes. I had already pulled out my phone and Google searched "deadly animals

WALKER TIP
BEST TO BE SEEN, OR, TO BE ABLE TO SEE

It may be overkill but I always had two small, bike mount flashlights mounted to my handlebars and almost always had one flashing forward. The only time I didn't have one on was when I was on a very desolate road where very few cars passed by. The batteries typically last about six hours which is why I had two. I would charge them at night and, if you buy quality lights, they will make it all the way across the country. Buy rechargeable ones, though. You don't need to waste money on batteries and they're heavy to carry.

near me." Did you know that the three deadliest animals on the Natchez Trace Parkway near me were smaller than a baby's arm? That's right. Number one killer animal was the cottonmouth snake. That sound was no snake, or scorpion, black widow, or fire ant, which were the next three on the list. In fact, not one animal in the top ten list could possibly make that sound. But it still scared me because what *could* make that sound was a zombie or an ax murderer who was walking around the forest on fire.

Stealth camping can really fuck with your imagination.

I can't conclude this story for a few more days, so we'll just leave the Natchez Trace Parkway for now with me scared to death in my tent, and all my weapons strategically prepared for the apocalypse. I didn't sleep well that night.

Oh, and I said I didn't kill anybody in Alabama. I didn't say that Wink didn't.

4,000 APRONS & A PLACE TO BURY TOENAILS

IUKA, MS

34° 48' 43.7" N

88° 11' 28.1" W

MILES WALKED: 892

esides Iuka (pronounced eye-you-ka) and the amazing family I met there, Mississippi sucked for me. Maybe it sucks for everyone. Perhaps not. But this is my story, and it sucked for me. Let me start with the highway shoulders - they don't pave them in Mississippi. At least the highways I walked. And that state, which is difficult to type over and over again, is pretty damned hilly.

Highway 72 in Alabama, despite the rolling hills, was an easy walk. The second I stepped into Mississippi I knew I'd gone back in time. The shoulders changed from smooth, wide blacktop to random sized, loosely packed gravel. Random, meaning as small as pebbles to about three inches in diameter. What the hell? The purpose of a shoulder is to provide a safe place for drivers to pull over, fix a flat tire, run out of gas or take a leak. They're also there to serve us few people who think walking on highway shoulders is a fun, enjoyable way to spend quality time alone. There is no chance of safely changing a tire on the shoulders of Hwy 72 in Mississippi. There's also no way to push a 120-pound cart on it. It was like trying to suck a golf ball through a garden hose. Or eat chicken wings. Too much effort, not enough reward. The juice just wasn't worth the squeeze. OK, I'm done with bad analogies, but you get my point, right? Walking in Mississippi sucked. And I can't wait to get through that state in this story so I can be done typing the name.

But I do have a good story and the conclusion to the Natchez Trace fright night.

My mom loved everything about my journey, and we talked nearly every day. It was kinda the deal with my parents. I had to have a GPS device so they could watch me move, and I agreed to call regularly. My mom also loved to research the towns I was approaching and send me tidbits of info about them. On my first day in Mississippi, I was headed to Iuka. I called the fire department ahead of time, and they agreed to let me sleep in their building (I slept in five firehouses, always alone, on my journey). A few miles from town, my mom called.

Mom: "Did you know that the world's only apron museum is in Iuka?

Me: "No, Mom, I did not know that.

Mom: "You know I love aprons, right?

Me: "Yeah, I do recall that.

Mom: "Will you get a picture of the museum for me?

Me: "Of course. I'd love to.

Iuka was a tiny town. The odds of me not walking by the museum were pretty slim. Snapping a shot of the sign for my mom was a for sure thing. We had hung up but, as I was entering the town, she called back

Mom: "So, I decided to call the museum to make sure they were open and ended up talking to the owners who were such sweet people. I told them you were staying at the firehouse, and they offered to let you stay at their Airbnb on their property for free.

Me: "That's great! I feel bad canceling on the firehouse, but a real bed in a real house would be better than my tent on a floor. I'll head to the museum and meet the owners. Thanks, Mom, love you.

I met Carolyn and Henry, the owners of this odd collection of protective clothing, at their museum. It was quite impressive. They had over 4,000 aprons going back to pre-Civil War days. I learned more than I ever needed to know about aprons, but it was cool because I didn't realize that, until recent history, the style and design of aprons said a lot about your social status. But I won't spend too much time on that subject because this is a murder novel and not the history of aprons.

After loading Alexa and Wink into their truck, we made our way to a very large property a mile or so from the museum. We turned down a long, manicured gravel road flanked by acres of grass, trees and small footbridges that crossed a creek that snaked around the property. At the end of the road were two large, brick homes. The one on the right was two stories with a porch wrapped around the bottom floor decked out with furniture and an outdoor fireplace. The one on the left was a single story but wide and sprawling. Henry drove the truck up to the carport at the house on the left and killed the engine.

Carolyn: "This one's yours, Thomas."

Me: "This whole house is mine?"

Henry: "Yep. We live in the house next door. Let's go in and I'll show you around."

Wink: *"Score! Way to go, Grandma."*

We spent about fifteen minutes going over the heater, cable TV, WIFI hookup, laundry and bathroom stuff. I wasn't feeling awesome and every minute passed brought on more and more exhaustion. I wanted the tour to be over so I could take a hot bath and go to sleep.

Carolyn: "So that's home for the night. We're pleased to have you, Thomas. Make yourself at home and pop on over if you need anything."

Me: "Thank you so much. We really needed a comfy bed tonight. Tent life can get to you."

By the time I was unpacked and filling the tub, I was burning a very high fever. Like 103 high. Boom! Just like that. Instant sick. My throat was swollen and burning, my skin hurt, my entire body ached, and my head was pounding. Was I having an apron allergy attack? I sweated myself through a sleepless night of pain and misery and ended up sweating through five more nights there. I didn't go to town again until my last night when I was finally feeling better. Carolyn and Henry brought me medicine and groceries and checked on me quite regularly. They were incredible people and, had my mom not done her mom things, I would have been infecting an entire fire department with my ick. On that last night, I went to dinner with Carolyn and Henry and finally got to talk to them about my journey and told them the story of the crazy sounds I heard just a few days earlier on Natchez and how I had laid awake all night fearful of being eaten by the bogeyman.

Henry, laughing through his words: "That wasn't a wild animal. It was a wood mill a few miles away. The sound you heard was a giant saw cutting through logs."

Damn! He was so right. That's precisely the sound I heard. OK, joke's on me.

SIDE NOTE:

In Iuka, there's a cemetery called Toenail Cemetery. Its
official name is Mount Evergreen Toenail Cemetery. It's not
a burial ground for toenails. Real dead people are buried
there. In researching this book, I emailed the city of Iuka
and asked for some history of the name since I can't find
anything online but, alas, I didn't get a reply.
The irony of Iuka having a cemetery called Toenail that
doesn't actually contain buried toenails is that it was during
my stay there when my first toenail fell off. I'm not kidding.
That is a fact, and I have pictures to prove it, although I
don't think you'd want to see them.

I was super rusty and lacking energy when I walked out of Iuka. Six days in bed can do a number on your body after walking twenty or so miles in all the days prior. My next goal town was Albuquerque. It's all I had to go on between here and home. Annie had some distant cousins in Mississippi and Arkansas, and Johnny was working on their where-abouts. If they were anywhere near my path, I'd pull out the Joshua Owens card again and approach them. But, for now, I was determined to finish Mississippi, make a pitstop in Memphis to check out Beale Street, eat some BBQ and head into Arkansas. That would take me to Oklahoma, where I'd pick up Route 66 in OKC, continue through the panhandle of Texas and, finally, into New Mexico and the last city where Kennedy Quinn Rose was known to reside. Between me and Albuquerque were 1,380 miles. If I could do twenty miles per day and take one day off every ten days, it would take me seventy-seven days to get there. That's a lot of days. I hoped Johnny would find something for me to do during that time.

It took me three grueling, painful, fatigue filled walking days to get within striking distance of Memphis. I had been warned about Memphis and the safety of walking through it, so I planned well in advance to enter mid-afternoon and get someplace safe. It was during that three day walk that I had my first real mental breakdown. It came behind a very old, small brick church in a nothing little place called Michigan City about forty-five miles from where I would cross into Tennessee. Rain had pounded me since the day I left Iuka, and lightning storms forced us to stop often for shelter. Twenty miles would typically take me about eight hours, but these distances were taking more like ten to eleven. I found the old church on the side of the highway and knew in an instant that it was home for the night. Large trees and bushes completely surrounded it, there were no buildings in sight, and it was a Friday night - perfect for church camping.

Wink and I made our way around to the back to find what appeared to be a perfect spot to set up my tent. The rain was still coming down but not quite as hard as earlier in the day. With severe thunderstorm warnings plaguing the weather app on my phone, I stupidly decided to set up against the wall of the church to get as close to a structure as possible. I was saturated by the time we made it into the tent. Although I dried us off as best as I could, our gear inside was damp and cold. Wink and I ate inside the tent as the sun started to set. I had changed into multiple layers of dry clothes, hoping to warm up inside my super-duper zero degrees sleeping bag. Wink was bundled up in his blanket, and, as night fell, I started to doze off. Within a few hours, my night went to shit. The storms rolled in heavy, and the thunder and lightning woke us both. Wink was nervous and barked profusely. Strange shadows and bursts of light hit the walls of the tent every few minutes. I felt safe, but Wink wasn't having any of it. I tried to get him into my sleeping bag with me, but his strength and anxiety outweighed my desire to calm him. I braced for zero sleep. What I didn't brace for was my stupidity in the placement of my tent. I should have looked at the pitch of the roof before placing it where I did right up against the wall of the church.

The gutters or rain deflection devices on the roof of the church failed around midnight. I didn't know if the rain gutter had broken or what happened, but a sudden deluge of water pounded down on top of the tent as if a swimming pool floating overhead tipped upside down. I could feel water rapidly pooling under me, and the sound of it crashing down upon us was deafening. The ground was swelling, the top of the tent was caving in, and my brilliant plan for tent placement failed. Water started to come in through the bottom near the flap door opening and the zippers near the top were bending with the force of water and sprung a leak. We were the Titanic minus the love story.

I clipped Wink's leash to one of the tent poles so I could climb out and attempt to survey the problem without worrying about him dashing off in the night. My campsite was a disaster. I had set up on a thick bed of leaves, which had become a puddle several inches deep that was threatening to turn into a lake. My tent, which I had fully tethered down earlier due to high winds, was like a small boat tied up to a dock. Looking up, I realized my error. I had placed my tent directly below two rooflines that met at a ninety-degree angle, and a makeshift board which was probably placed up there to direct water in a different direction was tipped over and not doing its job. I was sleeping under a fucking funnel during the worst thunderstorm I had ever encountered. It was pitch black; I was relying on the light from my head mount flashlight and knew there was no way to reposition in the dark storm. The winds were fierce, and I feared untethering the tent to move it. Tents act like a sail in the wind, and I was certain it would easily blow away or, at a minimum, tumble into a bunch of trees with all my gear and Wink attached to it. I stood in the downpour, looking at the mess, scolding myself for my careless mistake, and saw the straw that broke the camel's back. The tarp I secured over Alexa, our food, and all of my dry clothing had come loose in the wind and was gone. No clue where it was. Alexa was full of water. If I had been using her for her intended purpose, I'd have two drowned kids on my hands. It was that full.

I collapsed in the mud and leaves and let the rain pour over me. I cried and laughed and held Wink tight. We had hours to go before the sun would come up. I had nobody I could call for help, I had no dry clothes, most of our food was ruined, and temperatures were well below fifty degrees. Wink sensed my resolve, my desperate collapse into sadness, and he knew I was giving up.

Wink: *"Hey! Knock it off. You dragged me out on this dumbass adventure without ever asking if I wanted to walk twenty miles every damn day. And I killed someone for you. Snap the hell out of it. It's just water, man. Let's get back in the tent, cuddle up and ride this thing out."*

So, we did. I laid awake with Wink mushed up against me. He was suddenly unfazed by our current state of affairs and the storm of the century going on around us. He knew his job, and he was doing it well. Calm and warm. That was our entire to-do list. Be calm and stay warm.

I messaged Lindsay the next morning. The sun had come out, but it was soul-crushing cold, and we were still soaked. I was able to make coffee and, since Wink's food was now mush, I warmed it up in my JetBoil. He was pretty stoked to get warm stew for breakfast and wolfed it down. Then he got more because he deserved it.

'Lindsay, I need help. I'm in a shit situation in Michigan City, MS. I'm stuck behind a church in the middle of nowhere. Everything is soaked, I'm freezing, thunderstorms are all around us, lightning touching down way too close and I haven't slept. All of my food is ruined, but I'm good on water. Do you know anybody in this area?'

Before I left on my journey, I learned of a private Facebook group called USA Crossers. Most people who have crossed America on foot and many who plan to walk are members of the group. Being that it was private, I joined knowing that the public, specifically Annie, if she was stalking me on social media, wouldn't gain knowledge of my journey. It was in this group that I had met Lindsay, whom I've referenced many times in my story. Lindsay had walked across America a few years earlier, adopted a stray puppy in Arkansas, and, when she reached Oregon, got an electric bike and rode back. Her route was very close to mine, and she was an incredible friend and asset during my hunt. She had no clue that I was out killing people and hunting down a vicious murderer. She might have been a little less helpful if she had that information. On the other hand, Lindsay was a tough as nails and slightly crazy brewery owner from Boston, so maybe she would have dug it. Who knows? I didn't share.

My point in telling you about USA Crossers is that, through those connections, I met a community, albeit very small, of people I could call or connect with for help, advice, route guidance and just plain old support from like-minded people who'd done the walk and fully understood the physical and emotional impact of the journey. Lindsay was one of those people. She saved my ass that day behind the church in Michigan City, and, ironically, also almost got me killed in Arkansas. But I'm not there yet.

Lindsay's reply: 'I got ya covered. There's a guy who took me in, and he lives in Arkansas just over the state line from Memphis. I messaged him and he's waiting for your call. Here's his number.'

And that's how I met Jerry Harvey.

Message to Jerry: 'Hey, Jerry. This is Lindsay's friend Thomas. She told me she messaged you about my predicament. I hate to ask, but are you in any way able to come give me a hand? I'm in Michigan City, MS on Hwy 72 behind a church.'

Jerry: 'Hey, Thomas. Yeah, no worries at all. Tough place to be in this storm. I'll head that way, but it'll take me at least two hours. Send me your exact location.'

So, I did and, a few hours later, Jerry arrived. Wink and I had been sitting on a covered stairway on the side of the church, attempting to avoid detection. Any time the rain stopped, we would walk around a bit so he could do his thing, but, during those walks, I could tell he was ready for a break. After loading everything into Jerry's truck and getting the heat blasting on high, I fell asleep against the cold window and didn't wake up until we approached his home in Arkansas.

WALKER TIP

Test your gear a hundred times before you walk. You need to know where everything is in your cart, how to find it in the dark, and, more importantly, how to use it all in different weather conditions and with or without light. Before I left, I made sure I could set my tent up blindfolded. Then, luckily, we had a pretty big rainstorm in normally sunny Southern California and, in the park across the street from my house, I set up and broke down my tent a dozen times in crazy high winds with rain pounding down on top of me. It was one of the best learning experiences prior to walking because I ran into that exact scenario dozens of times and I would not have wanted to learn how to do it out on the road.

FOREVER TOGETHER IN A RIVER

MILES WALKED: 1,141

Up until Toad Suck, Arkansas was great. The shoulders were excellent, the roads were mellow with traffic, and it was relatively flat. The people were super cool, hospitable, compassionate, interested in what I was doing, and nearly every cop who passed by would stop to say hello. A few even circled back and brought me coffee.

I spent a few days at Jerry's house. Wink needed rest, and the weather was horrible. I was also a little upset that I had taken some help forward and had missed the state line crossing from Mississippi into Tennessee and then into Arkansas. I asked Jerry if he would drive me back to Mississippi so I could do both state line crossings, and he obliged. Although it was still raining a bit, we did exactly that on my third day at his house.

Memphis is located on the big river in the southwestern corner of Tennessee, where it meets Arkansas and Mississippi. You could easily do both state lines in a few hours. Stepping onto the Big River Crossing, a beautiful walkway that spans the Mississippi River, felt incredible. I stopped at the state line, dead center of the bridge, and watched the vast expanse of cloudy brown water flow from the north. To my right was the Memphis skyline with that ridiculous pyramid that dominates the city view. To my left were the flatlands of Arkansas as far as I could see. The clouds were relentless in their effort to soak my bones, and the sharp, cold air clawed at my face and hands. I stood on that line, contemplating that frozen moment of a life turned upside down. To think that I would see the massive expanse and beauty of America on a journey like this was challenging to wrap my arms around. For the past few months, I had been living in my own little universe, walking roads and highways, finding death at my feet, lost in a puzzle that was so small there was only one piece. Me. And here, on this bridge, life was happening all around me, and none of it cared about my problems or my adventure. The water below had places to go, and the big city people had jobs to do, groceries to buy, kids to feed, lives to live.

I had never felt more alone. It was on that bridge when I realized my meltdown behind the church needed to happen. It broke me down, brought me to my knees, forced tears from my eyes, and the heartbreaking loneliness and sadness, unbeknownst to me until that moment on the bridge, cloaked my soul and rendered me invisible. It fed me power, bravado, and determination. I became courageously, dangerously undefeatable.

I powered away from Jerry's house with new vigor. I was full of determination and fire to tackle Arkansas and continue west to Albuquerque. Although I knew I wouldn't find Annie there, ABQ represented a life shift for her. She left her identity of Kennedy there, and I wanted to know why.

I headed west on Hwy 64 and went through some towns with pretty cool names like Eerie and Bald Knob. Yes, Bald Knob, where there's a little dive cafe famous for their upside-down strawberry cake. Two, please. It was there that I headed south on Hwy 367 to a town called Searcy.

I bring up Searcy for a few reasons. First, Searcy is a dry town. That's right, dry, as in you can't buy alcohol. Unless you happen to know about the two places in town that have some magic permit that nobody else can get. But, to sip a beer, you have to join their club. What does that entail? Absolutely nothing other than writing your name on a small white business card that has a handwritten Club ID number on it, which they then hand back to you to keep as a souvenir. What the hell? This was not the first dry town I'd walked through but, after learning of this completely ridiculous loophole in the law, how could I not partake? Seems almost un-American to find a loophole and not power on through it.

I called my friend Lindsay. Not because I was *alone* lonely, but because I was *lonely* lonely. There's a difference.

Me: "Hey, Lindsay. Need a break from the bar?"

Lindsay: "Always. What did you have in mind?"

Me: "Meet me in Arkansas. You always told me you loved it. Get down here and walk a few days with me. I could use some company."

Lindsay: "No, shit? Thought you'd never ask. Hell yeah, I can do that."

Me: "I'm in Searcy. Left Jerry's three days ago. Thanks for that by the way. Dude saved my ass from that storm. Hey, did you know there's a weird rule in Searcy that allows you to join a club and get a drink in an otherwise dry town?"

Lindsay: "Of course. How do you think I survived the bible belt? I researched every backward drink law loophole when I was there. And, absolutely Arkansas. Head to Little Rock. I'll look into flights. I'll call you back in a bit."

Love that girl. Just like that, and she's all, "Hell yeah, I'll bail on life for a few days." Before I finished my third club drink, Lindsay called back.

Lindsay: "I bit the bullet. Your call couldn't have come at a better time. I'm leaving the day after tomorrow."

Me: "Sweet! What the hell did that cost?"

Lindsay: "Who cares? Money vs. getting the hell out of Dodge to walk with you? Easy decision."

Me: "Excellent answer. I'm two long or three short days away. I'll make it two long and arrive on the same day. Shoot me your flight info and

WHY ARE THERE STILL DRY TOWNS?

Most dry municipalities are in the south and Alaska. In the south, according to several internet sources that I believe to be at least fifty percent accurate, the laws are in place due to powerful religious lobbying, specifically from Protestants. Even though nearly every study by the Department of Transportation proves that vehicular deaths where alcohol is a contributing factor are three times higher in dry towns due to the far distances people are willing to drive to town lines for a drink, the need to flex their religious power reigns supreme. But, if you are willing to join a club in Searcy, a club that has no membership fee or, from what I could gather, any possible way of tracking due to the handwritten business card method of obtaining membership, drink up! Funny side note - when I was in Clarksville, another dry town in Arkansas, directly across the street from my motel was a McDonalds (complete with gigantic kids play center), a Kentucky Fried Chicken and a Waffle House. They all shared the same parking lot with X-Mart Adult Supercenter, which was also just a short walk away from Brick House Salon and Spa. I can't buy a beer, but I can get all the sex toys and videos necessary to enhance my already pleasurable journey.

To be fair and honest, Brick House Salon and Spa is a legit place to get all prettied up in what appears to be an old brick house. Clever. I know this because I walked there, hoping...

bring your gear. I'll carry it, but I'm low on funds, and we're camping."

Lindsay: "Oh yeah. Can't wait."

To celebrate, I had a fourth club drink. Membership has its privileges.

Two days later, I walked into Little Rock and continued towards the Bill and Hillary Clinton International Airport. I arrived at the doors in front of arrivals and thoroughly enjoyed the stares from travelers and security guards as I waited for Lindsay. I had purchased a few Corona tall cans and had them wrapped nicely in my cart to celebrate our first actual meeting in person. When she walked out the double sliding doors, Wink jumped up on her hips and started to lick her face as if they'd been friends forever. What's up with his sudden love of this complete stranger? Lindsay shoved her gear inside Alexa, we hugged, and off we went.

Lindsay: "Where to?"

Me: "We gotta get out of town. Little Rock is sketchy, and we're not camping anywhere near here."

Lindsay: "It's four o'clock. How far out of town do you think we're gonna get before the sun drops? No, we're moteling. Better yet, we're ho-teling. On me. Let's find a cool place in a cool part of town and let the brewery pay for our room."

Me: "Twist my arm. I haven't showered in two days."

Wink: *"It's pretty bad."*

Lindsay: "Yeah, I know, that's why we're doing it."

We got a room with two beds in the bustling downtown district, which was only a few miles away. Despite Little Rock being known for a pretty high crime rate, we loved it. At least the area we walked through. Downtown was cool with tons of restaurants and bars and more bars and a few more bars. I think we hit them all that night. We had Wink with us, and he enjoyed the party night out with lots of people and laughter from me. I guess he wasn't used to me being so jovial, silly and carefree. Besides the few months before our journey, we've been pretty much alone in some pretty tricky weather, not to mention the killing spree we had been on.

Lindsay, after downing a few quick beers: "So, what the hell? How has your walk been? I was surprised to get your invite. Is everything cool?"

Me: "Lindsay, you have no idea. First, thanks for all your help. This has been a rough walk, and you've gone way beyond the call of friendship. But, hey, I gotta cut loose and get some shit off my chest. I don't know you super well, but can I trust you with some heavy stuff?"

Lindsay: "Thomas, how many laws do you think I broke when I walked across America? You think this girl didn't bend a few rules along the way?"

Me: "I've killed four people."

Lindsay: "Bartender!" she yelled for another round. Then, more quietly and sincerely, "Thomas, what the fuck?"

Me: "Well, actually, I killed three, and Wink killed one."

Lindsay: "Wait, you're not fuckin' with me, are you?"

Me: "Let's get a shot and another beer. It's gonna be a long night."

I told her everything. No detail left out. We sat in the bar for nearly eight hours. Our faces were locked together as I recalled those four horrible events in great detail. I don't know if she told the bartender to keep our drinks full or if I don't remember continuing to re-order, but my glass was never more than half empty. I drank and talked and drank and talked, and Lindsay, unlike her usual character, never said a word. She just let me get it out.

Lindsay: "Holy crap! So many questions. Oh my God, where to start. OK, first of all, the thing with the cop in Shallotte and his Google Map obsession is fucking classic. Great story, true or not. People just don't get it. Second, what was down that road?"

Me: "I have no idea. I never saw anything. Either they were just being assholes, or they were cooking meth or growing weed. No other explanation."

Lindsay: "Wait, are you using me to test out some bullshit story that you're thinking about putting in a book or something? Is this all crap? Cuz you're a little buzzed, and I'm calling major BS on all of this."

Me: "I swear on all that is holy. No bullshit. No book."

Wink: *"He ain't lyin'."*

Lindsay: "You're not religious, so your swear means nothing."

Me: "It's just a saying."

Lindsay: "Show me your back. I wanna see where that guy tried to saw you in half."

I lifted my shirt and showed her my trophy scar.

Lindsay: "OK. Seriously. This is heavy. How are you doing? For reals, I mean. Walking across America is friggin hard enough. Most people don't last a week or two. You had to kill two guys in that much time and another one right after."

Me: "I'm perfect. I've never felt better. That's why I called you. I'm a pacifist. I've only been in two fights my entire life. I avoid shit like this. Yet, out here, I'm not the me I used to be. I can't say the road changed me because all this happened so early in my walk. It was something in me that I didn't know was there. The first two guys were self-defense. No problem. Had to do it, right? But that guy in Monetta? I just killed that guy. I mean, he did have his hand wrapped around Rosie's neck, and I'm certain that she and Hoover were in deep shit. No doubt Sally was often used as a punching bag. I don't know. That guy just needed to die. I don't feel bad at all for him. And that's kinda what's scaring me. But just a little if I'm being totally honest. I feel worse for the kid who stabbed me than I do Teddy."

Lindsay: "I don't know what to say. Honestly. Besides holy shit, I'm glad you're still alive, I can't relate to anything you must be feeling."

Me: "That's the thing, Lindsay. I'm not feeling anything. I know I'm not crazy. I know I don't have an insane desire to kill people. I'm not looking for trouble. But, for the first time in my life, I'm not afraid of it either. And if I have to kill again, I'll do it without a second thought."

Lindsay: "Yeah, but you just said four magic words that tell me you're OK and not going crazy. You don't even know you said them. You said, "if I have to", you didn't say, "when I kill again" or "if I want to kill again." You said, "if I have to." They're different. You may have to kill again and, dammit, I'm glad you won't hesitate. You saved yourself a few times, thank God, and you probably saved at least one other person from either a drunken love fest murder or, at a guaranteed minimum, one hell of a beating by some asshole who will no doubt take it too far someday. Don't beat yourself up. Hold yourself up and be proud of your courage and bravery."

Me: "I'm glad you're here, Lindsay. I've been spinning for days about all this stuff and needed some tough words and grounding."

Lindsay: "You're welcome. Let's do one more round and get outta here. We need to walk tomorrow."

We were seriously hurting the following morning. I hadn't had much to drink since I started my journey, and the shots and beers kicked my ass. I grabbed the Corona tall cans we never got to the day before and we had a little hair of the dog. We headed out of Little Rock towards Conway on Hwy 365. I made Lindsay push Alexa the first several hours after gulping down copious amounts of coffee. My usual 3.25 mph walking pace was not happening. Lindsay, who pours beers for a living, felt fine within a mile. She was also fifteen years younger than me, and I'm sure that helped her cause. We decided to do a little stealth camping that night near Conway Lake. There were legit campgrounds at the lake, but they were too far out of our way, and, when there's a lake, there's a place to stealth camp. We found a great spot, cooked some freeze-dried lasagna, and told road stories. Sitting next to the lake, watching the sun go down, and enjoying time with a great friend was exactly what the doctor ordered. It was perfect. We both crashed early, hoping to get out at sunrise and get in some good miles the next day. Past Conway, we turned and headed more west than the northern trajectory we had walked the previous day.

Me: "When I got out of high school, I went to work for my father. I had no idea what I was going to do with my life, but I thought maybe I was gonna become a rockstar. I played bass in a rock-n-roll band with three friends from high school; we all thought we were gonna be famous. We were just a bunch of punks with no direction, but, damn, we had so much fun. For five years I worked for my dad during the day and played music, drank gin and smoked cigarettes at night."

Lindsay: "You're a musician?"

Me: "No, I was more of the guy in the band that held us all together but couldn't really play my instrument for shit, but, because I booked all the shows, my buddies had to keep me around. Anyway, the band broke up, of course, and I lingered on at Dad's company. When I realized I wanted to go to culinary school I was pretty afraid of telling him that I was leaving his company. I didn't know him that well back then. We weren't super close when I was young, but we were starting to build a real relationship around that time. After I got accepted to the program, I went into his office, nervous as hell, and told him my plans. I was expecting major backlash, but, looking back now, I'm not sure why I felt that way. My father was always a very aggressive, successful businessman and I guess I just didn't know him to be someone very accepting of me wanting to find my happiness. So, with shaking hands and sweaty pits, I interrupted his work and laid it all out on the table."

Lindsay: "What happened?"

Me: "He came around his desk, gave me a hug, and told me he was proud of me. He paraded me around the entire building and was so excited to tell the whole company that I was heading off to become the next great chef. It was the moment that bonded our friendship. I had never really thought of him as my friend, you know? He was just my dad, whom I didn't know that well yet."

Lindsay: "What made you think of that, Thomas?"

Me: "All he ever wanted was for me to be my best self. He told me that if I wanted to be a garbage man then I should go be the best garbage man in the world and he wouldn't think any different of me. He loved me and that's all that mattered to him."

Lindsay: "Have you been your best self?"

Me: "I used to think so. I've certainly fucked up a lot, but I want to believe I've always been a good man and have always followed my heart. I don't know if that means I've been my best self, though. Here I am, right now, lost in America with nothing but this dog, this cart, a very broken existence back home and a long, long road between here and there. A road I don't even know why I'm walking on. I say it's to hunt down Annie but, really, is that why I'm out here or is she just my excuse to escape?"

Lindsay: "You'll know the answer soon. You'll know when you get to the ocean."

Lindsay suddenly stopped at the edge of a bridge, just outside of Conway, dozens of feet above the rushing waters of the Arkansas River. Tears swelled in her eyes.

Lindsay: "How many times have you crossed this river?"

Me: "This will be the third. Once walking into Downtown Little Rock, once walking out yesterday and now here, today."

Lindsay: "We'll cross this river four more times, Thomas. I've crossed it sixteen times, and this will be number seventeen. Yep. Seven times on each of my journeys across America and twice with you yesterday. I have a love-hate relationship with the Arkansas River. I hate it because most of the bridges we will use really suck for walkers. I love it because I spent so much time with it. It calmed me. It let me sleep next to it. I sat at its edge several times and let it talk to me. My dog played in it. I do love this river."

All I could do was hug her. She was having some serious memories flooding back to her, but she wasn't sad. She was longing for the adventure. She was missing the road. I was warned that post-walk anxiety was real and that it never goes away. I was advised to prepare for sadness and loneliness when I finished the walk. Here I was witnessing that sadness.

Lindsay: "When you're done, Thomas, people won't understand you. They can't. Relationships suffer from the walk. Your life after the walk is different than before because the road will change you. Your life at home, it's a big puzzle, right? You were a piece of that puzzle. You may or may not like the puzzle, but you were a piece of it. And then you left that puzzle for a little while, and, when you get back, you will realize that your piece grew, and it will no longer fit in the space it once used to. That's not bad or good; it just is. And everyone you love is still fitting snug in that puzzle, and they can't understand why you don't. And you can't expect them to understand why you don't fit because they didn't walk alone for eight months across a continent and survive to tell about it. And that's not their fault, and you can't make it their fault. They still love you; they just don't know you as well as they used to. And they never will. They won't relate to your feelings, and you can't reminisce about the road with them or anybody because nobody was there with you. All you can do is tell them stories that they will find amusing and amazing but couldn't possibly fathom ever happening to them. They will envy your bravery, perseverance and sense of adventure but know that they would never do anything close to what you did. There will be a large part of your life, Thomas, where you will always be alone no matter how many people are around you. No matter how much love you find. There will be emptiness."

It was my turn to cry. I wanted that empty space that only I was allowed to enter. That space where nobody dared to go. That space where people let me be when they knew I was visiting it. If there was any reason to hope for a safe finish to this journey, that was it - to have my very own one-piece puzzle.

Me: "You know what's cool? You and I will always get to reminisce about our time, out here, together. This will be our space."

Wink: *"Don't forget about me."*

I smiled at her, and she smiled back, and we hugged hard and cried together. Lindsay was always such a strong, loud, crazy girl I knew only on the phone, and here we were, together in the flesh, about to cross the Arkansas River for the third time in as many days. We walked onto the bridge, holding hands, taking up an entire lane without a worry in the world. Halfway across, Lindsay stopped again and went to the edge where I followed.

Lindsay: "Let's spit in the river. Together. I'd say let's pee in it, but that could get messy. Let's just spit in it, and then we'll be there, in the Arkansas River, together, forever. Two dumbass cross-country walkers adding to the rushing life down below. One, two, three!"

As our spit hit the water, we rushed to the other side to see if we could watch it flow away and pretended that we could. We laughed and high fived and got the hell off that bridge before we got run over.

Just across the bridge was Toad Suck. Not sure how it got that name, but I'll never forget that little nothing of a place because it's where death, once again, shattered my life.

MAY

THE WORST OF TIMES

CONWAY, ARKANSAS
TO
OKLAHOMA CITY, OKLAHOMA

TOAD SUCK & A MASSHOLE

Toad Suck is a small, unincorporated community just over the Arkansas River from Conway. The road we were on was pretty narrow and didn't offer much of a shoulder. I kept Wink in the grass on the left while Lindsay pushed Alexa on the blacktop. Cars went by very infrequently and at a much slower pace than on the bigger highways. For the most part, we were alone, and, when we weren't, we were always given lots of space by drivers.

Lindsay: "You ever think maybe you'll do this again?"

Me: "What?"

Lindsay: "Walk across America. What the hell else did you think I meant?"

Me: "Are you kidding? I'm barely a thousand miles in. I'm not even sure I'm gonna finish this time!"

Lindsay: "Oh, you will. I've met a lot of crossers and I can pick the ones that'll finish. You'll finish. Trust me. I wouldn't blow all that money to come walk with a quitter."

Me: "Would you do it again?"

Lindsay: "So fast. God, I would do it tomorrow. I say that yet, I could if I wanted to, I guess, but I'm not doing it."

Me: "I like it out here. I wish I was doing it only for me and not with this mission to find Annie. Maybe I'll do it again but just to do it and not because I'm fucked up in my head over what happened back home."

Lindsay: "I'd like to cross next time with someone else. At least part way. I don't know if I could go all the way across with one person and not want to kill them halfway through."

Me: "Let's make a pact. If –no, when I finish and sort my fucked up life out, I'll walk with you. We can make a deal now that we don't have to do the whole thing together if we end up wanting to kill each other after a few weeks. I wouldn't want to fuck up our friendship over a walk. Deal?"

Lindsay: "Hell, yes! Maybe I just need someone to poke the bear and it'll get me back on the road."

Me: "Alright then. We have a deal. You better not flake on me!"

Lindsay: "No chance. I've been looking for an excuse to get the hell outta Dodge. Now you just gotta finish."

Me: "Oh, I'm definitely finishing now!"

In the distance, we saw a big black truck approaching very quickly. Lindsay, getting a bit concerned for our safety, started giving the "slow down" gesture with her arms and hands, but we quickly realized that this truck was not slowing down and was narrowing the gap, not widening it. I moved as far left as possible, and Lindsay had only one of Alexa's wheels on the road. She was pushing the other two through pretty deep grass and some mud. As the driver neared, we could see him cursing at us with wild arm gestures through the windshield. The truck flew by within an inch of Lindsay and Alexa.

If I were alone, I would've just kept going, but I was with crazy Boston Lindsay, and she decided it was a good idea to speak her peace with the driver by spinning around and flipping him double birds. The next thing we saw were brake lights followed by the sight of the truck stopping very quickly and then white reverse lights.

Always thinking on her feet, Lindsay whipped out her cell phone and started recording the truck barreling down on us in reverse. I was shitting bricks. Lindsay was not, in fact, I think she was enjoying it. The truck stopped about ten feet away and sat idle for half a minute. The driver door opened and out stepped an older guy who was maybe in his sixties.

If I heard this story from a friend, I would be picturing a beat-up farmer truck driven by a scruffy redneck. Come on, admit it, you are, too. We were in the south, a guy nearly runs us down and then backs up for some more action. This is something I would picture Mr. Boot doing. But no. You are wrong. This was a really nice, big new truck and the guy that stepped out looked like my grandpa on his way to a casual church gathering. Except that my grandpa didn't carry a gun on his hip and, if he did, he certainly wouldn't have yanked it out and aimed it at a woman or any other person just because they flipped him off.

Man with gun: "Girl, you just made the biggest mistake of your life!"

What the fuck? Grandpa was seriously aiming his gun at Lindsay as he slowly walked forward. I've told you this before, I'm not a fighter. I'm a pacifist. My arms were way up in the air. Lindsay held firm with her cell phone held out as her weapon, and its lens pointed right at him.

Lindsay: "What are you gonna do, fuckin' shoot us for flippin' you off? You nearly ran me over, asshole!"

And that's when I heard the shot and watched the bullet that took her down. Wink was ferociously pulling on the leash, so I let him free to chase the shooter down. The guy turned to run from Wink but pulled off a few more shots towards me, but I was hiding behind Alexa, grasping for Lindsay's hand but afraid to give him a target. I heard Wink growling and barking, and then I heard the truck door slam shut, and his wheels peel away. I jumped over and straddled Lindsay and pulled her top up to see a hole just about dead center of her chest and blood pulsing from it. There was no blood under her, and I knew the bullet was still inside. Tears were streaming down her cheeks, but she smiled through her pain.

Lindsay: "I'm so sorry! What an asshole!"

Me: "Lindsay, listen, you're gonna be OK. I'm gonna shove a cloth into this hole, and it's gonna hurt like hell, but I gotta do it, OK? I'm gonna call for help but push right here. Now!"

Wink had run back and was trying to lick Lindsay's face. He knew this was bad. Probably knew more than I did.

I pushed Wink away and kissed Lindsay on her forehead, and, as she squeezed my leg, clawing into my skin through my pants, I shoved my glass cleaning cloth deep inside the bullet hole with my finger. I have no idea if that helped at all, but it seemed the right thing to do. She was struggling to breathe, and there was blood pooling in the corners of her mouth. I looked at my phone and cried.

Me: "Lindsay, I have to go get help. I don't have reception. Shit!"

Lindsay, struggling and gasping through her words: "No, wait, please just sit here with me. I know what's happening. It's OK. Fuck, I can't believe he shot me."

Tears were pouring down my face and my hands were shaking as I hugged Lindsay and kissed her cheeks. Our eyes were locked and we both knew what was about to happen. I squeezed her hands and my face told her how much I loved her.

Me: "Don't you fucking die on me! I don't want to cross this river anymore without you. And you just promised me you would walk with me next time. Fuck you, Lindsay! Don't you back out on our deal."

Lindsay: "I'll be there, Thomas. I promise. Fuck! Why did he shoot me? Where I come from, I flip you off, you flip me off then we go get beers. It's why they call us Massholes."

And that was our last moment together. Lindsay died on that asphalt, staring into my eyes, with a bullet in her chest after crossing the Arkansas River for the seventeenth time. She died in a place called Toad Suck.

Panicking, I pulled her off the road and down into a soft ravine and covered her with some branches. I couldn't put her in the cart because, well, it just wasn't built for an adult, and I wouldn't be able to push her.

Not that Lindsay was heavy because she wasn't, but it was a baby stroller, not a wheelchair. I made her as comfortable as possible, kissed her lips, grabbed her phone off the ground, and walked quickly back towards Conway.

Wink was quiet and walked with his head down and his ears flopped forward. He knew. He cried with me. My head was spinning out of control, and I didn't know what to do. As sad as I was, I began to fear the man's return. What if the guy was a local cop and I marched into the police station looking for help? What if he saw me walking on the road and finished me off? I found a secluded place where I could hide for a few minutes to think and cry. I was well off the road and I laid down on the moist grass and sobbed. When my tears finally stopped, and my eyes were clear, I took out Lindsay's phone and found that it was still recording. I didn't realize it was still going but I was relieved that it was. I didn't know her password to get into her phone and, had it stopped recording and locked down, I wouldn't have seen the Arkansas license plate on the back of that truck and the face of the man that gunned down my friend. There it was, in the video replay, crystal clear. I quickly sent the video to my phone via text, email, and airdrop. The text and email wouldn't go through, but the airdrop did. No way I was losing this video. Then I went into her phone settings and turned the screen lock off. When the video finally arrived on my phone, I opened it and watched it a dozen times. I studied the man's face and that truck and that gun, and I listened to her over and over again. "It's why they call us Massholes". Those were Lindsay's last words.

Me: "You are a Masshole, Lindsay."

Rage surged through my blood as I thought of that man. I grabbed all of my loss and gut-wrenching sadness and shoved it all in a box. I'd deal with that later. Right then, I had a video, a license plate from the state I was in, a black truck, a man's face, and furiously vengeful thoughts in my head. This changed everything.

Annie would have to wait. I had more pressing matters to attend to.

I decided to lay low for the night and think. I couldn't call anyone, and I had no way of jumping on the internet to start hunting that fucker down. Staying here, hidden, was the best option. The guy could come back out looking for me to finish what he'd started, or cops could show up if he had had a wave of guilt crash over him and had decided to give himself up. I set up camp in my little secluded alcove of trees, pulled out a bottle of wine that we had brought for our walk, and drank the entire thing. At some very late hour, the alcohol did its job, and sleep finally found a home.

I woke a few hours later with a screaming headache and sucked down four Advil and a pint of water. After some coffee and a pop tart, I wasn't feeling too bad. I crept out of the tree line and looked down the road a quarter mile where I had laid Lindsay to rest. I didn't see any police activity. She was still there, and I had to push away the fears that animals may have gotten to her. I must have had a dream the night before because my plan was locked and loaded. Today I would kill the man who took my friend from me.

I broke down camp faster than I ever had before. I had to look normal and not stand out, so I covered Alexa with branches and hid her well in the trees. I cleaned up, clipped Wink to my belt, and walked across the bridge towards Conway. I had cell reception as soon as I got to the other side, found a place under the bridge, and made some calls.

Me: "Johnny, listen, and don't talk. I'm in a very bad situation, and I need your help super-fast. I'll tell you everything later but first listen. Do NOT believe what you hear in the news. No matter what, do not believe it. Parts will be true but those about me are not. That's all I'm gonna say. Keep an eye on your email because you may get one from me tomorrow at noon. For now, I need you to work your internet magic and find the guy that owns a black truck with Arkansas plates 508KCD. I need this info right now."

Johnny: "OK, this is easy. Hang on. I'm not gonna ask."

Me: "Just get it. I'll wait."

Johnny: "Got it. Registered to a guy named Charles McEnroe. The address on file is 975 Brush Creek Lane, Conway, Arkansas."

Me: "Can you dig anything up on him? Quickly."

Johnny: "Calm down, man. I'm here to help. I don't know what shit you've gotten yourself into, but I'm here for you, man."

Me: "You can't imagine, Johnny. Can't imagine."

Johnny: "OK. A quick social media search shows nothing. DMV says he's sixty-two years old. Same address on file there for years. Give me a sec and let me see what else I can find."

While he searched, I did a quick map glance and found that I was about a mile away from his house, which was in the far west reaches of town where big homes nestled in the trees that lined the river.

Johnny: "Alright. Here we go. He owns a very large logging company based right there in Conway. His kids are also listed on corporate documents. It's a big company, so I'm gonna assume he's probably retired or close to it. He's been divorced twice, most recently eight years ago. There are quite a few local stories about his involvement in the community, but he also has a DUI from a year ago and an arrest for assault stemming from a bar fight but no charges, no conviction."

Me: "Thanks, Johnny. Hopefully, I'll talk to you soon."

Johnny: "That's not all, Thomas. That missing guy from Monroe? His body was never found but, after lying about my motivation for inquiring and then verifying my PI creds with the investigator on that case, I learned a few things. There was blood found in the living room at his house that trailed out to the garage. No attempt was made to clean it up. When I pressed him for prints or DNA, he balked and wouldn't share. I asked if they'd ever had a suspect, and he alluded to a female when he mentioned shoe prints found in the blood were a women's size eleven tennis shoes. I guess they can tell by the design of the sole that it was definitely female. That's a big print for an average sized female, Thomas, but just about spot on for a six-foot tall woman. This has Annie all over it."

Me: "Man, what is wrong with this girl? Thanks Johnny. I gotta run.

I'll be in touch. If you get an email, you'll know what to do. Just trust me on that."

My next and final call was to my son.

Holden: "Hey Dad, how's the walk?"

Me: "Hey, buddy. I'm not so great, but I'm going to be."

Holden: "Dad, what the hell is going on? Are you OK? I mean, physically, are you hurt?"

Me: "Yes. I mean, yes, I'm OK, no, I'm not hurt. I just want you to know that I love you more than anything in the world. You know that?"

Holden: "Yeah, of course. I love you, too. You're kinda freakin' me out, though."

Me: "I'm sorry, son. I don't mean to. Everything is gonna be OK. I promise. I gotta go, though. I'll talk to you soon."

I made two more quick calls to my parents but kept it cool like I was just checking in. No way I could have them thinking anything bad happened. They would worry and try to fix everything as any good parent would want to do. Totally understandable but I couldn't do that with them. Quick hello, road update, I love you, goodbye.

I pointed the lens on my phone at my face and recorded my message.

Hello family, friends, and the fine police of Conway, Arkansas. My name is Thomas Curran, and today I'm going to commit murder to avenge the death of a very close friend.

You will soon learn that, since I began my journey, I've had to kill three people in self-defense. Well, actually, Wink killed one of the people to protect me. God, I love that dog. Yesterday was a tragic day. Yesterday my dear friend Lindsay, who flew out to walk with me for a few days, was shot and killed on the side of the road, just a mile or so west of Conway in a place called Toad Suck, by a man in a new, black pickup truck with license plate 508KCD.

Lindsay recorded the entire event on her cell phone. There's a copy of that video on this phone and in my email. I had no cell service to call for help, and before I could sound an SOS on my GPS device, she had already passed. In a panic and fearing his return, I carefully pulled Lindsay into the ravine on the south side of the road and covered her with my jacket and lots of branches. This morning, before heading out to find the man responsible, I called the police with her location.

Fearful that the gunman would return, I was seriously spinning out of control and decided to hide out overnight in the trees. I stayed awake most of the night, eyes wide and tearful, holding Wink close for comfort.

Using the license plate number from the video and, with the help of a friend, I've discovered the identity of the killer. His name is Charles McEnroe, and he lives about a mile from where I'm sitting right now. Today, I'm going to find Mr. McEnroe and I'm going to kill him. I know this is wrong, and I will probably end up in prison or die in the process, both of which I'm OK with, so long as justice is done.

I know I should have handled things differently, but what's done is done. I'm going to schedule this video and the one of the shooting to be sent to you at noon tomorrow. If things change, I'll have time to stop the transmission. If you're watching, I probably need an attorney or someone to pick up my body. Either way, please make sure that Wink is taken care of. And please get in touch with Lindsay's family. I don't know how to reach them. We're friends on Facebook.

I guess that's all except for a huge I love you, and I'm sorry I've put you through this.

I winked at the lens, blew a kiss, and stopped the recording. Time to kill. Revenge killing didn't taste good in my mouth, but I had to do it.

HUNTING A (NEW) KILLER

hadn't done anything illegal yet, and the worst thing that could happen if I was found stealthing through the woods along the river would be some serious court-ordered counseling sessions. Perhaps I would look into those when I got home. The first thing I had to do was get a message to the police with the location of Lindsay's body. I couldn't stand the thought of her laying in that ravine and being attacked by animals.

Me: "Johnny. Need a favor. You're good with computers, right?"

Johnny: "You know I am."

Me: "Is it possible to call a police department without them being able to track the number or where it's coming from?"

Johnny "Easy. Want me to tell you how?"

Me: "No. I want you to do it for me. Game?"

Johnny: "This is right on that edge of illegal. It depends on what I'm calling about."

Me: "Here's what I want you to say: 'Hello. I'm calling on behalf of my friend, and I need you to listen very carefully. Yesterday a woman was shot and killed about a mile west of the Prince Street bridge on the Arkansas River Trail. The man with her survived, but the killer drove away. My friend, fearing for his life, dragged her body into a ravine on the south side of the road and covered her with his jacket and tree branches. Please, go retrieve her body ASAP. You'll learn what happened and who the killer was when my friend feels safe enough to come out of hiding.' Then hang up. Don't let them track you or ask a bunch of questions. Just hang up."

Johnny: "What the fuck happened, Thomas?"

Me: "Guy just shot her, Johnny. He almost hit us with his truck, and she flipped him off. He got out and shot her in the chest then fired three my way but missed because Wink was chasing him down. He got in his truck and bailed. She died within a minute."

Johnny: "So, why aren't you just going straight to the goddamned police right now? Are you crazy? You should have gone yesterday when it happened. And at what point will you realize that this little journey that you're on is an equally dumbass thing to do and you call it quits?"

Me: "I can't call them because I'm going to kill him."

Johnny: "Oh, dude, that is a bad, bad idea. You do that, there's no takesy backsies. That's life, man. In or out of prison, that will ruin you forever. Don't you ever watch movies and yell at the screen when people do dumb shit that you would never do like tiptoe down a dark stairwell into a pitch-black basement holding only a toothpick for protection when they know that Freddy fucking Krueger is down there? Don't you yell, "Why the hell are you doing that?" Right now, you are the dumbass with the toothpick. Just let me come get you. I can leave in, like, three minutes, and I'll drive straight through."

Me: "No, make the call in ten minutes. Making that call is not illegal. We didn't have the rest of this conversation. Call the police department in Conway, Arkansas. Say what I said to say and hang up so they can't ask questions and you won't have to lie to them. One mile west of the Prince Street bridge on the south side of the road. Don't mess that up. She's just laying out there, Johnny."

I hung up. No more drilling. It was almost noon, and I had work to do and cops to hide from. I had to get up the river closer to my target.

During my brief hike, my murder plot started to come together. I was going to somehow sneak into his house and kidnap him by zapping him in the neck with my stun gun, which should knock him out. Then I would drag him down to the river, weigh him down with rocks, pull him out as far as I could into the water, wake his ass up and watch the fear on his face as he sunk. What could possibly go wrong?

I was parked on my ass against a tree less than a hundred feet from the home of Charles McEnroe. As I waited, I continued to fine-tune my plan. I could see his garage, and I could glimpse through a few windows where lights were glowing. It was a good hour before I saw movement, and, when I did, conflicting sets of emotions fought for prime shelf space in my mind. I saw Charles pass a window of what appeared to be a dining room. It was a brief glimpse of the man who killed my friend. Immediately I was a man on a murder mission. But, I'm not a murderer. Not a cold-blooded one anyway. I guess I didn't have to kill Teddy back in Monetta, but I can still chalk that up to the defense of another. Lindsay was already dead. This was different. This was pure, unjustifiable revenge murder. In the eyes of the law, no more legal than what this asshole had done. As he passed across the window a second time, I saw the flaw in my plan in the form of a small child in his arms. And, again, when two young adults entered the room, and they all sat down at the dinner table.

I inched closer to the house stepping as quietly as possible. I'm certain they couldn't hear me, but creeping slowly and softly is what you're supposed to do when you're stalking a man that you're about to kill, right? I found my way to the edge of the woods about twenty feet from the killer's big black truck. Family meal was in full swing. Everyone was there, dishing food on their plates. I watched them join hands and say their prayers. I wonder if they went something like this in his mind: "Dear Lord. Please forgive me for being a murderous asshole. I shot an unarmed girl in the chest today, but I know you'll forgive me, so all is well." I would allow him one final happy family meal. He would soon die and, when he did, he would be able to ask his God in person for forgiveness. My job was to introduce them and make sure his family knew why.

Laughter filled the room as the little girl gesticulated wildly while telling stories. Her animated face and broad smile were joined by those of her parents and, presumably, her grandfather. My plan, up to that point, was shaky at best. I hadn't planned on extras at my party and certainly not a cute little kid with beaming parents. Watching that lying maggot laugh and have fun sickened me. I hated him, and he was going to pay for what he did. Kid or not, the tax man was comin' and had just declared it tax season.

It was still reasonably early, and I was hoping that the family would leave soon to get the little one tucked in for story time. Within forty-five minutes, the front door opened, and everyone walked out. As Charles walked his family to their car, he was less than twenty feet away, and I heard him say that he was going to meet a buddy "over at the lounge" for a beer after cleaning up. They left, I waited and reformulated. This new tidbit of info changed my plan altogether. I watched him scoot around in the kitchen, cleaning up after his very last dinner party. He was listening to music and appeared to be enjoying his evening. Did this man have no conscience or fear? He killed a woman a few hours earlier for no reason, he knew I was still alive and that I witnessed his senseless murder. I imagined he was so damned arrogant about his social status and power that he had in town and probably thought some guy pushing a cart on the side of the road wasn't going to come back to haunt him. Yet, here I stood, coming back to haunt; coming back to reap my revenge. As furious as I was, my new plan spread a smile across my face; this was going to be beautifully revengeful.

I fired up Google Maps and searched for lounges near me. There were three in the Conway area with the word 'lounge' in the name. Two were much further away on the east side of town. The Alibi Lounge was much closer, just a few miles away, near downtown. Had to be it, right? It would take me about forty-five minutes to walk, maybe less with so much adrenaline coursing through my veins. I chose a route that put me through a lot of residential neighborhoods to stay off the main roads. There was no way he would see me.

I made it to the bar, and it was ideally situated directly across the street from the university and appeared to be somewhat busy with college students. What does a sixty-two-year-old man think he's doing hanging out with his buddy in a college bar? I walked around the busy street and found his truck. He was there. Here we go.

Wink: *"He's here. I can smell him."*

Me: "You ready?"

Wink: *"Let's do this."*

Time to get my ass kicked.

THE ALIBI

I walked into the Alibi Lounge holding Wink very close. He had no room to move more than an inch from my leg. The room was only about half full, and I saw Charles and his equally old buddy sitting at the end of the bar. They were at least twenty-five years older than every other person here. Except me. Do they think they're cool?

Wink: *"That's him. That's our guy."*

Me: "I know, buddy. Be cool."

Wink: *"I can take him down right now."*

Me: "Hang tight. You'll know what to do when you need to."

I surveyed the situation, and it couldn't have been more perfect. I ordered an old fashion and gulped it down quickly. That definitely helped. Wink was getting anxious and was pulling on the leash; his ears were back, which meant he was in protection mode. Hunting mode. Exactly the way I wanted him. I took out my phone and started recording a video. I didn't need video, just audio; I put it in the vest pocket of my jacket for optimal microphone performance.

I ordered and received another drink, mustered up all my courage and walked down the bar to approach Charles from behind. I clipped Wink's leash to a bracket under the bar about six feet from my target. I told him to sit, which he did, but his eyes were trained on the man sitting in front of me. Suddenly, and without provocation, Wink lunged with a furious bark, his large, sharp teeth bared. His leash stopped him shy of Charles, who jumped off his seat and spun around. As he turned, he knew. His eyes leveled on mine and then on Wink. My hand was on the clasp attached to Wink's collar, and Charles had nowhere to go.

Bartender: "Hey, control your dog, or get out."

I held my hand up to the bartender as if to shut him up without ever breaking eye contact with Charles.

Me: "How you doin' old man? Remember me?"

I double flipped him to jog his memory, but he didn't need the hint.

Charles: "Well, well. Homeless junkie guy. You're a brave boy comin' in here."

Me: "Junkie? Is that what you think I am? I just came here to have a drink, think about life and here you are. We'll see what happens next, killer."

Charles: "So, this is how you're gonna handle this? Corner me in a bar with your dog and do what?"

Me: "I might have another drink. Are you packing your little dick pistol tonight?"

Charles: "Whatever you are, or she was, we don't need you walkin' through our town. Ain't that right, Mikey?"

Me: "So, you're the protector of the town? You're the big bad-ass everyone counts on to keep the bogeyman away? Or is that what you just tell yourself and your buddy Mikey"

Charles: "Boy, you're about as dumb as she was. Bitch shouldn't have flipped me off. I was just sending her a message with my fly by."

This was actually too easy. I pegged his arrogance perfectly. Just a little more push and I might just get him to tip.

Me: "Oh, I get it! Your ego is so fragile that you let a woman with a couple of middle fingers push you over the edge. Yeah, I bet that's it. Your little dick got its feelings hurt so you thought you'd just kill her."

Charles: "I was just gonna scare the two of you till she opened her mouth. She practically begged me to shoot her."

He laughed as he said it and, inside, I did, too.

Me: "Feel like finishing the job you started yesterday?"

Charles: "You say you're not a junkie. Who are you? Yesterday you were walkin' out of town, and now you're here. You shoulda kept on goin'."

Me: "Until you came along, I was just a guy walkin' across America with his dog and a good friend. Finding some peace. Doin' some soul searching. Takin' a little break in life. But tonight, I'm the guy who's gonna rip your whole life apart."

With a tilt to my head, I put on my best snarky, condescending smile and raised an eyebrow. I needed him to be the aggressor and would continue to pile on as many insults as necessary for him to attack. His ego was fragile; it shouldn't take too much.

Me: "How about I just get it out of the way and tell everyone in this bar what you did yesterday? Does your buddy know? Have you been bragging about it? Hey, Mikey, do you know what your friend here did yesterday? What's your name, anyway, killer? I wanna know the name of the coward that shot my friend."

Charles: "My name is Charles. You remember that when I smear your ass all over this bar."

Mikey: "You might wanna watch yourself there, fella. Not quite sure you know who you're dealin' with here."

Me: "Hello Charles and Mikey, my name is Thomas. So, Mikey, you do or don't know? Which is it? I would recommend you say you don't, even if you do. You see, Charles, that girl you killed yesterday? She was my friend. And she was no homeless junkie. You fucked with the wrong people."

I cleared my throat and raised my voice to a near shouting level.

Me: "Everyone, can I have your attention, please?"

The bar went silent and the crowd had turned to face me in curiosity. That's as far as I got. Charles swung hard, and I let it land square on my cheek below my eye. I purposely fell behind Wink, so he was between Charles and me. Outraged, Charles didn't see the setup and stayed on the offensive. As he cocked his fist back and got close enough to strike, Wink took him down with a hard bite to his calf and a fierce whipping motion like he does when we play tug-o'-war. Charles didn't stand a chance.

Within seconds, cops were everywhere, and we were both up against the bar being frisked. From me, they removed my knives, stun gun, and cell phones. From Charles, they removed his cell phone and a pistol from an ankle holster.

Me: "Officer, when we get to the police station, you're going to understand more clearly, but you will definitely want to put that gun and my two phones into evidence bags. I promise you're gonna need them."

I stole a glance at Charles and winked.

Me: "That was too easy, Charles. See you at the station, big boy."

We were cuffed and dragged outside, Charles limping and trailing blood. A paramedic arrived and, shortly after, animal control was on scene to deal with Wink.

Me: "Hey, my dog did nothing but his job to protect me."

Animal control person: "We're just here to control the dog, not hurt him."

I arrived at the station before Charles, who was tended to for a bit back at the bar. I was cuffed to a metal bench near a desk when he was brought in, limping and bandaged, and led to another desk about ten feet away. At that point, I assumed the cops just thought this was a simple drunken bar brawl. I smiled at Charles, and his face was nothing short of priceless; he was plagued with fear. His once stern rage had been replaced by shaky hands and a quiver in his lip. His bandaged leg protruded from his torn open jeans, but I doubt he was paying attention to the pain. They had his gun and a body with a bullet inside of it. He had no idea what was on those two phones.

The two officers who brought us in sat down between us.

Officer A: "Mr. McEnroe, surprised to see you here. Mind telling me what happened tonight?"

Charles: "This guy walked into The Alibi with his dog and attacked me."

Me: "Shut up, Charles. Tell them what you did yesterday. Tell them what you did to my friend."

Charles: "I don't know what he's talking about. He's clearly homeless and crazy."

Me: "I've heard great things about the police here in Conway and I'm sure you know how to do your job, officers, but you might want to have your Chief of Police come down here for this. It's gonna be a long night."

Officer A: "Are you the guy who called in about the body this morning?"

Me: "Yes."

Officer A: "Gentlemen, I'm holding this conversation for the Chief. Sit nicely, don't talk to one another, and be cool, or you're both going into lockup. Understood?"

With that, he picked up the phone and made a call. My eyes never left Charles' face, but he never looked up at me. Fifteen minutes later, a casually dressed man in his sixties stormed through the doors. Hello, Chief.

Chief: "Officer Michaels, mind explaining the urgent call? Good evening, Charles. Kinda surprised to see you sittin' here."

Michaels, aka Officer A: "We got a call about a bar fight at the Alibi. When we arrived, Mr. McEnroe was on the ground under a good-sized dog with blood pooling under his leg. Mr. Curran was also on the ground with visible bruising and swelling below his left eye. We collected a pistol and a cell phone from Mr. McEnroe. We collected two cell phones, two knives, and a stun gun from Mr. Curran. Mr. Curran claims there is something on his cell phone that we need to consider as evidence. Mr. Curran is the man who called in about the body this morning."

Charles: "Chief Barnes, this is all a load of crap. I was sitting at the bar, enjoying a beer when this guy came in with his dog and attacked me."

Me: "Come on, Charles, you have to know you're dead to rights by now, don't you? A smart guy like you? I can let him sit there and bullshit you guys all night, but I don't want to waste your time. Those evidence bags you brought in? Pull either of my phones out. It doesn't matter which one."

Officer B, who was far younger than his colleagues, put on a pair of gloves and retrieved Lindsay's phone. Attempting to turn it on, he seemed perplexed.

Me: "You're gonna need to take that glove off to work the touchscreen."

Officer B looked to Chief Barnes and got a slight nod of approval. Officer B removed one finger from his glove and used his knuckle to fire up Lindsay's phone.

Me: "Good. Now, go to the photos app and click on the folder for videos. You'll see one that's forty-three minutes long. Should be right there at the top. Let's play that video, sound all the way up for full effect."

The two officers huddled behind the Chief as he hit the play button.

Lindsay: "Ok, ok. I'm recording. Fuck me, what's this guy doing? Can't handle a girl giving him shit for being an asshole?"

Me: "Just chill, ok? He probably just wants to scare us."

On the video, they saw the truck flying towards us in reverse and then skid to a stop. Then there's the pause and then Charles getting out while pulling a pistol from his waist.

Charles: "Girl, you just made the biggest mistake of your life."

Lindsay: "What are you gonna do, fuckin' shoot us for flippin' you off? You nearly ran me over, asshole!"

Then came the shot and the phone hitting the ground as it continued to record the overcast sky.

We could hear three more shots, running footsteps, Wink growling, and barking, the truck door slamming, and the truck drives off. Then my final conversation with Lindsay and the sound of me dragging her to the ravine, grabbing the phone, shoving it in my pocket.

Me: "You can turn it off. I didn't realize that it kept recording. The next thirty minutes or so are pocket sounds of me walking and sobbing under a tree. But, if you want to hear that, feel free to keep going."

Charles: "What you don't see is what they did before I pulled over. That bitch provoked me."

Me: "Really? That bitch? Officer, take out the other phone, would you?

The code is 224466. Go to the videos and play the one from the bar. You won't see anything because it was in my pocket, but you'll hear plenty."

On the recording, they heard our entire bar conversation, which pretty much sealed the deal. I didn't attack him at the bar, and he admitted to the killing.

I looked at Charles, whose head was down, and tears were running down his cheeks.

Me: "What are you crying for, asshole? An hour ago, you were suckin' down beers in a bar with Mikey having a grand ole time. You weren't sad then."

Charles looked up at me and all I saw was a scared little boy.

Charles: "I'm sorry."

Me: "Fuck you, you piece of shit. Apology not accepted. I suggest you guys call your mayor because you're gonna have one hell of a media shit storm in a few hours. Your local good ole boy is a murderer, and I'm gonna make sure he pays for it. You wanna save your face from being plastered on every media outlet nationwide, Charles? Sign a confession, right now. Chief, what's the crime here? First-degree murder? Second?"

Everyone in the room was completely caught off guard. They knew this man. Officer B was relatively young and had probably grown up with his kids. I was anxious to see if they would do their jobs.

Barnes: "That's not up to me, Mr. Curran, and that's not how this works so I need you to calm down and stop barkin' orders. We have process and, despite what you have been through, you will respect it."

Me: "I'm sorry, Chief. It's been a crazy twenty-four hours."

Barnes: "The prosecuting attorney files charges and negotiates pleads. The police gather evidence and support. I will call her shortly and get her here in the morning. Charles McEnroe, you are under arrest for the murder of..." he was fumbling through the police report from earlier in the day.

Me: "Lindsay Monroe. Her name is Lindsay Monroe."

Barnes: "...for the murder of Lindsay Monroe."

And then came the Miranda rights, full cuffs, and an escort into the back of the building to the holding cells.

Me: "What kind of man does what you just witnessed? Where's my dog?"

Officer Michaels: "Your dog is at animal control, but he's fine. He's in his own run and probably asleep."

Me: "Chief Barnes, am I under arrest?"

Barnes: "No. Not yet anyway. Nothin' to hold you on just now."

Me: "I need a motel room. Can you line that up, please? If not, I'm calling my friend from Fort Smith to come to pick me up, but I won't be back here tomorrow if that happens."

Barnes: "We're gonna need you to stay in town for at least one more day to sort this out. Maybe longer. What's your budget?"

Me: "I don't have one. I typically camp every night. What's yours? I'll stay as long as you're paying for the room."

Barnes: "We don't normally pay for motel rooms, Mr. Curran."

Me: "Then I gotta go. I don't have the money to sit around while you guys figure things out. I'm gonna need my phones. I'll send you the video files while I wait for my friend."

Barnes: "Fine, we'll pick up the tab. There's a place nearby where we sometimes put people up. I'll have Officer Michaels take you to get your dog. Where are your belongings?"

Me: "They're in a cart that I push. I had to hide it in the trees on the other side of the bridge. I'll need to go there first. We're gonna need a pick-up truck. And a flashlight."

Barnes: "Can I just ask, why are you here in Conway? What brought you and Ms. Monroe here?"

Me: "I had a rough year and needed a break, so I decided to walk across America. Lindsay joined me in Little Rock, and she was going to walk with me to Fort Smith. She walked across America a few years ago, and we became friends through the community of people like us that do that sort of thing."

Barnes: "Hold up. You're walking across America, and your path was through Conway?"

Me: "Correct. Ocean to ocean. It's a thing, and I don't expect you to understand, but some people need an adventure in life, and it's the one I chose."

Barnes: "That's actually pretty cool. I didn't know people did that."

Me: "Not many of us do. I chose this route because Lindsay had done a similar one, in fact, she walked right through this town. She told me how incredible the south was and, up until yesterday, I'd say she was right. The south has been good to me. Two nights ago, we camped out at the lake and made our way through town yesterday. About a mile west of the bridge, well, you know the rest from there."

Barnes: "Did Ms. Monroe have a dog with her when she walked through here a few years back?"

Me: "Yes, Thina. And she pushed a cart similar to mine."

Barnes smiled and was taken aback.

Barnes: "I remember hearing about her. Damn, I had forgotten all about that. She met some locals who told us about a real nice girl walking through town with a cart and a dog. I remember being disappointed that I didn't meet her. I've got some wanderlust in my soul, believe it or not. Small world. I'm very sorry about your friend. I'm shocked by that video and even more shocked at who I see pulling the trigger. Mr. McEnroe has always been an upstanding community man and business owner. This is going to get ugly no matter which direction the prosecutor takes it. If you promise not to leave town tomorrow, I will get you that motel room, but I need a day with the prosecutor to sort this out. I also need to talk to Mr. McEnroe after we're done here. His version of events will help decide next steps."

Me: "I'll make that deal. But I gotta get out of here ASAP. Despite what you might say, I am not safe in this town. Not with Mr. Upstanding Community Man sitting in jail for defending his small town from, as he put it, homeless junkies. I don't think I'm gonna get much help or support around here. I'll be surprised if I can get a cup of coffee."

Barnes: "I understand your concerns, I'll see to it that you're safe. We'll figure this out quickly. Get your dog and cart and go get some rest. I'll pick up the room. Right now, I need you to send me those video files. I'm sure one of my younger officers can figure out the best way to transfer them to us."

With that, Barnes was gone. Officer B, the younger one, came in with the phones and a laptop, linked them up and transferred the files. He gave me back my phone but kept Lindsay's. Officer Michaels then took me to pick up Wink and rescue Alexa from the woods.

Michaels: "We're just two guys in a truck, right?"

Me: "As far as I can tell."

Michaels: "Well, between us, Mr. McEnroe isn't that great of a guy."

Me: "Yeah, no shit."

Michaels: "I guess I don't have to tell you that. This town has a few guys like him. Big money, donations everywhere to look good, church members blah, blah, blah. But he's also a womanizer and arrogant prick. Because of his money, he can get what he wants around here, he knows it, and he abuses it. He's burned through every single woman in this town and a few married ones, too. His kids are good people, though. They took after their mom. She was, is, a good lady. She left Conway when Charles married his second wife within a year of their divorce. I don't know exactly why she left, but I can imagine it was because Charles was the money and influence, and his second wife was much younger. She no longer had pull in town, and I think she was embarrassed for him and the kids. Anyway, it doesn't surprise me he's ended up in this mess. I hope he gets what's comin' to him."

Me: "How's Barnes and your prosecutor. Are they softies for the locals or maybe in his pockets or open to bribery? I'm not making any accusations, but a guy with that kind of money goin' up against a guy walking with a dog and a cart might just try to purchase some sympathy."

Michaels: "I'm sure Charles will hint at that possibility, but he's in quite a bit of trouble and knows bribery could backfire. Barnes is a law-man. Through and through. Raised in a family of cops. I can't see him taking the bait. He also owns a lot of land and has plenty of money. He would have no reason to ruin his reputation. I don't know the prosecutor that well personally, but I will say this, there is no way she would take a bribe. She covers three counties, so she's a busy woman. She moved up through the ranks putting away some serious dirtbags. She's young and aggressive and lives here in Conway, which means she knows Mr. McEn-roe. Not sure how that works, to be honest, but with the evidence you have available to the press, I'd say Charles is gonna pay for this one. He may plead down to something lesser than murder, so don't be surprised if that happens."

Me: "If that happens, that video gets out. I will be on every TV station that'll take me."

Officer A: "I don't blame you a bit.

We got to the motel and, after a beautifully long, hot shower, I let Wink up on the bed with me.

We crashed out within minutes and were yanked out of our deep sleep at 8 a.m. when the phone in my room rang.

Barnes: "Get dressed, Mr. Curran. An officer is coming to get you in one hour. Get some coffee and breakfast in your belly cuz it's gonna be a while till lunch. The county prosecutor is going to meet us at the station where she'll take statements from both you and Mr. McEnroe. I know you've been through it, but you're gonna need to do it again."

Me: "I need someone to look after Wink. I can't leave him in the room."

Barnes: "Bring him along. We'll take care of it."

I was introduced to Carla Crow, prosecuting attorney for Faulkner, Searcy, and Van Buren counties. She was young, maybe thirty-five, well dressed, and had long brown hair. She had a firm demeanor but had a softness when she spoke. She sat down across from me and started the recording device.

Carla: "Hello, Mr. Curran. My name is Carla Crow. I'm sorry your visit to Conway landed you here. I'm a prosecutor, which means that I work for the citizens of the three counties I represent. Better said, my job, to protect the community and provide justice, is to make sure that people that should be incarcerated are. My job is to gather evidence of a crime if one was committed and determine what charges, if any, are levied against a suspect. To best do that, it would be helpful to hear your story. Mr. McEnroe is meeting with his attorney this morning and is not speaking to us at this time. Your account of what happened, along with the evidence collected, will help me do my job. Of course, you are under no obligation to speak to me, and you have the right to have counsel present. I am recording this interview. Do you understand everything I just told you?"

Me: "Yes and thank you. Please call me Thomas. I will choose, for now, not to have an attorney. I don't believe I need one. Can I call you Carla?"

Carla: "Yes, Carla is fine. Can you please tell me your version of events starting the day before you walked through Conway?"

I told her every detail. No Cliffs Notes version this time. I painted the picture of two innocent, adventurous souls who found themselves face to face with a killer and how one of them died at his hands. I cried a few times when I spoke of our time on the bridge together and when Lindsay died.

Me: "That's it. Everything up till this morning. Nothing left out, nothing added."

Carla: "Can we see the video of the crime and hear the audio from the bar?"

Barnes picked up a remote control and, suddenly, my nightmare was on a large flat-screen TV to my right. I didn't watch, but I couldn't escape the sound. They ran the entire video, all forty-three minutes of it. In the background, through the black screen, were thirty-three straight minutes of nothing but crying. Then one sentence filled the room.

Me: "That man needs to die, Wink, and I'm gonna do it."

Sadness and rage-filled my heart. I wished, at that moment, that I had just killed the bastard and went on my way. But I knew this was better. If Carla did her job, he would suffer far more than eight inches of steel penetrating his heart.

Carla: "We have an issue here, but it's one I'm not too concerned about. Technically, the shooting occurred in Perry County, which is not in my jurisdiction, but the bar incident was here. Perry County sits in the sixth district, and I will need to confer with the prosecuting attorney for that county. He works out of Little Rock; however, we have a good relationship and, since crimes occurred in both of our counties, we will decide together where the trial will take place. Is there anything you want to add here, Thomas?"

Me: "That last line? I was stressed, scared, and sad. It was just talking with my dog. Are you gathering evidence on Mr. McEnroe or me?"

Carla: "Telling your dog you're going to kill someone is not a crime, Thomas. I'm looking for evidence, period. It's what I do with the evidence that matters. In Arkansas, there are six types of criminal homicide: capital murder, murder in the first degree, murder in the second degree, manslaughter, negligent homicide, and physician-assisted suicide. Capital murder is off the table completely. First-degree murder is a longshot but the best place to bargain from. It is typically hard to get a conviction if there was no premeditation. Second degree and manslaughter, although similar, carry extremely different sentences. The jump from manslaughter to second-degree murder is in the determination of the circumstances leading up to the killing, in this case, Ms. Monroe flipping Mr. McEnroe off. If it were determined that a reasonable person would become so emotionally or mentally disturbed that they would disregard the value of human life, we would have to consider manslaughter. Flipping someone off should never, in my opinion, cause a reasonable person to commit this crime. Based on the evidence I've seen and heard in the videos and the apology he made to you that was witnessed by three sworn officers, I'm going to push for first-degree murder and make a case that the premeditation came when he tried to run you both down."

Me: "What if he wants to bargain?"

Carla: "I don't tread lightly on the lives of reckless killers. I never wanted to do anything in law except prosecute bad guys. If I can win, I don't deal. Not with murderers. However, I always leave myself room to wiggle."

Me: "I want to believe you, Carla. You, Chief Barnes, and the officers involved have been nothing but kind and compassionate. But now you're saying there's another prosecutor with a say in this matter. Lindsay loved Conway and that dumb river for some reason; it's why she met me here, and I have no desire to bring media hell down upon you. But justice better happen for her and her family. If Mr. McEnroe pleads down to anything I consider unacceptable, those video and audio files go straight to national media outlets. He's an arrogant, narcissistic murderer, and this is your chance to show the world that nobody will tarnish the great name of your town."

Carla: "I'm going to make you an offer, Thomas. Assuming Prosecutor Bigley from the sixth agrees and assuming Mr. McEnroe doesn't save us all some time and confess to first-degree murder, which he won't, you give us the wiggle room to plead down to 2nd degree if I can get a long enough sentence that almost ensures us that he dies in prison. Anything less than a minimum of fifteen years is a no go. We go to trial. He's sixty-two years old, Thomas. A fifteen-year minimum sentence in prison at his age is pretty much a life sentence."

Me: "I'd be more comfortable with twenty, but you do what you need to do. He needs to die in prison, or I'll have no choice but to share what I have with the media. I don't mean to be an ass, Carla, but you have to understand where I'm comin' from."

Barnes: "Actually, I can't possibly imagine where you're coming from, but I know it must be a very sad place. I will get the best possible sentence, or we will let a jury decide. Now, you said in your interview that you had

WALKER TIP
THE DIGITAL LIFE OF A WALKER

I used a lot of apps on my iPhone during my walk. Google Maps, of course, was used every day while walking and every night while planning the following day. But I also used a few others:

Weather Underground and NOAA - these are the two apps I used to track weather, tornado warnings, thunderstorms, etc. There are lots of apps for this but these two worked the best for me.

Couchsurfing and Warm Showers - these apps are to find free, friendly homes to stay at while adventuring. The only issue with them is that you have to send out about twenty requests before you get any replies, even rejections. People just don't check them that often. However, I stayed with about a dozen hosts using these apps.

Trail Link and All Trails - these apps will show you all of the bike and walking trails across America that are closed to cars. It's brilliant. Anytime you can jump on a paved trail, do it.

Rails to Trails - similar to the one above but focusing on old rail lines that have been converted to walking/riding trails. No cars at all and they generally touch each town they pass. Walking is fast and typically flat because rail lines rarely had more than a 3% grade. The Silver Comet Trail runs from Atlanta to the Alabama state line where it changes names to The Chief Ladiga Trail. It's one such trail I walked, and it was awesome. Use it.

X Hunt - this app is designed for hunters, but I used it because it shows every inch of land in the US and whether it is private, public, Bureau of Land Management (BLM) or national forest. Know that on most BLM and forest land you can legally camp and mostly for free.

iOverlander - a stealth camper's dream app. It's curated by the users and people plot places on maps where they've stealth camped, what services are nearby, whether it was dangerous, etc. It's also used by car campers and people that live a van life. It's very useful. I tagged several places myself.

emailed a copy of the video to a private investigator. How do we know that video is not going to be leaked by him?"

Me: "I guess you don't — no way to take back that email. We're just gonna have to trust each other. You need to call Lindsay's family. I don't know them, but I'm sure you can find them in her phone."

Barnes: "We've already contacted them. They're coming here to-morrow. They are aware of the situation, the possible charges, and your involvement."

Me: "Damn. I haven't thought much about them through this whole thing. How'd they take it?"

Barnes: "As you would expect. It wasn't a pleasant call to make."

It was approaching noon, and I needed to stop the transmission of the email to everyone. They didn't know that I had never sent the video to those I said I did, and they never called my bluff.

Me: "Chief, I need a computer for a few minutes. I set up an auto transmission of the videos to a group of selected people to occur at noon. I gave myself enough time to be able to stop the transmission. Can I sit down at a desk somewhere so I can do that?"

Barnes: "You really thought of everything."

Me: "I had no idea who he was or what was going to happen to me. Honestly, my initial plan did not involve the police, if you know what I mean."

Barnes: "I think I do. I'll bring you a laptop. Carla, if there's nothing more with Mr. Curran for now, I'm going to get him back to his motel to await further word from us."

Carla: "I'm good. Thomas, again, I am incredibly sorry for what has happened here. I hope you can find some peace. Chief Barnes, please make sure that Thomas' motel is taken care of by the county."

Me: "As long as you're paying for my room, I'll stay. Also, I'm broke and normally eat top ramen on the road. There's a buffet next to the mo-tel, think maybe you can swing by there and open up a tab for me? I don't eat too much."

Barnes: "You're getting a little greedy, Thomas."

Me: "No, it's not greed; it's survival. I don't have any cash. I normally stock up on top ramen and beef jerky but, since I'm in town and all, a few big meals could go a long way."

Barnes: "Unofficially, yes, I'll take care of you. I know the place, and I'll call over there now. That's it; we're done."

He smiled and apologized again, which was unnecessary. I think he was feeling pretty bad that something this horrible happened to two innocent travelers in his town, and he took it very personally. Officer Michaels was right, Barnes was a good lawman and a good person.

Carla: "I need to call Prosecutor Bigley. Let's go see Mr. McEnroe."

Wink and I were chauffeured to our motel. I left him in the room and headed to the buffet, where I powered through a massive plate of spaghetti and meatballs, garlic bread, and two trips to the salad bar. I grabbed a few dessert items to go and headed to the cashier. After giving the woman my name, I was handed a zero-balance check and a stare down that I quickly lost. I left a few dollars with the check and headed to the door. The cashier called out to me.

Cashier: "You should check out of that first-floor room across the street and get out of town, Thomas."

I guess the word was out. She said my name with just enough vitriol hoping to scare me. I turned around and made my way back to the much older, tough-looking woman with a full head of silver hair pulled severely tight into a ponytail.

Me: "Is that any way to speak to a tourist visiting your fine town?"

Cashier: "We're not big on strangers comin' through here, stirrin' up trouble, tearin' families apart."

Me, chuckling: "Oh, is that what you've heard? That I just wandered into your podunk town and decided to tear a family apart? You're not real bright, are you? You must be the only woman in town that Charles hasn't screwed over. Let me guess, family?"

Cashier: "I'm just suggestin' you leave pretty quickly. You are not welcome in this town or this restaurant."

Me: "Nah, I kinda like it here. Good spaghetti. I'll be back for a late dinner and probably again for breakfast. Chief opened up that tab for me and, well, I'm plannin' on using it. Have a nice night, and you might wanna check your facts before you start flingin' accusations. Sweet dreams."

I spent the rest of the day in the motel room. There was no way in hell I was going back to that buffet. I cozied up with Wink and Netflix. Barnes called me bright and early.

Barnes: "Thomas, we're gonna get you out of here, but we need to have you down at the station to go over a few things, first."

Me: "Sounds good but I need a ride. I haven't had the warmest of welcomes from the locals. Word's out and a lady at the restaurant made it clear I wasn't welcome."

Barnes: "I'll send an officer over to get you and your dog."

Me: "Thanks, Chief."

At the station, we went straight to an interrogation room where Carla was going over some paperwork.

Carla: "Good morning, Thomas. We've negotiated a plea bargain with Mr. McEnroe. They offered 2nd degree with a chance of parole in ten years. We countered with first and twenty-five. We met in the middle at 2nd degree and seventeen. He'll be seventy-nine when he's eligible for parole. It's the best offer we'll get without going to trial where it could be difficult to find a jury that isn't familiar with Mr. McEnroe to some degree. That could be good or bad, and it's a gamble. We have not presented the deal to the judge yet; we wanted to discuss it with you first. Please understand that we do not need your permission to make or accept any offers; this is purely out of respect."

Me: "Respect or fear of that video getting out?"

Carla: "Call it both."

Me: "I'll hold the videos for now. Let's hope he dies in prison. The day he breathes free air, that video goes viral."

Carla: "Understood."

Me: "Chief, I'm going to need a ride far, far out of town, at least a few counties away. I didn't get a real warm welcome at the buffet last night and had quite a few slow drive-bys on my walk over. I don't think you want any more roadside shenanigans, am I right?"

Barnes: "No problem. If that'll be all, let's wrap this up. Thomas, I'll get an officer to drive you where you need to go."

I shook their hands and made my way to the lobby to wait for my ride. Officer Michaels was my driver.

Michaels: "I seriously cannot believe the events of the past few days. The town is already in an uproar, and it's good you're gettin' out of here. Nobody wants to believe that Charles would kill someone like that and there was a lot of talk about goin' to get you in your motel room. We had cops keep an eye on it all night."

Me: "Thank you. I'm happy to leave."

Michaels: "I'm gonna take you to Russellville. It's about forty-five miles away. You should be unknown in those parts, and you'll be on a major highway, so it should be safer than the back roads. And, Thomas, if I may be so forward, I think this journey you're on is pretty awesome and incredible, but haven't you had enough yet? All this danger and death following you?"

Me: "I gotta do this. I'm gonna finish this walk for Lindsay. She wouldn't quit."

I asked him to drop us off on the west end of town at a Holiday Inn Express. I needed a night to wash all my clothes and stock up on food before hitting the road. He got out and walked with us to the lobby and plopped his card on the counter.

Michaels: "This one's on me. I don't know why, but I like you, Thomas. Let me donate the room and a few hot meals to your journey. Hell, enjoy a few beers, even. Just don't go crazy on the room service."

Me: "Thank you. I greatly appreciate that, officer. Keep an eye on that old man for me. I'd sure hate for anything bad to happen to him in prison."

We both laughed and shook hands.

I was determined to cover eighty miles and get to Oklahoma in two days. Normally impossible, but paranoia was pumping through my veins. I couldn't shake the fear of being found by one of McEnroe's buddies or family members. Every car that passed was a potential revenge killer. I left Russellville at 4 a.m. and covered forty-one miles, found a grove of trees, slept for six hours, and was out the next day at 4:30 a.m.

I had a good forty miles to go, but I was hurting quite a bit from the previous day's outing and I was certain that Wink was, too. The rain began early, and it was accompanied by fierce winds. Thunder and lightning were in the distance to my left and crept closer every hour. Wink and I were drenched as we entered a town called Mulberry. The wind was so intense I struggled to keep Alexa moving in a straight line. I took a break on the steps of a small business and looked up the number for the local firehouse. I was eventually patched through to the town mayor, who also happened to be the fire chief. He agreed to let me stay at one of their volunteer houses not too far away and met me there about an hour later. We got inside and, when we entered the garage where the trucks were parked, a smile covered my face ear to ear. This was the first firehouse I had stayed in that had a real pole that came down from the second-floor bunk beds.

Me: "Where are all the firemen? Is this a volunteer house?"

Chief: "It's volunteer house #2 in this town. Doesn't get much use; it's more for storage and tornado season when all hell breaks loose. Which is right now, by the way. You know you're walking into tornado alley in the middle of tornado season, right?"

Me: "Yeah, I'd heard something about that. Bad planning."

Chief: "Be safe and follow the warnings. Hate to have to send a truck after ya."

Me: "I will. And, Chief? You know the minute you leave I'm going down that pole, right?"

Chief, laughing: "You do what you want, Thomas. Just don't get hurt.

You'll be alone here tonight, so make yourself at home and lock up on your way out. There's laundry upstairs, and a few beds made up. The kitchen is downstairs."

The chief left, and I was alone. I showered and immediately set my camera up on a tripod. I went to the wall where all the fire gear was hanging, put on a jacket and hard hat and shot at least six videos of me making up dumb fire drills where I'd slide down the pole and rush past the camera as if I was on my way to an emergency. I sent one of the videos to a friend who replied that I should do it naked. So, I did. I stripped down to nothing but the hat and went down the pole a few more times till I got the shot. I sent it to her, and her reply was, "Uh, I was kidding! Don't you think maybe there are some cameras in there?" Sure enough, there were. Oh well, maybe Chief would get a kick out of it. I got a pretty funny video, and it was during the review of those shots that I saw the horror that was four months of not manscaping. Wow.

I left the next day and made it to Fort Smith, which sits on the state line of Arkansas and Oklahoma, by sundown. During that three day stretch, I crossed the Arkansas River three times. The following day I crossed it the final time entering Oklahoma. Seven times in total. I stopped halfway across the bridge, spat into the river, and allowed myself to cry for Lindsay.

TORNADOES 101

PRAGUE, OK

35° 29' 11.4" N

96° 41' 12.4" W

MILES WALKED: 1,474

I f you asked me to give you only one piece of advice about walking across America, it would be this: do not, under any circumstances, walk through Oklahoma in May.

Let's start with the easiest part of my insanely long trek through Oklahoma: the incessant and unrelenting thunderstorms. Yeah, that was the easy part. The rain rarely stopped, and it wasn't normal rain. The temperatures were warm but fierce and coming from the southwest up from Texas, which was also being pummeled by storms. Wind and water barreled into my face, making walking furiously difficult. Luckily the road had only rolling hills and shoulders that were solid and wide.

So, if that was the easy part, what was so hard about Oklahoma in May? Tornados. They were everywhere. Tornado Alley runs from the Gulf of Mexico in Texas up through Oklahoma all the way to South Dakota through Kansas, Nebraska, and Eastern Colorado. The season for tornadoes is late spring. Awesome. Just awesome. I learned early on that the warnings I got from my weather app on my phone needed deciphering. I

249

learned this from the first farmhouse door I knocked on during my third day in the Sooner State.

I received a tornado advisory on my phone for the area I was in. My eyes shifted to the skies but, unless there was a funnel coming at me, I really had no clue what I was looking for. All I had was a big red box on the screen of my phone that said tornado and advisory. Enough for me. I knew that most homes in tornado alley had shelters, so I hoofed it to the first house I saw and, luckily, there were no stray dogs or scary ass signs warning would-be trespassers to stay the hell away. I got to the door and knocked. A middle-aged man answered with a kid clinging to his legs. He appeared friendly but certainly had a concerned look on his face when he eyed his visitors.

Man: "Can I help you?"

Me: "Maybe? I'm walking across America with my dog here, and I was hoping to get in your shelter with you and your family?"

Man: "Why?"

Me: "I got a tornado advisory on my phone? I'm from California, and we don't have tornadoes there. Isn't that what you do?"

The man laughed and stepped out under the covered porch.

Man: "You don't need shelter right now. An advisory just means that the weather is right for tornados and one could occur. There is no tornado yet. You wanna sit and have a cup of coffee and hope for a break in the rain?"

Me: "Yes, please."

We sat, drank hot coffee, and I was schooled on tornados.

Man: "Just know that if you get an advisory, you're going to be really wet, and you'll probably deal with a lot of thunder and lightning. Advisories are almost always followed by a Severe Thunderstorm Warning. Down here, near the gulf, you're also going to be pretty warm. Tornados happen when the warm wind comes up from the gulf and clashes with cold wind coming down from the north. Right now, it's windy, wet, and warm. But up north, the wind is headed our way, and it's cold. Those are ideal conditions for a tornado to form. What you really need to look out for on your phone are tornado warnings and tornado watches. If you see a warning, start considering finding cover not just from tornados but, more than likely, big ass balls of hail. Walking out there you do not want to get pummeled by hail. If you rent a car in this area you are required to pay for hail insurance. Why? Because the hail that comes down is so big that it will destroy a car. Imagine what that would do to you and your pup. We're good folks down here, and we take our tornados seriously. Back in 2013, just outside of Oklahoma City, a tornado buried an elementary school in the middle of the day. Seven kids were killed. They had very little warning and no shelter. Things have changed since then. I can't imagine that anybody will refuse you shelter should you get a warning. If you get a tornado watch, no matter where you are, you get your ass covered cuz a funnel has touched down, and it'll find you.

Me: "OK, I feel a little dumb for rushing up to your house, but I appreciate the info. Advisory, warning, watch. Got it. Shelter for sure at watch. You think this rain will lighten up any time soon?"

Man: "Nope. Hate to tell ya that but no, it ain't gonna."

Me: "Well, I can't just sit forever then. I gotta keep going, be wet, and find my next camping spot. I appreciate the coffee, sir."

Man: "You are welcome to camp here but, if you gotta go, you gotta go. Godspeed, my friend. Don't ever hesitate to knock on a door for help. Not during a tornado."

We were off, and I kept my phone at the ready. This whole tornado thing was freaking me out. For the next few days, we walked, dried off, ate, slept, and walked again. For the most part, Wink and I camped behind churches and barns, hoping for as much overhead cover as possible. We got a few motels in Sallisaw and Henryetta. The rain never stopped, and we took cover four times when my weather app alerted to tornado warnings.

On one particularly rough day, we rolled into a town called Checotah. We had already put in about eighteen miles, and we were dead tired. A few blocks away was the police station and firehouse. The weather was actually not too bad. The rain was barely a sprinkle, and the sun broke through the clouds. I met two officers outside and asked for some assistance. I started with the usual introduction of myself and what I was doing. I was not met with the normal warm hospitality I had grown accustomed to in the south.

Me: "Can you recommend a motel in town?"

Officer: "I cannot. We don't have any motels open right now. One burned down last year, and we closed up the other one due to, shall we say, unwanted and illegal adult activity that was happening there."

Me: "Shit. I've camped out at a few firehouses and behind one police station on my journey. Do you think I could pitch my tent back behind your station? I'll be out early tomorrow."

Officer: "No, you cannot do that. There is nowhere in town that you can legally camp."

Me: "Officer, we've just walked eighteen miles. The next legal campground is Gentry Creek, and that's another ten. Can't you help me out? I don't think we have ten more miles in us today, and the weather could turn at any time."

Officer: "I suggest you head west until you get to the truck stop on 266. From there, you can figure out where you're going to sleep tonight, but you cannot camp within city limits."

Me: "Wow. I've walked over a thousand miles on my journey, and this is the first town where the police weren't willing to help. I hope you're proud of that accomplishment. I'll make sure to mention you personally in my memoir. Officer Williams is it? That's what your tag says. I like to give credit where credit is due."

Williams: "Keep walking, sir. We'll keep an eye on you to make sure you get to the truck stop safely."

Wink: *"What a jerk."*

Asshole! I was completely caught off guard by his blatant disregard for humanity. Checotah, Oklahoma: motel-less home of the Wildcats and asshole cops. And now, right below Augusta, on my list of places I would never live. We walked to the Flying J Truckstop, plopped down on a bench, and ordered some hot food from Denny's take-out.

Me: "Hey, you got 8 more miles in ya?"

Wink: *"Do I have a choice?"*

Me: "I wish we did. I'm sorry."

Wink: *"I know. It's cool."*

I gave him two Slim Jims and a big bowl of water. The rain had stopped, and we were quite warm for the remainder of the day. By the time we reached the campground, which sat on the edge of Lake Eufaula, we were both in pain and had nothing left in us but shower, eat, and sleep.

While munching on a now warm sandwich, chips, and cold beer that I had purchased at the truck stop, my thoughts wandered to Annie and how I had managed to end up next to this lake. What happened to that girl that made her become Annie Fox? I hadn't found a trail of bodies that she'd left behind, but there were a few curious incidents that needed clarification. How did her brother really die, and why? What really happened to that missing guy back in Monroe? It reminded me that I had to get back with Johnny to see if he had learned anything more about him.

Me: "Johnny, were you able to dig up any more info on that guy back in Monroe with the bloody trail through his house and the shoe print?"

Johnny: "Well, hello to you, too. How about a, 'Hey, my buddy Johnny, how are you, my friend?' before you start firing off questions."

Me: "Sorry, man. I had a moment of intense clarity the other day, and I have this newfound energy."

Johnny: "Dude. I'm messin' with you. I did get the guy's name, but it went nowhere. Then I started to follow a totally different lead that I'm not ready to share with you yet, and I kinda forgot about the guy. Let me get back on that."

Me: "Wait. What other lead?"

Johnny: "Not yet. Don't want to send you down a rabbit hole until I know more. Keep your head on the road and staying alive out there. Let me do the legwork."

Me: "Fine. Talk soon, buddy."

OK, I get his point about keeping my eye on the road but, damn, he has a lead, and he won't share it? Does he understand that I lay in my friggin tent every night with nothing but time for shit to roll around in my head, and now I'm gonna have this to think about? Jerk.

A few days later, I met a family in Prague, a small town sixty miles east of Oklahoma City with a few cool spots to eat and an archery range. Dee and Alex Capron owned a place called Destinations, which was a converted gas station turned old Americana style diner. They also had a warm bed and a lively, possum and kid-filled home. Yes, they had a pet possum. And it smelled horrible. Storms had picked back up, and they encouraged me to wait it out at their house. Very late during my second night there, I got to experience the fear and adrenaline rush from being in the middle of a real tornado.

We had been on tornado warning all day. The rain was relentless, and funnels had been touching down all over Oklahoma and Texas. Dee recommended I put together a little bag of things I wouldn't want to lose should something terrible happen. I didn't have much with me that would qualify for a spot in the bag, but I made one anyway. At 5:12 a.m., the sirens in town went off. I jumped out of bed, threw on my clothes, grabbed Wink and my bag of goodies, and ran into the living room to find the entire family sitting around the TV watching the news. There was a map showing the path of a particular tornado coming up from the southwest, making its way towards Oklahoma City and Prague. I was ready to go to the shelter, but they said it was too far away still. Watching that map with that red rectangle inching towards us and the sirens blaring outside was utterly surreal. At one point, the tornado turned directly towards Prague, leaving Oklahoma City safely behind but with us in its sights. It slowly made its way across the screen, which zoomed in so that only the word Prague was seen across it. The rectangle made its way over the P.

Me: "OK! Let's go! It's here!"

Wink: *"Yeah, it's time!"*

I was assured we were still OK. It was still several miles away. We waited. I went out the front to the porch to see and record the storm. It was so dark, but a light across the street showed the rain coming in from the south on a nearly horizontal plane and trees bending and twisting in the wind. In the background of the video, you can hear the eerie sirens screaming and see the pre-tornado storm racing through the small community.

The rectangle crossed the R.

Me: "Now?"

Nope, not yet. They knew the map. The youngest boy, Izzy, started to get anxious and was clearly afraid. As the rectangle neared the A, Alex made the call.

Alex: "Now. Let's go!"

His sudden shift in demeanor was all business. Izzy was shaking from fear. We went through the house, gathered up all the pets (including the possum), flew through the back door into the storm, and down the shelter stairs. My veins were pumping with adrenaline. I wanted to feel and hear that storm but, of course, didn't want it to find its way through this community. The door slammed shut and there I was, in a concrete bunker with a strange family who took me in, several dogs, a possum, one candle and jars of pickled vegetables. Outside the sirens could be heard and, inside, there was nothing but communal silence. It was eerily straight out of a movie. The only voices were those of Dee calming her young son. We were going to be OK, Izzy. We'll be OK.

The sirens stopped after ten minutes. We waited a few more minutes before Alex opened the hatch. Massive raindrops like I had never witnessed beat us down as we made our way back to the house. They were like mini swimming pools falling from the sky. Just one hitting your head drenched your entire body. When we were safely back in the living room, they all announced that they were going back to bed. Huh? You can sleep after that? Not me. Or Wink. We were buzzing. There was no falling back asleep. I made a pot of coffee, fed Wink and wrote in my journal. When the sun came up, I went outside to see the damage and was both surprised and relieved to see none. There was debris from the wind everywhere, but the tornado had skirted the edge of town.

I said goodbye to the Caprons the following morning. Walking out of town, I saw the swath of land where the tornado had travelled. On both sides of the road, brush and grass was twisted and flattened and fences were torn to shreds. Even on the road I could see a mark across the asphalt. I stood there, looking left and right, directly on top of a potential killer's path who had fizzled out before claiming a victim. I continued on through Meeker and into Oklahoma City. A few days later we walked through the town of El Reno, which had not fared as well. El Reno had been hit the same night that we were in shelter back in Prague, and the damage was devastating. Several buildings, a car dealership, and two motels were leveled. Two people died in one of the motels. Just six years earlier, the largest tornado in history with the second-highest wind speeds ever recorded on earth had graced the edges of that same small town, killing eight and injuring hundreds. Had I not stopped for a few days in Prague, I may have been in that town that day.

I'm not sure that many people, especially walkers, would ever say these words under normal conditions, but I couldn't wait to get to Texas.

JUNE

WHAT ARE YOU DOING IN MY ROOM?

ACROSS TEXAS
TO
BOISE, IDAHO?

THE TEXAS PANHANDLE

SOMEWHERE IN THE MIDDLE

35° 12' 51.8" N

101° 22' 59.0" W

MILES WALKED: 1,820

crossed the state line on Route 66, which I had picked up in Oklahoma City. The nostalgia of the Mother Road has deep history, and I was looking forward to seeing all that she offered. As I made my way across the Texas panhandle towards Amarillo, I visited Cadillac Ranch where some old crazy artist had sunk a bunch of old Caddies nose first into the ground. Tourists from all over the world visit daily and spray paint the cars. Of course, I stopped and added to the living art piece. I also walked by the insanely large cross on the edge of I-40, which you start to see from about fifty miles out. I was getting a little anxious for some Annie updates from Johnny, but he was struggling with getting hard facts on his new lead, which he still had not shared with me. Without a firm destination, I continued west. It's all I knew how to do.

I stopped at a roadside motel that shared an offramp with a truck stop. With nowhere to camp that felt safe, I made my way to the office where I met the owner. She was a very kind woman in her mid-40s from India. From the look of the empty parking lot, I was pretty sure I was the only person there. It was a classic L-shaped, single-story motel like hundreds I had seen already. In the middle of the L stood a defunct cafe with a collapsed roof. It took nearly an hour to get my room key because the friendly owner was dead set on telling me her entire life story of how she emigrated to America after losing her husband and daughter in an explosion in India. She made her way across our country and, somehow, ended up buying that beaten-down place.

The room was small and reeked of a thousand years of body odor, stale smoke, and bathroom cleaner. I had gotten used to the smell of these old places and knew I would acclimate soon enough. Alexa wouldn't fit through the door, so the owner offered to let me park her inside the cafe. Inside the boarded-up eatery, time had stood still. Everything was exactly where it should have been as if they were opening up for dinner in a few hours. Porcelain mugs were perfectly aligned on the counter next to the coffee pots, menus were stacked neatly next to the cash register, every table was set with standard issue salt/pepper/napkin/creamer assemblies and, inside the glass front cashier cabinet, were a dozen brands of candy bars and t-shirts waiting to be sold. Watching over the perfectly preserved diner were about a hundred cats lounging everywhere. There was a small window propped open where they entered and exited at will and, on the floor, dozens of litter boxes and bowls of food and water. The place gave me the creeps. Was I in an episode of the Twilight Zone?

I eventually climbed into bed to watch some TV and, minutes later, nice owner lady came to my door with a spray bottle filled with a pink liquid. She barged in when I greeted her and told me she was going to spray down the floor so it would smell better. I told her it wasn't necessary, but she insisted. OK. It's her place, right? Her magic potion did nothing to cover up the smell, which I had already grown accustomed to, but it did add a layer of bubble gum to the ambiance and, since the carpet was now wet, added a stickiness to the bottom of my socks. I could do nothing but laugh a little. I finally made it to sleep but was rocked out of my slumber when, around 2 a.m., my door opened, and there she was again. I grabbed

Wink to keep him from attacking. She was unfazed by his bark.

Me: "What are you doing in here?"

Lady: "Just checking on you. I like to make sure my guests are OK and see if they need anything."

Me: "Uh, yeah, I'm good, lady. You can leave now."

Lady: "Oh, good. I'm glad you are happy and comfortable."

And then she turned and left.

Wink: *"That was weird."*

What the hell just happened? Did I dream that she actually walked in my room, uninvited, at 2 a.m. to check on me? I've often wondered what her true intentions were that night but stop myself before allowing any disgusting details to find permanent residence in my imagination. I found her spraying down her driveway as I left the next day. I didn't know what to say to her other than to ask if she would open the cafe so I could retrieve Alexa. It was the most bizarre motel experience on my journey.

I made my way across the panhandle, with Amarillo being the only major city I walked through. The weather had shifted from the thunderstorms to dry, windy, intense heat. Walking was not easy and the rumors of boring, long, flat Texas proved to be nothing but understated.

Through Texas, Route 66 has a tendency to up and disappear often and without reason. It just stops being a road and forces you to either hoof it through private land (no thanks) or get on the interstate. Neither seemed like good options to me but I'd rather have been run over by an eighteen-wheeler than cornered in the middle of a private dirt road in an open carry state. I chose the interstate and, although it was super-fast and insanely dangerous, I found the incredibly wide shoulders to be quite an easy walk. Texas also has some of the most incredible truck stops along I-40 so there were perks to interstate walking.

In Amarillo, I made a stop at The Big Texan, which is like Disneyland for steak lovers. It's a Route 66 landmark and, if you're willing to sit at a table on an elevated stage in the middle of a dining room filled with a few hundred more people, then this is your paradise. However, to get a seat at that lucky table, you have to attempt to devour a seventy-two-ounce steak, salad, shrimp cocktail, loaded baked potato, and a roll, and you have to do it in under an hour. If you accomplish the challenge, you get it for free and you take home a t-shirt. I did not make that attempt knowing it would be a futile one, but I did have one super tasty dinner compliments of my buddy Tracy back at home.

A week later, near the New Mexico border, and after walking dead straight, mostly in the early morning and early evening due to the insane heat, I got the call that changed my entire trajectory.

Johnny: "OK. I'm ready to share the new lead, but you're not gonna like it. I think your girl is up here, Thomas."

Me: "Shit. How do you know this?"

Johnny: "Because I'm me, and I'm awesome. There's a town near central Oregon, just north and east of Bend, called Prineville. About six weeks ago, a barista at a place called Prineville Coffee was found dead in the dining room when the morning manager showed up to work."

Me: "People die all the time. Why does this matter?"

Johnny: "His body was hacked up, Thomas. There's some grainy video of a tall woman entering the rear of the building long after closing hours and hastily leaving about fifteen minutes later. They found the guy's parts all over the place the next morning. You can't see her face in the video, but, man, there's just no way this is a coincidence. Too many similarities."

Me: "OK, that was six weeks ago. So, why wouldn't I like this info?"

Johnny: "A few reasons. First is that nobody knows who she is or where she came from. The police have more footage of a very similar-looking woman pumping gas at a 76 station on the east edge of town on Highway 26 about fifteen minutes after the video was shot of the lady leaving the coffee shop, but they can't get a clear shot of the plates. The car was a late model blue Honda Civic. All they can tell is that the plates weren't from Oregon. Prineville Coffee is on the west end of town, the gas station on the far east. Then there was nothing. Zip. She disappeared until yesterday."

Me: "What happened yesterday?"

Johnny: "The same car was found abandoned in a strip mall parking lot. They've recovered footage from a credit union and then a Ford dealership of the car traveling east. She's either hiding out or she stole a car and she's on Hwy. 26. She's probably headed towards Idaho. Maybe Boise. Towards me and your family."

Me: "You said there were a few reasons. What's the other one?"

Johnny: "You're in Goddamn Texas, and that's a long walk to Oregon."

Me: "Alright. You're still bored??"

Johnny: "Always, why?"

Me: "Hang on a sec."

I pulled up Google maps and routed the drive.

Me: "Come get me. Now. Kiss Shannon goodbye, get in your car, and get down here. I'm in a town called Wildorado, which sits on Route 66. I'm gonna continue west. You head to Albuquerque and then east on I40. It's an eighteen-hour drive so do it in two days. I'll camp one night and keep walking. Call me when you get to the Texas state line.

Johnny: "Thought you'd never ask."

Wink: *"We're getting out of this heat? We're leaving Texas?"*

Me: "Tomorrow."

Wink: *"Thank you. Besides that creepy motel lady, Texas has been friggin' boring. And hot."*

My adrenaline was at an all-time high. This was my first real lead on Annie since I started hunting her. I packed up my gear, ate a quick bowl of oatmeal, and hit the road. The sun was baking me, and walking west was met with strong, gusting winds that carried desert sand that lashed at my face and hands. Wink walked with his head down and slightly behind to my left to avoid the suffering. Thirteen miles took us six long hours. We found a secluded spot behind a roadside billboard where I set up the tent with no wind fly attached so I could get as much breeze as possible. The heat barely broke overnight and I woke up sticky and dehydrated.

Eleven miles into our day, we stopped to wait for Johnny at a landmark

Route 66 cafe in Adrian, TX, home of the official halfway point of the Mother Road. It was just past 1 p.m., and I made up a bullshit story about being stranded and waiting for a ride and asked if we could park ourselves in one of the back booths. The owner looked at Wink, who gave her his cutest sad dog eyes. She smiled and obliged. We were only there for a few minutes when Johnny called. I gave him our location, ordered some food, bacon for Wink, and cold beer. I got lost in deep thought about the Pacific Northwest.

ROAD TRIP

ADRIAN, TX

35°16'15.7"N

102°40'22.4"W

MILES WALKED: 1,896

Johnny: "Dude, we need to have a serious friend to friend talk. First, you look like hell. How much weight have you lost? And what's with the beard and hair? No wonder people think you're homeless. Are you even eating out there?"

Me: "I never stop eating. Three packs of top ramen a day, bags of trail mix, beef jerky, gas station sausage biscuits, and pretty much anything else I can shove in my mouth. Did you know you can buy a thirty-two ounce can of Dinty Moore beef stew at Dollar General for a buck? You don't even have to heat it. Straight from the can."

Johnny: "You're a chef. A good one, too. You're eating that crap?"

Wink: *"It's actually not that bad."*

Me: "Yeah, I eat that crap — a lot of it. I'm not pushing around a mini-fridge and BBQ, and I'm a little shy on funds right now. I eat what I can get."

Johnny: "It's your heart, bro. Tell me about Arkansas. There's gotta be more than what you've told me."

I told him everything, just as I had said it to Lindsay. And then I told him about Toad Suck and Charles McEnroe. I was in the driver's seat and, by the end of my narrative, we had traveled at least sixty miles, and I couldn't remember one of them. Do you ever do that? Drive to a destination and, when you arrive, not remember driving there? That's some scary shit.

Johnny: "Who the hell are you? Let me see if my scoreboard is accurate. One dead guy at home. Not on you. The dead guy in North Carolina, two in South Carolina, one in Alabama, a dead girl with a bullet in her chest and nearly a revenge murder in Arkansas till you pulled your head out of your ass and wised up. At least one dead guy on Annie, three on you and one on Wink. Still unexplained and highly suspicious are her little brother and the missing guy from Monroe. And, just for an added bonus, you got a killer locked up for eighteen years for shooting your friend. Does that sum it up?"

Me: "Well, almost. You know Rosie, the girl in Monetta that I saved from Teddy? She met me a few days later in Athens, Georgia."

A sly smirk appeared on my face.

Johnny: "Someone actually found you attractive? God, I hope you showered. The wanna-be rinse you did prior to me arriving didn't do much. You're kinda ripe."

Wink: *"Ha! Good one, Johnny."*

Me: "Thanks for that. So, yeah, I think your scoreboard is accurate."

Johnny: "Here's what I'm thinking. You've dodged a lot of bullets on this little midlife crisis hunting expedition. Your friend was shot dead right next to you. Dude, you had to drag her body into a ravine and then went on a revenge-seeking murder rampage that, luckily, didn't quite pan out. When we get to Boise, I'll hook you up with a detective friend of mine, and you hand it all over to him and the cops. As long as your friends in Monetta don't crack under pressure, you're a free man and, more importantly, you're still breathing. How about we keep it that way?"

Me: "No chance. I don't know how I feel about Annie right now. I mean, I lost everything because of what she did, but maybe I needed to. I was chasing the wrong dream back then. I feel that now. Despite all the horrible stuff that's happened on this walk, it's changed me for the better. I love the road and the freedom it provides. I haven't thought about bills or Yelp reviews or payroll or employee bullshit since I took my first steps. No, I need to see this through."

Johnny: "I get it, man, but maybe you should walk for you and not to find Annie. Let go of the hunt and allow the road to heal you. You think that finding her and getting answers is going to solve all of your problems, but you might be setting yourself up for a hard, disappointing fall. Regardless of whether you find her or not and regardless of what she says or doesn't, you're still going to get home, you're going to be broke, and you're not going to have your restaurant."

Me: "I hear you, Johnny. Maybe the change in scenery in the Pacific Northwest will calm my heart a bit. I'm not turning anything over to the police, though. If I can find her walking on a damn road, they should be able to with all their resources. It's been six months, so I doubt they even care anymore, to be honest. So, here's the deal I'll make with you and Wink. I'll walk out of Boise and head west into Oregon. I'll focus on healing and try to release the need to find Annie. I'll always want to, but I'll try not to allow it to consume me. And I'll try not to kill anybody along the way. That's the best I can do."

Johnny: "Buddy, I know you think that everything that's happened to you was justifiable and that you're in the clear. Mr. Boot, Yellow Man, and the kid in Priceville were all self-defense and shouldn't come back to bite you. But that guy in Monetta, that was murder. You left your tent, from behind a damn police station, after you turned your weapons over to the chief and purposely walked over to that market. You put yourself in the middle of a domestic dispute, you broke into a man's house, stole a knife, and then murdered him. Then you let the local stoner take the fall for it, you lied to the police about your whereabouts and left. Then you hooked up with the girl you were supposedly defending when you did it. In a small town like that and with some vagabond outsider as the defendant, it won't be hard to convince a jury that what you did was premeditated. Malice aforethought, my friend. You are not in the clear, and the more shit you drum up, the more likely it is for the truth to come out."

Me: "You're right. I am a murderer. I'll probably leave that off my resume when I get home. But I would do it again, Johnny. He was gonna hurt Rosie, and no doubt, beat his wife again. Who knows what he was going to do to Hoover? Yeah, I'd do it again. Not sure what that says about me. I'll have to think about that on my walk."

We made it to Boise, and I crashed at Johnny's place. The next day I walked over to my mom's house. She wasn't expecting me and rolling up to her place, which shares a property with my little sister, unannounced, was an excellent surprise.

JULY

HELLO & GOODBYE, MOM
HELLO, BROOK

BOISE, IDAHO
TO
PRAIRIE CITY, OREGON

KNOCK, KNOCK!

BOISE, ID

43° 36' 23.3" N

116° 10' 14.9" W

MILES WALKED: 1,896

I was only in Boise for a day, which upset my mom, sister, and her family who live in two houses built on the same property in the old downtown area. I hadn't told them I was coming, so when I walked up and knocked on the door, my mom about fell on the floor.

Mom: "Oh my gosh! What are you doing here? How did you get here? I thought you were in Texas?"

Me: "Hey, Mom. Surprise! Yeah, turned my GPS off so you wouldn't know I was headed up here. My old buddy Johnny picked me up in Texas. I'll explain later. Wanted to see the look on your face when I knocked on your door unannounced."

After a month-long hug and her tears wiped from her face, I walked into Mom's house and grabbed a beer. My sister, brother-in-law, their two kids, and my nephew came barging through the front door. Then we did the whole long hug thing again, and I finally got to sit down and explain myself. Of course, it was mostly lying. I couldn't show up unannounced hundreds of miles from where I was supposed to be and unload a bunch of murderous shit on my family. Especially with the kids around.

Me: "OK, here's the deal. It was way too hot down in the desert, so I called my buddy Johnny, you all remember him, and asked him to drive down to pick me up and bring me up here to finish my walk. Oh, and this really horrible thing happened to me in Arkansas…"

Before I got into the whole thing, we got my older sister, who lives in Vermont, on a video call so she could join the party. Then I told them the whole story of Lindsay, minus my psycho revenge murder plot break from reality, which, naturally, provoked a pretty long, obnoxious cry fest. Well, not with my younger sister. She's a tough chick with a bit of a dark side, and I think that, although she found sadness in the horrific death of my friend, she kinda liked the thrill of the whole thing.

Me: "So, when they let me out of town, I just kept walking until I couldn't handle the heat anymore. I decided to come up here, head west into Oregon and down through California to finish up."

After the conversation that you could imagine would happen in this scenario was over, Mom decided to make dinner.

Me: "Mom, I know you're excited that I'm here, but I have to leave tomorrow. I can't explain why right now, but I have some pressing stuff I gotta take care of, and I can't do it here."

Mom: "What stuff can you possibly deal with walking on the side of the road."

Wink: *"I'm with you, Grandma."*

Me: "Will you just trust me when I say I have to leave and that there's a good reason, and I'll explain later?"

Mom: "Just tell me you're OK. Look me in the eyes and tell me you're OK. I'll know if you're lying, Tommy. I always know when you're lying."

Wink: *"He's lying."*

Shit. She was right about that.

When I was a little boy, maybe nine years old, my mom was dating a guy who ended up being my stepdad and the father of my much younger sister. I stayed home sick from school one day, and there was a watermelon in the fridge. I wanted a piece, so I hauled it up on the counter, grabbed a big knife, and tried to cut through it, but I wasn't strong enough. So, I put it back in the fridge. Later that day, my mom came home with her boyfriend and saw the watermelon with the big gouge in the top of it. Of course, I said I didn't do it. Not sure why I thought that would get me in trouble but, you know how kids are, they lie about stupid shit, right? Well, the next day, the watermelon was in a large clear bag, and the knife was in another clear pouch on the counter, and they both had little white stickers on them with long numbers. They proceeded to tell me that they called the police because someone must have broken into our house, and unsuccessfully tried to steal a slice of watermelon. The police had sent over a detective to dust the knife and melon for fingerprints and I lost it, broke down in tears and admitted to the attempted grand theft and watermelon butchery. They laughed, and I got grounded.

Luckily for me, the question my mom just asked me point blank and told me to look her in the eyes when I answered was just a simple "are you OK?" To that, I could be honest.

Me: "Yeah, Mom, I'm OK. I promise."

Mom: "I don't believe you."

Wink: *"You shouldn't."*

Me: "I know. But I am. You'll understand later."

I had my mom drop me off on the far north-western edge of the massive sprawl that had taken over Boise the following morning. It would have taken me two days to get past all the new planned communities, which are a bitch to walk through because you absolutely cannot camp anywhere without some uptight homeowner's association do-gooder calling the cops on you. She cried as she said goodbye, we hugged and off I went.

The possible Annie sighting happened on Hwy 26 coming out of Prineville, which continued east through Ontario, Oregon, where it crossed into Idaho. I would be at that state line on that highway in a few hours. My goal for the day was a small town called Vale. As if hoping I would miraculously spot Annie driving by, I walked with my eyes trained on the driver of every single car that passed me.

Where are you, Annie? Are you out here? Are you near me? Do you know I'm here looking for you?

What were the odds of me spotting her at a stop light, sipping a coffee with a giant, bloody chef's knife dangling from her rearview mirror?

SLEEPING BURRITOS & TIGER TOWN

PRAIRIE CITY & MITCHELL, OR

44° 27' 46.6" N
118° 42' 34.8" W

MILES WALKED: 2,084

Turns out, odds were just about zero. With over three-million registered passenger vehicles in Oregon, perhaps I was a bit ambitious with my hopes. But the odds didn't stop me from darting across roads and highways anytime I thought I caught a glimpse of Annie. I was nearly run over dozens of times from not paying attention to the road. People honked and several drivers had to swerve to miss the crazy-homeless-cart-pushing-dog-lover bouncing back and forth across the road.

Wink: *"I'm not sure what you're up to but can we just go straight and knock off the curb jumping and highway crossing? You're gonna get hit by a bus and I'm chained to your hip. Not cool."*

Alas, my first few days were total strikeouts and my hopes of finding Annie were fading quickly. Honestly, had she driven past me and I happened to recognize her, what the hell would I have done anyway? Turn around and chase her? Whistle loud and hope that she'd hear me and pull around to say hello? I didn't know what my plan was, but I wasn't going to stop looking. I made it through Brogan, Ironside, and Unity before hitting some pretty legit mountains.

Oregon allowed me freedoms I hadn't had elsewhere, and they came in the form of National Forestry and protected land owned by the Bureau of Land Management (BLM), aka "camp wherever the hell you want, legally and free." I loved it. Once I was in the mountains, and as long as I was a hundred feet off the road, I could pitch my tent wherever I wanted, and the only thing that might have a problem with it was a big ass bear or mountain lion. I took my food precautions at night quite seriously by hiding Alexa and all my grub across the highway. The only rule I broke was my nightly ration of Reese's Peanut Butter Cups.

Did I tell you about my insatiable sweet tooth I developed on my walk? Oh, yeah, it was crazy. Within the first two weeks of my journey, I woke up every night craving chocolate. CRAVING as in "if I don't eat some damn chocolate, I might do something dangerous." I don't know where it came from, but it was intense. Snickers were my go-to for quite a while but got boring around Georgia. I made the jump to Reese's and never looked back. The perfectly balanced blend of sweet, melty chocolate mixed with salty peanut butter did it. I wished I'd bought stock in Hershey's before I left because I'm quite certain I did wonders for their shareholders. Imagine this commercial:

Wink runs into the tent, eating a jar of peanut butter and bumps into me while I'm eating a Hershey's bar.

Wink: *"Damn, Dad, you got your chocolate in my peanut butter!"*

You know the rest. I really needed a life because shit like that was in my head all the time by that point in my walk.

So, I would bring my daily allowance of one 4-pack Reese's in my tent, devour them watching Netflix and then I would crawl out of my zippered, nylon house and walk across the road to put the wrappers inside my rubbish bag. Then I would thoroughly wash my hands and brush my teeth. Maybe that was overkill, but if I liked Reese's that much, maybe bears did, too. I wasn't taking any chances.

I always slept better after Reese's.

NOTE:
I did not receive any endorsement money or free peanut butter cups from Hershey's.

A few days from Prairie City I got a call from my friend Brook. She was a former employee of mine long ago, and we had remained very close friends. She had moved to the Seattle area but still worked in LA, so she commuted quite a bit and made the drive often. It turns out she was driving back up to Seattle, and we decided to meet. I was super stoked because Brook and I always had a very special friendship that was forged through years in the kitchen together and a few business trips to NYC and Chicago. Brook was going to set her course for Prairie City to hang out for a day and a night.

I was on Hwy 26 all the way across eastern and central Oregon and it's the same highway as the path of the Trans-Am Cycling trail that goes coast to coast from Oregon to Virginia. Since I walked on the same side of the road westbound as cyclists used riding eastbound, I met dozens of cool adventure seekers. Every single one stopped to talk, tell stories, eat some food, or see what the hell I was doing out there. You have to understand that the area I was in was very desolate, so seeing a guy chained to a dog pushing a stroller was not what they were expecting. They all had different life stories, but one thing they all had in common was their love of a place called the Spoke'n Hostel in an upcoming, small town called Mitchell. It was just a few days away and I was excited to experience the hype. I put it on my must-do list.

Brook and I had dinner and drinks at a local brewery where we met one such cyclist and enjoyed an awesome night of laughter and storytelling. It was wonderful to have such a surprise visit from someone I hadn't seen in a few years and in the oddest of places to meet up.

Brook is one of those friends who couldn't possibly judge a soul. She found interest in everything in front of her and was open to any and all experiences. When you spend hundreds of hours within inches of another person in a kitchen, you get to a point where you can finish their sentences and accurately predict their next move. Brook and I were like that and it went both ways. As we laid in bed, I shared my experiences with her as she cried tears on her pillow. She was feeling my pain with me. Brook could do that. She was an empath and she was intuitive. She used to call me out of the blue when I was at my worst. She always knew when to call. We had this deal, this code-phrase, we shared when we worked together that we still have today - if either of us sent a text message to the other that said "I'm craving a burrito", we knew the person needed help and we would stop everything and go. In bed, that night, she knew where I was and where I was headed. When story time was over, we embraced like spoons, turned on some music, and slept. Two burritos in a bed in Prairie City.

Unfortunately, there was a killer on the loose, and it was my job to find her, so I had to leave my friend the next day. I would send her the burrito text several times over the next few months and she got me through some pretty rough nights.

I continued the next three days over steep passes with little to no shoulder at some points, and the walk, as beautiful and exciting as it was, brought me close to death several times. The highway was often flanked by deep gorges and rocky drop-offs that ended hundreds of feet below. It took me five days to travel the eighty-four miles along the Ochoco Hwy until I made it to the crazy small, very cool town of Mitchell, where I found the place that all the cyclists had told me about.

The Spoke'n Hostel was an oasis of friendly, generous, compassionate, adventurous, and transient people. It was an old church that was granted to a couple from Eugene a few years earlier. Mitchell was a town in swift economic decline when Patrick and Jalet Farrell picked up their busy city lives and took over the building. It was still a practicing church, and Patrick was the pastor, but the building had been converted to a hostel full of beautiful bunk beds and a few private rooms. There was a game table, comfy and cool furniture to lounge on, a piano, and a kitchen downstairs where everyone convened for breakfast, ate tons of free ice cream of every possible flavor, told their stories, and then left to continue their journeys. Every day during cycling season, a new batch of a dozen or so people would ride in, shower, eat, drink beers at the local brewery, stock up at the market, crash early, eat breakfast and plan to leave the next day. Plans, of course, are often broken which was fairly routine when you visited Mitchell.

That's right, I said brewery. In a town of barely one-hundred people, Tiger Town Brewery Co. called Mitchell home. They did some bang-up business and their beer is legit. Townies, cyclists and tourists (and one random guy walking with a cart) regularly gather for cold local craft beer on the patio and in the small, quaint dining room where they enjoy the tranquility of communal peace and storytelling. And they made a very good burger. With cold, fresh beer, great food and the comfort of the hostel, it's no wonder people had a hard time cycling (or walking) away.

I stayed for three nights and it was awesome. I needed some time to think and there was no better place to do it. I was certain I had missed Annie on the road, and, with no real destination in mind, I took the time to get to know some new friends.

I told Patrick and Jalet everything. Everything. My intuition told me that I could trust them with my fears, my anger, my desire for revenge, the sadness of all my loss, and my fear of emptiness I knew I would experience when I got home. They never judged me for what I had done nor for the lack of religion or a God role in my life. We were three people, huddled around a table late into the night, listening to me unpack my life's luggage. I think I ate three very large bowls of ice cream during my confession.

When I finally left, my departure was met with great sadness. The hostel provided a peaceful, safe comfort, and I didn't want to leave that feeling behind and venture back out. The place is operated by volunteers, and I told them I would like to return and give back for what they had given to me. I'll never forget Patrick and Jalet and hoped to see them again soon.

I had less than a thousand miles before I would be home, and I was beginning to believe I would never find Annie. In a few days, I would pass through Prineville, where the last murder had occurred several weeks earlier. It was the closest I would feel to her. I would see where she had taken another life, but my selfish pursuit of her would prevent me from being any help to authorities.

Annie was still mine to find. I had to ask her why she ruined my life. And why she killed that kid in Prineville.

AUGUST

SLEEPING IN A TEEPEE
DOWN BY A RIVER
ON A HEMP FARM

PRINEVILLE, OREGON
TO
COTTONWOOD, CALIFORNIA

THE PRINEVILLE COFFEE MURDER

PRINEVILLE, OR

44° 18' 09.4" N

120° 51' 26.0" W

MILES WALKED: 2,131

The journey to Prineville was two days of incredible beauty through the Ochoco National Forest, through which I covered four pretty respectable mountain passes. Despite the intense daily climbs up and down winding highways, the distance was never a concern because I could stop and camp anywhere. I was feeling very lonely for the first time in several months, and moments of sadness and failure plagued me often. The serenity and beauty of the mountains was my only saving grace. I was beginning to accept that Annie and I would never meet again, and she would continue to kill people around the country, and I would go home to nothing and be nothing.

Prineville sat at the bottom of a very long, twenty-five-mile downhill slope from the Ochoco Pass, where I had camped the night before. I was relieved, as I'm sure Wink was too, that we had zero hills to climb that day, especially because the wind coming up the mountain, although quite warm, was strong and angry. We abandoned our walk several times to hide for cover behind rock formations and the large trees that lined the highway. There were moments where walking downhill felt like an uphill battle. That all changed when we got to the foot of the mountain and made our way into town.

On my left, I passed the Ford dealership that had picked up the blue Honda on their cameras that may have had Annie at the wheel. Then, on my right a few blocks up, the credit union Johnny told me about. I booked a motel in town so I could clean up after four nights of camping and get to some real detective work. It was late in the day, and I wasn't able to visit Prineville Coffee till they opened the next morning.

Coffee girl: "Hey there. Welcome to Prineville Coffee."

There wasn't much excitement in the girl's voice. There was an expected sadness about her, and I felt like an intruder. Prineville Coffee was a small town, community cafe where a stranger had destroyed a life and then vanished. Although I felt her pain, all I could think about was the divine smell of rich coffee. I had grown used to Folger's freeze-dried instant crystals and had forgotten how delicious real, craft roasted coffee tasted. I sat in the corner with Wink at my feet, sipping away in hopes of hearing some gossip at the counter. It was busy and mostly with locals offering condolences and filling up a large jar where they were collecting donations for the victim's family.

After the rush had died down, and I had consumed plenty of coffee, I made my way to the counter.

Me: "Excuse me. Hi. My name is Thomas, and I'm walking across America with my dog. I couldn't help but overhear all of the conversations about some tragedy. Do you mind me asking what happened?"

Coffee girl: "One of our employees was murdered here several weeks ago. Right there near where you're standing."

Me: "Oh, shit, I am so sorry. And sorry I brought it up, sincerely."

Coffee girl: "It's OK. It's pretty much all anyone talks about in town these days. Some lady walked right through the back door when Spider was cleaning up. She cut him up and scattered him around. His real name was Mark, but everyone called him Spider. I don't know where that nickname came from, but he liked it a lot."

She had a slight frown and tears in her eyes that were focused on something a few feet away that wasn't there. She stayed there for a few seconds, wiped her eyes, and forced a small smile.

Coffee girl: "They still haven't found her. The video sucks, but you can see her get out of the passenger's door of a blue car, walk in the back door, and about fifteen minutes later, she walked out, got back in the car, and drove off."

Passenger's side? So, she wasn't alone?

Me: "I'm terribly sorry. Really, didn't mean to do that to you."

Some customers came in behind me and good thing because I wanted to wrap this up.

Me: "You take care of yourself. My heart is with you and your community."

I bolted outside with Wink and grabbed my phone.

Me: "Johnny, she wasn't alone. Not sure where you got your info, but they left out a detail. She got out of the passenger's side door at the coffee shop. Annie's got a buddy."

Johnny: "Shit. Yeah, didn't get that part. Sorry man. Not sure how that helps but would have been good to know in case you strolled up on her."

Me: "Probably doesn't matter anyway. We passed each other somewhere or she went west or another direction. I doubt she's still in town. Fuck. What am I doing out here?"

Johnny: "I've been asking you that question for months, my friend."

I hung up. I was pissed off for no reason I could logically attach to that emotion. Who was I mad at? Johnny? Me? It had to be me. I didn't have much money to begin with and I had pretty much gone through every penny I did have. I was no closer to success and had no future that I could sort out in my mind. I went back to the motel, ate some peanut butter cups, and went to sleep. I needed to get out of that town and walk to something familiar. I needed a friend. I needed someone I could unload all my shit on; I needed someone who wouldn't judge me. I needed to get to Bend.

A TEEPEE, LEIGH? REALLY?

BEND, OR

44° 03' 33.1" N

121° 18' 53.8" W

MILES WALKED: 2,154

Two days, thirty-six miles, one sleepless night "camping" under the trailer bed of a big-rig and endless thoughts of hacked up bodies later, I was there. I called my old buddy, Leigh, and asked if I could crash at his house. Although completely surprised by getting a random call from me and shocked by my predicament, he sounded genuinely stoked to have a house guest. I walked to his place and poured a huge glass of wine.

Leigh: "So, what are you doing here, man? You could have given me a little warning. I would have planned a party or something."

Me: "No party needed. Take me somewhere we can talk and drink."

Leigh and I went way back to my days when I thought I was going to be a rockstar. Leigh had played guitar in our band for a few gigs back in the late eighties. Gone now was his long, curly Hollywood ballad-rock-band hair. His new look was hip, grey older guy. He looked much better now. I told Leigh everything; I trusted him like I trusted Brook. I let it all out, but it took a few old fashions. Leigh didn't open his mouth once until I drained number three.

Leigh: "I don't even know where to begin. That's either one hell of a bullshit story you're cookin' up for a Netflix mini-series, and, if that's not the case, I'm with Johnny on this one. Quit chasing this crazy bitch. There is absolutely no upside to finding her."

I was beginning to believe that Johnny and Leigh were right. I knew I was hunting her purely for personal gain and not necessarily for justice, even though rotting in prison for what she did to Jesse would be an appropriate conclusion to the story. Was putting myself in danger worth a face to face meeting with a cold-blooded killer? I knew she killed Jesse, and I was pretty damned sure she was the Prineville Coffee killer, but that was based purely on coincidental evidence. Then there was the truth about her brother that I kinda wanted to corner her about and, hell, while I was at it, why not bring up the missing guy in Monroe?

Me: "The upside is...dammit, hang on."

My phone dinged and vibrated in my pocket, telling me I had two text messages. The photo and message from the blocked number froze the blood in my veins.

The photo showed a brownish colored coffee cup nestled in a car's cup holder. On the seat next to the cup, you could see the front page of a newspaper. On the side of the cup was a white sticker with a red coffee mug in the center. It was turned just enough so that you couldn't read the logo, but I knew where it was from. I had taken one of those same stickers out of the basket at the cash register at Prineville Coffee and stuck it on Alexa just a few days earlier.

The message attached read, "Hello, Thomas."

Me: "Holy shit. Leigh, order us another round. I need a drink. I just sobered up."

Sweat immediately soaked my forehead as a rush of heat swarmed my body. I jumped up and started pacing around the bar, struggling to catch my breath. I handed my phone to Leigh and showed him the picture.

Leigh: "OK, it's a coffee cup. I don't get it. What am I looking at?"

Me: "Prineville Coffee. The day of the murder. Look at the date on the newspaper. It's the same day that kid died. She fucking knows I'm looking for her."

While Leigh was zooming in on the photo to search for any more details, my phone dinged again.

Leigh: "Thomas, you've got a very serious problem. You just got a new photo from her. Another newspaper shot but, dude, this is a bar right here in Bend and she took this photo yesterday. She's here, in town."

I grabbed the phone and sat down. The new photo was of a half-empty glass of beer and, like the coffee cup picture, it was sitting on top of the local paper. Behind it, laying on its side and barely visible, was a brown bottle with a white label and blue writing. Zooming in, I could see a side view logo of an Icelandic Viking. It was a bottle of Einstok White Ale, my favorite beer, which was always on tap at my restaurant. The restaurant she stole from me.

The new message read, "I would walk 500 miles, and I would walk 500 more just to be the man who walks a thousand miles to fall down at your door".

That bitch. I hate that song.

Who was hunting whom? I was an easy target. She could find me just by driving around. She obviously knew where I was, or at least my general location. What was she doing? Was she taunting me? Flirting with me? Warning me?

Leigh: "You have to stop; this has gone too far. You have to call the police, tell them everything, show them those photos and get yourself someplace safe. You can stay here, or I can get you a hotel close by — my treat. But you cannot continue this walk. This chick is nuts."

Me: "No, I have to keep going. It's the only chance I have of getting close to her. If I can't find her, maybe she'll come to me."

Leigh: "Can you hear yourself right now? Are you a fucking idiot? I'm seriously worried about your ability to make a rational, sane decision."

Me: "I hear you, Leigh. I get it. But this thing that's in me, this need is killing me more painfully than she ever could. I have to see her. I have to find her."

Leigh: "What you're gonna do is finish your drink and sleep on this. I'm gonna introduce you to a friend of mine tomorrow. Her name is Erika. This may sound weird, but she's this hippy chick who works on a hemp farm and lives in a teepee right on the Deschutes River. You're gonna go hang out with her for a night and listen to her. She's intuitive, and you need to spend some time with her. I know it sounds nuts, but I know this girl and she can just see shit. I mean it, OK? Just one night. See how you feel after. At least do that for me."

Me: "A teepee, Leigh? Down by a river on a hemp farm? Really? You think that's the answer to all my problems?"

Leigh: "No, not an answer. But maybe some direction."

Me: "What's your deal with her?"

Leigh: "You know I've been through plenty of shit in my own life. I met Erika a few years ago through a friend and spent some time with her out at her teepee and, I don't know, she just has this way of making a difference in your head. You don't even know she's doing it but, somehow, she makes you think...I don't know, maybe more clearly? I don't know how to explain it, but I think she can help. If not, you'll still have a cool experience but I'm a big believer in Erika and think you need to meet her."

I reluctantly agreed after finishing my fourth drink. Maybe a night in a teepee on a hemp farm down by a river would do me some good.

Leigh drove me to Erika's bungalow in town the next day. As we walked up, a short human figure fully dressed up in what I thought was a HAZMAT suit came from around the side yard. Through the mask, the face inside blew a kiss, told us she had to tend to her bees and for us to wait on the patio.

Wink: *"What the hell was that?"*

Me: "Really, Leigh?"

Leigh: "I know. It's weird. Just go with it. I'll take Wink for the night; you focus on you. Be open minded, Thomas."

Wink: *"Thank you, Leigh. Good luck, bro. We're outta here."*

ERIKA

MILES WALKED: 2,154

A few minutes later, the white suit walked around the corner, minus the helmet. Now uncovered was an angelic face with long, flowing silver hair and piercing blue eyes. Erika's aura was wise and flirty with a slight smile and gaze that landed softly. She stripped out of her beekeeper suit and revealed a very petite woman wearing shorts and a loosely knit tank top that did nothing to hide her tiny braless body underneath. She was remarkably beautiful, poised and confident.

Erika: "Hello, Thomas. Leigh has told me that you could use some guidance. Would you like to spend an evening with me and see what we can do about that?"

Me: "I thought you lived in a teepee down by a river."

Erika: "I do, and I live here sometimes when there's room for me. People stay here as they need to. The door is always open, and I don't ask questions. I sit with people, and we listen to each other's bodies, and we heal. Most of my time is spent in the teepee outside of town. We'll go there in a few minutes, OK?"

I wasn't sure what I was feeling. It was confusing. I was in the middle of a major crisis of the life-threatening type yet, when Erika looked at me without ever flinching or even blinking, I was quite peaceful.

Me: "Yes, let's go to the teepee."

I looked at Leigh, who smiled, gave Erika a hug, and said he'd pick me up the next day. I had nothing with me but a toothbrush in my pocket. I helped Erika load a box of honey jars into her trunk and off we went. We didn't speak the entire way to the teepee, but, at one point, she turned my hand, so my palm was facing up, and rested it on my leg. She then put her palm on mine and gently pressed down and closed her eyes. We were moving at a pretty good rate on the road heading into the hills, her eyes closed for half a minute or so, but I wasn't worried. The car never drifted from its lane and I felt surprisingly safe. She opened her eyes, pulled back her hand, and let out a long, soft breath.

Erika: "That was good, Thomas, thank you for sharing."

You're welcome?

We arrived at a dirt road to our left that took us about a quarter mile to a group of small buildings. As we passed them, Erika explained that the small community of thirty or so people was off-grid and self-sufficient. She assured me they weren't a cult or anything like that. They were just a community of farmers that grew hemp as a business and all the food they needed. They lived on solar and had cell service, which allowed for decent internet connection.

Me: "Why don't you live in these buildings."

Erika: "I prefer my teepee, the river, and the stars. That's mostly all I need. We all go to town often and have dinners and drinks. We don't like to be secluded. That's not what this is. We just prefer our homes to be quiet and peaceful. We actually party quite a bit in town with the locals. We eat fast food sometimes and occasionally order pizza which always freaks the delivery driver out. We're not weirdos, just different. You'll like it out at my place."

Me: "What will we do?"

Erika: "The water is wonderful right now. We can swim a bit then build a fire. Once the sun goes down, we won't talk, though. That's when we'll work."

Me: "I don't have a swimsuit."

She looked at me like I was a fool.

Erika: "You won't need a suit, Thomas."

We drove through the hemp fields, through a gate and down a rough, bumping dirt road to a clearing where I could hear rushing water. And there it was, Erika's massive teepee she called home. It must have been twenty-five feet tall and fifteen feet wide with tall, beautiful wood poles sticking up through the top, pointing in all directions. Behind it ran the Columbia River.

We got out of the car, and Erika took my hand and led me to the flap door. Inside was nothing but a very large foam mattress sitting on top of dozens of colorful rugs that lined the floor. On top of the mattress were quilted blankets and, on the side hanging from the slanted canvas walls were old, iron candle sconces. You could easily fit a king-size bed, dresser, and maybe a desk inside. It was huge.

Me: "This is unbelievable. I've never been in a teepee."

I turned to find Erika without a stitch of clothing and the sunlight from behind radiating around her body. She reached for my hand and told me to get undressed. It was time to swim. I had to remember that this was not what I might be thinking, and perhaps hoping, and to get those thoughts out of my head. That was not easy. Erika was beautiful and peaceful, and I was a guy who'd been on the road for a long time. I took a deep breath and got naked. Luckily, there was no hard evidence of attraction happening, if you know what I mean.

We walked hand in hand to the river, where she abruptly departed our togetherness and walked, without hesitation, through a break in the bushes and into the water. I watched as she disappeared under the sur-face. I waited to see her face emerge and, when it did, I followed her in. We were in a small, cool pool of the river nestled between large boulders that allowed the soothing water to collect and be calm. The bottom was pebbled with the occasional large rock that lightly scraped my toes as I walked around. We were together in the water, but I felt alone as Erika spent long moments at the mouth of the pool looking out into the rushing river.

Erika: "Come here, Thomas."

I joined her side and looked out. She put her hand on the small of my back. She put her other hand on my chest and slowly caressed up and down my spine, occasionally stopping to press firmly against my back as her other hand held me in place. I was looking out at the river but could feel her gaze strong and focused on my face.

Erika: "That water is life, Thomas. It's your life and mine and everyone's. It's been many places. Right now, it's here with us until it rushes by and goes on to someone else. Somewhere else. Like our lives, right? Yesterday you were somewhere, today you are here, tomorrow you will be there. Nobody knows if a drop of water in a rushing river tries to stay right next to another particular drop of water all the time. For safety. For companionship. There are too many drops to know for sure. But, collectively, they are always together. Sometimes they might be holding hands as they rush through life, other times they might be with strange drops of water. Like now, you and me."

Me: "I've never thought of a river like that. Everything is living, right? So why wouldn't they want to be together?"

Erika: "Because they can't always be with whom they want to be with. Just like you. You're missing somebody, Thomas, but right now you are here with me. How does that make you feel?"

I sat with that question. I reached up and held her hand and tried to focus on one drop of water and follow it. It made me think of Lindsay and the time we spat from the bridge. Was our spit still clinging together for companionship? I wanted to believe they were.

Me: "Peacefully lonely."

Erika: "That's very present of you, Thomas. Can you feel the life of the water around your body? Can you feel it be near you, then leave to be replaced by more water? Or do you feel the presence of one, singular, powerful life upon you?"

Me: "I don't understand."

Erika: "The water is a metaphor I'm using to understand your heart and your life where you are right now."

Me: "My life at home was one mass of energy and, in hindsight, complacency. Comfortable in my mind, I guess, but transient, fearful and lonely. Then I left it and everything, every day, was new and exciting and scary all at the same time. People and places came and went so quickly. I experienced them for a moment and then they disappeared as quickly as they came. I guess, before my walk, my body of water was one, singular, powerful life but it was missing so much. Now, seven months on the road alone, it's been like this river. It presents itself, is with me for a speck of time, then it rushes by to be replaced but not forgotten."

Erika: "That's tough introspection when you dig that deep, isn't it?"

Me: "Yeah, it is, Erika."

Erika: "We're done swimming now. We need fire to continue our work."

She turned and walked to shore, leaving me to feel for a moment. The sun was inviting the moon to take its place, and, with only a few hours of daylight remaining, I made my way to Erika, who was waiting on the bank with her hand held out.

She created a fire just outside the teepee and surrounded it with rugs. We were still naked but draped in blankets as the air cooled, and the night fell. Erika took my hand again and closed her eyes. I watched her breathe and a small tear form and run down her soft cheek.

Erika: "Are you ready to learn your truths, Thomas?"

Me: "I don't know what's really true anymore. I started this journey..."

Erika: "Ssshhhh. Leigh briefly told me about your journey, but I stopped him. I wanted to hear about it from you. But tonight needs to be about purpose and feelings — not months of details. We don't have time

293

for that, nor is it important. I don't want to know exactly what you are doing; I want to hear from you why you are doing it. Leigh told me you were in some kind of trouble. I asked him not to tell me anything; he knew he didn't need to. I've done this with him before. Tell me where your life journey has taken you and where you hope it will lead you."

Me: "I was happy eight months ago. Or, looking back, I thought I was. I thought I had everything except someone to love. I did have somebody to love but I lost her. Then another woman stole my only happiness and my business, and then disappeared. I've been walking thousands of miles looking for her to find out why she did that to me. And now I think she wants to kill me."

Erika: "How did you lose the woman you loved?"

Me: "She wasn't the woman I thought she was. And then she was gone."

Erika: "And how did the other woman take your business from you?"

Me: "Annie was my employee. I trusted her; I liked her. She murdered a young man in my restaurant and then disappeared. I lost everything."

Erika: "Did you love Annie?"

Me: "I don't think I ever thought of her like that. I guess if I had met her under different circumstances, I would have been attracted to her. She was beautiful and tough and street smart. I like ambition in a woman, and she had a lot of that. You know, I've never sat with my feelings about her as a woman. She was my employee so, if I did have feelings for her, I certainly never allowed myself to feel them. I'm just careful that way."

Erika: "Do you believe finding her will bring you peace?"

Me: "No, I don't. I don't think I'll ever be at peace again. Except right now, sitting here with you, I'm at peace, but this is just a moment."

Erika: "Thomas, I'm going to do something, but it's for a reason that is not sexual. I'm going to kiss you, and I want you to kiss me back. Don't be nervous. I want you to let go and kiss me deeply. I want you to feel me because I need to feel you. I want to feel the peace you say you are experiencing right now. When a person is open to communicating through sensual touch, messaging is far more clear than words can ever be. Can you do that? Just kiss me?"

Without waiting for an answer, she leaned into me, our lips met, our mouths opened, and we explored each other through a long, deep connection. It was different than any kiss I had ever had in that, although it was physically stimulating, it was not a sexual connection, we were communicating in a way I never had before.

Suddenly, Erika stopped and stared deeply into my eyes, holding my face in her small, warm hands and allowed her eyes to release several tears. It was the most powerful and sensual twenty seconds of my life.

Erika: "I didn't feel peace, Thomas. I felt sadness and fear but also a strong sense of determination. Your heart is very troubled, but not from loss; its trouble is fear of not knowing how to fill the void from the loss. You haven't allowed your determination to take control and guide you; you're still allowing your fear to do that. That will change tomorrow."

Me: "How will that change?"

Erika: "It will because you will make it change. The sun is down, and you need to be in silence tonight. Is there anything you want to say to me?"

Me: "Thank you."

We left the fire and moved inside the teepee and laid down under the blankets. Our bodies were warm next to one another, our fingers interlocked, and we stayed in silence for some time. Erika seemed to be experiencing something deeply emotional as her breath flowed in and out of her body in long waves. Slight moans escaped her lips from time to time. I could feel her intensity and our skin was warm against each other. Just as I began to think about kissing her again for very different reasons than before, she opened her eyes and released my hand.

Erika: "Thomas, this woman you are seeking, although you will find her, is not who you are chasing. You will discover your true quest when you think you are done walking. You will discover that Annie had a much more important purpose in your life and that she is not the woman you believe her to be. I cannot tell you more without clouding your judgment as you continue your journey, which you must do. You will not find your answers unless you finish your walk and, when you do, you will realize that your journey has just begun. You've traveled many miles to get here, and when you finish, you will learn that you've only just taken your first steps. Tomorrow you will rest in silence and then you will walk. You will discover your truths. Finding Annie will only be the icing on your cake, finding your truth is your cake."

Those were the last words Erika said to me. The next morning, I found her by the water wrapped in a blanket. She turned as I approached and held her finger to her pursed lips to silence my words and make me sit with my thoughts. We walked the half-mile to where the dirt road met the highway where Leigh was waiting. I climbed in the car as he got out to talk to Erika.

Erika: "I told Thomas to rest today in silence and continue his journey tomorrow."

Leigh: "You did what? There's a psycho killer bitch out there taunting him, and you told him to keep going?"

Erika: "He needs to find her to find himself."

Leigh: "I hope you're right about this Erika."

Erika: "Have I ever been wrong?"

Leigh sighed, shrugged and hugged her goodbye. My eyes were locked in a stare with Erika as we drove off. And then she was gone.

I did as I was told and sat with my thoughts. Leigh talked a lot while I listened, drank wine, and ate a lot of great food, but I never spoke a word that day. The following morning, I loaded up Alexa, clicked Wink to my belt, and made my way down the driveway. Leigh called out to me.

Leigh: "Hey, you don't have to listen to her. You can stop. You should stop."

Me: "No, something tells me I'm gonna be OK. I gotta go. I'll call you."

We walked down the driveway, out to the highway and continued south towards home; towards my truths.

Wink: *"Anything you wanna get off your chest? You're acting kinda weird."*

Me: "Can we not talk today?"

Wink: *"OK. I understand. You know where I am if you need me."*

For six days, we walked in silence: no music, no phone calls, no podcasts, no Netflix in my tent. The only person I spoke with was Wink, and he didn't have much to say. I found myself checking my phone for new messages several times a day, but none were delivered. On my sixth day, I crossed the state line into California, and I felt like I was right around the corner from home.

I hadn't killed anybody since Monetta. I had eight hundred miles before I would be home, and I wanted to keep the scoreboard where it was.

California was my worst stretch.

WELCOME TO CALIFORNIA

expected balloons and a ticker-tape parade waiting for me at the border of my final state line crossing into California. What I found were a few park benches blazing under the heat of the sun. Across the highway was a small, full parking lot and a bus that had unloaded a bunch of tourists. People were lining up to snap a photo in front of a royal blue sign with the words Welcome to California scrawled across in bright yellow cursive writing. Was that really a tourist destination? It was a road sign.

I had a bunch of miles to cover, it was hot, and I just wasn't in the mood for camping. Leigh had helped replenish some funds so I could get a few motel rooms on my southbound trek. I booked a shitty little room in a town called Dorris and moved as quickly as possible.

My head was spinning from my time with Erika. What truth was I chasing, and how did Annie play into them? What did she mean when she said that Annie wasn't the woman I thought she was?

When I made it to the crappy little motel in Dorris, I was pleasantly surprised by the company I would keep for the next few hours. It was another single-story, L-shaped place, and I was right in the crook of the bend. Outside all of the other rooms were beer coolers, BBQs fired up, and the smell of the food was outstanding! There was music blaring from one of the rooms, and twenty or so field workers were out milling around, talking, laughing, drinking, and having a great night. They all stopped to watch the guy with the cart and dog roll into the middle of their party. I said hello as I weaved around the fiesta and made my way into my room.

Not a minute later, there was a knock on my door. Outside were a few guys, and a cold beer held out.

Beer guy: "Hola amigo."

Me: "Hola. Lo siento, hablo poquito Espanol."

No clue if I said that right, but they got my point.

Beer guy: "Come eat tacos with us. Drink cerveza."

Twist my arm. I joined the lively crowd in the courtyard parking lot and devoured several of the best tacos I had ever shoved inside my face. I struggled with my best kitchen Spanish and most of my new friends laughed at my horrible attempt to communicate. Those in the group who spoke English helped me out and even translated some of my stories from the road. These workers were what they called travelers. Unlike many day laborers I would meet in the coming month during my trek through central California, these field workers moved around from town to town for different seasons, not sticking to a particular farm or crop. A month earlier, they were a little further north "pineconing," which I did not know existed. They were stationed in a town that was the gateway to an area of the forest that grew incredibly large and beautiful pinecones. They would work the season there and then head to another city for work. In a month, they were headed back to the same pinecone town to forage mushrooms. They were migratory day laborers, and they stuck together. They had their little community and preferred life on the road rather than living in one rural town, tending the same fields season after season. I did my best describing my life on the road for the past six months, why I was out there and where I was headed. I told them all the great stories of the road while leaving out the gory details. I didn't want to scare my new friends.

I said my goodbyes, thanked them and made my back in my room with Wink and climbed into bed. About fifteen minutes into watching a show, my phone dinged. A text had arrived. It was a picture with no message. It didn't need one. The shot said all it needed to say.

The picture was taken from across a highway looking over at a few dozen people who formed a haphazard line in front of a big blue sign that said Welcome to California. In front of the sign was me taking a selfie.

Annie, what are you doing? Why are you doing this to me? I had no way of communicating with her. The number was blocked, and I couldn't reply. I wanted to say, "OK. I quit. Kill people, I don't care. I just wanted to ask you why you killed Jesse." But I couldn't. Or could I?

I logged into Instagram and brought up the only digital place I knew of that Annie had once used, CarbonEdgeKenn. Annie was not a very socially active person when she was Kennedy. Most of her photos were of obscure food shots, and what appeared to be odd trinkets she would find interesting scattered on the road or near trash cans. There were no shots of people, no signs of friendship or family or vacations. She never tagged anybody, used hashtags, check-ins, or geotags. It was nearly impossible to understand where or when she had taken the photos and how they made her feel. The food was usually of half-eaten tacos or burgers after the contents of the plate had been scattered around. I wondered if her message was, "Yum! I'm halfway through the best taco ever!" or "Meh, not worth finishing." In some of the trinket shots, she had zoomed in so far that it was nearly impossible to identify the object.

Without really considering the potential consequences of what I was about to do, I fired off a private message.

"Hello, Annie."

I sat and watched the message, hoping that, at any moment, I would get a reply. I woke the next morning with my phone on my chest and drool running down the right side of my cheek. I hadn't moved an inch.

I walked south with Mt. Shasta flirting with me for days. I first caught sight of her a week earlier when I was still in Oregon. I knew all the way back in Idaho that, at some point, I would see her. One very cold and windy day south of Bend as I approached Klamath Falls, I was heading down a very steep hill on an insanely busy highway. The road curved as it hugged the mountain and all I could see around me were tall, beautiful, mighty trees. As I turned one bend, there was a clearing to my left, and, suddenly, the snow-peaked beauty presented herself through the trees. She was magnificent. One tall, white peak against a majestic blue sky and a smaller peak begging for attention a bit lower to the right. It was so far away still, but in that spot where I had stopped suddenly to admire her stunning presence, she felt right next to me. She winked with a sly, flirty smile and asked if she could join me for a while. I obliged with flushed cheeks. She was the most beautiful thing I had seen in, perhaps, my entire life.

I spent the next six days walking to and then around Mt. Shasta to the west. I stayed in a small town called Weed, and they really know how to capitalize on that name. Tourist shops dominated the downtown area with every possible clothing item and trinket you can imagine emblazoned with the town name in clever ways to promote their hippy, pot-smoking persona. I have no idea if Weed is a hippy, pot-smoking town because I didn't spend much time there, but they definitely want you to think so. I would, however, guess it to be true. In reality, the town was named after the founding family with the same surname back in the earlier part of the last century — something to do with forestry, not cannabis.

Between Weed, Shasta City, and Dunsmuir, I met dozens of Pacific Crest Trail hikers who hitched off the trail to get to the small towns for restocking and much, much needed showers and cold beer. I hadn't realized I was so close to the trail, and many of the hikers told me about the campsite at Castle Crags, so I made my way there. It was south of Dunsmuir on the west side of Interstate 5, so I had to do a little bit of illegal walking on the eight-lane asphalt monstrosity, but on that day, luckily, I didn't encounter any cops.

Castle Crags is a big National Park with lots of campgrounds and one set aside for PCT hikers. Although I wasn't a PCT hiker, the guards at the gate allowed me to only pay the five-dollar PCT fee rather than the thirty-dollar camping cost. They either wanted to keep the cart/dog guy with the other smelly, dirty riffraff, or they were just being cool because I looked like I could only afford five bucks, which was true. I was the only one in the camp when I arrived, so I picked the best spot and set up my tent. I opened the bear cage next to the fire pit and picnic table to put my stuff in and found a veritable pharmacy full of goodies; PCT hikers kinda share everything. There was a white plastic basket full of toiletries, bags of food, top-ramen, books, and even gear like a flashlight, some gloves, a pair of pretty decent shoes, and a bunch of maps. There was even a small box of condoms. Not opened. Poor hiker. Must have given up hope.

I mentioned before that many people had asked me why I didn't do the PCT or Appalachian Trail instead of a trans-con, and, honestly, I just hadn't thought about it. I wanted to walk roads across America. But, sitting in that camp, where thousands of thrill seekers and soul searchers spent countless nights telling trail stories around that firepit caused a stir, the PCT bug bit me. Also inside the bear cage was a large stack of shower tokens. I had purchased two for a buck at the gate, which would give me a total of four minutes in the shower. Discovering the magic stash of tokens was like ripping into a Wonka Bar to the glare of shining gold. The stacks were at least a hundred tokens deep, so I took a handful and made my way to the bathhouse. My last shower had occurred a few days earlier, and, with no luxury time added in, I used at least five tokens to get the road off my body. I blew another half dozen basking in the heat and steam. The tokens were like poker chips; I was goin' all in. If any of you PCT hikers are out there reading this and you were one of the cool cats that left some tokens behind, I thank you. And to that one hiker who gifted a can of turkey chili, you are my hero. Oh, that chili was so good that night.

I met a few hikers in the camp when I returned. They were a couple from Austria and appeared to be about thirty-five years old or so. They were grungy and dirty and exhausted. They sat and talked as they peeled off clothes to reveal grime and dirt and trail deep in the crevices of their skin and feet. Their hair was a mess, and their clothes were near disposable at that point. Before my walk, I probably would have gagged at the sight and smell, but all I could do was smile and appreciate it. I wanted to be dirty and smelly like them again. I felt rather wimpy for having taken a twenty-minute shower earlier. But that passed rather quickly when I showed them the shower token stash and watched two of the biggest smiles I'd ever seen spread across their faces. Even after they grabbed a good handful, there were still dozens and dozens of tokens for the next folks coming through. I ventured to guess that the park rangers probably kept it well stocked. They returned from the showers looking and smelling fresh and carried with them soaking clothes that they had hand washed. After getting comfy, they pulled out some semi-cold beers, and we traded stories from the trail and the road. I wanted to hear about their journey, and they wanted to hear about mine. The shifting stories from road to trail would have been an interesting side by side story to write.

After a few hours, they got up from the bench and started to put their now dry clothes back in their packs. They announced they were leaving and not staying the night. I was confused and also a little bit sad. They had to get another five or so miles in because the following day had a specific destination with some steep inclines, and they needed to get a little closer that night, or they wouldn't be able to make it. We said goodbye, promised to stay in touch, and off they went into the woods. I almost left Alexa behind and followed them. I could disappear into those woods, forget about Annie, forget about money and, I don't know, build a cabin and live on the land. Because I know how to do all that shit, right? I slept alone that night. Human alone, but not animal alone. I had a late-night rendezvous with a curious deer that found the scent of my tent somewhat attractive. I laid in absolute silence with my arms tight around Wink to keep him calm as I peeked through the mesh and spied on my visitor. Just as we were getting comfy together, Wink let loose a furious frenzy of barks that made my guest feel unwelcomed. We were alone again, and I told him to stop being such a bully.

July was winding down as I made my way through Redding, the hottest city in California. It was several digits higher than the one-hundred mark for most of my days and nights. Walking was hard, Wink was exhausted, water was never enough, and my daily miles crept lower and lower. On one particular day, Mother Nature, stupidity and one giant asshole nearly killed us.

LOST IN DEHYDRATION

MILES WALKED: 2,481

The highways that run north-south in California are forbidden to pedestrians, and they are well patrolled. There aren't many frontage roads like bigger towns have, and the only way to get through that part of the state is to head east or west a mile or so to a parallel road that, for the most part, are not paved. These roads are well-traveled by field trucks and tractors and, south of Redding, have only scattered homes or buildings. The land was well-protected farmland and finding what I considered to be safe places to camp was a challenge, so finding cheap interstate motels became my daily mission. I stayed in one such place in a town called Cottonwood and, the following morning made my way a mile back out to the side road and started to head south again. It was supposed to be a twenty-one-mile day, and it was well over one-hundred degrees by 10 a.m. My phone rang at mile thirteen. It was my mom.

Mom: "I think you're going the wrong way."

Me: "Not possible, Mom. There's only one road out here, and I've been on it for a long time."

Mom: "I don't know, Tommy. You might want to check your GPS. You're not headed south; you're headed west back towards the interstate."

She was crazy. There was no way I had made a turn westbound. I hadn't seen any turns anywhere. I had crossed over some railroad tracks, but that was it. I fired up my GPS, and whadda you know, she was right. How the hell had that happened?

Me: "Dammit, Mom. I gotta call you back. I need to figure this out."

Wink: *"Way to go, genius."*

After careful review, I saw my mistake. When I had crossed the tracks, the road curved a little left but, right next to the tracks, was my road, the one I was supposed to stay on, but it was narrow and less traveled, and I didn't see it. I was heading northwest towards the interstate. I was two and a half miles off course with nothing near me. If I stayed moving forward, I would hit the interstate in a few miles and be stuck. I guessed I could have turned around and backtracked thirteen miles to the motel but, no, that was not happening. So, I decided to get back on course. I was getting a little worried because we were scorching hot. Scorching. And my twenty-one-mile day was turning into a twenty-six, and, in that heat, I was not happy about it.

Worry of my additional miles was completely trumped with absolute fear when I realized how low I was on water. I had only a few pints left and at least eight miles before civilization. I was literally alone, baking in an earthen oven, without enough water to keep Wink and me alive. I sat under a tree and cursed myself for screwing up so horribly. Bad water management in the worst possible conditions and even worse navigation. I took a sip, gave a sip to Wink, settled my nerves, and walked. A few miles in, I found a house, and what played out there crushed my hope for humanity if only for a moment.

I rolled Alexa and Wink up the driveway of the only place I had seen standing for miles. Near the garage were a few young guys getting stuff out of a car. One of the guys who hadn't seen me yet made his way into the house. I called out to the other.

Me "Excuse me? Sorry. I'm walking to Red Bluff, and I'm low on water. Mind if I fill up my bottles from your hose?"

The hose, by the way, was ten feet away, connected to a spigot, and coiled up next to the house.

Asshole: "No, you can't."

Me: "What? I just need some water. You have a hose right there!"

Asshole: "This is private property, and I can't let you be here without a badge."

To this day, I have no idea what he meant by the need for a badge. I would've thought that a piece of crap redneck like him would not be so inviting to the police, but that's what he said.

Me: "Dude, it's over a hundred degrees, and I'm walking. The next town is eight miles away. Are you seriously denying me water?"

Asshole: "Yeah, get off my property."

I couldn't believe it. I was seriously shocked and thought maybe he was kidding. I stood there for a second, waiting for him to say, "Dude, I'm just fucking with you! Of course, you can have some water" because that's what 99.9% of normal, caring, compassionate, intelligent people would do. I guess if you're the .1% Neanderthal piece of crap like him, you let a guy and his dog walk to their death.

I turned and walked down the driveway and felt his stare the whole way. I turned at the bottom, gave him a Lindsay Monroe greeting, and told him to fuck off. I didn't even care if he shot me; I was probably going to die anyway.

Within a mile, I was completely out of water and parked under a tree. It was the first time on my walk where I was genuinely fearful that the earth was going to kill me. I knew I couldn't walk seven more miles without water. Even if I waited until the sun went down, it would still be in the nineties. Wink was panting and decided it was a good time to share his feelings about our situation.

Wink: *"Uh, why didn't you pack more water?"*

Me: "I know. I know. I'm sorry. I thought we had enough."

WALKER TIP
WATER, FOOD, REST

WATER - far more critical than food and you must NEVER underestimate your needs, or you will die. I don't want to sound dramatic but it's true. Although this is a book of fiction, the part you just read about the heat, running out of water and being denied by that guy in Cottonwood, know that that happened to me in real life and I almost died. The weight is worth it. Carry it. I also used Nuun electrolyte tablets. You will burn through fluids and you must replace those cute little electrolytes. Although I never needed it, bring a way to purify water. Tablets, pump or a LifeStraw, it's worth having if you need it.

FOOD - You will require far more calories than you are used to eating. You will eat constantly, while you're walking, sitting, and, for me, many times in the middle of the night. Top ramen, beef jerky, tuna pouches, trail mix, protein bars, instant oatmeal, dried fruit, almonds. Those were my daily staples. I hardly ever cooked the ramen or oatmeal. I bought a pint of Talenti gelato at the grocery store and devoured it. I then used that little plastic jar to cold soak both the ramen and oatmeal. It's easy. For the ramen, break it up and put it in the jar with the seasonings and enough water to fill. Shake it up and walk for thirty minutes. Have a seat, shake again and voila! You have perfectly "cooked" top ramen. Same process for oatmeal but measure the liquid to what the packet recommends. When you can get your hands on fresh fruit or vegetables, eat a ton of them. They're heavy to carry but you will miss them on long stretches where they just don't exist or in towns where fresh produce will seem to be illegal.

REST - In the south, go to church for a good seat. They almost always have steps, awnings, and, if you're lucky, a playground area out back that will most likely have benches. Just know that you will encounter churchgoers on Sundays and Wednesdays so appear friendly or avoid loitering around God's house on those days, especially near the playgrounds. Better yet, if you're willing to carry an extra pound, buy an ultralight folding chair. I had a Helinox Chair Zero. I found it used for $20.

Wink: *"I'm glad you're not paid to think. You'd be broke."*

Me: "I am broke."

Wink: *"See? So, what are you going to do?"*

Me: "I don't know, dog! Dig a well? Shit, I don't know, leave me alone."

I hugged him. He didn't mean to hurt my feelings; he was just saying what any dog would in that predicament. But he was right. I had no reception, I couldn't call for help, and there was no way, not yet anyway, that I was pushing the SOS button on my GPS device for some water. I wasn't dying yet. As we sat in the blistering hot shade contemplating how agonizingly slow and miserable it would be to die under that tree, I saw a puff of dust come up off the road far in the distance. I watched as the puff moved closer and knew there was a car coming. I jumped up, clicked Wink to Alexa so he could stay in the shade, and made my way out to the middle of the road.

A little black car was headed towards me, bouncing along the dirt road. I waved my arms and stood dead center; the car was either going to stop or run me over. I noticed it slowing and inched my way to the side as it made its way to a stop next to me. The driver, a guy barely in his twenties, rolled down the window.

Driver: "What in the hell are you doin' way out here?"

Me: "Walking to Red Bluff. Thanks for stopping. How far is it to town or where I can get some water? We're stranded out here, and I've run out."

Driver: "It's your lucky day, man. I have a ton."

He reached into the back seat where there was a big cooler full of cold bottles of water.

Driver: "I'm headed to an event. Here, take a few."

I couldn't believe my luck. He handed me two large quart bottles of ice-cold water as I thanked him profusely and watched as he drove away. I'm not sure what would have happened if he hadn't come by. Maybe another person would have driven down that road or maybe not. I had enough water to get me to town, it was cold, and that's all I cared about. Not that I cared or that it mattered but I was curious what kind of event that kid was headed to out there in the middle of nowhere and why on earth wasn't he on the interstate? For a moment, I allowed myself not to hate that kid back at the house that denied me an hour earlier. If I wasn't on foot, in that heat and, given my experience of the last few months, I know I would have gone back and killed him. I kept telling myself that he'll get his someday, and that was just enough to get me by.

Or, maybe I'd rent a car in Red Bluff and head on back after nightfall. I didn't do that. I couldn't because I was busy killing somebody else.

MY OLD LAW SCHOOL BUDDY

RED BLUFF, CA

40° 10' 57.7" N

122° 14' 00.2" W

MILES WALKED: 2,496

When I rolled into Red Bluff, I made my way to a motel where I'd booked a room. I needed to get out of the elements, into a cool shower and soft bed. I had walked nearly twenty-five miles in intense heat, and Wink and I were both in horrible shape. I needed to cool him down as well. When we got to the motel, the guy at the front desk was a thirty or so year old self-absorbed craphead who barely looked up from his cell phone when I walked in. If you could have seen me, you would know that I looked pretty bad. He eyed me and glanced out the window where he saw Alexa and Wink.

Craphead: "Is that your dog and...cart? What the hell is that thing?"

Me: "Yes, it's actually a stroller with my gear in it."

Craphead: "No, I don't think so. You can't roll that thing into our rooms. You'll mess up the floor. Either leave it in your car or leave it outside."

Me: "I don't have a car and it has everything I own in it so I can't leave it outside."

310

I heard him clicking away on his keyboard.

Craphead: "Well then you can't stay here. I just canceled your reservation."

Me: "What? I just walked twenty-five miles in this heat and I've already paid for my room. I'll collapse my cart, carry it in and everything will be fine. I've stayed at dozens of motels, and my cart has never damaged anything."

Craphead: "You'll get your refund in about ten days from the app you booked it through. You can leave now."

Me: "You're a real piece of shit, you know that? You better hope I don't run into you outside this dump you call a motel."

Controlling my anger but giving him my best intimidating look, I held the stare for a minute, turned around, slammed the door hard enough that the glass should have shattered and sat down next to Wink. Two times in one day I had encountered horrible human beings who had zero regard for other humans. Both were guys under thirty years old in Northern California. What the hell was happening to our society? Was the age thing a coincidence, or was this how that generation is growing up? I guess I have to give huge credit to the kid in the black car that saved my ass. I'll walk back my judgment of the younger folk, but just a little bit.

I sat under the carport outside the motel doors to calm my nerves before firing up my phone to find a new place to stay. While zooming around on Google Maps, I heard the doorbell chime, and the guy walked out to confront me.

Craphead: "You can't sit here."

Me: "Listen, asshole, I'm looking for a new motel. It'll only take a minute so back off."

Craphead: "You have one minute, then I'm calling the cops."

Me: "What's your problem with me, anyway?"

Craphead: "My family doesn't like homeless people living here."

Wink: "We're not homeless, asshole!"

Me: "I'm not homeless."

Craphead: "Of course, you're not. Just leave, alright?"

My rage was beginning to boil over. Wink was sensing the hostility between us and took a hard position in front of me with his ears back and chest flexed. The guy looked down with a bit of fear and quickly retreated to his office. I contemplated gutting him right there and shoving his phone straight down his throat but thought better of it. Too many cameras, too much rage, and I would certainly go to prison for this one. So, I got up and walked away. Good job, Thomas. Way to turn the other cheek.

Wink: *"Yay for you. I was ready to take that guy out, but I didn't feel like going to dog jail tonight."*

I found a place about a mile away that was more than happy to take us; it was a nice little motel with excellent management. Next door was a Denny's, and I had my sights set on a nice big juicy burger with fries. I was hoping that this was one of those cool Denny's that served beer. I showered, fed Wink, put down a huge bowl of water, and left him in the room. I needed a moment alone to decompress and try to fully absorb what would turn out to be the worst walking day of my journey.

Denny's made the best burger I had ever tasted. Or maybe I was just starving. It was hot and juicy and loaded with bacon, cheese, and avocado. I don't think it lasted more than three minutes on my plate. I devoured the fries and a few glasses of water and, start to finish, wolfed down my dinner in eight minutes flat. I asked the server where I could get a cold beer within walking distance, and she recommended a cool little spot just a few blocks away. I paid my check and made my way there.

As I approached the curved driveway and parking lot to E's Locker Room, which sat right on the Sacramento River, a small, beat-up red truck flew around me, barely missing my arm and barreled into a parking space. One step further, and I would have been toast. What the hell was going on today? Was the heat getting to people and making them aggressive and unkind? I watched the driver jump out of his truck and head to the entrance. I smiled with great anticipation. It was Craphead and he was alone. He had seen me sweating profusely a few hours earlier wearing shorts, a dirty shirt, sunglasses, and a wide-brimmed hat. I was now cleaned up in long hiking pants, no hat, no dog, and no cart. No chance he would recognize me.

I strolled into the bar like I owned the place and had been there a thousand times. It was pretty busy with happy people and happy hour winding down. I didn't look around, and nobody paid me any attention, which was fine by me. I went straight to the bar, ordered a beer, and sat down two seats away from Craphead. He had his back to me and was talking and flirting with a young woman. I momentarily reminisced about this exact scenario back in Arkansas, and a wave of both sadness and power surged through me. I had avenged Lindsay's death without harming a soul. Tonight was for me, and it could have a very different outcome. I was ill-prepared for a confrontation as I was not expecting to be in this situation. I had no weapons and no Wink. If something were to happen, I was going to have to dig deep and circle the courage wagons. If anything was learned from walking for months on end it was that I was a lot tougher than I thought.

I casually sat, sipped my drink, looked at my phone, and listened to him make his moves. Craphead was not a discrete talker, and learning the story was quite easy. He had met this girl recently, and it seems he had asked her out before, and maybe this was a first date, or he was still trying to get her out. Despite his arrogance with me at the motel, he came across as a little bit desperate, asking her several times if he would get to see her again. He lied about his career, claiming he was an attorney who helped people in need. At first, I gave him the benefit of the doubt and that perhaps he was helping the family out at the motel. Maybe he was an attorney, but no way he did so to help people in need. Excellent work, Mr. Compassionate Samaritan. But then he lied and said he was late arriving because he had spent his day with a family who had lost their home to foreclosure and was helping them sue their lending institution. What a sack of crap liar. This was clearly just an attempt to get this girl into bed because there was no way he was going to be able to back that story up long term. I hated this guy more now than I did a few hours earlier.

I wanted to see if he would recognize me, so I leaned into his space and pretended to reach for a napkin off a stack that was placed in front of him. The woman looked at me, and I winked at her. She smiled a bit, which caused him to turn and check out the guy who stole a moment of interest from his target. My face was only a few inches from his as I encroached well into strange human comfort zone, and we caught eyes. There was a moment of possible recognition, but I think he was more concerned about someone moving in on his girl than he was worried about the homeless guy he kicked out of his motel.

Me: "Excuse me, just grabbing a napkin."

Craphead: "Yeah, I can see that."

Me: "Is that ok with you?"

Craphead: "Yeah, just do it."

I grabbed my napkin, pulled back, and gave him a 'Don't I know you from somewhere?' look.

Me: "You look familiar. Do we know each other?"

I glanced over at the woman. She had an inquisitive look on her face as Craphead showed signs of worry. Not a look that would say he possibly recognized me but one that showed he was afraid his cover was about to be blown.

Craphead: "No, we don't; I'm sure I would remember you."

Annoyed at my intrusion, Craphead turned his entire body towards the woman and sat up extra high on his seat to create the biggest wall he could with his back. I glanced over his shoulder to the woman who was focused on me, waiting for my reaction. I smiled, raised an eyebrow, and nodded. This got a slight smirk of approval, which must have infuriated him. Enjoying this quite a bit and wanting her to see what a phony ass-hole he was, I decided to keep going. I walked around, so I was standing between them with my beer in hand.

Me: "I think I remember. Are you an attorney?"

Craphead: "Yes, I am, but I'm kinda busy, so…"

Me: "Sorry, I just love it when I know I know somebody, but I can't figure it out, then I do figure it out, and I have to let them know. I knew it was something to do with law, but I can't put my finger on it. Where did you go to school?"

He looked at me then at the woman. I followed his gaze to her eyes, which begged for him to answer. She was enjoying this. I think she had already called bullshit on his lies, and maybe I was helping her out. We both noticed him squirm in his seat.

Craphead: "Listen, I'm quite certain we don't know each other from law school. I got my degree in Chicago."

Me: "Chicago? Me, too. What school? That must be it. Was it the University of Chicago?"

No way this moron would pull this out of his ass quickly enough to sound believable.

Craphead: "No, Illinois State."

Me: "Well, I must be wrong then. Maybe we met at some law thing in Chicago at some point. My name is Joshua, by the way. So, you're practicing out here now? I couldn't pass the California bar the first time, so I'm studying for it again. Well done, man."

Craphead was showing severe signs of desperation, and it was clear to the woman that he was in a tight spot, so she intervened.

Woman: "My name is Claudia, and this is Sean. Nice to meet you, Joshua. Sean was telling me about his career and the people he helps, weren't you, Sean?"

Me: "Pleasure to meet you, Claudia, and see you again, Sean. Listen, sorry I barged in on your date. Listen, Sean, what's your last name? Mine is Owen. Maybe we can grab a beer sometime and figure it out. I'm new in town and would love to meet some people."

Sean: "O'Grady. I know, I don't look Irish, that was my dad. I look more like my mom's side of the family. Now, if you don't mind?"

Me: "Yes, of course. Sean O'Grady. All good. Sorry to bother. Claudia, nice to meet you."

I made my way back to my spot at the bar and Googled Illinois State

University, searched their list of academics, studied the location, and knew all I needed to know. I couldn't have been happier. I ordered another beer, paid my tab, and thought about what I wanted to do with that information. As I drank, I occasionally glanced over at Claudia and made eye contact a few times. Then I did it one too many times. Sean turned around and, suddenly, after seeing me through hateful eyes, he made the connection. With a shitty, condescending grin on his face, he laughed and nodded.

Sean: "Now, I remember you."

Me: "There you go. I knew you'd figure it out. Why don't you tell Claudia how we know each other."

That stopped him. He knew he screwed up. Any mention of kicking me out of the motel would completely blow both his lawyer and compassionate Samaritan covers. He now had to decide what was more important: getting this girl into bed or confronting me. He chose the former and did a reasonably good job of backpedaling.

Sean: "It was Chicago. Law school conference or something. I can't remember much, but I do recall grabbing a drink together at a beer cart. Did you mention something about a dog? I remember the cart and the dog, but that's about it."

His eyes were begging me to agree with him and move along.

Me: "No, that's not it. I know exactly where it was that we met."

His begging, pleading eyes were priceless. I probably could have negotiated a year's worth of free meals, the winning lottery numbers, and his firstborn at that point. He was desperate for me not to fuck up his night. I didn't care; this was too much fun.

Me: "It was just three hours ago. Come on; you don't remember? You were working behind the counter at that shithole motel at the end of town. I'm walking across America with my dog, we had a reservation, and you kicked me out because you thought I was homeless. In fact, you said your family didn't want homeless people staying at their motel."

Claudia: "Sean, is that true?"

Sean: "Listen, asshole, I don't know you, and you're full of shit. Leave us alone."

Me: "Fair enough. Maybe I'm wrong. I'll leave you be, counselor."

I turned to leave, but not quite ready to end this little game, turned around one more time, called his name and waited for both of them to look over.

Me: "Hey, Sean. Illinois State doesn't have a law program, and it's a good two-and-a-half-hour drive from Chicago. Oh, and Claudia? You should swing by the Classic Inn and see what Sean really does for a living. Have a nice night."

I couldn't help but smile as I walked towards the door. What an asshole. No way he was getting that girl into bed. His body blindsided me, and I hit the wall with devastating force. For a little guy, he had a damn good punch. His fist had come from my rear right and landed hard on my jaw, and his body propelled into mine. My already pained face was planted against the wall, and blood was pouring from my mouth. I was on the floor with my head jacked up against the wall as his fists pummeled down on my face and ribs. It seemed like forever passed before someone pulled him off me.

I was a mess. Blood was soaked through the top of my shirt, my lips looked like I just had ten rounds of collagen injections, my eye was nearly swollen shut, and my ribs hurt like hell. But I was grinning from ear to ear as I stood and watched Claudia slap Sean across the face and storm out the door. Sean was being held back by a few big guys, and I stood tall and stared him down.

Sean: "Your lucky I didn't kill you, motherfucker!"

Me: "Perhaps."

I moved closer, so we were just a foot apart. I leaned in and gestured that I wanted to tell him a secret. I put my hands up to show I was not going to harm him, lowered my head, and gave him a quiet, whispering warning in his ear.

Me: "You'd be wise not to fuck with me."

I pulled back and spoke in a normal voice.

Me: "I know everything about you, Sean O'Grady."

I smiled, winked with my good eye, and strolled out.

Battling through intense pain in my ribs and face, I quickly walked the few blocks back to my motel. I could barely see and was fumbling with my room key when I heard a car scream into the parking lot and pull to a stop. With a quick glance as my door finally opened, I saw the red truck at the end of the lot, and the driver's door swing open. I casually stepped into my room and latched the deadbolt. At that point, I had no desire for further confrontation. I was beaten down and easy prey. Wink immediately sensed a problem as I carefully bent down to kiss him. He wanted to lick away the pain from my face, but I held him steady to avoid his need to provide medical aid. In the mirror, I saw a decent sized cut on my right cheekbone below my eye, and my lip was split open. Both cuts had begun the healing process already, and the bleeding had nearly stopped. I knew the minute I washed the dried blood from the openings, they would flow again but knew I had to do it at some point. I went to the blinds and peeked through in hopes of seeing Sean and, sure enough, he was pacing near his truck, having what appeared to be a fairly heated conversation on his cell phone. I wondered if it was Claudia and, if so, if he was telling her that he'd followed me to my motel and for what reason.

I grabbed my knife from its sheath and went back to the sink to start wiping the blood off my face. I wanted to look presentable for my visitor if he chose to come knocking. I cleaned up pretty well. No knock had come in the past ten minutes, and I began to think he'd decided that wasting any more time on me was poor decision making. After I got my face in somewhat decent order, I went back to the blinds and peeked out to find his truck was gone. I downed four Advil, a quart of water, and took a hot shower. The searing heat soothed my skin, where bruises were forming on my back and sides above my ribs. There was no swelling, so I felt pretty confident that nothing was broken. Then again, I wasn't a doctor. What the hell did I know about broken ribs and what they look like? I carefully washed, rinsed, and toweled dry. Stepping into the room near the bed, I was startled by a sudden pound on the door. Really? Now? I was clean and naked. I guess this is how it's gonna go. Maybe answering the door in the buff was a good way to throw him off guard.

I walked to the door and saw Sean through the peephole. I grabbed my knife and held it tight, sticking up and out above my right thumb. I dropped the towel and, keeping my knife hand hidden behind the door, I swung it open for all the world to see. Sean, naturally, was stunned, and my plan to shock him worked perfectly.

Sean: "What the fuck?"

Me: "What are you doing here, Sean? Wanna come in?"

Sean: "Screw you, asshole!"

Sean very suddenly charged through the door with his hands up and aimed for my throat. My knife met his skin, and I shoved it straight into his heart and jerked it sideways. Our eyes locked, mine full of anger and hatred, his swelled with shock and tears as I watched his dark soul vacate his body. He was dead before he hit the ground, and one of us was gonna need another shower. I dropped the bloody blade to the floor, picked up my phone and called 9-1-1.

9-1-1 Operator: "9-1-1 what's your emergency?"

Me: "Hello. I'm in room 174 at the Comfy Inn. A man broke into my room and attacked me, and I killed him. It's a bloody mess. I'm sitting on the bed, unarmed, awaiting your arrival."

9-1-1 Operator: "What is your name, sir?"

Me: "Thomas."

9-1-1 Operator: "Sir, did you say a man broke into your room and you killed him?"

Me: "Yes."

9-1-1 Operator: "Officers are on their way."

Me: "Thank you."

9-1-1 Operator: "Why did you say you killed him?"

Me: "He knocked on my door, I answered, and he charged in after me. So, I stabbed him."

9-1-1 Operator: "Why did he charge you, sir?"

Me: "It was either because we got into a fight earlier at E's, or it was because I was naked."

9-1-1 Operator: "Why were you naked answering the door?"

Me: "I thought it would throw him off."

There was a long pause.

9-1-1 Operator: "Sir, do not touch the body and do not leave the scene. Do not approach the officers when they arrive. Please have your hands visible. Officers will be there momentarily."

Yeah, yeah. I know the drill. Last time I heard that order, however, I was under a bridge three thousand miles away eating cold chili and Ritz crackers looking at a dead yellow man.

Me: "Can I get dressed? I'm still naked."

9-1-1 Operator: "Yes. Please do. I want you to stay on the phone until officers arrive. They will know you're on the phone with me. When they arrive, they'll ask you to put the phone down. Please keep your hands visible at all times."

Me: "Understood."

9-1-1 Operator: "Where is the weapon now?"

Me: "On the floor, next to the body."

After throwing on some shorts, shirt, and socks (I walk barefoot on cheap motel carpet as little as possible), I sat on the edge of the bed with my hands in full view, phone near my ear. I didn't need some trigger-happy cop thinking I had a weapon. I had locked Wink in the bathroom for his safety and, from the sounds coming from behind the door, he was not liking that. A lot of cops arrived really quick.

RITA THE SHRINK

ystanders were forming a collective huddle not far away with their cell phone cameras no doubt live streaming the action. The sirens broke the crowd, and several squad cars came to a screeching halt just outside. The cops more than likely saw the bloody body long before they entered. It's hard to miss a wide-open motel room door and a lifeless body straddling the jam. I knew they would approach with weapons drawn, and my hands were already way up in the air.

Officer: "Sir, please set the phone down on the bed, slowly go down to your knees and put your hands behind your head."

Dammit. Bare skin on the carpet. I should have thought of that and put on hiking pants instead of shorts.

Me: "Yes, officer. Sir, I am the victim here. I called 9-1-1 after being attacked by this man. I mean you no harm, and I'm not holding any weapons. My dog is in the bathroom, and he's very anxious. He witnessed the attack, and he's one hell of a protection animal, so please be careful. I can help you with him when you're ready. He's friendly, but he's also worried."

Officer: "We'll get to the dog in a minute. Thanks for the heads up. As a matter of safety and policy, I'm going to cuff you and get you back up on the bed. Then we'll talk about what happened here."

Me: "Of course. No offense taken. I know you can't see it on this beautiful burgundy carpet, but there's blood everywhere, so watch your step."

One officer carefully entered the room and surveyed the path to me while two others held their positions at the door, guns pointed directly at my chest.

Officer: "Instead of coming to you and contaminating this space, I'm going to ask you to slowly get up and walk as far around the body as possible. We'll get you outside and talk there."

Me: "Can I put some shoes on? I don't want to wear blood-soaked socks all night. They're right there on the floor. Just a pair of running shoes."

Officer: "Yes, but please move slowly and keep your hands visible."

I got up and went to my shoes. I could feel the muzzle of his gun trained on me and prayed like crazy that he was having a good day and understood the situation. One flinch, and I was dead. I kicked the shoes out to the space where he could see them and sat down on the edge of the bed, slid them on, and laced them up. Hands in the air, I shuffled past the side of the bed, around the body, and out the door where I was quickly cuffed and asked to sit on the curb. It was still hot as hell outside, and I positioned myself as best as I could so the least number of bystanders could see me as possible. I wondered how many people were watching this live on Facebook.

Ten hours earlier, I was a lost man with a dog on a dirt road. An hour later, I believed I was going to die of heat stroke or dehydration. I was kicked out of a motel for being homeless. I flirted, purposely, with the wrong girl to antagonize the asshole from the motel who, in turn, beat the crap out of me. Now that guy's dead body was straddling a door jamb five feet away, and I was sitting on a curb in handcuffs — what a day.

The scene had been taped off, and cops were everywhere. A few news vans had arrived, and cameras were jockeying for position. I called over to one of the police officers who appeared to be in charge.

Me: "Excuse me, officer?"

Officer: "We'll get to you in a minute."

Me: "I know, I just have two favors to ask. I'm sorry, I know you're busy, but I think you'll understand."

He walked over and stooped down.

Me: "Listen, I know you have a job to do, and I respect that. I really do. And I will cooperate fully. I just ask if there's any way I can get my dog out of the bathroom and maybe sit somewhere away from all these cameras. I know you don't know this now, but I really am the victim of this assault, but I'm sitting here in cuffs with all these cameras rolling, looking like a goddamn murderer. Please, is there anywhere else I can sit with a touch of privacy and dignity? I'm gonna have to walk away from this, but every second they're showing me sitting here in cuffs is going to follow me for the rest of my life."

Officer: "I understand. Let me see what I can do."

And he did. He went to the motel manager and was back in a few minutes.

Officer: "Alright, I'm going to uncuff you, and we'll go in and get your dog. I'll then lead you to the manager's office and have an officer stand guard. The cameras will see that you're walking uncuffed and with your dog, and hopefully, that will mitigate any damage. I'll head down to the office in a bit, and we'll start our talk. I need a few more minutes here after I take you down there. Is that a deal?"

Me: "Absolutely."

With that, he did what he said he would. Wink was a basket case, and I had to carry him out so he wouldn't trample all over the blood and stop to sniff the body. Once outside, I realized how big the circus had become, and all I could think was how soon it would be before Annie saw this on the news.

After fifteen minutes in the office, the lead officer returned with a very attractive woman in her forties. She dressed and looked like all the good-looking female detectives that appear in all the Netflix Original Series I had been glued to for months. I always wondered why they made male detectives so obviously cop looking and females so hot. Hollywood. Whatever. I had been on my best behavior, and I think they trusted that I wasn't a danger.

Officer: "Mr. Curran, this is detective Fowler from our homicide division. She's going to take over from here."

Detective Fowler: "Good evening, Mr. Curran."

Me: "Not really. Look at me. But thanks. Nice to meet you."

Detective Fowler: "Let's get to it. What's the story with the dead guy in your room?"

Me: "I've been walking across America for the past six months or so. I came down from Oregon, heading to Newport Beach, where I live. Earlier today, I tried to check in to the Classic Inn, where I had made a reservation. The dead guy, who told me his name was Sean O'Grady, wouldn't let me check in because he thought I was homeless. I'm not homeless, but I can see why he thought that given my cart and my dog, and I probably smelled pretty badly because I had walked twenty-six miles in today's heat. Anyway, we argued a bit, but I left and found this motel. The people here were cool, unlike Sean. I showered up, left my dog in the room, and went out for a bite and a beer.

"I was at the bar at E's something or other down the road, and he happened to be there next to me talking to a girl, but he didn't recognize me. He was lying to her and giving her a bullshit story trying to get her into bed or something, so I fucked with him a little bit and blew his cover. He was claiming to be some bigshot attorney who, ironically, helped people in desperate need. As I walked out of the bar, he jumped me from behind and beat the shit out of me. That's where all this mess on my face came from. There had to be a few dozen people who saw him attack me from behind, and I did not fight back. Someone pulled him off, I got up and walked out. When I got to my room, I noticed that he had followed me here in the little red truck you'll find outside. I took a shower, cleaned up a bit, and figured he'd left. As I settled in for the night, he knocked on my door, and, when I saw him through the peephole, I grabbed my knife for protection. I probably shouldn't have opened the door, but I did, and he charged me and took the knife in his heart. It happened suddenly. I didn't try to stab him, but the knife was in my hand, and it just happened. I dropped the knife, called you immediately, and didn't move until you arrived."

Detective Fowler: "Do you have any alibi that can corroborate that you walked into town today?"

Me: "Yes, I can hand over a few assholes out on a dirt road, about eight miles out of town, whom I met earlier today. I asked them for some water, and they kicked me off their property. You can probably get some video from the Classic Inn that shows us meeting there then maybe some more of me checking in here a half hour or so later. I ate dinner, alone, at Denny's, then went to the bar. I'm quite certain that people will remember a guy with a cart and a dog strolling into town, but you'd have to hunt them down. I'm kinda hard to miss."

Detective Fowler: "Can I ask why you're walking across America?"

Me: "I don't know, I guess I just needed time to think. Maybe I'll write a book, and you can read the full version. It's pretty benign, really. Well, it's not, but it's irrelevant to tonight's situation."

Detective Fowler: "Mr. Curran. There's blood splatter everywhere. Yet, I look at you, and your clothes are clean. Did you change after you killed Mr. O'Grady?"

Me: "Oh, yeah, I forgot that part. I answered the door naked. There's a lot of blood on my body."

Detective Fowler: "Naked?"

Me: "Shock and awe. I don't know. I knew it was him; I didn't know what he was going to do, so I figured throwing him for a loop might make him laugh or reconsider whatever bad thoughts he was having. He'd already beaten the crap out of me, I was sore and tired and just wanted to eat some peanut butter cups and go to sleep."

Detective Fowler: "Why did you answer the door? Why didn't you call us instead?"

Me: "Damn good question. I'm out here walking to experience life like I never have before. I'm opening myself up to everything regardless of consequence. I've never lived like that. When you force yourself to be vulnerable and brave, you learn a lot about your values and boundaries. The guardrails get wider and wider, and the world you find comfort within expands greatly. I've done things on this journey I never knew I could do. For example, a year ago, I never would have opened that door. I would have cowered behind it. Tonight, I approached him naked as a newborn baby willing to accept anything. It might not be the smartest approach, but it is incredibly liberating."

Detective Fowler: "So you don't believe you provoked him in any way?"

Me: "Absolutely not. I didn't allow him to lie to an innocent woman, and he had a fragile ego. If we can't call people to the carpet for their bullshit, we all become victims, and people like Sean will always win. I allowed him to take his anger out on me, and I left. He decided to follow me here, and he decided to confront me. Either one of us could be lying on that disgusting carpet with a hole in his heart. He chose to put himself between a bullet and a target. I am not happy that I killed a man tonight, but I will not apologize for it, either."

Detective Fowler: "Interesting way of putting it, Mr. Curran."

Me: "Would it surprise you if I told you this wasn't the first time this has happened in the past few months?"

Detective Fowler: "Is killing people becoming a habit for you?"

Me: "Not a habit. No. But it has happened before."

I spent the next half hour filling Detective Fowler in on the details of Annie, Jesse, my journey, the four men before Sean who had died, and, of course, about Lindsay. She sat in silence, not even taking notes, as I cried through my Arkansas story. There was a long moment of despair as I closed my eyes and allowed months of pain to pour from them.

I was nearing my rock bottom. I hadn't processed what I had been through until this woman sat in front of me, without judgment, and allowed me to lose my shit. I had never wanted home more. I wanted my bed, my friends, my family, and my restaurant back. I wanted to feel consequential and special. I wanted someone to touch me. God, I wanted someone to hug me. I was hundreds of miles away from any soul I knew that could hug me. I slid off the chair and hugged Wink. I couldn't stop the wave and had to succumb to its need to crash down upon me.

Detective Fowler patiently waited until I was done and composed. I got back up and sat down.

Me: "I'm sorry. My reality just hit pretty hard."

Detective Fowler: "It's ok. Mr. Curran, I'm going to leave you for a few minutes and talk to the other officers. You won't be alone here. Please, don't try to leave. Just stay put, ok?"

I looked at her with broken desperation.

Me: "Where would I go?"

It felt like hours had passed. I had moved over to a sofa and laid down with Wink on the floor next to me. I woke to a hand shaking my shoulder.

Detective Fowler: "Mr. Curran. Wake up, please."

Startled and momentarily confused, I slowly sat up, looked around, and reality settled back in.

Me: "I'm sorry. Everything that happened today must have wiped me out. I'm a mess and not feeling well."

Detective Fowler: "I understand. A few things are going to happen, and then I want you to meet somebody. First, a medic is going to check you out. We need to make sure you are physically ok even though you say you're feeling alright. I have to say, you don't look good. Your face is pretty beat up. He'll determine whether you need to go to the hospital. We also have a psychiatrist from the crisis center here who wants to talk to you for a few minutes. For the same reason the medic is going to check your body, she needs to check your brain and take a temperature of your mental well-being. Depending on her evaluation, we'll decide whether you need some attention."

Me: "OK. Who am I meeting after that?"

Detective Fowler: "There's a local family that helps battered women and homeless people in times of crisis. They've been following the news and drove over to offer assistance. I know you're not homeless and clear-ly not a battered woman, but they're good people who are known to us and, if we allow, they are willing to help. If the doctors approve, we'll introduce you to them and see if it's a good situation for all of you. We're going to need to keep you in town for a few days, and, rather than have you cooped up in a motel, they might be able to help. Do you understand everything I just said to you?"

Me: "Are you saying there are people in this town that are willing to help a guy with a dog who's just killed someone?"

Detective Fowler: "They're good people, Mr. Curran. They've seen bad stuff like this before."

Me: "Thank you. Send the doctors in."

After examining my face and applying a few butterfly bandages to the cuts, the medic removed my shirt to examine my ribs and concluded that there was heavy bruising but didn't believe there to be any broken bones. He told me to keep an eye on it for a few days, gave me some symptoms to look for, and told me to get to a hospital if I noticed any of them. He cleared me to go and sent in Doctor Rita Romero, a feisty, petite woman in her early fifties who was dressed nicely in very stylish *going out to dinner on a hot date* outfit. Considering the circumstances, the town I was in, and the time of day, it seemed like overkill. But, then again, there were cameras everywhere.

Dr. Romero: "Hello, Thomas. Can I call you Thomas?"

She had a familiar, comfortable voice and demeanor that immediately calmed my nerves. There was something about her, but I couldn't put my finger on it.

Me: "If I can call you Rita. I hate the formal approach."

Dr. Romero: "Of course. This is some pretty heavy stuff here."

She waved her hand around, and I was happily surprised by her light-hearted approach to emotional interrogation.

Me: "Yeah, you could say that."

Rita: "No, for reals. This is some crazy shit you've gone through. And Detective Fowler briefed me about the rest of your walk. I gotta say, I haven't seen this before, Thomas."

Then it hit me. I smiled.

Me: "I'm sorry. Has anyone ever compared you to Rosie Perez?"

Rita: "Has anyone ever compared you to Forrest Gump?"

Me: "Touché. I think I'm ok. I don't know. I'm so close to home, and I can't seem to shake all the shit off of this walk and get there without people messing with me. I think tonight just allowed it all to come crashing down. There's a dead guy out there. I did that. It's just sad, and I know it will haunt me forever. All of this will."

Rita: "My job is to determine whether I can let you walk away from here tonight, no pun intended, or check you in at the hospital for observation. How do you feel about that?"

Me: "I understand. Does this mean I'm not being charged with anything?"

Rita: "That's not my decision but, since you're sitting here with me, my gut says no. Detective Fowler will be back shortly to talk about the case itself. I'm just here to talk to you about you."

Me: "Is everything I tell you going to be replayed to the detective? I mean, do we have any room for privileged information?"

Rita: "That's a little tricky. I'm an independent doctor and consult for the police department. Anything you say to me regarding this case or that I feel might be related to this investigation will be shared in my assessment. However, if there's some stuff you want to talk about that may or may not be relevant to the case, I will determine whether it will be helpful in my decision making and whether the details need to be included in my report. I guess the best I can say is that you are free to tell me anything you want but, if I believe that what you tell me is relevant, I am required to share it. So, tread lightly if you're concerned."

Me: "OK. Well, I kinda need to get some stuff off my chest, and so I guess I'll just put it out there and see what happens. I think I hit a wall today and need to release some of my anxiety. You seem like a nice person, and this could take a while. You're dressed nicely, did I ruin plans you had for the evening?"

Rita: "Thank you, but, no, I'm one hundred percent here for you as long as you need me to be."

I sighed deeply, leaned back into the sofa, raised my eyes to meet hers, and allowed the words to free flow, unabridged, from my heart.

Me: "Rita, I've been hunting a killer. A murderer. A woman who ruined my life and was never caught. In doing so, I have become a killer. A different kind of killer than the one I'm hunting but a killer, nonetheless. I know you're aware of what's happened during my journey, but what you may not know is why I'm out here walking."

I spent nearly an hour, uninterrupted, telling the doctor all the details of Annie/Kennedy. I started with Jesse, my loss, my decision to walk, Johnny (but I called him Jack to protect him), my meetings with Jenny, Peggy Lee, and Lester. I offered my belief that Annie had killed her older brother and possibly the guy who disappeared from Monroe and the kid in Prineville. I told her of my desire to kill Charles in Arkansas and how that turn of events played out, my knowledge of Annie's real name, why I re-routed to Oregon, the Prineville Coffee murder, the blue Honda and, finally, showed her the pics that Annie had been sending me the past few weeks. I told her I believed that Annie was nearby and following me but wasn't sure of her intent for doing so. The only thing I left out was my attempt to communicate with Annie via her Instagram page. I needed to keep that line of communication open and untainted.

Rita: "Thomas, that is the most unreal story I have ever heard. I'm not even sure where to begin. Do you feel you're in imminent danger?"

Me: "Oddly, no, I don't. I've been walking these highways alone for so long and faced many challenges. Annie has been close enough to me in the past few weeks that if she wanted to hurt me, I think she would have done it by now. I've certainly offered her many opportunities where it would be easy. I don't know what her intention is."

Rita: "Besides the pictures, has she communicated with you?"
Me: "No."

I'm glad she didn't ask me if I'd communicated with her. Lying would have been tough to pull off.

Detective Fowler entered the room and motioned for Rita to follow her outside. I was exhausted and needed sleep desperately. I laid down on the sofa, closed my eyes, and rested my hand on Wink's back. A few minutes later, they came back in.

Detective Fowler: "Mr. Curran, here's the situation. The medics have cleared you on the condition that you keep a close eye on your ribs over the next few days. I know they've explained that to you. Dr. Romero, however, is concerned about your state of mind and would like to see you again tomorrow. I don't believe you are a threat to yourself or others, and I'm willing to release you, your dog, and your belongings, but only to the care of the family I had mentioned earlier. We will need to do a follow-up interview tomorrow at their home after Dr. Romero meets you, which will also happen there. If you agree to their care, I'm willing to let you go. This means you cannot leave their home, and you cannot leave town until I release you. Do you agree to all of these conditions?"

Me: "Yes, I agree, and will stay put."

The detective opened the door and motioned two people inside; two people who had no idea I was luring a murderer to their home.

GETTING MOORE

etective Fowler: "Mr. Curran, I'd like you to meet Mr. and Mrs. Moore. Dario and Julia live on a property about fifteen miles away. It's a nice, fairly secluded place up in Cottonwood. I think you said you walked through there."

Great. Cottonwood. Home of that prick who wouldn't give me water.

Me: "Oh, yeah, I know Cottonwood. Nice to meet you both. I can assure you I'm no threat to you or your family. This incident was horrible, but, as I hope you know by now, it was not perpetrated by me. I did nothing to that man except call him out for lying to an innocent girl. Maybe I should have just kept to my own business, but I can't change that now."

Dario: "We're not here to judge, just here to help if we can."

The Moore's loaded Alexa and Wink into their truck since I was pretty much useless, and we got on the highway headed back north to their beautiful home. We didn't speak much for the twenty minutes it took to get there. Julia asked what I liked to eat and drink, we had a conversation about how we hoped Wink would get along with their two dogs, and they told me a bit about their daughters, who both lived somewhat locally. It was late, and they knew I was exhausted. At their house I was shown to my room, I thanked them profusely, introduced Wink to their dogs and let them run around in the backyard and take care of business. I asked if he could sleep next to me on the floor in my room. They understood and allowed it that first night. Sleep came fast, and it was deep and long. Neither of us woke up until after nine the next morning.

My body felt like it had been dragged behind a freight train for a few miles. Sitting down to take care of morning business sent shots of pain through my ribs that nearly put me on the ground. After finally getting up off the toilet and performing other necessary morning bathroom chores, I followed my nose to the source of the smell of strong coffee and bacon. Julia was in the kitchen, cooking up a huge breakfast while Dario was out in the backyard. I let Wink out to play and gingerly sat down where a cup was waiting for me.

Me: "Good morning, Julia. Thank you for the coffee and for opening your home to me."

Julia: "Good morning to you. I hope you're hungry and no thanks needed. Dario and I have been through a lot of stuff in our lives, and we like helping those in need. Don't feel like you need to tell us anything or open up. We're just here to offer a roof, hot food, and a safe place until you're ready to leave."

Me: "Well, I appreciate it very much, and I'm sure my mother will, too. Which reminds me that I need to call her this morning. She tracks me on GPS and is probably wondering why I've backtracked and why I'm not walking today."

Julia: "Yes. Call your mother!"

So, I did.

Me: "Hey, Mom. How are you?"

Mom: "I'm doing ok. I was thinking about you. I looked at your GPS and was wondering what was going on with you today. Did you meet a girl and end up back in Cottonwood?"

Ah, my mom, she's such a joker.

Me: "Ha! Yeah, I wish that was the case. No, I had a pretty rough night, Mom, but I need you to know that I'm ok. So is Wink. But I'm going to be in Cottonwood for a while. I'll be staying with a nice couple named Dario and Julia Moore. I'll send you their info, so you have it."

Mom: "Tommy, what happened?"

I told her everything that had happened since she had called me when

I was lost. In telling the story, I couldn't believe everything that had happened in one day. I could hear her crying and assured her that I was ok, that I wasn't in trouble, and that she could check on me as often as she needed.

Mom: "Do you want me to drive down there? It's about a ten-hour drive."

Me: "No, no. It's ok. I have a few interviews with the detectives and a shrink today and, assuming all is cool, I'll take off as soon as I can push my cart. The Moore's have offered their home for as long as I need it."

Mom: "I'm so proud of you, son. This has been an amazing journey, and you're almost home. Truly remarkable."

If only she knew. Maybe someday I will tell her about everything else that had happened. I had to tell her about the previous night because it was all over the news and she didn't live too far away. I wouldn't want her to hear it that way.

Me: "Thanks, Mom. I love you. Don't worry, ok? I know you will but don't. I'll call you later."

We hung up, and I ate six pancakes, four strips of bacon, two eggs, and downed at least three cups of coffee. I thought about asking Julia to follow me for the rest of my walk and cook like that for me every day.

Detective Fowler called shortly after breakfast, saying they were on their way to the house. As I was on the phone, Julia came from a back room with all of my clothes washed and folded in perfect little stacks. I thanked her, not knowing how she had gotten them without me noticing. It was nice to have super clean smelling gear again. It had been a while since those garments had seen the inside of a washing machine. Despite their cleanliness, I could still smell the road on them, and it brought some comfort. I took a long hot shower, threw on some shorts and a tee, poured another cup of coffee, and waited for the cavalry to come lock me up. Detective Fowler and Dr. Romero arrived shortly after I got dressed, and we gathered at the dinner table. I wondered if that was the last hot shower I'd ever have in a civilian bathroom. I should have enjoyed it longer.

Detective Fowler: "Good morning, Mr. Curran."

Rita: "Good morning, Thomas."

Me: "Good morning. Detective, can you call me Thomas?"

Detective Fowler: "Of course. So, here's where we sit. Last night we went to E's and spoke with the manager who provided us with video footage of the events that occurred there. We then obtained more footage from outside the motel. Both videos clearly show Mr. O'Grady being the aggressor and attacking you, as you claimed in your version of events. We were also able to speak with Claudia Clay, the woman Mr. O'Grady met at E's. She's married to a big-shot insurance guy and mom of two kids. She claims she was there for a girl's night out and arrived a bit early. She ordered a drink, and that's when Mr. O'Grady sparked up a conversation. The manager confirmed that Mrs. Clay regularly meets her friends there and that he has no reason to think that her story wasn't true."

Me: "So Sean was hitting on a married woman who was just playing nice. Any idea what brought him there in the first place?"

Detective Fowler: "No clue, but the bartender had seen him there many times before, always alone and often buying drinks for women. The bartender called him a classic "player." He wasn't a big fan of the guy, but hey, he's a bartender, so he serves the guy drinks and, as long as the women don't seem bothered, he doesn't get involved. Although he didn't like the guy, he's never seen him get out of hand."

Me: "Where does this leave me?"

Detective Fowler: "This is where it gets a little sticky, Thomas. Concerning Mr. O'Grady, we will not be filing any charges. Last night was self-defense. However, you've told Dr. Romero a pretty wild tale that involves a murderer who's crossed many state lines, and the local FBI office is now involved. They're on their way here to speak with you. Dr. Romero had no choice but to report your conversation to us, which required us to call the FBI."

I looked to Rita for some support and confirmation. She had a look on her face that begged for forgiveness.

Rita: "Sorry, but I'm required to inform law enforcement if, during my interviews, I believe a crime might be committed. In your case, although you are not the person I am concerned about, you have knowledge of imminent criminal activity of the worst kind and, therefore, I was compelled to share."

Me: "It's cool, Rita. I had a feeling it would go this way. We're good."

Rita: "Thomas, I'm very worried about you. I've counseled hundreds of people who've experienced extreme trauma, but I've never encountered a story like yours. I honestly don't know how you've continued this journey with everything that's happened to you. No sane person can experience so much death and destruction up close and personal without having severe emotional distress. You have both witnessed and caused death many, many times, yet your determination to find the woman responsible for most of it is unnerving and worrisome. At some point, you will crash, and you are out here walking through unfamiliar land on a desperate search. And you're alone. And when that crash occurs, you will have no support."

Me: "I have Wink."

Rita: "Yes, and he is a very loyal companion. However, Wink is not enough for something this big."

Me: "Detective, before they arrive, is there anything I've done that I should be worried about? Have I broken any laws?"

Detective Fowler: "The FBI takes obstruction of justice very seriously. You've gone on this little detective expedition knowing the identity of a murderer whose walking free and you failed to share it with any proper authorities. You have information about multiple murders yet, for your reasons, you've not come forward. That said, no law requires civilians to intervene or even report a crime that's been committed. Since you had no forward knowledge of the Prineville Coffee murder, assuming it's Ms. Rose who committed the crime, you cannot be charged as an accessory. Your problem, however, is that you haven't been cooperative with the authorities, and most involved at this point aren't too excited about helping you out of your predicament."

Me: "Let me see if I understand you correctly. In a matter of a few months, while walking on the side of a goddamned highway and with the help of a former private detective in a completely different state, I'm able to figure out who murdered my employee, fucked up my life, where she's from, and who her family is and I'm supposed to feel bad that an entire police department couldn't even figure out that they bungled up her name? How confident should I have been that any help from me would have accomplished anything more than what I've been able to? Bring in the FBI, I'll talk to them, and then I'll get back to my walk. No disrespect to you, Detective, or you, Ms. Romero, but I don't give two shits if the FBI isn't too keen on being my friend right now. You have both been incredibly kind and compassionate. My frustration right now is certainly not directed towards either of you or the police department here."

Detective Fowler: "I understand how you're feeling. It's not uncommon for civilians to have distrust towards police."

Me: "Oh, no, you've greatly misunderstood me. I trust police officers emphatically. I respect them immensely. This is not about me having distrust for the police. I wanted to find her. I didn't want them to. I need answers, and that's the only way to get them."

Detective Fowler: "I see. And what are your plans for Kennedy when you do find her?"

Me: "Gameday decision, Detective. I'm gonna have to go with my gut. But I'll tell you what, if my gut says turn her in, I'll call you first."

Detective Fowler: "Out of my hands, Thomas. You'll want to call the FBI."

As if on cue, the doorbell rang and, upon being answered by Dario, in walked two suited up feds. The Hollywood stereotype was close: they were in suits, they did have short trimmed hair, they did not have any facial hair, but their suits weren't black so shame on them.

Why was I so angry with these guys already? I had no reason to be. I hadn't even met them yet. I probably should have called them a long time ago and I guess they have every right to be a little pissed-off. I was feeling completely unreasonable but, for some reason, didn't care at all.

Special Agent Lewis introduced himself and Special Agent Morgan and sat down across from me where Fowler and Romero had been a minute earlier. They did not have smiles on their faces, they were not welcoming, they were not friendly, and their suits looked stupid. I couldn't wait to get this conversation going.

Me: "Coffee, gentlemen?"

Kill em with kindness first, right? Let them make the first asshole move. That was my plan.

SA Lewis: "We don't drink coffee."

Me: "Agent Morgan, do you corroborate that statement?"

SA Morgan: "It's Special Agent Morgan, and, yes, I do. No coffee for me."

Me: "OK. Let's start over. I was just messin' with you guys. My bad. I know I haven't done anything illegal and that I don't have to sit here and talk to you, but I want to help. Sincerely."

SA Morgan: "Mr. Curran, illegal or not, which is yet to be determined, you're involved in some serious, twisted crimes, and had you come forward months ago, perhaps a kid in Oregon would still be alive. Maybe even a few other people who've stopped breathing since you took to the road. So, forgive us if we do not see this morning as a nice little coffee chat. We have a lot of questions and hope to get a lot of straight answers."

Me: "In a very narrow context, that is a fair assessment, Special Agents. Very narrow, however. Before you start, what's the difference between Special Agent and garden variety Agent, anyway?"

SA Morgan: "Special Agent means I can arrest you."

He answered with a 'so screw you' smile. OK, let's play. I haven't done this in a while, and I have all the time in the world.

Me: "Fair enough. Let's do this."

SA Lewis: "Mr. Curran, do you know Kennedy Quinn Rose?"

Me: "Yes, and no. I know her as Annie Fox. I only learned her real name about a month after she murdered one of my line cooks earlier this year."

SA Lewis: "That would be Jesse Gutierrez?"

Me: "That's correct."

SA Lewis: "Did you ever feel compelled to reach out and share the information you had with authorities?"

Me: "I shared everything I knew about her when I was interviewed countless times back home."

SA Lewis: "But, as you learned more information, you didn't think to call that in?"

Me: "Never."

SA Lewis: "May I ask why?"

Me: "Because I needed to find her. I wanted to talk to her. I wanted to know why she killed Jesse in my restaurant and ruined my life. I knew that if the police caught her that I may never know those answers. And, I'm sorry, but I need those answers. Plus, I was one guy walking on the side of a road. Certainly, if I could figure stuff out, an entire force of seasoned detectives should be able to."

SA Morgan: "Mr. Curran, I understand your need for answers, but don't you think that protecting innocent people is more important than your selfish curiosities?"

Me: "Yes, I do. I didn't think Annie was a threat to the public. I've been running on the assumption that Jesse was a heat of the moment thing, and it wasn't until Prineville when I started to think that maybe she was dangerous to others. I should have called then. In hindsight, which we all have at times in our lives, I should have called in Oregon."

SA Morgan: "No, you should have called the minute you knew her name and where she may have gone."

Me: "Special Agent, are we going to sit here and have a civics lesson, or do you have questions that might help your cause? I don't need you to tell me how I should've handled things. I get it. But you're not me, and your life didn't get jacked up by some crazy bitch, so don't think that you can understand how I'm feeling or my state of mind."

SA Lewis: "Do you know where Ms. Rose is right now?"

Me: "No. But I think she's close and I think she's following me. And, as you know, she's not alone."

SA Morgan: "How do you know she's not alone?"

Me: "If she is the Prineville Coffee murderer, she drove away from the scene in the passenger's seat of a blue Honda Civic."

SA Morgan: "We know that. I'm asking you; how do you know that?"

Me: "My buddy is a former private investigator. He's bored and jumped back in the game to help me out. Don't even ask if I'll give you his name cuz that ain't happenin'."

SA Morgan: "Mr. Curran, we can drag your ass in front of a judge and force you to tell us who he is, so don't get cocky."

Me: "You see, Special Agent, that's why I had no faith in coming to you. You're completely unfocused. Why the hell do you even waste a moment of time caring what the name is of a random PI who's just doing what he's licensed to do legally? Focus. Like I have. On Annie or Kennedy. Sorry to be such a prick but you asked why I didn't come to you and, well, there you have it. I'm willing to help you guys with information, but not if you're gonna act like an arrogant ass."

SA Lewis: "How about we all calm down a bit. We may have different motivations, but we have a common goal, and that's to find Ms. Rose. I apologize for our arrogance, Mr. Curran. We both know what happened to you last night and that you must be under amazing stress right now."

Morgan stole a glance at Lewis that did not convey happiness about the change in tone from him.

Me: "She's sent me photos. Recently. Taunting photos. Photos that just about prove she was the Prineville Coffee murderer, that she's tracking me and that she's quite possibly very close by."

I picked up my phone to show them the pictures. As the screen powered up, there was a new photo message from a blocked number. I pretended to be scrolling through messages, but what I was really doing was taking a huge shit in my pants as I stared at my screen. There were three pictures and a four-word message. The first photo was a fairly close shot of me, my face inches away from Sean O'Grady's as I reached for the napkin. The second was of me handcuffed outside the motel room with Sean's body splayed out behind me. The final shot was the clincher. It was the front of the house I was sitting in right now. The cars parked out front were not there last night; they were those of the four people here questioning me at this table. The message read: "Be very careful, Thomas."

I'm not a poker player. I can't calculate odds that quickly but, even if I could, my poker face sucks.

SA Morgan: "Everything ok, Mr. Curran? You look like you've seen a ghost."

I thought of all my options before responding. I could lie to them and only show them the photos I had mentioned earlier and not include the new ones. I could come clean and show them what I had just received. Or I could be a jerk and not share anything without a search warrant, which they would more than likely be able to get. I had evidence that they should have. Maybe I should be done and hand it all over or, perhaps, I could convince them to use me as bait to lure her out.

Me: "Gentlemen, I want to help. I'm sorry I've been a jerk. I have been on this mission for so long and have suffered tremendous loss. I've been stabbed by a tweaker and shot at by gun-toting Arkansas redneck who murdered my friend just inches away from me. I've killed four people and watched my dog take down and kill another. I've lost my business, all of my money, and I had to file for bankruptcy. I have nothing to go home to, and I'm completely broke. A year ago, I was the happiest man in the world with everything he ever wanted. Now, I have nothing but deep, calloused scars on my soul and an empty bank account. The only good thing that's happened on this journey was a weekend in Georgia with a woman I barely knew. So, letting go of the hunt is hard. But it's time. I'll give you everything without any more attitude if you promise me one thing."

SA Morgan: "What's that, Thomas."

It was the first time either agent had used my first name. I think, if only for a moment, they were attempting to feel my pain.

Me: "If you catch her alive, I want ten minutes with her."

SA Lewis: "I think we can make that happen."

I slid the phone over with the most recent message showing. As they scrolled, I described what they were seeing.

Me: "That message arrived while we were talking. That's me at the bar where I first encountered Sean O'Grady last night. The next picture is obvious. And the third, well, as you can see, she's been outside this whole time."

Both agents and the detective brandished their weapons and, just as you would see in the movies, strategically made their way to the front door, opened it, cleared each other from different angles, and made their way outside. I heard Detective Fowler call for backup and, within minutes, the street was buzzing with activity, and there was a chopper hovering overhead. Julia and Dario were in the kitchen, crouched down next to the refrigerator. I was standing at the front door in plain view, almost begging her to come for me. She was an up-close, personal kind of killer, and I wasn't too concerned about a sniper shot to the head.

I stood there for what seemed like hours waiting for bullets to fly and bodies to drop, but the only sounds I heard were the whir of the chopper blades and radio crackle. My phone chirped from the dining table. I snatched it up and clicked the notification. It was an Instagram message from CarbonEdgeKenn.

"DO NOT LEAVE THAT HOUSE!"

A KILLER'S KILLER

replied quickly. "Annie, please stop! Why are you doing this to me?"

"It's not me. DO NOT LET THEM LEAVE YOU ALONE."

"Annie, I need to see you. I need to know why you did this!"

"If you see me, you will DIE!"

"Why, Annie?"

Nothing. No reply. I was pacing, debating sharing this with the agents. For the first time since we sat and had a beer outside the back doors of my kitchen, I connected with Annie. What did she mean it wasn't her?

"Annie?"

Nothing. Screw the feds. Annie was mine.

When the agents and detective made their way back in, while the street remained abuzz under blinding light from the chopper above, we made our way back to the table.

SA Morgan: "I need you to send me those messages, photos, and any other communications you've had with Ms. Rose since the murder at your restaurant. Here's my card with my email address. Please send them right now. There will be patrols out all night. If there is any new communication from her, you must call me immediately. Is that clear? Mr. Curran listen to me. There is a killer right here in this community. Do you understand the weight of our department that will crash down on you if you do not cooperate?"

Me: "I do. You'll be the first."

I got up and paced around the house. I had just lied to an FBI agent, which I'm pretty sure was obstruction and could land my ass in jail.

Me: "Wait. Agents, I lied. Well, kind of. Not really a lie, but there's something else. While you were outside, I got these messages from Annie on Instagram."

After looking at my phone, both agents offered up their scariest glare.

Me: "Yeah, yeah, I know. I was going to keep them to myself, but I thought better of it. I'm sharing it now. I just got them five minutes ago, so chill out."

SA Lewis: "Mr. Curran, it's crap like this that makes us not trust you."

Me: "You know, you guys and your idealistic expectations of what every single person should do every single time something bad happens can go to hell. It's really easy on your side, with all your training and experience, to say what should be done in every circumstance and then pretend to be ultra-surprised when normal people under extreme distress don't follow through. That's complete bullshit, so back the fuck off with your condescending glares. She's here, in town, go find her."

Could I get arrested for being aggressively honest with my feelings? Before the freezer incident, I was very cooperative with the cops. Now that I've been on the not-so-good side of things with them more than once, I see how they can get a little testy and unsavory. Or, maybe I was just more of an asshole since all this started. I didn't want to be an asshole, but I was finding it much harder to practice patience and understanding. When I eventually get to sit on a nice comfy sofa in some shrink's office, I'll have to get to the bottom of that.

I was put on lockdown at the house. Legally speaking, of course, I didn't have to stay put and I could leave anytime I wanted, but with Annie's threat of death and the local cops and feds all up my ass for bringing that bitch to their town, I decided to cooperate and not be a nuisance while they sorted their crap out and figured out what to do with me. That and I was in no condition to walk. My face was a wreck; I could barely walk fully erect and pushing Alexa was out of the question. It was going to be a lot of time, rest and Advil before I would be ready to head out.

Everyone left after securing the house and following Dario and me as we took the dogs on a quick walk in the backyard. We were then locked up tight and realizing that we were hungry.

Julia turned out to be an excellent cook. We put together some pretty mean dishes over the course of the following week. We made a bunch of the Mexican recipes from my restaurant, grilled steaks, had a three-person appetizer party, watched movies, and they taught me a fun rummy style card game at which I whooped their butts the first time we played. Julia, Dario, and I became quick friends and many cold beers into our nights, talked about some pretty heavy stuff.

Within a week, it appeared the feds were giving up on trying to keep me in town. We met at the house, along with Detective Fowler and Dr. Romero. They updated me on the zero updates they had, encouraged me to stay longer but knew that wasn't going to happen. There was no trace of Annie in Redding, Red Bluff, or Cottonwood. No tall women that were unknown to others or checked into any motels, no reports of stolen cars, no more dead bodies, no more messages, and no more pictures.

So, after seven days of heal and chill time, I decided to enjoy one last night and head out. Julia and I made a huge dinner, and Wink and I retired early. The road was calling, and we were ready for it. I set my alarm for 4 a.m. and woke as excited as an overachieving kid on his first day of school. I hadn't realized how much I had been missing walking and was eager to lace up my shoes and hit the blacktop. Wink and I both ate a big breakfast that Julia had made. I downed lots of coffee, sucked down a bunch of Advil and grabbed Wink's leash.

As I opened the front door to the still dark, hot morning outdoors, Wink unexpectedly and, entirely out of character, bolted with great force, and I lost my grasp of his leash. With only early morning moonlight, I could just barely see him charge the tree line, and I could hear his ferocious barking. Figuring he was chasing a squirrel or some other furry creature, I charged after him. Yelling for Wink to return, I ran to the edge of the driveway and listened. To my right, I could hear him running and, suddenly, a piercing scream of horror, loud growling, and wrestling on the ground.

I ran into the trees towards the screams when the unforgettable sound of a dog yelping in agony broke the darkness. I was close and could see Wink and another figure on the ground rolling and screaming. I dove on top of the heap of flesh and rolled in the warm, wet dirt trying to separate Wink from the person below me. I pushed Wink off, where he collapsed and whimpered, and I started to ferociously beat down on the body beneath me. Something blunt and hard crashed into my skull, and I lost my strength. Instantly, the attacker was on top of me, bleeding through a massive torn open gash in her neck that Wink must have inflicted. She was tall and strong and, in her hand, cocked high above her head ready to plunge was a large hunting knife a lot like the one I had gutted Mr. Boot with. Her teeth were filled with blood, and her deep crimson saliva poured from her mouth upon my face. I looked up with utter shock as I realized it wasn't Annie attacking me. It was Peggy Sue.

Peggy Sue: "You did all of this! You were supposed to protect her. She loved you!"

My head was spinning, my ribs were taking a beating, and the pain was at Defcon 4. I was barely conscious and horribly confused. I wasn't even sure if what was happening was real. I looked over and saw Wink on his side, his breaths labored, and blood slowly pooled under his belly.

"Mother! Stop! Don't do this!"

My energy and attention sprang back to life. I knew the voice of Annie, and it was coming from behind my head from somewhere far back.

Annie: "Mother, please, stop. You have to stop this. We've gone too far, Mom, please, stop!"

Her pleas were cracking under intense sobs, and I heard her drop to her knees not far from my head. I couldn't see her, and I wanted to see her so badly. Annie was desperately pleading as Peggy Sue screamed back with hate and vitriol.

Peggy Sue: "Don't do this? Don't do this? I've been doing this for you your entire life!"

Annie: "I've never asked you to do any of this!"

Peggy Sue: "You've always needed me to save you! Why stop now? I've been saving you ever since you let your brother hurt you. I killed my only boy for you!"

Annie: "I just wanted you to stop him; Mommy, I was just a little girl."

Peggy Sue: "I had to save you from every boy that broke your heart."

She looked down at me with fury and resolve. I could see blood slowly pulsing from her neck and watched more trickle down from her mouth. She knew this was her final act of vengeance, and she was going to make it count.

Peggy Sue: "And you, Thomas. You come into my bar, pretending to be a man I had beaten to death years earlier. I knew what you were up to. My little girl loved you, and you didn't protect her from that Jesse boy. If you weren't going to stand up to him, then I had no choice but to cut him up and ruin your life. And here you are, hunting her when you should have been hunting me."

She brought the knife down quickly. I barely had a flash of time to jerk my body away as the blade drove straight down the edge of my head as I felt my scalp and the flesh of my ear slice clean away. I could feel the skin pull from my head and, despite the hot morning, the gash felt ice cold as blood flooded my face and hair. I was fighting like hell, bashing her neck and face as she raised the knife to finish the job. Four shots rang loud and thunderous. The bullet that passed through Peggy Sue's head and the one in her chest dropped her on top of me. I heard Annie screaming and, in the distance, sirens blaring. I couldn't move. My body had given in to the pain, and I was helpless. Peggy Sue's lifeless body was too much weight for me to manage, so I just laid there, barely able to breathe. A few seconds later, her body was pushed off me, and I could see Dario and Julia, both armed, keeping Annie on the ground. Peggy Sue wasn't getting up.

I rolled over to Wink and held his paw.

Me: "Hey, buddy. Hang in there, OK?"

Wink: *"I probably should have stayed in the house."*

Me: "You saved my life, again. I love you, big guy. We're gonna be OK."

He was still breathing, and we waited, locked in a loving stare, as the cavalry arrived. By the time I was put in the ambulance, my lights were out, and I slept.

HELLO, AGAIN, ANNIE

REDDING, CA

40° 34' 18.5" N

122° 23' 42.8" W

MILES WALKED: 2,496

I t was two days of surgery and sleep before I was awake enough to understand what had happened. Dario and Julia were in my room, as were my mom and my son. Both had flown out the day before after Detective Fowler had called them with the gory news. My mom was a face full of tears and smiles as she realized that I would be ok. It would take a bit, but I was gonna make it. I had dozens of stitches in my scalp and a few dozen more holding my ear together. I was a pathetic pile of bruised and swollen bones and felt like I'd gone a full ten rounds with Mike Tyson. One strong coughing attack could break me forever. Drinking water was difficult, but it soothed my dry throat and helped me feel a little bit whole. Detective Fowler and SA Morgan walked into the room and asked everyone if they could meet with me privately. I asked my family to get me a cup of strong coffee, and they all left.

Detective Fowler: "You're one hell of a lucky man, Mr. Curran. Half an inch. That blade missed your right eye by exactly one half of an inch. If Dario and Julia weren't such good shots, we wouldn't be having this conversation. Dario took out the mother, Julia took down the daughter. Still pleased with your decision to hunt her down?"

Me: "Annie wouldn't have done that to me. I thought I was hunting Annie, not her psycho bitch mother."

Detective Fowler: "Either way, you're lucky, and we're happy we only have one dead body on our hands and that it belonged to a real killer."

Me: "One body? Annie survived?"

Detective Fowler: "She did. Barely."

Me: "Where's Wink? My son told me he's gonna be ok. Is that true?"

Detective Fowler: "He's gonna be OK. He's at a local vet hospital where he underwent surgery to repair two stab wounds. One was a pretty deep penetration in his rear right upper leg, and the other was shallower and up near his right shoulder. Like you, he missed death by a fraction of an inch. The shoulder wound just missed a major artery. He may not want to walk back across America any time soon, but then again, why would you in the first place?"

Me: "You know the saying 'Not all who wander are lost'? Well, Detective, some are."

Detective Fowler: "To each his own, I guess."

Me: "So, are you here to live up to your end of our deal Special Agent Morgan?"

SA Morgan: "You still want to see her, huh?"

Me: "Like you don't even know."

SA Morgan: "Before that happens, I think you should listen to her recorded testimony. She was very forthcoming. She's a broken woman, Thomas. It was difficult to hear her story, to be honest. She's not the woman you thought she was and, before you see her, I think you should listen."

Me: "Does she want to see me?"

SA Morgan: "Just listen."

SA Morgan approached the bed and handed me a small digital recorder.

Me: "Can I do this alone?"

SA Morgan: "Of course. We'll leave you be."

I stared at the small silver device in my hand. His words, "She's a broken woman, Thomas", were stuck in perpetual replay in my head. I wasn't sure if I wanted to hear what was on the device, but I had to know.

Play.

SA Morgan: "Ms. Rose. I'm special agent Morgan. Also present in the room is your attorney, Ms. Vandale, and Detective Fowler from the Redding Police Department. This conversation is taking place inside your hospital room in the ICU at Mercy Medical Center in Redding, California. You have been read your Miranda rights and are agreeing to this interview. Is that correct?"

Annie: "Yes."

SA Morgan: "Ms. Rose, instead of hitting you with a lot of questions, would you like to tell us your story and we'll ask questions as we need to?"

Ms. Vandale: "My client has survived a lifetime of severe trauma at the hands of her brother, father and mother. She's suffering from post-traumatic stress and will be under the care of a team of doctors over the days to come. As of now she has not been charged with any crimes and this interview is..."

Annie: "Ms. Vandale, it's ok. I need to let this go. I need to tell my story. Agent Morgan, I'll cooperate but I need you to be gentle right now. Can you do that?"

SA Morgan: "Yes, Ms. Rose. I respect what you're going through and understand you have quite a story to tell."

Annie: "Will Thomas be able to hear what I'm going to tell you?"

SA Morgan: "Yes, everything you say here today is evidence and it sounds like maybe Mr. Curran will deserve to hear it."

Annie: "That's good. I want him to hear it. Would you mind sitting down? You're making me nervous. When I was a very little girl, my daddy taught my brother how to hurt me. When Mom wasn't around, Dad would tell me how much I ruined his life when I was born. He would say that there was no more room in our home for another woman and that, when I came along, all of Momma's attention shifted to her little girl. Before me, Christopher was her boy and she loved him and played with him and protected him from Daddy's swift kicks and lashes. But when I was born, everything changed; my father stopped hitting him and started loving him in the way only he could - he taught him how to hate women. He taught him what to do to me and Momma when he didn't get what he wanted. Daddy had always beaten up on my mother for any reason he saw fit and he wanted Christopher to learn the game. My memories are just chunks of stories but with brutal clarity. I'm sure I had some fun as a little girl, but I mostly remember the bad times and they are so clear and focused like they just happened yesterday."

There was silence for several long moments of swelling anxiety. I envisioned Annie gazing at a slow, methodical IV drip leashed to her arm as her brow furrowed, lips trembling as tears welled in her eyes. After a few moments lost in the past, she returned to the room and wiped the pain from her face.

Annie: *"You may be thinking they hurt me sexually, but they didn't. They hurt my body in many ways but never touched me like that. They needed to break me down so I would obey them and let them be powerful over me. But I was a scrappy little girl. Ironic, really, because I got that from Daddy. My mom, back then, had already lost her will and fight and accepted a life of obedience through violence. As much as she wanted me to be her little girl, my personality, my perseverance, was all Daddy, and he hated that. He made sure there were no strong women, or little girls, in his home, and he wanted his boy to follow his lead. I don't remember a single day that I didn't fear both of them. And then, suddenly, Daddy was gone.*

One night, my parents had a horrible, bloody, fist-pounding fight and he stormed out of the trailer, drove away, and never came back. I actually missed him in the beginning. As much as I feared him, I knew, even as a small child, that I was like him and he was my father. He's all I knew as a little girl. After Daddy left, Christopher became more violent towards me and Momma. He would scream at us constantly and tell us that Daddy was gonna come back and kill us all. He and Daddy were gonna fix us women and run away together. One day, Christopher took a knife from the kitchen and chased me out the door and down to the creek. I was so scared; I was screaming for help, but nobody came. He pinned me up against a tree, held that long blade up to my little face and told me he was gonna cut my throat out. I think he would have if Momma hadn't shown up with her hands beating down on his body. I never saw her hit anybody and, watching her strike blow after blow upon my brother, shattered everything I knew about my timid, scared mother. Although she was trying to save me, she had become a monster and, suddenly, I was alone in the world. I died that day but not from the blade of a knife.

I never saw Christopher again. Momma told me the next day that Daddy had taken him away in the middle of the night. It was years later, after another one of my friends, a man a little bit older than me, had disappeared that she told me how she killed my brother and left him in the woods for the animals to get him. She said she was protecting her little girl, but she was really just killing me slowly. We left Whiteville a few years later and settled down in Monroe where I tried to be a normal girl. It was hard to blend in quietly because I was tall, gawky, and had a big chip on my shoulder. And I was pretty. Tall, pretty girls get a lot of attention and I couldn't escape it. So, I did what I could and took what I wanted. I pretended and played nice and, as soon as I knew what to do, I started to sleep around and control boys by playing with their fragile little hearts. Control. It's what I learned from Daddy. But I never loved any of them.

When I was twenty, I escaped. A man I'd been playing around with a bit disappeared and I knew it was Momma. I fled to New Mexico to try to start a new life away from her. I don't even know how many men she had killed before I left New Mexico. I was numb to it by then. I would find a job; maybe try to have a boyfriend and she always knew when I was sad. I always let her hear it in my voice on the phone no matter how hard I tried to sound happy. Then, as before, a boy would die or disappear. And, like always, I would leave and try again somewhere else. I left Kennedy in

Albuquerque a few years ago. I wanted to escape my mother's reach forever, make it impossible for her to find me. I chose the name Annie Fox because it sounded edgy and cool. I had never been edgy or cool. I wanted to find a new woman inside of me that could love and hurt and love and hurt like everyone else without fear of her retaliation.

I bounced around restaurants in LA and Orange County, and I read about Thomas's place in the newspaper right after he'd opened. He seemed like a passionate chef with big dreams. His place was near the ocean, which I had grown to love. I actually sat at his bar a few times with sunglasses and a great big ugly hat on so he wouldn't recognize me when I got up the nerve to show up at his back door looking for a job. He and I talked while he served drinks or chatted up other customers. He never hit on me, he was never inappropriate, his staff seemed friendly and genuinely happy to be there, and I noticed a few of the same people sitting at the bar each time I was there. He had regulars who loved what he had created. I wanted to be a part of that.

Once there, I felt whole and happy and free. I loved my job and my line mates. In hindsight, I know I was also falling in love. Then I screwed up. In my new life of happiness, I was missing the family connection. I wanted to share my happiness with someone who had known me as that scared little girl. I couldn't call my parents, so I called my cousin Jenny. I had told her about Thomas, and maybe I admitted to having a crush on the chef. I told her about Jesse and all the fights we would get into, but I also shared that he and I were friends and that the fights meant nothing. I told her about throwing his knife roll in the deep fryer and nipping his nose with my knife, and all the times he would try to hit on me. I guess there was an occasion for her to talk to my mom and, thinking she was sharing an innocent con- versation that she had had with me, told her everything. Told her where I was, told her that maybe I had a boyfriend who owned a restaurant that I worked at, that there was another cook who had hit on me a few times but nothing seriously and who knows what else. She thought she was just sharing family gossip. She didn't know my mom's violent history; she didn't know what she was starting. I didn't know any of this until that awful night when she showed up and Jesse and I were closing up the kitchen.

I was in the office on the phone placing the produce order when I heard some commotion. I figured one of the boys had come back to drink some beers and thought nothing of it. I heard Jesse start yelling, and then I heard my mother's voice screaming over his and then his cries for help. Oh, Jesse, he was crying out agonizing screams begging her to stop and then it was silent. I dropped the phone and ran into the kitchen to find her standing over his dead body. I ran out the back door and down the street and dropped down on some grass and cried until I couldn't anymore. I knew then, once again, that I was trapped. I walked back to find his body gone, and my mom starting to clean up the floor. She had stabbed him several times, and there was a lot of blood, more than what you would think. I asked her where he was, and she said she had put him in the trunk of her car and not to worry, Mommy was taking care of everything. I didn't know why she was cleaning, but she insisted on getting the place all spotless so nobody would know anything had happened. I didn't help her. I sat outside, losing my shit. Then she came out and, with a proud smile on her face, tried to hug me and tell me everything was better. I hated her. I wanted her to be dead, not Jesse. I walked through the kitchen one last time and said goodbye to what I felt in my heart had been my new home. She took me to a motel and never let me return to my apartment. She left when I got into bed and returned about an hour later, looking happy and satisfied. She said that Jesse had been dealt with, she climbed into bed, and was asleep within a few minutes.

We drove back to Georgia the next day, stopping only once in Albuquerque. I didn't speak to her the entire way. She kept me locked up inside her home, right there in Monroe, for months. I was less than a mile away when Thomas sat in her bar, doing shots, pretending to be Joshua Owen, a boy I knew as a teenager. A boy Momma had murdered years earlier. She'd been waiting for the man claiming to be Joshua. She knew he was coming. Jenny had told her that a man named Joshua Owen had come around asking about me and that she had told him where to find my mom in Monroe. Mom was excited and anxious for the mystery man to arrive. Then, Thomas gave himself away. After a few shots with Mom, he referred to me as Annie, not Kennedy, and she knew exactly who he was. She wanted to kill him right there but knew the consequences. She figured she'd just let him go. She knew he'd never find me there, so she let him walk away.

And then, Arkansas happened. She read about a guy walking across America and a girl that was with him who was shot and killed. She read everything she could and, in her crazy head, allowed herself to get all worked up, and she was so upset with herself for letting Thomas leave. She knew in her heart that he'd let that girl get shot and that he should pay for it. I begged her to let it go, and she did, for a while. After a week or so, I made my escape again. I stole her car during one of her late shifts and drove till daylight. Then I ditched the car and hitchhiked to Bend, Oregon, to start a new life. I made another huge mistake. I called her from a payphone outside the shitty little motel to ask her to leave me alone and let me have my life. We argued and fought, and I hung up on her. Three days later, I walked out of that motel, and there she was, at the curb, leaning against a rental car waiting for me. It was at that moment that I gave up on life and conceded to her control. I was too tired of running.

I gathered my stuff, and we drove out of town. We went to a drive-thru coffee house in Prineville. The place was a cute, small-town family-owned shop, and while we were waiting for our drinks, that young man who she killed later that night was outside sweeping up the patio. We made eye contact, and he was pretty flirty through the window. My momma saw him, and she saw me smiling back, and she was furious. We drove out of town up into the hills and sat in silence for hours. She refused to talk to me. We had no food, and I had no idea what was going to happen. I was just letting her cool down. I thought about running into the woods and never turning back. I wondered how far I would get before getting eaten by a bear or starving to death. But when I'm with her, I find it very hard to run. She's always had that hold on me. She suddenly got up and told me we were leaving. She told me to drive and told me where to go. I knew what she was going to do, and I didn't try to stop her. There was no stopping her. Ever. My whole life and I could never stop her. I could have called the police many, many times, but I wasn't strong enough. Every time I considered turning her in, I would remember that she saved me from my daddy and my brother and, as despicable as her form of saving was, I just couldn't do it. We didn't even know if that boy would be there, but, sadly, he was. We could see him through the window, cleaning up the dining room at that coffee shop. I pulled into the back and, well, you know the rest. We left and drove back to Bend and got a room at a sleazy little motel in a not so great part of town. If anything, my momma was careful. She knew that place would never talk."

Annie went silent, probably lost at the IV drip again when the flood gates opened. Her wails and cries from years of emotional abuse became fierce and, listening to them, brought tears to my eyes.

Annie: "Agent, I'd like to see Thomas. Do you think he would see me? Is he here?"

The recording stopped, and I took a breath. I spent a moment in silence and reflection attempting to compose myself. I called SA Morgan back into the room who was followed by Detective Fowler and Dr. Romero.

SA Morgan: "She's here, in ICU, just like you. She's right down the hall. She's under arrest with multiple jurisdictional charges pending as we sort through the mess. If the doctor says we can move you, and, after hearing what you just did, you still want to see her, we can head down the hall to her room."

Rita: "Hey, Thomas. Welcome back to the living. I'm happy to see you breathing."

Me: "Hello, Rita. I'm happy to be breathing."

Rita: "Thomas, you're probably going to experience severe post-traumatic stress, and I'm very concerned about how you're going to deal with it. I know you want to see Ms. Rose but I'm not certain that's the best idea."

Me: "Good idea or not, I'm going to see her."

Rita: "With your permission, I'd like to talk to your family and put together a counseling plan for you when you get home. Is that alright with you?"

Me: "Sure, Rita. And thank you. I feel pretty good, to be honest. I know the symptoms will come later. I'll keep an eye out for them."

SA Morgan called in the doctor treating me and explained what was going to happen. The doctor, who was also treating Annie, unenthusiastically agreed to allow me out of bed and to be wheeled down to her room.

SA Morgan: "Ms. Rose and her attorney have agreed to a brief meeting. Ms. Rose is recovering from two gunshot wounds to her shoulder and leg and is a bit fuzzy headed like yourself. This meeting is ill-advised by all parties, but a deal is a deal and Ms. Rose wants the same. You won't be allowed to be alone with her or touch her in any way. Everything you say will be recorded and can be used as evidence. I would strongly recommend that you keep this little meeting simple and brief."

Doctor: "Mr. Curran, we're going to attempt to get you in that wheelchair with as little discomfort as possible. You don't have any broken ribs, but they are beat to hell, and this is going to hurt. Are you sure you want to do this?"

Me: "I'm sure. Let's do it."

Five minutes and two long moments of excruciating pain later, I was wheeled out of my room. I grabbed a coffee from my mom's hand and swallowed as much as I could. A minute later, I was sitting next to Annie. SA Morgan set up a digital recording device between us, and he and Annie's attorney gave us some space.

Me: "Hello, Annie. Fucked up year, huh?"

Annie: "What were you thinking, Thomas, coming after me like that? And walking? That doesn't even make sense."

Me: "I lost everything, Annie. I thought you killed Jesse. I mean, you kinda did but, you know what I mean. I had to find you and ask you why you would do that to me. To him. I thought we were friends or at least work friends, you know? It just didn't make sense to me. I had to know."

Annie: "My mother has been ruining my life since I was a little girl. I'm so sorry, Thomas."

Me: "I'm sorry you had to lose your mom that way, but she was pretty fucked up, Annie. I heard the recording. Unbelievable. I seriously cried so hard."

Annie: "Yes, she was."

Me: "I would never have guessed you were anything but courageous, strong, and ambitious. You were a rock in the kitchen. But on that recording, you were none of those things growing up. I never saw you as a timid, shy, fearful woman. You're a hell of an actress, Annie."

Annie: "I was all of those things, Thomas, until I found my way to your place."

Me: "Annie, how did she know where I was? How did she track me?"

Annie: "Jenny gave your number, Joshua Owen's number, to my mom. She was a resourceful woman, my mother. With your number, she had figured out how to track you all along, keeping an eye on you. When you disappeared from Texas and popped up again in Oregon, we had been staying in Bend but driving up and down the coast. She thought we were mending our relationship, but, in reality, I was starting a long, slow, lonely death. I thought of jumping out of that car any time we were near a cliff. I prayed that she'd lose control, and we'd fly off an edge like Thelma and Louise. Then, out of nowhere, there you were, on the map, walking directly towards us. Directly towards Prineville. She couldn't believe it. She kept saying that she had big plans for you. That's when she took the picture of the cup sitting in the holder in the car. That's when the taunting began."

Me: "I had a private investigator helping me find you, and he had read about the Prineville Coffee murder. The grainy video showed a tall woman coming out the back of the building, and he knew it had to be you. It was just too coincidental. So, he came and picked me up in Texas and brought me up here so I could try to find you in Oregon."

Annie: "She wasn't planning on killing you, Thomas. She was hoping to scare you enough with those photos to get you to go home and stop chasing me. Then she got greedy and got too close. When the FBI showed up, she knew you had finally told them everything. She knew we were stuck, but I couldn't stop her. I'm so sorry. I'm sorry. I'm so happy you were in that home with that good family when she made her move. She would have killed you, and I'm happy they shot her dead."

SA Morgan: "One more minute. Say your goodbyes."

Me: "Annie, can I see the tattoo on your shoulder, the one you always try to hide."

Annie smiled ever so slightly and pulled her gown down to expose her entire upper body. Stretching from behind her shoulder, across the bottom of her neck and down her chest was years of work done by different artists. Years of darkness, evil and her story of emotional imprisonment.

Annie: "Everything she's done, that I know of, in the name of saving me is right here. I showed it to Jesse once. He thought I was coming on to him letting him see my breasts but, it wasn't that at all. I liked Jesse; maybe even loved him like a little brother. I felt connected to him and I wanted him to see it. He didn't know what it meant but he spent long minutes studying every inch. He never asked me what it meant. Or maybe he was pretending to look at it and he was just checking out my tits. You know Jesse."

Me: "Yeah, that sounds like him. He was a good kid. He survived a crazy life only to be murdered by an even crazier woman."

Annie: "I miss him. I'll pay my price for what my mother did. I won't fight that. Had I been a stronger woman I could have stopped this a long time ago."

Me: "I don't think you could have, Annie. She owned you and she overpowered you from the day you were born."

Annie: "Perhaps. But I should have tried."

Me: "Annie, did you love me? Before she died, your mom said you were in love with me, and that I didn't protect you."

Annie: "Head over heels, Chef. It's why I told you I was married to a woman. I wanted to get close and you would never let that happen. You're so damned by the book. If I wasn't a threat, I felt I could get closer and, maybe, someday, tell you that I love you."

Me: "What about your husband?"

Annie: "Yeah, I guess I gotta deal with that, too."

I leaned over and kissed her shackled hand.

Me: "Goodbye, Annie. I'll try to fight for you."

SA Morgan grabbed his recording device and wheeled me out of the room as Annie began to cry. I didn't want to see it or hear it. My heart was broken for both of us.

SEPTEMBER

ARE THESE THE TRUTHS YOU'RE LOOKING FOR?

RED BLUFF, CALIFORNIA
TO
NEWPORT BEACH, CALIFORNIA

IF I NEVER TOUCH THE WATER...

NEWPORT BEACH, CA

33° 36' 26.7" N

117° 55' 46.6" W

MILES WALKED: 3,235

My mom wanted me to recuperate back in Boise, my friends wanted me to go home and get my life in order, and the Moore's offered their place and hospitality for as long as I needed to heal. It was rather nice having so many options! With the hunt over, I wanted to stay close to the investigation, regain my strength, heal my wounds, and finish my walk. I had been so focused on finding Annie that I didn't quite grasp the enormous accomplishment that I was so close to finishing. Walking across an entire continent, over three thousand miles, is done by very few people, and I was only a few hundred miles from accomplishing it. With Annie in custody and Peggy Sue dead, the killings would stop, and I had the clarity I had been walking for. I needed a new goal, and it became finishing my journey at the Newport Beach Pier, where I had spent many nights as a teenager and young adult. For the first time in eight months, the ocean was calling my name.

It was two weeks before I was strong enough to walk crazy-ass long miles and push a cart every day. Wink was another story. His walking days were put on hold. My mom took him back to Boise with her and promised to have him at the finish line, where he would plunge into the cold ocean water with me. I missed him by my side.

The day after they took the stitches out of my head, I hit the road. I woke up early to the smell of a full breakfast smorgasbord. Julia had prepared a feast for my departure day that included bacon, sausage, eggs, pancakes, yogurt with granola, two kinds of juice and lots of coffee. She also had a little to-go bag with PB&J sandwiches, bags of trail mix, bananas, oatmeal, top ramen packets and, of course, a few 4-packs of Reese's. With wet eyes we hugged and said good-bye. Dario and Julia stayed on their porch and waved me off until I was out of sight.

I was alone, again, but with nobody to hunt. With only a few hundred miles to go, my thoughts on the road were rich with fear and sadness. I was going to finish my walk with no money in my pocket, no restaurant to open, no lover to hold and no clue what I was going to do with my life. When I set out seven months earlier, I thought I would figure out the second half of my life, but I was no closer to that revelation than I was when I left.

For these and many other reasons, California was a tough walk for me. Was home still my home?

One day, on a very long, dirty road that ran through the middle of Nowhere, California, I saw a bicycle in the distance coming towards me. I was hot and nasty and was a little miffed that the road I'd been sharing with only my thoughts was about to be violated by a stranger. You can go hours on those dirt roads without seeing anybody. After the guys who wouldn't give me water, the sideways glances from many more people on the roads than in any other state, a man and a woman who'd both separately tried to kill me and my utter loss for words with regards to how I was feeling about Annie, my hope for humanity was broken. I walked because I had to. I wasn't smiling much or enjoying the beautiful valley of abundance that surrounded my every step. And there, ahead of me, was that damn guy on a bike. As he pedaled rather slowly, his bike wobbling towards me, my alert level jumped a notch. He wasn't a cyclist, rather, a tired-looking guy on a BMX bike. Twenty feet away, I noticed a big heavy bag hanging around his neck, swaying from side to side with each leg rotation. Ten feet away, I moved left so he could pass on my right. His right hand went into the bag around his neck; my hands went to my weapons strapped under my handlebars. Five feet away, his hand rummaged around in the bag seeking purchase of...? Four feet away, my hands tightened around the weapons and readied them for release and defense. Three feet away, his hand emerged, holding a large peach. One foot away, he held it out at arm's length, and I snatched it with my right hand. We never made eye contact as he rode past.

That man was a field worker who saw a guy walking on a hot, dusty road and, selflessly, offered a moment of kindness. He wasn't the first or the last person on my journey to show me unconditional compassion and humanity, but that day, during that horribly sad and challenging month, he raised my spirits with the simplest gesture. He will never know how important that sweet, juicy peach meant to me. I stopped Alexa, took the time to assemble my folding chair, plopped my ass down on the side of the road and ate that peach as I watched him ride off in the distance. I wanted to chase him down and thank him but, someone like that, he knew. He didn't need thanking.

The next few weeks I walked in silence. I listened to my heart, the earth, the pains in my body and the sounds of farming and agriculture all around me. I continued down long, straight, dusty frontage roads until, eventually, I turned west and went up and over the hills near Paso Robles. As much as I wanted to enjoy some winery hopping, my spirits were low and focused on finding some peace before getting home.

I took a bike trail through a small town in the hills west of Paso on a warm, early September Sunday, that sent me meandering through fields of trees and herds of cattle that seemed miles from where they were supposed to be. As far as I could see, there was nothing but yellowish-brown hills, occasional outcrops of trees and lots of cattle who didn't seem to mind the human intrusion along their fence line. As I neared the top edge of a hill, a new yet familiar smell reached my nose; it called me forward and I moved quickly to the crest to find its origin.

As my eyes cleared the top and around the trees, I saw the deep blue of the Pacific Ocean in the distance and I could smell the salt in the air. My altitude and clearing allowed a view that stretched dozens of miles both north and south on the shoreline. I'd waited nearly eight months to see those waters again and the only thing missing was Wink. He would have liked this view. He would have known we were close to home. I missed him dearly but would see him soon enough.

I took out my phone and called my father.

Dad: "Hey, Son, how are you? It's been a few days. How are you feeling?"

Me: "I'm really good, Dad. I'm standing on top of a mountain, staring at the Pacific Ocean in the distance and I needed to tell you something."

Dad: "What's up? Are you ok?"

Me: "Yeah, I just wanted you to know that I think I'm finding my best self. Out here, on these roads, I realized that it's yet to come because I'm going to finally let that happen. Not for anyone else, just for me."

Dad: "What do you mean by that?"

Me: "There are these lyrics to one of my favorite songs by Jane's Addiction that go *'I chip away, cuz I'm not ok. So, I... I chip away. Poked a hole right into myself and inside I found someone who said I was ok. Still I don't feel easy.'"* I think what they mean for me is that, on this walk, I found a man inside of me who I didn't know was there. A man whose desires are so different that they scare me. A man who needs to break free. I'm not sure where or when it was on this journey that I met him, but he's here with me now and he's ready to live. I love you and I wanted you to know that I've finally met him."

Dad: "He sounds like a good man. I look forward to meeting him. I love you, Son."

Me: "Love you, Dad."

In late September, around 11 a.m. on a sunny Southern California Saturday, I met my son at a little cafe a few miles from my finish line. He knew the moment was going to be a bit overwhelming for me. We ate mostly in silence as I contemplated the next hour of my life. We walked a few miles to gather Wink at the house he'd been staying at since my mom made it to Southern California to see my finish.

Wink: *"Oh my God, Dad! Where did you come from? Wait a minute, what's with the leash? Nope, count me out, not doin' it. I like it here. A lot."*

Me: "Calm down, buddy. It's just a short one."

With only one mile to go, the reality of my journey's end nearing started to settle in. As we approached the pier, I saw dozens of friends and family members cheering me on. The beach was busy, and people not there to see me were curious about the commotion.

Me: "Wanna do this with me?"

Wink: *"You go have this moment alone. I'll meet you down there."*

I rolled to the sand, handed Wink to a friend and slowly made my way closer to the water. I had seen this in my head for eight months and, after living near this massive body of water for over thirty years, it never looked more beautiful than it did during those final steps. I waited for my courage to gather. If I never touched that water, my journey would never be over. The minute I got wet, that was it. Do I jump in? Turn around and go back?

I took the plastic jar full of Atlantic Ocean water, sand and that one lonely seashell and stepped cautiously forward; tears broke free and streamed down my cheeks. I could hear crowds of people cheering me on, and people I had never met were taking my picture and shooting video. I took off my hat, threw it to the ground, ran to the water, and dove head first.

As I rose from the cold Pacific Ocean that defined my journey's end and turned around, staring back at the beach, at my family, friends, and strangers cheering me on, I was lost yet again. I unscrewed the lid from the jar, poured its contents into the shore break, and married the two oceans. Over the heads of the crowd that had formed, I could see the mountains in the distance, where I had just walked 3,235 miles from. To get home. To find Annie.

And there I was, back at the puzzle and that empty space waiting to be filled once again. As I searched my soul, I no longer recognized my piece. It had shifted and it had changed, just as Lindsay told me it would back on that bridge during her seventeenth crossing of that big, beautiful river. What she didn't tell me was how much I would love my new shape, my new form, and how desperately I would need to find or create a new space within which it might fit.

I smiled as I reminisced about my night in that teepee with Erika. She was right. One long, deep kiss and she knew I was chasing the wrong demon but that I would figure it out at the right time. That time was now.

My eyes found the road that led away from the beach towards the mountains in the distant east. That nameless road of many faces that cradled me for countless days and nights. She was hot and cold, slick wet and desert dry, long and straight as a taut wire, as twisted as a coiled snake and one real bitch. The most beautiful bitch I'd ever met. We were in love and I was leaving her. Another in my lifelong series of break-ups.

Eyes swelling with motionless tears, gazing at the path that led to where I once was, away from what I feared and no longer recognized, I wondered what Rosie was doing.

Wink: *"Don't even think about it."*

Monetta was only 2,400 miles away.

Certainly within walking distance.

THE HUGE THANK YOU PAGE

THE ROAD ANGELS WHO GAVE ME ROAD MAGIC

Holden Curran, Leslie & Brett Vandale, Josh Holden, The Entire Holden Clan in NC, Lisa, Richard & Jessie Morgan, Mary & Brent Wheatley, Dr. Kibler & his awesome team, Officer Joseph Henry, David & Nicole, Kimberly Hynes, Amber & Jessie, Melissa Byrd, the Wall family, The City of Monetta, Tammy & Joel Hanson, Pamela Eli, Jenn & Terrie Krauss, Madison Ryan, Duck the Harley Guy, Mark & Mindy at VFW Post #6445, Del at VFW Post #5899, Sonja at Chicken Coop, David in Athens, Steve & Pat Milby, the entire Lolo/Tovar clan in Atlanta, Kenny, Carla & Kenny Jr. Stephens, Just Wayne, Amanda Kilgus, Kevin McCarley, Philip Castillo, Carolyn & Henry Terry, Jerry Harvey, the Glen Fire Department, Sha Johnson, the Adams family, Ken & Sherrie Sowers, Tanya Sanders, Audrey House, Mulberry Firehouse, Pastor Ryals, First Assembly Church, Steve Longacre, Melissa Zabecki, Marval Resort, Kelly & Jodi Cox, Hippy Larry, The Capron Clan, Rebecca & Adam Moser, Rachel & Sean Vogt, Courtney Charton, Will Smith, Misty at KOA, C. Tracy Davis, Janel Broderick, Caroline Smith, Jr. Little & his family, Mom, Dad, Mary, Donna Sperl, Brook Gossard, Jeannine Sibley, Spoke'n Hostel Crew: Pat & Jalet Farrell, Rosie Day & Timi Knight, The Town of Mitchell, OR, Tiger Town Brewery, Noah & Jill Carr, Leigh & Erinn Meyer, Erika Kightlinger, Donna Araiza, Julia & Dario Moore, Black Car Kid with Water, Bike Guy with Peach, Cal Fire Wilbur Station, Gatlin & the Blakely Family, Lisa Cervone, Maureen, David Nguyen, Porter/Meltzer Family, Sarah Bergez, Vyes Family, Cousin Heather, St. Theodore Church, Chronic Cellars, Marge & Dick Griffen, Jack Lockhart, Allison & Craig Brandum, Sharon & Martin Suits, Amy & Don Keuffler, Pam & Joe Waltuch, Jack Lockhart, 3000 Kylie, El Capitan, Christen and Jason Munninghoff, Mike & Leslie Fallon, Katie Fallon, Erin, Nick, Emma & Kaitlin, Jennifer & Mark Sommer, Geoff & Tracy Yeaton, Zach Galifianakis, Katy Clark, Claudia & Gabe Stubin, Jim Asher

TO MY FELLOW TRANS-CONTINENTAL CROSSER FRIENDS WHO HELPED ME PLAN AND SURVIVE

Tyler Coulson, Lindsay Monroe, Eric Keeler, Jonathon Stalls, Kait & John Seyal, Brett Bramble, Chris West, Jessie Grieb, Pete Miljevic, Tyler "Biddy" Bidwell (RIP Biddy), Angela Marie Maxwell, Tom Griffen, Noah & Joanne Barnes, Steve LeSage, Dr. Terrie Wurzbacher, Mario Landeros, Matty Gregg, Keoni Smith, USA Crossers FB Group

PEOPLE BACK HOME THAT HELPED MAKE THE JOURNEY AND THIS BOOK HAPPEN

Mom, Dad & Mary, Nick Curran, The Wongdock Clan, Michele Curran, Jane & Glenn Fowler, Christie Frazier, Shelby Coffman, Karen Musselman, The Hood Kitchen Space, Joanna & Adam Hutchinson, Heather Thorne, Katherine Coltrin, Greer Wylder, Sean O'Grady, Pediatric Cancer Research Foundation, Jeri Wilson, Julianne Ludwig, Tyler Muzzy @ ASICS, Rick & Amy Gann, Julie & Groovy Rothenberger, Paul Guidotti, The Entire Village People @ Taco Brat Crew, Tosi Health, Lucille Salter Packard Children's Hospital @ Stanford, UCSF Benioff Children's Hospital, Black Magic Tattoo, Gold Rush Tattoo, Lululemon, Kevin Morby, Jane's Addiction

THE BOOK LAUNCH TEAM

Asef, Brett, Britta, Cassidy, Christie, Andy, Jenn, Kari, Katie, Lisa, Kat, Karen, Lacey, Erin, Mary, Missy, Rory, Sean, Holly, Natalie, Karyn, Tim, Tina, Trevor, Wendy, Tiffany, Katherine, Jamie, Amanda, Lori, Britt, Cassidee, Christine, Maddie plus many more already listed above.

THANK YOU TO EVERY SINGLE PERSON WHO DONATED TO THE PCRF DURING MY JOURNEY

ABOUT THE AUTHOR

THOMAS CURRAN is a father, chef, author, artist, and trans-continental walker. For his 50th
birthday, Thomas rescued a dog named Wink,
flew to the east coast and walked home—3,235
miles across America from the Atlantic to the
Pacific. His son, Holden, lives in North Carolina and walked his first day with him. During his
journey, Thomas raised $21,220 for the Pediat-
ric Cancer Research Foundation. This book was
written most nights in his tent, a stranger's home or super cheap motel.
Thomas lives in Costa Mesa, CA where he is working on his second novel.

Now that you've thoroughly enjoyed this masterpiece, Wink and I would
greatly appreciate it if you'd leave a review on Amazon. Thanks!

Made in the USA
San Bernardino, CA
28 May 2020